The Mercy of Wolves

Lane Bristow (signature)

Lane Bristow

authorHOUSE®

AuthorHouse™
1663 Liberty Drive, Suite 200
Bloomington, IN 47403
www.authorhouse.com
Phone: 1-800-839-8640

First published by AuthorHouse 11/6/2007

ISBN: 978-1-4343-4187-7 (sc)

Printed in the United States of America
Bloomington, Indiana

This book is printed on acid-free paper.

For Kaela.

"*The wicked is banished in his wickedness,*
But the righteous has a refuge in his death."

Proverbs 14:32

Introduction

Continental Yukon, located in the southeastern hemisphere of Canadian Exodus, is the most heavily forested landmass known to man. In the early days of colonization, it was very sparsely populated, as opposed to the mountain and prairie continents of Manitoba, Ontario, and Alberta.

In late June 2167, on the verge of Canadian Exodus's centennial celebrations, a rogue militia unit led by terrorist general Cole Dallas Kressel, great-grandson of planet's discoverer Lawrence Kressel, captured Continental Yukon's single military base, Port Yellowknife, a training camp for Canadian Infantry, and experimental air defense facility. General Kressel, self-proclaimed Heir of the Planet, made a televised statement, specifying that Continental Yukon was under the ownership of his militia, a guerilla force known as the Bloodline. Possession of the base gave the Bloodline virtual control of the continent.

On July 1, 2167, Canadex Prime Minister Fredrick Martenson identified the Bloodline as "… the greatest single threat to the peace of this planet." On the following day, he secretly assigned Captain Maxmillan Towers (Canadian Northern Eagles, Commando

Team Four), the most decorated Special Forces war hero in Canadian history, the task of forming an elite paramilitary unit, dedicated to matching the Bloodline's abilities in discretionary warfare. The unit would work in cooperation with the Canadian Armed Forces, yet exist outside of its purview and, to the extent possible, outside of its awareness.

Out of the thousands of Canadian soldiers and civilians who volunteered for this special unit, only one hundred passed the preliminary requirements of the Towers Program, the most rigorous and dangerous training exercises ever executed. From the one hundred qualifiers, only twelve successfully completed the two-year course.

These twelve men, and Captain Towers, vanished from existence, and every one of them was listed as deceased in the Canadex Census Registry Databanks. Working from an undisclosed location, they formed the most deadly covert operations unit in the history of mankind. They were known as Track and Pursuit.

Prologue

The 7-3-0

07:00, January 1, 2171.
Track and Pursuit Headquarters,
Somewhere in the western forests of Manitoba,
Canadian Exodus.

In daydreams, a soldier will imagine a world without war. At night, a soldier will dream of facing a loved one on a field of battle. Both scenarios can be dismissed as unlikely, or even impossible, and yet both can still be very troubling.

Captain Maxmillan Towers had seen many soldiers die in battle, some fighting him, others fighting beside him. In more than thirty years of service in the Canadian Armed Forces, he had killed more men than he could ever remember, and had watched more of his own men die than he could ever forget. He had fought the Bloodline since the day he had first worn his private stripes at the age of eighteen. Captain Towers was no

3

stranger to death, but there were only forty-five deaths that he could ever fully blame on himself.

Forty-five portraits hung side-by-side in a long corridor which Captain Towers stood in every single morning. Forty-five Canadian soldiers smiled at him in pressed uniforms, fresh from graduation and promotion ceremonies, all too young and full of courage. Towers looked into each face as he slowly walked down the tope hall in his forest green uniform, his shoulders glistening with the brass lion and tiger insignia of Track and Pursuit. His polished black shoes clicked with hollow volume in the emptiness of the dimly lit tunnel that opened the way to TAP HQ, the only world that Captain Towers knew anymore.

Maxmillan Towers had black hair, buzzed to military perfection, and a thick moustache that covered his upper lip. His medium built body was strong, and his height was just over six feet, but he always felt as though his entire form was falling and weakening as he passed the few words inscribed in the center of that long wall, just above numbers twenty-two to twenty-four:

THE 3-6-5.
THEY CHOSE THE IMPOSSIBLE
TO FIND THE BEST.
JANUARY 1, 2169-JANUARY 1, 2170.

Towers could not walk past that inscription without pausing to trace his fingers along the golden impressions of the letters, his teeth lightly gritting behind closed lips.

No one ever entered the corridor while Captain Towers was there. They knew better. No army on Canadian Exodus could lay claim to a soldier greater, or more revered, than Maxmillan Towers, and yet the men and women under his command all knew that in the one minute and thirty seconds that it took for him to travel the length of that hall every morning, the captain was not to be interrupted.

Captain Towers thought of the faces behind each one of those photos. In his mind, these were the only people he had killed to whom he was obligated to stare into the eyes of. He had killed enemies with rifles, knives, cords, his bare hands, or the push of a button. Soldiers had followed his orders to their own deaths, without question. Towers had seen men at their best, and most vile, but only the faces in those forty-five eight-by-ten oak frames haunted his dreams.

Even while preoccupied, nothing escaped the notice of Captain Towers. From a distance of fifty-seven feet, he heard the young communications lieutenant approaching the hallway from the adjoining corridor. With the corner of his right brown eye, he recognized the woman as Lieutenant Johansson Murtaub, sonar chief in Comm. She was waiting for him to approach, not wanting to intrude on the sanctity of the 3-6-5 Wall.

"You walked quickly to stop so suddenly, Lieutenant," Towers commented, still staring into the eyes of a fallen soldier. "What is the urgent matter?"

"You startled me, sir. I was on my way to contact you at home."

"I am here. Good morning, Lieutenant."

"I apologize, Captain Towers, but I think you should see this."

"You work sonar and frequency. There is a strange sound?"

"Yes, sir. We've picked up a transmission from the forests of Continental Yukon, twenty kilometers north of Fort Lawrence. I do not recognize the frequency."

Towers sighed and folded his arms, turning on one heel to face the young soldier.

"How long have you been stationed here, Lieutenant?"

"Almost a month, sir."

"Do you believe that this transmission was meant for us to find?" The question was several different tests.

She nodded, hesitantly. "I do, sir. Fort Lawrence has no capacity to produce a signal like this. Whatever is sending it is not Bloodline technology."

"Very well. Stand by in Comm."

"Yes, sir." She saluted smartly. Towers returned the salute, then turned back to the wall, as Murtaub's footsteps faded away. The captain stood for another moment in silence, rubbing his brow with his fingertips.

"Happy New Years, kids," he grunted, striding down the hall. "We're gonna get'em."

Like most of the underground facility, buried deep in the heart of Manitoba's western mountain range, Comm was running on a skeleton crew that day. Even in Track and Pursuit, the beginning of a new year merited at least one day away from assignments and missions and killing. The eleven TAP operatives were on leave for the week, although all of them had informed Towers that they would return that evening for the first annual memorial of the 3-6-5 victims. Most of the operational staff was also off for the weekend, and the remaining personnel had not even expected Captain Towers to report in that morning. Towers smiled at the surprised looks that the communications officers gave him as he entered the nearly vacated Comm. Most of the staff was newly appointed, and obviously did not know him well if they had expected him to not be there on this of all days.

"Captain present!" Murtaub announced, standing at attention.

"Carry on as you were," Towers said dismissively. "Corporal Mendez, anomalous reading."

"Aye, sir," the young Latino man replied, tapping the keypad in front of him. "Monitor up, main screen."

The enormous screen on the far wall lit up with a green map of the four hundred square kilometers of forest surrounding the Bloodline garrison and city of Fort Lawrence. A blinking red dot indicated the location of the transmission.

"The frequency pace alone leaves anything the Bloodline has in the dust, sir," Lieutenant Murtaub said, shaking her head. "It's one of ours, or an independent of some sort. Comparison analysis is running."

"When did this start?" Towers wondered, his brow furrowing into three deep creases.

"Four minutes ago, sir," Murtaub replied. "On the stroke of seven a.m."

"I've got audio translation," Mendez called out. "Coming up on overheads now."

The grey speakers in the low ceiling began emanating a shrill series of rapid clicks, sputtering in and out as the signal grew and waned. Towers eyes betrayed nothing, but he knew the signal immediately. He also knew that most of the others in the room would not know what it was.

"Atmospheric impedance," Mendez was saying, twisting the enhancement dial on his workstation. "I'll try to clear it up."

"Impossible," Towers murmured, eyes fixed on the red dot.

"Sir?" Murtaub was the only one who heard him.

"That's not atmospheric," Towers said. "Those are definite breaks."

"Faulty transmission?" Murtaub suggested.

"More like coded. Corporal Mendez, switch to Morse code translation."

"Aye, sir."

"Opinion, Lieutenant?" Towers inquired mildly, cocking one eyebrow, almost playfully.

Another test. Murtaub knew better than to hesitate again.

"I have never seen this before, sir," she replied frankly. "However, I understood that only TAP operatives used Morse coded transmissions."

"Very true," the captain agreed. "Forget comparison analysis. The signal is a 3-6-5 Cuff."

"But, sir, all of our operatives are on leave. We don't have anyone in Continental Yukon, and this frequency is too fast for a Cuff."

"But, forty-five soldiers were pronounced dead in Continental Yukon, wearing those Cuffs," Towers explained. "Only forty-two bodies and Cuffs were ever recovered or accounted for. That's the old frequency. We changed it ten months ago."

"You think it's captured, sir?" Murtaub ventured. "A trap?"

Towers snorted, still staring fixedly at the central monitor. "I designed the Cuff. It would have blown up any Bloodline fool who tried to remove or tamper with it."

"I've got Morse translation," Mendez said. "Central monitor."

The Morse coded message began flashing across the green satellite map, a single word in bold black letters, blinking on and off repeatedly.

CHECKMATE

"Checkmate?" Mendez said, puzzled. "Is that an assigned retrieval code?"

Towers lips parted as recognition set in, and he took a slow step toward the blinking monitor.

"Contact Falcon," he said, still shocked. "We need an evac for a 3-6-5 operative."

"Someone survived?" Murtaub was incredulous.

Towers nodded. "There should only be forty-four pictures on that wall."

"Patching in Lieutenant Falcon's home frequency," Mendez informed them. "One minute to holo-conference."

"Send it to my office," Towers muttered, shaking his head. "Chess...."

Murtaub nodded. "It looks like we have a number twelve, sir, if he really survived the game."

"Oh, he won," Towers assured her. "But I was not referring to the game." He chuckled slightly. "The man who is sending this signal is named Chess. That is why I assigned him that evac code. Irony, Lieutenant. Irony."

"Corporal Chester Conrad Bradley," Murtaub remembered, impressing the captain. "Canadian Northern Eagles. Number four on the 3-6-5 Wall."

Towers nodded his agreement. "If I'm right, he'll have a TAP name by the end of the day." He could not help but shake his head again. "Chester Conrad Bradley...."

"I still can't believe it, sir," Mendez confessed. "I mean, Corporal Bradley was pronounced dead over a year ago."

"No, Corporal Mendez," Captain Towers said with a cold smile. He turned and began to walk out of the room. Everyone watched him go, knowing that he was not finished speaking yet. They heard his last words after he was already out of sight.

"He was pronounced dead *exactly* a year ago."

Part One

The Stake

Chapter One

January 1, 2191.
Office of the Prime Minister,
New Shilo, Manitoba,
Canadian Exodus.

For almost one hundred years, every Prime Minister of Canadian Exodus had given the people they governed the same vow, and that was a pledge to eliminate the Bloodline threat from the planet. Prime Minister Dee Robertson Stone had been the nation's leader for less than a year, and she had made her own private vow to be the first one whom history would not judge a liar.

"Thirty seconds, Madam Prime Minister."

Dee Robertson Stone was a tall, thin woman, nearly sixty years old, with twenty-year-old blue eyes and greying brunette hair. Her angular features and tight mouth always looked ready for a fight, but, on this day, she felt very tired, and very old. Even so, her fierce determination was all that she would allow her face to reveal. The people of Canadian Exodus needed strength and decisiveness, and Dee Robertson Stone was not going to deny them that. Seated behind the huge black desk in her empty office, with quietly folded hands and cold eyes, she stared unflinchingly into the blue steel monitor which was about to send her words into every television on the planet.

"Ten seconds, Madam Prime Minister."

The intercom voice was annoyingly robotic, but it did remind Stone to quickly adjust her deep-burgundy pantsuit, and take one more long, deep breath.

"I know you can hear me, Alvardo," she muttered. "You had better be right."

"I am," a second robotic voice promised her.

"On live in 5 ... 4 ... 3 ... 2...."

The Prime Minister closed her eyes for the final second, then turned them back to the monitor. She had waited her entire life to give this address, and, now that the moment had come, she was afraid. She refused to let that show. Her country had seen too much fear.

"Fellow Canadians...."

The greeting sounded hollow and false. Stone had to start over, as more than thirty million people watched from four continents.

"The Home Base calls Canadian Exodus 'The Planet of Light.' Our two suns do not allow that which is known as night to fall, and yet we have been consumed by a brilliant, shining darkness for almost a century. The darkness of war, hatred, and violence. Our ancestors migrated to this planet in search of a new home, a fresh start. War followed us here, in the form we know as the Bloodline. They have struck at us with the weapons of terror and atrocity, seeking dominion and a bloodright that was never their own, and never will be. This planet belongs to the people of Canada, not to any tyrannical

'Heir.' Port Yellowknife belongs to the people of Canada, as does the entirety of Continental Yukon. For twenty-three years, the Bloodline has claimed ownership of both, and their claim is no more valid today than it was when they shed the blood of the captured Canadian soldiers at Port Yellowknife. That spilled blood will yet be avenged. That was my vow to all of you when I assumed this office. It stands to this day.

"The Bloodline has no valid claim to a single handful of soil from our planet. The people of Canada grew this soil from dust and oblivion. The Bloodline cannot see that this collective effort gives way to collective ownership. They can never see this, blinded by greed and hate.

"The Bloodline troops are required to take the Oath of Denunciation before being admitted to this terrorist faction. They denounce their country, their national allegiance, and their citizenship. It is their right to denounce this, under the articles of the Canadex Bill of Rights. However, what they have failed to realize is that their collective denunciation has made them illegal aliens within this sovereign nation. General Cole Dallas Kressel has repeatedly stated that his army will have no part of Canadian Exodus as a nation. Well, General Kressel, my reply to you is that you are absolutely correct. You shall never again have part of, or place within, Canadian Exodus.

"People of Canada, the day of the Bloodline has passed. I am herewith implementing and ratifying Legislative Motion B-478, known throughout the Legislative Assembly as The Banishment Act. By rejecting Canadian Exodus, the Bloodline has rejected the only home they have ever known.

"The Banishment Act will be carried out as follows:

"Part A.   General Cole Dallas Kressel, terrorist leader and self-proclaimed Heir of the Planet, once captured, will be banished from Canadian Exodus to an equatorial region of The Desert.

"Part B. The Bloodline Seconds, once captured, will be banished from Canadian Exodus to equatorial regions of The Desert. This includes all living Bloodline officers confirmed present at the Port Yellowknife massacre: Major Powers Bourgeouis, Captain David Whitefeather, Colonel Milo Curtis, and Captain Garrett Baxter.

"Part C.   The Heir Defenders, personal security unit of General Cole Dallas Kressel, once captured, will be banished from Canadian Exodus to southern polar regions of The Desert. This includes Commander Robert Flaxton, who has personally claimed responsibility for atrocities such as last year's terrorist bombings in Toronto Exodus, executions at the Port Yellowknife massacre, and the sexual assault and murder of eighteen female Canadian soldiers over the past two decades. Also included in this section of the Banishment Act is the Heir Defenders Command Second, and any Heir Defender Deputies subsequently captured.

"Part D. The fate of the aforementioned Bloodline personnel is henceforth set in stone. They will be shown the same mercy that they have shown to Canadian soldiers and citizens in times past. They will be left to the mercy of wolves.

"Part E.   Subsequent to the banishment of the aforementioned Bloodline personnel, any person found bearing arms in the name of the Bloodline, or inciting insurrection against Canadian Exodus in the name of the Bloodline, will likewise be banished from Canadian Exodus to that planet which we call The Desert.

"Part F. Once banished, the names of the banished persons will be permanently removed from the Canadex Census Registry Databanks. The banished persons will never be permitted to return to Canadian Exodus. For all legal and moral purposes, the banished persons will no longer exist.

"I speak now directly to the soldiers of the Bloodline. Discard your uniforms and pledge anew your allegiance to Canadian Exodus, and you may yet be pardoned for prior acts of war. The Bloodline dies this very year. Do not die with it.

"People of Canada, let us look to this new year with renewed hope and courage. This year will be remembered as the beginning of an era of peace for our planet. That is my new vow to you. Happy New Year, and may God strengthen us all for the final battles to come."

Chapter Two

January 1, 2191.
Bloodline Controlled Military Complex,
Port Yellowknife, Continental Yukon,
Canadian Exodus.

"She sounds very confident, General." Major Powers Bourgeouis seemed abnormally nervous.

General Cole Dallas Kressel gave a slow nod, but he was smiling.

"Very confident," the old man softly agreed, leaning back in his command chair and stroking his short-trimmed white beard. "Very."

The enormous Tactical Center at the heart of the complex was more crowded than usual with technicians and red-and-black uniformed young troops, most of whom had come only to watch Prime Minister Stone's announcement on the central holographic monitor. In spite of the crowding, they all stood a respectful distance behind General Kressel and his Seconds.

"We have seen confidence before," the general said with quiet dismissiveness. "The confidence of the Canadex has been the biggest threat that we have faced in twenty-three years. I am not cowering under my bunk just yet. Posts."

"Posts!" The wiry, seventy-year-old Major Bourgeouis barked, standing at the general's side.

The troops stood raggedly at attention, but all managed to touch their chests in salute before filing out of the room. The general was left alone with Bourgeouis, and Colonel Milo Curtis, a short, beefy man in his late fifties, with red hair and moustache, flabby jowls, and sunken cheeks.

"Confident, yes," Curtis noted, his voice deep and resonant. "Pity that the disguise of her voice does not also mask her eyes. She doubts her own words."

"Which means that someone else is confident in her stead," Kressel murmured. "Someone who knows more of military operation than our dear prime minister does."

"A strike?" Bourgeouis hated the sound of the words as he fitfully rubbed his thin jawline.

"They've been planning strikes for as long as we have held this port," Kressel snorted. "We're too well dug in for any strike. They're plotting something else."

"Let them plot," Curtis said with a shrug. "We control more than a quarter of the planet's landmass with this one continental claim, and our recruitment is at an all-time high. Let them plot."

General Kressel stood and stared into the cold blue eyes of Dee Robertson Stone, her final holographic frame frozen in the center of the room.

"Ordinarily," he said slowly, "I would let them plot. But this woman is no ordinary pirate leader. Her threats are specific, not vague. She is working from a simulated timeline, and she's backed by Krunnion. I will not underestimate Krunnion."

"What do you want me to do, sir?" Bourgeouis requested, standing at attention. Kressel turned to face his Second, placing a comforting hand on his friend's bony shoulder.

"Recall, Powers," the general instructed kindly. "Recall every insertion and strike team from Manitoba and Ontario. Full abort and fallback. We need to reinforce our holding here until we know what Krunnion is up to. I'm not chancing anything. If it is a strike, he will find himself facing the entire Bloodline legion."

"The Canadex has never threatened banishment before." Curtis was uncomfortable with the thought.

"The Desert is a fear tactic," Kressel said, folding his hands behind his back. "Demoralizing, the thought of being left on the one habitable planet that no one wants to inhabit."

"Leaving us at the mercy of wolves," Curtis muttered. "Give me death first. Have you ever seen The Desert, General?"

Kressel managed to smile again at the unpleasant memory. He had indeed seen the archival film footage of the burning sand world.

"Have hope, Milo," the general chuckled. "We're going to the equatorial regions. We'll die a sandblasted death in a matter of hours. Quick and easy."

"Inspiring, sir," Curtis sighed, with half a smile.

"Recall," Kressel said again, as he strode from the center to a waiting elevator. "Full abort and fallback. Have Xander issue the abort codes."

Major Bourgeouis leaned across the command console to touch the comm link to the officers' barracks.

"This is Major Bourgeouis. Lieutenant Xander, report to Tactical. Repeat, Xander to Tactical. Initiating abort contingency. Respond and verify."

"Xander here, sir, reporting to Tactical," the lieutenant's garbled voice crackled from the console audio pad. "Verification code 981-B46 Beta. Out."

"What are they plotting, Powers?" Curtis asked, as they continued to stare at Stone's frozen image.

"They're plotting to banish us to The Desert," the major snarled. "Initiate comm links to all off-site teams. We've got to get them back here."

Chapter Three

January 1, 2191.
Office of the Prime Minister,
New Shilo, Manitoba,
Canadian Exodus.

Canadian Armed Forces General Alvardo Krunnion was a patient man, but he knew that the prime minister was deliberately making him wait in the marble corridor outside of her office. He knew that she was angry right then, angry about making vows that she did not believe that she would be able to keep. Krunnion himself had doubts, but he understood that this was the best shot they would ever likely have to end the disgracefully long reign of the Bloodline terrorists. Krunnion had fought his share of battles to earn command of the Canadian Army, and he was not going to let his boys and girls down.

The general had been sitting calmly in his hard chair for over an hour, but Stone was mistaken if she thought that she was teaching him some sort of lesson. Alvardo Krunnion had hunkered down in foxholes for days, waiting for Bloodline troops to emerge from bunkers or barracks, and step into the sights of his Ion-57 Snipe. He knew how to wait.

"Alvardo."

The prime minister's voice could still sound angry, even when electronically distorted. General Krunnion stood up, tall and straight in his navy blue uniform, as the office doors in front of him gave a hydraulic hiss and then silently parted. Trying not to smile was difficult.

"Madam Prime Minister," he nodded, as he stepped into the round office, standing at attention before the black desk. Prime Minister Stone rose from her seat and motioned for him to be seated. The general knew her well enough to just shake his head and remain standing.

"It's a start, Madam Prime Minister," he said.

"The press isn't listening, Alvardo," the prime minister muttered, turning to stare out the window, overlooking the towering Parliament Building across the plaza. Her arms were folded, which was never good.

"It's a start, Dee."

"This is my career, if I don't deliver Kressel now."

"We had to issue the ultimatum first. You knew that."

"It's a prototype, Al," she snapped. "We're basing the future of this country, and this government, on a prototype. We are a fledgling nation, still. Grand total of four satellites over our heads. We can't spare them."

"You approved Kage to CSIS. You knew my opposition to that, and now you're going to question me for actually agreeing with him? It will not happen very often."

"You want me to risk losing a satellite!"

"I want you to help me end a war," Krunnion clarified.

"Every country faces terrorist actions. We fight them, we kill them, we move on."

"Terrorist actions?" Krunnion was disgusted, and made no effort to hide it. "You think the Bloodline can be dismissed that easily anymore?"

"It's what they are."

"We know that. The people used to. Not anymore. They have survived the only test required for public acceptance. Time. No one remembers the start of this war. Bloodline activists are petitioning us to recognize these 'opposing thoughts' as a new political party! Apathy and tolerance are fueling the Bloodline. Cities on this very continent have banners up on campuses, urging Canadians to forgive Port Yellowknife, and support 'the Kressel Cause.' Terrorist actions are becoming a civil war. People are either choosing sides, or just not caring, and this is our best chance to stop it. We cannot wait anymore. They'll be pulling back to Continental Yukon as we speak. How long do you think they are just going to sit there? Our window is less than a week."

Stone turned and rested her palms on the desk. Krunnion knew that she was inwardly grappling with the decision, knowing that it could spell the end of her administration if something went wrong. The history books on Dee Robertson Stone would begin with what she decided on that day.

"We have no guarantees, General," she said quietly. "And you can't give me a guarantee."

"Guarantees don't exist," the general replied. "History will know that you at least tried."

The Mercy of Wolves

"History remembers winners and losers." Stone sank back into the chair. "I really wish that there was a broader range of options, more than two one-word headings to be placed under for all posterity, but it just doesn't happen. Terrorist actions, civil war, or public apathy, it doesn't matter. We have to win. The only other option is to lose."

"Then give the shuttle the go-ahead," Krunnion implored. "Twelve hours, and this could all be ending."

"Twelve hours." The prime minister could barely force herself to digest such a short time frame. After so many years of conflict, a twelve hour solution sounded impossible.

"Twelve," Krunnion affirmed. "Once in orbit, we can have Sweep installed in under thirty minutes. One pass around the planet.... We're done."

"No." Stone could not yet resign herself to the decision. "Aerial test sweeps had enough residual effects to immobilize the host, as well as the target. Standard shielders are not holding up against the directionality model. We almost lost two good pilots. From space ... we lose the satellite, and, once the shielders are overwhelmed, it shuts itself down before reaching critical mass. Then it's over. We're shut down. Do you think the Bloodline won't exploit that?"

"Madam Prime Minister." Krunnion was having a harder time sounding patient. "We are out of options. We cannot invade them, we cannot bomb them. We can do nothing until their air defense is down. So, here's the pretty version. The chances are that this mission will fail, costing us a multibillion dollar satellite, while disrupting countless lines of communication, surveillance, and public broadcasting. We will be set back years in our efforts to replace it, and the Bloodline will take advantage of the chaos. More blood, innocent blood, will be shed, and will continue to be shed for another hundred years. But, if we do nothing, we will save some money, and more people will still die. And you will sit in that chair, knowing that you could have tried to stop it! The choice is yours. You can sit there and be a politician, or you can stand up to Kressel and be a leader."

Krunnion knew that the prime minister's resolve was growing weaker when she said, "Just assume, for a moment, that it works. What then?"

"This is my vow, Dee," Krunnion said solemnly. "If this works, it will take the head off the Bloodline. Right at the neck."

Krunnion had not intended to make a clever metaphor, but it still annoyed Stone.

"Alvardo, did you know that Home Base cockroaches can survive even after their heads are removed?"

The general sighed, finally settling into one of the black sofas. "I did not know that."

Stone was assuming the scholarly tone that accompanied her lectures. "They can live and move about for days after decapitation. Starvation is their chief adversary after that."

"As I said. I did not know that."

"June 15, 2120, we destroyed Fort Kressel Mountain, northern Ontario. The Bloodline was scattered, their forces decimated, every aircraft in their possession

26

destroyed or captured. We said they were destroyed. Twenty years later, they came back.

"May 4, 2150, CNE-CT4 Lieutenant Maxmillan Towers kills Frankwell Kressel, *The Heir himself.* We cut off their head, General. They came back. June 28, 2167, they came back."

"I am familiar with our history books, Madam Prime Minister," Krunnion said irritably. "I wrote several of them. And, with all due respect, I have never met a man, or army, who could withstand the kind of demoralization we are talking about anywhere near as well as a cockroach. CT4 moves in, and we will do a lot more than take heads off. We will crush the Bloodline to pulp under our boots. And not even a cockroach can survive that."

Stone closed her eyes, wanting to believe.

"Alvardo.... General Krunnion, I am only going to ask this once."

Krunnion only smiled in his mind. He knew the question, and the answer.

"Can you do it?"

"Yes," the general said with a nod.

Prime Minister Stone's blue eyes opened again.

"Then do it."

Chapter Four

January 2, 2191.
Stormy Coulee Ranch,
50 km west of White Rock, Alberta,
Canadian Exodus.

The log ranch house was a place of perpetual silence, but the steely-haired man in the firelit den, darkened by tinted windows, was used to that, and he preferred it. Silence had kept him alive in the woods for seventeen years, while many others had died with the snap of a twig.

He looked at his silver-bearded face in the mirror over the green metal filing cabinet, and then he looked back down at the personnel file in his hands. That was how he started each new day. First, he looked into the eyes of people he had killed, and then he looked himself in the eye. Once that was done, he could face whatever the day would hold.

Staring into the mirror, he noticed how many wrinkles lined the corners of his grey eyes, and they were not laugh lines. He could not remember the last time he had laughed, or even smiled, for that matter. He had determined to live out his days as a good man, but had known for many years before that he could never truly be happy. He had served his country for two decades, and took solace in the knowledge that Canadian Exodus was safer because of him. His joy for life had to be an acceptable loss.

The file folder in his hands had taken him years to find, but Track and Pursuit had taught him how to hunt down more than just humans. No matter how long the search took, he had never stopped until he had the military service file and picture of every person whom he had taken the life of.

The cabinet held one hundred thirty-seven files, and five of them had the faces of women on them, including the one he had just withdrawn. Her name had been Danielle West, and she had been one of the most beautiful women he had ever seen, a twenty-five-year-old redhead with brilliant green eyes. She had also been a Bloodline Hitter, on a mission to assassinate the Canadian Minister of Defense. The silver-eyed man had tracked her to a New Shilo hotel room, moments before the planned hit. He had double-tapped her with an M-1911 Colt .45 semi-automatic projectile pistol, letting the recoil from the heart shot carry the pistol eight degrees upwards, so that the second round caught her squarely in the forehead. He was already walking back down the hallway by the time her body finished its slow slide down the glass partition to the carpet.

That had been seven years and twenty-six days earlier. He remembered the smell of the perfume she wore, mixed with the smell of copper. There was often a smell attached to the memories.

Danielle West had been number one hundred eight, but the man could not afford to allow her, or anyone else, to become a number. People needed to remain more than just numbers. West had Canadian parents, who were retired and living in Toronto Exodus, and an older brother who was a firefighter. She had loved dogs and sculpting. Her graduation yearbook had voted her "Most likely to become a movie star."

The aging cowboy slowly pulled the file drawer back open, and slid Danielle West's file into the back. The next day, he would read file one hundred nine, which was now at the front. Today, he had a broken section of fence that needed mending. The worst chores never seemed so daunting after his daily file reading.

He locked the cabinet, and hung the brass key and silver chain around his neck, under his faded plaid shirt. Turning to the fireplace, he lifted the black canvas gun-belt off the mantle, and strapped it around his waist. The same Colt he had shot Danielle West with was on that belt, and strapped to his left forearm was the sheathed knife he had used to kill thirty-four Bloodline terrorists. He had been a civilian for five years, and he still never left the house without those simple tools of war, or the 3-6-5 Cuff he still wore on his right wrist.

As he walked to the slab door, his left knee was even stiffer than usual, and his limp was much more pronounced. The stiffness made him grimace as he pulled on his leather boots, and then a long brown denim coat and faded grey cowboy hat. In spite of the occasional ache in the joint, he never grew weary of limping. That limp had been his deliverance from a life of killing. It was a blessing.

Chapter Five

January 2, 2191.
Primary Conference Room,
Towers Program Training Base,
87 km north of New Shilo,
Manitoba Badlands,
Canadian Exodus.

Twenty-four Canadian soldiers sat at a long, dark green table in an otherwise empty room, and they were all confused. Most of them did not know each other, and even those who did had no idea why they had been gathered there.

Their orders had been issued directly from General Krunnion on New Years Eve, instructing each one of them to cut their New Years leave short, and report to the New Shilo Infantry Garrison by 23:00, January 1. From there, a tall black man in civilian clothing, who identified himself only as Mr. Kale, had ordered all of them into an unmarked forest green bus. The bus was then driven by Mr. Kale nearly one hundred kilometers north into the forest, on an unpaved road, to an unmarked adobe training base, which none of the soldiers had ever seen before. Parking in front of a rather small grey complex, Mr. Kale had marched them directly to the tope-coloured conference room, and then ordered them to be seated and not to speak until spoken to. Without another word, he had exited the room, and shut the door behind him. That had been over an hour earlier.

The suspense was excruciating. Although only a few of the soldiers were known to one another, they all knew each others uniforms very well. Seven of them wore the beige uniforms of the New Canadian Airborne, twelve wore the dark green of the CNE-CT4, and the remaining five were attired in the deep blue fatigues of the Navy Special Tactical Unit. Every man and woman in that room was elite, the best that the Canadian Armed Forces could produce.

When the only door into the room finally reopened, every elite soldier seated at that table drew in a collective, shocked breath. They had all met the tall, beefy Cree man in his fifties who entered silently, but they had not seen him as they did now.

Every one of them had been introduced to a Mr. Ridgely during the previous year, but none of them had been told anything about him by their superior officers, except that he was an "observer." At the time, he had been dressed in civilian clothes, and had struck them as being powerfully built, but apparently non-military. That judgement had been incorrect, as all of them were now instantly aware. Mr. Ridgely wore an unfamiliar forest green uniform, with gold shoulder and collar insignia in the shape of a lion and a tiger. Looking at the imposing man at the head of the table, each one of them was amazed that they had not immediately recognized him as military the year before. Instinctively, every soldier rose to stand at attention.

Mr. Ridgely did not even look up at the open-mouthed soldiers. He set an open file folder on the table as he seated himself, and scanned absently over the list of names and service divisions on the first page.

"Be seated," he muttered, still not looking up. Uncomfortably, the soldiers took their seats. Mr. Ridgely was in no hurry to speak again.

"Captain Steven L. Morgan, CNE-CT4," he eventually said, as expressionlessly as before, still reading the file.

"Sir!" The young captain was instantly on his feet again.

"Quit standing up," Mr. Ridgely said irritably, glancing up for the first time. "Captain Steven L. Morgan, CNE-CT4, you are the senior ranking officer in this room. That will mean very little, or nothing, in the days to follow. Do you understand?"

"Uh ... no, sir," Captain Morgan said awkwardly, sitting down.

"Good answer," Mr. Ridgely chuckled, leaning back in his seat. "You all know me as Mr. Ridgely. We have all met. You are all wondering who I am, and why you are here, and why you did not guess that I was military on our initial meeting. The answers to your questions are quite simple. It is the job to look like something I am not. It's how I survive. Furthermore, I am technically not military. Technically, I do not even exist. The Canadex Census Registry Databanks have me listed as deceased, so skip calling me 'sir' for the time being. I'm dead. Should you succeed in what follows, you will be dead too. Your life will be death. My name is Captain Ridgely Falcon. Welcome to Track and Pursuit."

The man turned his attention back to the folder in front of him until the flabbergasted murmurings had faded into stunned silence.

"You're surprised?" he inquired to no one in particular, raising an eyebrow.

"Sir...." Captain Morgan stammered. "Mr. Ridgely ... Captain Falcon, I thought Track and Pursuit was a myth."

"I'll accept that as a compliment," Falcon smiled. "Every one of you has been specially selected by me to be trained as a hunter, should you chose to accept this position. You will be TAP Charlie Unit, the third class to be trained in the Towers Program. TAP Alpha trained at this base in 2168, and the eleven other men who completed the course served with me, hunting the Bloodline wherever they tried to hide. Last year, TAP Bravo was trained here, after we were ordered by the Prime Minister's Office to begin annual recruitment."

"Sir?" an NCA lieutenant ventured, cautiously raising his hand.

"Lieutenant Ray Felsted, NCA." Falcon nodded at the young man, who looked no older than nineteen, although his file placed his age at twenty-five.

"Sir, my father took the '68 Towers Program, but never completed it. My understanding was that Captain Maxmillan Towers himself was in charge of the training."

"That is true," Falcon said. "However, Colonel Towers is soon to retire. The Towers Program has been placed under my command."

"*Retire?*" Captain Morgan blurted. "Captain Towers committed suicide more than twenty years ago!"

"And what a lovely closed-casket ceremony it was," Falcon chuckled.

"So ... it's all true?" Felsted said slowly, still shocked. "You survived the 3-6-5?"

"As did eleven others," Falcon said solemnly. "Twelve out of sixty-four. Eight were disqualified, and forty-four died. For our own good, the world was told that we had died as well, and we were given new names. My name is not Falcon. Sergeant-Major Kale Hawk, whom you all know as Mr. Kale, is not named Hawk. Your identity is one of the many costs of Track and Pursuit. You will find it to be one of the most trivial. As I said to you before, and as the colonel said to us often, your life will be death. Death, and oblivion. I have been promoted pointlessly to my present rank of captain, because, in TAP, you do not report to anyone, and no one reports you. You live alone, work alone, and kill alone. All you will have is yourself. Your identity will be fabricated, your country and government will not recognize your accomplishments, and, when you die, only we will know about it. If you succeed, you will do great things for your country, but these are the costs. Each one of you must decide whether or not you love what you believe in that much. Now, I'll leave you to discuss that."

As suddenly as he had entered the room, Captain Falcon was gone.

Chapter Six

January 2, 2191.
Canadian Northern Eagles Squadron,
En route to Port Yellowknife,
Over Saskatchewan Ocean,
500 km north of Continental Yukon,
Canadian Exodus.

"Command, this is Rosewood One. ETA to target, fifteen minutes. Edmonton Strike standing by for go."

"Copy that, Rosewood One. Sweep installation complete, awaiting confirmation of detonation. Stand by."

"Roger that."

In spite of the danger, there were few sights more awing than a squadron of Northern Eagle Chops screaming through the air in tight formation, just above sea level. The tandem-seated fighters raced over the endless plain of blue water, drawing ever nearer to Port Yellowknife, and the heart of the Bloodline. Missiles were armed, and ready to go active at the push of a button, nose guns were fully charged. This was their time, command had said, and the brave pilots of the Canadian Northern Eagles were ready to claim it.

Holding back about fifty kilometers behind the Chops, the supporting fleet of CNE Runners followed, each long transport loaded down with artillery, landing craft, ground vehicles, and commando units. Once the Chops did their work, it would be up to the Runners to launch a full-out invasion of the Bloodline stronghold. Every man and woman, pilot and gunner, knew what was at stake.

"Command, this is Rosewood One. We're going to be in range of Yellowknife air defense in five minutes. Do we have a go?"

"Stand by, Rosewood One. Sweep is reaching critical mass. We've gotta wait it out."

Thousands of kilometers overhead, the newly upgraded Montauge satellite was passing over Port Yellowknife. The Blackout Chimney Sweep was locked onto the continent, and the pulse emittors were building up to detonation.

"Command, this is Rosewood One. They are going to start swatting us down in two minutes. We need the go!"

"Stand by."

Chapter Seven

January 2, 2191.
Bloodline Controlled Military Complex,
Port Yellowknife, Continental Yukon,
Canadian Exodus.

"General, we've got incoming!"

Cole Dallas Kressel felt a chill throughout his body. Every monitor in Comm was illuminating, casting a pink glow over the black room, turning every officer's face into the colour of a rose. Rotating sweeps on every screen revealed nothing but empty land, sea, and sky, yet the tone of Comm-Sergeant Coweller's voice told The Heir all that he needed to know. Port Yellowknife was under attack.

"Report," Kressel said quietly. Calmness was a soldier's closest ally, essential to survival.

"Sonar skips, 500 k north, closing fast. ETA, fifteen minutes."

"Propellents?" Kressel inquired.

"No, sir. Impacts, water on metal, high velocity, too fast for aquatics. I'm trying to tag them."

"Skimmers," Major Bourgeouis supplied anxiously, ever at the general's side. "Sir, they knew we would pull back. They wanted us to."

"Full alert, man all posts," Kressel intoned. "Continue rote sweeps, sonar, radar, and thermal. Charge all batteries, stand by to launch on tagged coordinates. I want every movement in a five hundred kilometer radius, tag them all."

"Aye, sir. Full sweeps."

"Sergeant Coweller, how many?" Bourgeouis demanded.

"Skips indicate at least thirty, fighter sized, at least six larger craft holding behind, 50 kilometers."

"Chops running offensive for Runners, invasion formation," Kressel murmured. "They really want me, don't they, Powers?"

Bourgeouis looked at his general, and tried to force a smile.

The main doors slid open, and six soldiers rushed into the room, all clad in the black tactical gear of the Heir Defenders, Kressel's personal bodyguards. Each one held in his hands a bullpup model of the Ion-57 Particle Assault Rifle, and short swords were sheathed on their hips, along with ion sidearms. At their head was Commander Robert Flaxton, a lean, handsome man in his mid-thirties, who had served Kressel since his early teen years. The team instantly fanned out to the perimeter of the room, providing a protective ring around the general.

"Ready to serve, sir," Flaxton greeted The Heir, touching his own chest in salute.

"Serve well," Kressel acknowledged, returning the salute. "Stand by."

"The rest of my deputies are manning the perimeter towers," Flaxton reported. "General, we should move you underground. We do not know what the Canadex are planning, but they would not fly in to their deaths. They don't have the courage."

"Perhaps they are not," Kressel said, still gazing fixedly on the central monitor, which revealed only red emptiness. "If this is some new stealth tech ... we may not be able to tag them."

"That's impossible, sir." Coweller was disturbed, but still certain. "They're too small. Definitely Chops. They're under radar, flying silent, but their low contact with the ocean is giving away their positions. If they're maintaining speed and formation, we can lock on. I'm working on it."

"Are they in range?" Bourgeouis wanted to know.

"Not yet," Coweller replied. "No indication of swapping.... I've got a lock."

"Get me Tactical," Kressel ordered.

"Tactical, on-line, sir."

"Captain Whitefeather, we are locked on?" Kressel demanded into the comm speaker.

"Affirmative, General," the captain's voice crackled back. "Standing by for launch. Confirm, please."

"Launch confirmed," Kressel said. "Fire on Sergeant Coweller's mark. Waiting for range."

"Range, 300 k. All batteries, stand by!" Sergeant Coweller barked. "Speed-form holding, we've got a positive lock."

"Anything else on sweeps?" Bourgeouis asked, rubbing his knuckled nervously.

"Screens clear, sir. Just the sonar skips. The woods are quiet."

"Krunnion, what are you doing?" Kressel muttered, his brow curving downward.

"Perimeter outposts! All Heir Defenders, check in and report!" Major Bourgeouis was rarely convinced by computer monitors, and Kressel admired that.

The static-laden reports followed on each other's heels.

"Northeast quad, all clear. No activity."

"Southeast quad, all clear."

"Southwest quad, all clear. No movement."

"Northwest quad, all clear. It's quiet. Maintaining full alert."

"Where is your Command Second stationed?" the general inquired of Flaxton.

"Southwest quad, sir," Flaxton replied. "He's the best choice to keep an eye out for monsters."

"Very well. Coweller, time to range?"

"Under a minute, sir," Coweller assured him.

"Eyes sharp, Sergeant. Your mark."

"Aye, sir. Standing by for launch. Battery Command, this is Sergeant Coweller. Report."

"All batteries charged," Gunner Hucio reported from Battery Command, at the north end of the base. "Ion pulse detonation rounds on your mark, Sergeant."

"What is wrong here?" Kressel growled. "Why are we still so blind?"

"They're burning fuel," Bourgeouis slowly realized. "Why can't we see it?"

Almost immediately, Sergeant Coweller was in a panic.

"Corporal Luis, run a thermal diagnostic, *now!* Over!" he shouted into the intercom. "General, I think thermals are down. The major's right. Flying under radar cannot block out heat signatures."

"How can they be down?" Bourgeouis demanded. "When were they checked last?"

"Two hours, sir. We run a complete system check every four. We haven't seen a single glitch." Coweller was confused, scrolling through his system files. "Something's wrong."

"Coweller, I want a full system diagnostic before your launch," Kressel instructed firmly. "If there's a pilot light out in a galley stove, I want to know about it. Do it now!"

"Aye, sir. Corporal Luis, this is Sergeant Coweller, priority message. Run full system check, repeat, run full system check. Confirm and verify, over."

The only response was complete radio silence.

"Corporal Luis, respond! Confirm and verify. Over!"

The radio was silent.

Coweller slowly turned to the general, stunned. "Sir, we've lost comm. Comm is down."

"Try holoconference," Bourgeouis snapped. "Hurry!"

"I just did. Not response. Nothing's happening. We're losing our systems, one by one. Thermals were the first."

"*How?!*" Kressel roared, slamming a fist down onto the command console before him. "They're going to be over us any minute!"

"Try running the check from here," Bourgeouis sighed. "And switch over to emergency generators. This could be some kind of electrical short. We need power, fast. General, I would advise you get to the lower levels, and escape tunnels. The Heir Defenders will escort you. It's not safe here."

Kressel hated running, but knew that pride often hindered true victory. However, he also knew that he had nowhere to run to. Port Yellowknife was Kressel Mountain, and he was too old to try to find a new one.

"If they can get here, they'll find me, one way or another. Can we get the systems back online?"

"Sir, emergency generators are non-responsive. They're all fully fueled." Coweller was turning red with frustration, the veins on the side of his temples emerging. "Nothing's working!"

"Sir, we can't stay here!" Flaxton snapped. "Let us do our job! You're in danger!"

"Sir...." The voice of Corporal Machlin was weak, and scared.

"What?" Kressel hissed.

"You can't leave, sir. The doors...."

Kressel stared down at the frightened man.

"The doors are electrically powered hydraulics," Bourgeouis wearily finished the hanging sentence. "We're trapped in this room."

"Sergeant Coweller," Kressel said quietly. "Opinion, please."

As if on cue, every monitor and overhead light began fading, leaving the windowless room in darkness within five seconds. Kressel had never heard such silence.

"Opinion, Coweller." Kressel's low voice sounded so loud in the blackness. "We have no eyes, no ears, and I am willing to bet no anti-aircraft."

"It has to be some sort of microwave or EMP, sir. Every operating electrical or plasma system on this base has been neutralized. That includes launch activation, comm lines ... even small arms, sir. The weapons in our hands are useless. I have no idea how they could have planted an EMP on the base. There was no source signature."

The Heir did not know why he closed his eyes. In the darkness, it made no difference. He felt tired.

"Major Bourgeouis ... is there any possibility of manually activating the self-destruct sequence from Comm?"

"Not without some power source, sir. The charges require an electric current to detonate."

"Clever pirates...." Kressel muttered. "Very clever, Krunnion."

Robert Flaxton's gravelly voice was still strong.

"Ready to serve, sir."

"You have all served me well," Kressel said stonily. "I swear to you that the Bloodline and The Mountain will not end here. Serve well."

Silence hung in the emptiness, making the tomb-like room into an absolute void. The whirring engines of the first wave of Chops could be faintly heard through the thick wall and ceilings of the compound as they screamed overhead, nose-guns spitting volley after volley of plasma flares into the heart of the Bloodline.

* * *

There was not a single pilot in the Canadian Northern Eagles New Edmonton Squadron who had not dreamed of this moment for most of their lives, the moment when Port Yellowknife would be retaken.

"Command, this is Rosewood One. We are moving inland over Continental Yukon. Bloodline air defense is confirmed neutralized, resistance zero. Preparing for strafing runs. Over."

"Roger that, Rosewood One. Begin your runs, eliminate all defenses and ground vehicles. O Canada, boys."

"O Canada, sir."

Most of the Bloodline troops could not have left their posts, even if they had tried. The doors would not open and weapons would not fire. Just like the Canadex troops captured there more than twenty years earlier, the Bloodline was a fish in a barrel.

The attack lasted minutes, only as long as it took for the squadron to make their passes over the hangars, airstrip, barracks, outposts, and primary complex. Port Yellowknife was a flaming ruin, and ninety-seven percent of the of the occupying forces were killed, constituting over eighty percent of the Bloodline army. It was a devastating end to a war with the single overhead pass of a satellite. The satellite was undamaged, and Continental Yukon was in blackout.

"Command, this is Rosewood One. It's high noon, and the commandos are a go. Port Yellowknife airstrip is retaken, all defenses neutralized. Let's drive the last stake. Over."

"Rosewood One, this is Command Peak," General Krunnion's voice acknowledged. "Form perimeter holding pattern, stand by to provide air cover. Commandos a go, repeat, commandos are a go."

"Command Peak, this is Silver One," the foremost Runner responded. "Roger that, we're moving into L.Z. now. Preparing to disembark."

"Silver One, be advised that enemy weapons are down, repeat, weapons down. Do not fire unless fired upon. Secure and hold the perimeter, begin sweep of the complex. Find out who's still alive."

"Roger that, Command Peak. We're on final approach, resistance zero."

"Make no mistake, Silver One. If primary target is still alive, maintain that. He will not want to be captured."

* * *

General Cole Dallas Kressel had no intention of being captured, but he would wait until he was facing his enemy, to die in the way that he had lived. He knew that most of his men must be dead. Although blackness was still all around him, he knew that some of those in the comm room could not have survived the barrage. He himself was lightheaded from a blow to the head from a chunk of the collapsing ceiling, the steel and concrete shaken loose by the seismic effect of the plasma flare detonation.

Kressel was never without weapons, but the dagger on his belt was the only one that would be of any use in the aftermath of an EMP. Its deer antler hilt was in his hand as the sound of rushing feet filled the corridor on the other side of the seized doors.

"Powers?" the general called out, concerned.

A low moan was the only reply that Major Bourgeouis could offer, having been all but buried under pitch black rubble. Kressel could not follow the sound of his friend in the darkness, and hated himself for being so incapable of rendering any sort of aid. He had never been so helpless, but never would he let his enemies see that in his flaming eyes.

"Commander Flaxton?"

Kressel heard the ring of steel as Flaxton drew his sword.

"Ready to serve, General."

"Come, you pirates," Kressel growled, tightly gripping the curved knife. "Come!"

* * *

CNE-CT4 Colonel James Reynolds did not believe in leading troops from a comm center frequency. He led the commando team with a weapon in his hands and his troops at his back.

The once grand corridors of the domed Port Yellowknife Complex had been shattered, and the corpses of many Bloodline troops had fallen there. Reynolds and Alpha-Team had to step over the bodies of men and women, finding their way through the complex with the aid of night-vision, under-barrel flashlights affixed to their weapons, and phosphorous flares. The air was choked with lingering flame, smoke, and concrete dust, forcing the Canadian troops to proceed with the aid of hazard masks. Reynolds knew that the building's structural stability was a definite point of concern, but his orders were clear: Find General Kressel, and bring him back alive.

It took Alpha-Team several minutes to arrive at their Comm Center objective, in the very heart of the complex. Thus far, they had seen no living Bloodline.

Reynolds touched his shoulder frequency on his armored vest. "Bravo Six, this is Silver One. What's your twenty?"

"Have reached Tactical, breaching now," Captain Ed Wallace replied from the eastern wing of the dome. "Negative on survivors."

"Report when cleared," Reynolds instructed. "We're breaching Comm now."

The double steel doors into Comm were jammed shut. Reynolds knew that Comm and Tactical were the least likely locations to have been severely damaged by the strafing Chops, and were the most likely to contain one self-proclaimed Heir of the Planet and his bodyguards. Both rooms would have to be hit hard and fast.

Reynolds deployed his twelve men to set charges on the western and southern entrances to the communications room. He had a tightness in his stomach, knowing that the outcome of a war, which few living people had seen the beginning of, lay just beyond those wedged steel doors.

"Alpha-Six, report," Reynolds whispered into his frequency. The men around him seemed anxious, and he could not blame them.

"South side charges are set, Silver One. Standing by to clear. Charlie-Team in support, waiting your mark."

"Move on my signal. Take cover for detonation."

"Roger that. All covered."

Reynolds licked his dry lips as he gently armed the remote detonator, his gloved thumb coming to rest on the green button.

"All teams, stand by. Breaching Comm now." The colonel took a deep breath, his thumb brushing over the detonation button. "O Canada, boys. *Fire in the hole!*"

The sub-zero charges instantly deep froze and shattered the heavy steel doors as though they were glass, the metallic shards blasting into the Comm Center.

"Green light, green light!" Colonel Reynolds shouted. "Team Alpha, Team Charlie, breach! Go! Go!"

"Flash bangs!" Alpha-Six, Captain Morgan Rows, roared, standing beside the shattered doorframe and hurling the grenade into the black interior. The high-pitched stun grenade detonated with a blinding phosphorous light, momentarily incapacitating everyone in its blast radius.

"Move in! All teams, move in!" Reynolds yelled, charging around the corner and rushing into the room, his ion pistol's under-barrel flashlight illuminating his way. Both commando teams fanned into the enormous room, weapons trained on the twenty or more Bloodline soldiers who lay moaning amongst the rubble. Reynolds immediately recognized the black uniforms and curve-hilted swords.

"Heir Defenders!" he yelled, kicking a sword away from Robert Flaxton's weakly groping fingers. "Primary target on location! Alpha, find and secure! Charlie, secure Defenders! Move, move!"

Even as he was speaking, his flashlight swept over General Kressel, who stood from behind the command console, having used the instrument panel to shield himself from the flash bangs. His knife was raised high over his head, daring anyone to approach it. Reynolds felt a chill. He had never seen The Heir in person before. Very few Canadians had.

"*Kressel!*" Reynolds bellowed, leveling his pistol on the fiery-eyed old soldier. "Drop it! It's over!"

From all corners of the room, laser sights began throwing red points of light onto the flashlight-illuminated uniform of the Bloodline general.

"Hold your fire!" Reynolds ordered. "Kressel, drop the knife!"

"Pirates do not command me," the general rasped. Without blinking, he dropped the knife down to his own throat.

"*No!*"

With more speed than he had shown since his youth, the thin form of Major Powers Bourgeouis lunged forward from the rubble behind the general. The palm of Bourgeouis's right hand was sliced open as he placed it between the blade and Kressel's jugular, while simultaneously tackling his friend to the concrete floor. The Canadian commandos charged toward them.

"Let it end, Powers," the general pleaded, the breath driven hard from his lungs by the force of the fall.

"While you live, hope lives!" Bourgeouis shouted his defiance, slapping the dagger from Kressel's grip. "The Mountain lives for hope! It will not end. *It will not!*"

He shook the general by his collar as Reynolds team seized him and yanked him to his feet. In an instant, Kressel was also in custody, his bodyguards disarmed and helpless.

The Heir was carefully raised to his feet, his captors appearing shocked to actually have him before them in magnetic shackles. Several of the commandos could not help taking a cautionary step back, staring at him with unbelieving eyes. For a long moment, he stared hard at each one of them, his gaze finally coming to rest on Silver One.

"Colonel James Reynolds," Kressel mused. "Canadian Northern Eagles Commando Team Four, Garrison Commander, New Edmonton. What a chapter in the history books you just wrote for yourself. Be proud, but be sure to share the credit evenly amongst your own."

Reynolds was more than a little surprised that his country's chief nemesis knew him by name.

Kressel chuckled. "No, we have never met, Colonel. Only by electrical and verbal means. And yet I know more about you than you know about yourself. Do you wonder how?"

Reynolds cleared his throat, finally lowering his pistol as he touched his shoulder patch.

"Bravo Six, this is Silver One. Report."

51

"Tactical clear," Captain Wallace's voice replied. "All secondary targets acquired, intact. Unarmed resistance only."

Reynolds wanted to smile, but could not bring himself to do so.

"Cole Dallas Kressel," he said, "you are under arrest for 342 counts of murder in the first degree, and for treason."

"And an excellent job you've done," Kressel acknowledged, nodding his admiration. "Your men are disciplined and elite. No soldier could ask for a more worthy capture."

"You will not receive what you have dealt," Reynolds said coldly. "As an unarmed prisoner of war, you will not receive 342 bullets in your skull on public television. Just though that would be."

"You still thirst for vengeance for that day," Kressel stated, almost sounding delighted. "I wish for you to take it, Colonel. Please. Raise the pistol. Avenge them. Save us all the trials, publicity, the banishment. Fulfill your dream."

Reynolds had never heard such an inviting offer, but he would not even raise the ion pistol. He holstered it and touched the frequency once more.

"Command Peak, this is Silver One. The coffin is sealed. Mission complete. All teams, complete sweeps, pull back to rendevous point one. Medical, stand by on the ground for wounded acquisitions. Over."

As Commando Team Four escorted the thirty-six surviving prisoners from the complex, three Chop pilots were already on top of the dome, running up the

Canadian flag. For the first time since June 28, 2167, the red maple leaf fluttered over Port Yellowknife.

The Edmonton Strike was the most successful military operation in the history of the Canadian nation, effectively shattering the Bloodline without the loss of a single Canadian life or plane. However, the mission did not end with the raising of the flag, although most of the people of Canada would always believe that it had. The events which immediately followed the retaking of the base were never reported to the public. The Canadian government decided that the citizens of the planet should only ever remember January 2, 2191, as a day of heroism, victory, patriotism, and, above all else, closure. Yet, for certain of those involved in the aftermath, tragedy would be the only remembrance.

The following media coverage was delivered to the Canadian public: After the retaking of Port Yellowknife, and the complete electronic neutralization of Continental Yukon, the Canadian Navy moved into the port, disembarking supporting Infantry ground forces. Briefly, sensational reports were also made of a previously unrecorded Canadian special forces team being sent in to aid with an important manhunt, but nothing more was ever mentioned of them. Inquiries into the reports were later answered directly by CSIS Director Jonathon Kage, who denounced the story as a tasteless hoax. After a six day delay that was never adequately explained, the military reinforcements joined the CT4 units in a massive sweep of the continent, capturing the dozens of camps, fortresses, and supply farms held by the remaining Bloodline troops and supporters, including the Bloodline capitol of Fort Lawrence, in the heart of the Yukon forest. All of these enemy controlled posts were taken without a single shot being fired, the defenseless Bloodline troops surrendering readily, and, in many cases, denouncing the Bloodline and offering their allegiance to Canadian Exodus. An era of peace did begin on January 2, 2191, but, unbeknownst to the public, the conflict was not finished, nor was the bloodshed.

Five Canadian soldiers died over the course of the three days following the retaking of Port Yellowknife, and the event was never made public. The government did not want the people asking questions about tragedy during such a time of relief, particularly because the men who died were not ordinary soldiers. They were soldiers who, for the past twenty years, had not existed.

Part Two

Hunters

January 1, 2168.

An open letter to the volunteers of the Towers Program, and Track and Pursuit Unit.

Towers Program, Day One.

Good men and women died at Port Yellowknife. They died at the hands of evil men and women, vicious terrorists dedicated to the destruction of our nation and world.

Track and Pursuit has a simple mission statement. We will defeat the Bloodline at their own game. They hide in the woods. Track and Pursuit will teach you to find them there. Be under no illusion. Those of you who have made it this far are reputed to be the best. It is my job to make the best better, and even the best may not survive the process. Many of you may die. Only the best of the best will complete this program, let alone the missions to follow.

You will be alone in the woods. No one will be covering your back. If you do not get yourself out, no one else will.

Can you do what is required? Can you kill like a bloodthirsty ghost, and disappear the same way? Could you hunt and kill me? Only Track and Pursuit will answer these questions, and give you the chance to find out.

Your life will be death. We will kill the evil so that the good may live. Whether we are considered good or evil in the process will be of no consequence, because we will not exist. Our judgement will not be in this life. Each one of you must decide, in your own heart, what the limit of righteousness is.

We do not kill out of hate for our enemies, but out of love for our country, and families, and those slain in the service of the same. Our love will give us the strength to freeze our own blood for the tasks that await. Love always, in the midst of a world of hate.

We're gonna get'em.

Captain Maxmillan Towers,
CNE-CT4.

Chapter Eight

Jonathon Kage knew that Prime Minister Stone had faced severe criticism for appointing him to his present position of authority. At the age of thirty-one, Kage was the youngest ever CSIS Director, and his marriage to Prime Minister Stone's niece had not earned him any more respect from his critics. General Alvardo Krunnion had reportedly laughed out loud upon learning of Kage's appointment, but the young man knew one thing for certain. No one would laugh at him today, or ever again.

Kage had ordered the construction of the Blackout Chimney Sweep, a project which most scientists and military personnel had deemed borderline lunacy. Now, as he reclined smugly behind his large desk in his large office, the fit blonde man could not stop chuckling. He was a hero. He had just saved Canadian Exodus.

"Laugh, General Krunnion," he muttered gleefully. "They'll still need me long after they use you up. Just laugh now."

Reaching leisurely across his desk, Kage tapped the comm to his receptionist in the adjoining room.

"Yes, Mr. Director?" the intercom replied. Kage still loved hearing that title.

"Belinda, get me Auntie Dee on holoconference. Now."

"I'll patch you right through, Mr. Director."

"Good."

A minute later, the holographic face of the prime minister glowed in the center of the room.

"Director Kage," her blue face greeted him, smiling. "Congratulations are in order for you."

"Save it for later, Aunt Dee," Kage grinned. "How goes the battle?"

"Yellowknife is confirmed retaken. Kressel and his staff are in custody, as are the surviving Heir Defenders. Containment is almost one hundred percent."

"*Almost?*" Kage was disgusted. "Why not one hundred percent? Why not?"

The prime minister shrugged dismissively. "Apparently, a lone Bloodline escaped, a perimeter guard. It's no loss to us. We have what we need, and then some."

"No!" Kage snapped. "That is not good enough. No one gets away! It has to be one hundred percent. It has to be. It *has to be!*"

"Jonathon, it's one man. Alone in the woods, armed with nothing but a sword. I am not concerned."

"Well, I am!" Kage exclaimed. "If he had a sword, that makes him Heir Defender. We need to send men after him. No Heir Defender is going to mess this up for me. I want complete containment, nothing less!"

"You're overreacting. You have your victory. Let it go, Jonathon."

"Put me through to Alvardo, Aunt Dee," Kage demanded. "I want guys sent into the woods. Lots of guys. Now."

"Calm down," Stone said, annoyed. "Colonel Reynolds has a CT4 team in the woods, but they don't have a trail. He's running, and we need our commanders to start focusing on leading the continental sweep. I'm pulling the team back."

"Aunt Dee!" Kage protested. "Come on! Don't you want to be the prime minister who let no evil escape justice? And Heir Defenders are evil, all of them."

"Jonathon, this is not up for debate. We have a continent to retake, and our commandos need to be ready, not out chasing squirrels."

"Then let me send someone we don't need!"

Stone rolled her eyes. "Such as?"

"Track and Pursuit. They're doing diddly-squat in the middle of all this, and it's time they earned their way! Let's send them in. Get me Maxmillan."

"Track and Pursuit has done more in the Bloodline War than any of the other armed forces combined!" Stone snapped. "They have more than earned their New Years leave. They have earned more than we can ever repay. They kept the Bloodline in check for twenty years!"

"Fine, fine. I'll make it up to them. I'll blow a few trumpets, jazz 'em up a bit, give them some well-deserved publicity. That ought to keep them happy. Just send the recall order, okay?"

"You want to use the media?" Stone sounded cautious. "Colonel Towers will not like that. TAP is supposed to be our greatest secret."

"Let's face reality, Dee," Kage snorted. "Our greatest secret just outlived their purpose. They're obsolete. I just did their job. All they have left to do is catch one little Heir Defender, and then they can have all the leave they want, living off oversized pensions."

"I don't know...."

"Hey, you gave me this position. Don't question it."

Stone was still hesitant. "Jonathon, you may be right, but I don't want to act impulsively at a time like this."

"A time like what? Like national glory, jubilation? Track and Pursuit had better be honoured that I want them one last time. I'm doing them a favour. And you owe me one. You know that."

"All right," Stone agreed reluctantly. "I'll recall Major Shark, and have him deploy to Port Yellowknife. He'll hunt the Heir Defender."

"No." Jonathon Kage was adamant. "This is their last job, and I want no stone unturned. Send in all the guys. All of them. I don't care about their 'work alone' crap right now."

"That's not feasible in the time window we have," the prime minister reminded him. "Captain Falcon and Sergeant-Major Hawk are overseeing the new Towers

Program, and only six of the other operatives are still in Manitoba and Ontario. You'd have to fly the other two in from Alberta."

"Then we'll close the Towers Program."

"I will *not* close the Towers Program!" Stone snapped.

"Fine! I'll send six. But they'd better find this guy. I'll have their pensions if they mess this up."

"Director Kage, we need to have some intel for them. Colonel Towers will balk if I just tell him 'Heir Defender, south of the port.'"

"There's six of them, Aunt Dee. Tell them to look for footprints, or broken grass, or whatever. They should be able to handle that much. I want containment. I deserve it. Good day."

"Take care, Mr. Director. I hope you're right."

"When have I not been?" Kage retorted as the prime minister's image faded away.

Chapter Nine

January 3, 2191.
Track and Pursuit Headquarters.
Somewhere in the western forests of Manitoba,
Canadian Exodus.

As far as the Canadian public was concerned, there was no such thing as an elite covert operations unit called Track and Pursuit. Some remembered that such a unit had been suggested in 2167, as a response to the Bloodline invasion of Port Yellowknife, but the official story was that too many soldiers had died in the training exercises, and the entire program had been terminated before official formation of the unit. A few soldiers who had passed the preliminary tests, only to be rejected before completion of the course, remembered the degree of eliteness required by the Towers Program, and spoke wistfully of what an unstoppable force Track and Pursuit would have been, had it only been given a chance.

The Bloodline did not know that Track and Pursuit existed either, but they knew that there was something bad lurking in the woods of Continental Yukon. Over one thousand Bloodline troops and officers had either been inexplicably killed or simply vanished into thin air since the unit commenced operations in 2170. The Bloodline forces told legends of the "Hidden Hunters," men who were never seen, never heard, and never lost. There were many of these legends, and one of them was that each Hunter carried a unique and unbreakable knife, bearing the image of a wildlife predator, whether that be a wild cat or bird of prey. Out of all the Bloodline's fantastic bedtime stories, that legend was one of the few that was completely true.

Twelve men had completed the Towers Program, and the nearly impossible 3-6-5. Eleven former Canadian soldiers and one civilian recruit had been accepted into Track and Pursuit, while the Canadex Census Registry Databanks listed all of them as having been killed in action during the 3-6-5. Towers had requested absolute covertness within the unit, and that meant that neither Track and Pursuit, nor its operatives, could officially exist.

Track and Pursuit was quietly fed information from every military and intelligence branch of the Canadian government, but every operative worked alone. The unit was not a division of the Canadian Armed Forces, or any specific government agency. Track and Pursuit was officially known to Parliament as "Independent Manitoban Mining Research and Development Grants." At every annual opening session of Parliament, an excruciatingly boring "Mining and Prospecting Report" would be read, and funding would be approved for another year. That was the subtle cycle of Track and Pursuit. In a world of incredible technological advancement, TAP was a unit which knew that there were times when technology was not enough. Sometimes, one man still had to be sent out to find one man. It was a unit of stone tools in a world of plasma energy, but, in 2191, that would all change, and the operatives involved would be changed forever.

After more than twenty years, TAP had only ten of the original twelve members remaining, and Major John Shark, formerly known as Lieutenant John Marcus Skyler of the New Canadian Airborne, would have been the first to assure anyone that the two members who were gone had been the two deadliest men on the planet. However, he had no time to ponder the unit's greatest losses on this second day of January as he entered the Track and Pursuit Briefing Room, still in civilian clothing. Colonel Towers had contacted Shark on his much-needed week of New Years leave with a succinct message.

Emergency recall. Come as you are.

John Shark was six feet, two inches tall, every inch of it hard muscle. His forty-fifth birthday was approaching with depressing speed, but age had yet to slow him in the field, although he did wonder how much of his hair would grow back if he ever stopped shaving his head every couple of days. He had killed almost forty high-priority Bloodline officers, Hitters, and defectors in his career, and captured nearly one hundred more. Shark had earned his position as senior ranking operative in the unit, although he was fully aware of the pointlessness of rank in TAP. No one reported to him, and he only reported directly to Colonel Towers. After all, with the exception of a very select and high-ranking handful, everyone else thought that he was dead. Ranks were merit badges, nothing more.

The empty Briefing Room was a small oak-paneled auditorium, circular with a sloping floor, and descending rows of desks, three rows of four, all facing the curved monitor built into the wall at the bottom of the run. A small touch-screen was raised on each desktop, each one the flat blue colour of stand-by mode.

Shark was early. He adjusted his knife belt, shifting his long, slightly S-curved knife, the dim overhead light panels glinting on the intricate shark outline stenciled into the blade. The desk at the near corner of the back row was his, and had been ever since the very first briefing of the unit. Only today, something was different. As a man trained to spot every anomaly in an instant, he noticed the absence immediately.

"Where's my plaque?" he said loudly, his voice echoing slightly in the emptiness.

"Talking to yourself, John," a sonorous voice replied from behind him. "A dangerous habit in the field."

"Just like walking with your feet hitting the floor heels first," Shark retorted. "I don't call that stealth."

"Feeling like a dinosaur, John?" Sergeant Hussaff Lion, once surnamed Kam, inquired with a chuckle from the doorway. "We finally get a second class in the unit, and the first thing they do is tell us that our desks are no longer ours anymore. Kids are probably going to be asking to borrow our knives next."

"Chrystanium better not be that rare," Shark muttered. "Kids.... This new government is getting way too involved. Life was easier when no one acknowledged us."

"The colonel says they're making us bake cookie-cutter troops," Lion agreed, sitting in the center desk of the middle row. He was a huge Arab man, over two hundred fifty pounds of power, with neatly trimmed black hair and beard. On his belt was a knife that looked like a meat cleaver, which had been used as one on countless Bloodline sentries. On the scale of pure, undiluted power, no one in TAP had ever been able to measure up to Hussaff Lion. He, too, was in civilian clothes, except for his knife belt. No operative of TAP was ever seen without that, on the occasions when they were seen at all.

"I just don't like the exposure, Saff," Shark admitted, booting up his desktop with the press of his thumb. "First a new government, next thing it's annual recruitment. We can't hide annual. It tells me that they don't think we're valuable enough to hide anymore."

"We're still under wraps, John," Lion consoled him. "They know we can't hunt if the entire Bloodline is hunting us."

"How long can they keep us wrapped with an annual recruitment program?" Shark grumbled. "It's too big, it's bringing in too many faces, and I don't like it. And aside from the breach risk, I don't want some grubby little punk sitting at my desk."

"Look, John, they terminate the 3-6-5, but the rest of the Towers is the same. Only the best are getting in. Besides, the youngest 'grubby little punk' is twenty four, and he was Navy STU. I was younger than that when I took it."

"Saff, I was the happiest man on earth to hear that we've got Yellowknife, but don't you see what it means?"

"The end of a war?" Lion guessed, not without some sarcasm.

"The end of our jobs."

"Well, between this and the Princess Pats, I've put in twenty-three years. If it comes to that, pension quality living is not an unpleasant thought. If you still need to kill somebody, hire out to the private sector. Lots of big suits will pay top dollar for Hitters of our grade."

"I do feel like a dinosaur," Shark sighed. "Drain the Bloodline, and we dry up too. I'll have to put in for a teaching job with Ridge and Kale."

"You'll live, John," Lion laughed. "Twenty years of the job hasn't killed us, I doubt post-war retirement will. I think it's time we hand these desks over to a new crew. We'll all be teaching sooner or later. You teach improvisation, I'll teach unarmed, Python teaches bladed weapons, Cobra on the snipe course. We all have our calling."

Shark rubbed his face between his hands. "Teachers.... I don't know. Every time the word comes up, I get this image of me with a bowtie and glasses on the end of my nose. I'd rather get hit."

"That can be arranged, too. Next hunt, just step on a dry leaf and hesitate. All the problems of this life go away."

Lion paused to boot up his own desktop. When the index display came up, he touched 'Mission Profile.' The sub-screen came up blank.

"No updates," he grunted. "Must have just come in before we got the call. Haven't even uploaded yet."

"So, what can be so important?" Shark wondered. "We got Kressel, whole staff, Defenders, and swabbies are moving in to mop up. We should already be getting decommissioned."

"Six recalled for one job?" Lion sighed. "That doesn't happen." He was bothered by a thought. "You think they're putting all of us on the same one?"

Shark tapped his monitor, scrolling through his mission archives. "That would be the only thing that makes sense, unless this is some kind of breach precaution. I mean, really. Who's left to hunt?"

"But Bruin and Python never even got contacted," Lion noted. "Forget it. I have no clue what's happening."

The four remaining recalled operatives all arrived over the next few minutes, all early and out of uniform. The first was Captain Martin Tiger, previously Lieutenant Martin Calvin, who had volunteered for the Towers Program from the New Shilo Armored Division. Calling himself the unit's trapper, rather than a hunter, he would go out of his way to bring his targets in alive. He firmly believed that the law should be the final judge of all terrorists. Although he had killed when the Bloodline forced his hand, he had captured ninety percent of his targets, often under circumstances which would have persuaded any other operative to activate the Cuff's evac code while sticking a knife through the target's throat.

Following on Tiger's heels was his closest friend, Captain Gerald Eagle, formerly Lieutenant Gerald

Grimms of the Toronto Exodus Navy Special Tactical Unit. A redheaded Irishman with a rather non-stereotypical cool temper, he was arguably the best pistol shot in the unit, ion particle or projectile. He had written his own chapter in the TAP legend book by being the only unit member to infiltrate Port Yellowknife, as far as the outer stockade, to capture one of General Kressel's favorite Hitters, Alexander Blue, an assassin responsible for the deaths of Canadian Justice Minister Rosalind Pike and three of her personal bodyguards. Eagle was the joker. He made everyone laugh. Laughter was a rarity in TAP. Every operative needed more.

Sergeant-Major Thomas Darcy, New Canadian Airborne, had been given the name Cobra, and had risen to the rank of Lieutenant. As an NCA sniper, his weapon of choice was the HK-80 Ion Particle Snipe. He had twenty-eight long kills to his credit, fifteen of them officers above the rank of captain. However, he was also highly efficient at capture missions, and had brought many troops and officers in for trial and incarceration. He called himself bi-planetary, the son of an Ottawa businessman, who had been raised for most of his teen years on the Earth Home Base.

The last to enter the room was Gunner Alphonso Manetti, now known as Alphonso Cheetah. He was a munitions and espionage specialist, often utilizing improvised traps or bombs to acquire his targets. He had never accepted a single promotion, wanting to retain the last shred of his RCHA identity. As he liked to say, "A cheetah can't retract his claws." Repeatedly proving himself to be the fastest long and short distance sprinter in the unit, he had more than earned his predatory namesake. Fine blonde hair and a lean build added to his cat-like appearance.

Every man wore a knife, either in a belt sheath or boot, each one vastly different, and the most cherished of all their possessions. TAP operatives did not have dog-tags. Their knives were the only identification the hunters carried.

After the usual banter and questions that no one could answer, there was nothing to do but sit in silence and wait for the colonel.

Chapter Ten

January 3, 2191.
Holding cell of Cole Dallas Kressel,
HMS Sovereignty,
Saskatchewan Ocean, off Yellowknife harbor,
Continental Yukon,
Canadian Exodus.

Kressel was handcuffed to the steel arms of his chair, and his tiny cell was dark. Creaks and groans of metal fatigue filled his ears, sounds which he had always hated. The general had not been on an aquatic vessel since his own amphibious assault on the port. He believed in keeping his feet in his great-grandfather's soil.

There was coffee in the room. A tin mug had been placed on the cold metal table before him when he had first been taken aboard, but no one had loosed his hands to allow him to sip from it. The aroma made his throat feel all the more parched.

Kressel had been sitting in black silence for nearly six hours when a blinding overhead light was switched on, and the heavy magnetic door swung wide open.

Dressed in camo fatigues, General Alvardo Krunnion stepped into the cell, holding his own mug of java and a pad of paper. He did not say a word, but made firm eye contact as he sat across from the table between them. Then he looked down at the paper, and began writing, ignoring the prisoner in front of him. Kressel raised his brow as he looked on the face of his most formidable adversary for the first time.

"Where are the bodies?" Krunnion asked quietly.

"You could say hello," Kressel ventured. "I will begin. Hello General Alvardo Diaz Krunnion. I am honoured to finally meet you."

Krunnion's voice was flat, and he never looked up or stopped writing.

"Port Yellowknife, and most of Continental Yukon, has been neutralized by a satellite-affixed aerial directionality electro-magnetic pulse cannon, a prototype that we call the Blackout Chimney Sweep. Your men are housed below decks, and are being fed and well cared for. Thirty-six survived, including yourself. Twenty-two are being treated for non-life threatening injuries, the others are relatively unharmed, and only one is confirmed escaped. Where are the bodies?"

"I believe in civility, Alvardo," Kressel replied coolly. "Talk to me. How is your wife?"

In one swift motion, Krunnion was on his feet, and the back of his closed fist was striking Kressel's mouth. The Bloodline general spat blood, his head snapping to one side.

"Don't ever tell me about civility, *Cole*," Krunnion whispered fiercely. "Every Canadian soldier captured here in '67 has been confirmed dead by way of your televised executions. That is three hundred forty-two of my troops whose bodies have never been recovered. Where are they?"

"Your passion is inspiring, General," Kressel rasped, gingerly licking the blood from his teeth.

"It may prove to be overwhelming if you do not answer my question," Krunnion said, walking slowly behind Kressel's chair. "Do not force my hand again, or the blow that follows will be crippling in the most literal sense."

"Loose my hands, General," Kressel snarled. "What a comical sight that would be! Two old men, settling differences like children on a playground. I cannot escape, but see how well I can still hold my own!"

"Save your breath for rotting in The Desert," Kressel said, sitting back in his own seat and taking up his pen. "I want the exact plot location. Where are the bodies?"

Kressel smiled at the memory. "We retained twelve pirates to dig a mass grave. Very commendably, they did the job with vigor, knowing that their own fate was sealed, but acting in the interests of giving their fellows a decent resting place. You train them well, Krunnion. You may remember those twelve. They were the ones who prayed and then sang your national anthem as they died."

"I want a location." Krunnion's voice could barely be heard.

Kressel nodded. "Beneath the airstrip, north end. The bodies were left with all dog-tags. You should be able to confirm the identities of all three hundred five men and thirty-seven women. Is there anything else you would like to beat out of me? I am very vulnerable at the moment."

Krunnion stood. "I would like to beat one hundred years of war out of you, but I don't have the time. However, I will ask you about the single Bloodline troop who got past us. Apparently, the Prime Minister's Office has an interest in the man. Out of a unit of one hundred, you have fourteen surviving Heir Defenders. We cannot find one, and one of my commandos was wounded with a bladed weapon, most likely an Heir Defenders Blade. Tell me who I'm looking for."

"The man escaped into the woods?" Kressel clarified.

"Southwest quadrant," Krunnion confirmed. "You had a supervisory Defender stationed in each outpost tower. Who is he?"

"Southwest quad...." Kressel mused, thinking back. He stiffened as the memory came back to him, but then he was smiling even wider than before.

"I want a name," Krunnion snapped.

Kressel was laughing. He was laughing very hard.

"My Defenders Command Second was posted at the southwest, Alvardo," he eventually chuckled. "And even your Hidden Hunters can't find him. Good day, General."

Krunnion stared for a long time at the Bloodline Heir. He knew that further questioning would be pointless. Kressel was facing banishment and death, and he would still treat life as a game.

Krunnion gathered his mug and pad, and headed for the hatch, leaving Kressel cuffed to the chair, the mug still out of reach.

"Good day, General Kressel. Enjoy that coffee."

Chapter Eleven

January 3, 2191.
Briefing Room,
Track and Pursuit Headquarters,
Somewhere in the western forests of Manitoba,
Canadian Exodus.

The operatives of Track and Pursuit had been briefed on missions time and again by Colonel Towers, and they still never tired of rising to their feet in complete respect every time the aging soldier entered the room.

Shark, Lion, Cobra, Tiger, Eagle, and Cheetah were all standing at attention when the colonel appeared in the upper doorway. He nodded to each one of them as he crossed the sloping run, setting his mission folder open on the podium next to the wall monitor.

"As you were," he said dismissively, gesturing for the unit to be seated. Towers hair was getting whiter every day, but he had lost none of his poise. He gripped the edges of the podium and looked up from the folder. "To the point, boys. Two apologies. I'm sorry that you were called in after only two days of leave, and I'm sorry that your plaques have been removed from your desktops. Annual recruitment was not my idea, but our new government, in all its wisdom, is beginning to take a personal interest in the command procedures of our unit. You're working for the Minister of Defense, CSIS Director Kage, and the Prime Minister's Office now. Not me. I'm sorry. The second graduating class will be reporting in for duty next week, and Captain Falcon is welcoming the third class to the Badlands Towers Program. We have to face some facts. The government does not respect our need for covertness anymore. And now that Yellowknife's been taken ... there's already talk of disbanding us. We've done our part, boys, but we're getting political. I'm beginning to wish that I had come up with a cover that would have allowed the entire government and military to believe that we were all dead back in '70, but it's too late for wishful thinking.

"You're going to hate this, kids, and I don't blame you. The Prime Minister's Office, and CSIS, want some kind of spectacular finale to the Bloodline War, and they're running reckless. We've been assigned to join a manhunt in Continental Yukon."

"'Join?'" Shark cringed, shocked enough to speak out of turn.

Towers sighed. "I fought it. You men work alone, definitely not as part of a mop-up crew. But they aren't budging on this one. They have issued a press release, naming Track and Pursuit as unsung heroes, flying in to save the day. It's drama, boys. Nothing else. We are officially in the open. Your face's are all over the news."

"*What?*" Shark could barely control his voice.

"Kage is calling it 'declassification.' At least, that's the word the public is hearing. Valerie Kine, that hot little number on Parliamentary Six has apparently got the exclusive this evening, talking to Kage as though we were his idea. As far as I know, none of you are invited."

"Great," Eagle quipped irritably. "They skyline us, and then we don't even get to meet Valerie Kine."

Towers smiled grimly. "Afraid not, Gerald."

"Are they insane?" Lion demanded. "Just because we've got Yellowknife does not mean that the sky is clear!"

"I know, I know," Towers muttered. "They've put every one of you in danger by giving you the recognition you all so justly deserve. They think this is over, that Johnny's ready to come marching home again. We know better, and General Krunnion knows better, but they're going over his head, too. They want a triumphant return with the one that got away. We're the climax. It's all a show."

Cheetah leaned back in his seat and stared disgustedly at the round ceiling. "They put us on TV...."

"Which is why we have to proceed with the utmost caution," Towers was adamant. "This could be our last job, let's do it right. John, we may need to pull a few strings that we don't actually have."

Shark raised an inquisitive eyebrow. "How do you mean, sir?"

Towers grinned slightly. "I've been informed that you are all to be placed provisionally under the command of Colonel James Reynolds and the other strike team commanders. Reynolds and I go back a long way. He's a good man, and he owes me one. He'll play along with the ruse that Major Shark has complete operational command. I can probably get General Krunnion to back that as well. John, I need you in charge of this op. I do not want over-zealous commanders and politicians screwing this up. To the rest of you, I know that you've never actually had to answer to John before, but you know that it will be better than listening to a bunch of hotshots looking for reputations. Are we clear?"

"Yes, sir," they all replied with affirmative nods.

Tiger raised a questioning finger.

"Marty?" the colonel acknowledged.

"Who's the target, sir?" Tiger inquired.

"Well, that's the best part of all," Towers chuckled. "We have no name, and no real intel. All we know is that he is an Heir Defender, most likely Flaxton's second in command."

"Most likely," Shark emphasized, still wary of the entire mission, and not finding the colonel's words very reassuring.

Towers shook his head helplessly. "The Bloodline doesn't log in personnel files as meticulously as we do, although I do admire their screening program. Inside men have just not been an option. The bottom line is that we're blind. You all know that I would never send you on a hunt with only this much intel. We've stayed alive by knowing exactly what we're doing and what we're getting into. The Prime Minister's Office is impatient, and it's out of my hands. You are all free to refuse this mission, and I emphasize that. However ... the way Kage likes to throw his weight, it could be the end of your careers."

"Sir, what's the significance?" Cobra had to ask. "An Heir Defender who has done so little that his name isn't even on our scope? Why do they need him?"

"They don't," Towers said frankly. "Kage wants him. Apparently, that's what matters."

"So," Shark said reflectively, "all we've got is a faceless Heir Defender in the woods, and he's good enough to get through a CNE Commando net."

"And wound one of the commandos, at close range, with a sword," Towers added emphatically. "Do not underestimate this man. We've all seen the kind of things that Defenders are capable of. Close range ... *with a sword.*"

"The colonel's right," Eagle agreed. "I'm the only one here who's ever had a Defender job before. They're good, the best even, but how many are good enough to get through a net with just a sword?"

"You've all got five senses," Towers reminded them. "Use six for this one. The target is somewhere in the forest south of the port, heading for any of the nearby camps or fallback points. You're going back into monster territory. The next major Bloodline stronghold is Fort Lawrence, but that's nearly four hundred k to the southeast. There are three known locations to the west and southeast that will have a contingent of troops, as well as Bloodline loyalists. We're watching what roads there are, but all of those points are within walking range in two to three days, so we've got a day and a half. He's got a twelve hour head start, and that will probably be sixteen by the time you're on the ground. As far as we know, the entire continent is neutralized, and I doubt they have the technology to recharge weapons and electrical systems, but it is a possibility, so we need to find him before he gets to a populated area. Full topographical maps will be uploaded to your monitors on the Runner. Ignore everyone else who will want to help with the hunt, find the trail, mark out a twenty kilometer perimeter, and do a grid search. Once the target is acquired, call for evac with the Cuff. Oh, and since you'll all be playing the same field for the first time … don't shoot each other. Clear?"

"*Yes, sir!*"

"Outstanding," Towers said with a proud nod. "Watch out for monsters, boys. We're gonna get'em!"

"*We're gonna get'em, sir!*"

"Suit up and armor up," Towers instructed. "Runner leaves in an hour.

November 1, 2168.

An open letter to the volunteers of the Towers Program, and Track and Pursuit Unit.

Good day, boys and girls.

In two months time, those of you who have made it this far will begin the 3-6-5. That will be the most difficult training exercise ever attempted, and many of you who choose to embark upon it will die. Be under no illusion.

Before the 3-6-5 can be attempted, the second most difficult exercise must begin. You had to be good to get to this point, but good is never good enough. Most of the enemies you will hunt will be unaware of your presence, but you must never allow yourself to believe that, ever. You must be able to hunt those who are hunting you back.

Over the next two months, every one of you will have the opportunity, and the rare privilege, to hunt me. While the successful completion of this exercise is not a prerequisite to the 3-6-5, it is still one of the most important tests you will ever face. I'm told that I am very good.

You will be judged on how well you perform, and on whether or not you survive, metaphorically speaking, of course.

Happy hunting, kids. I've always enjoyed laser-tag.

We're gonna get'em.

Captain Maxmillan Towers,
CNE-CT4

December 31, 2168.

Final hunt exercise results, out of 64 attempts.

Successful hunt: 2 of 64.
Cpl. Chester Bradley, CNE.
Vance Coolidge.
Successful survival: 4 of 64.
Cpl. Chester Bradley, CNE.
Vance Coolidge.
Lt. Ridgely Tumbler, CNE.
Lt. John Skyler, NCA.

Chapter Twelve

January 3, 2191.
Canadex retaken military airstrip,
Port Yellowknife, Continental Yukon,
Canadian Exodus.

The mood of the Canadian troops at Port Yellowknife was both tense and excited. Most of the soldiers had heard whispers of the Hidden Hunters, but they had never heard anything concrete until that day. Now, there were two stories dominating every newscast on the planet. The first was that the Bloodline War was over. The second was about a covert unit called Track and Pursuit, which was making its first public appearance in a volunteer mission to aid their allies in one final hunt. A photo of the original twelve operatives aired constantly, and the public was desperate to know who these reclusive heroes were.

The TAP Runner was flying over the last miles of ocean, and Major John Shark was getting angrier by the minute as he watched the footage from the cargo bay.

"We fought for twenty years to defend the system that's blowing our cover on national TV," he muttered, sitting on the seating racks that ran along each side of the long bay. "Remind me to move to another planet when we get back."

"They're just giddy," Sergeant Hussaff Lion chuckled, checking the action on his HK Ion-57 Particle Rifle, and slinging the weapon over his shoulder. Like Shark and the other operatives, he was wearing forest green combat gear and an armored vest, magnetically charged to protect against projectile, fragmentation, and pulse weapons.

"Giddy," Captain Gerald Eagle snorted, filling his ammo pouches with freshly charged ion clips. "I call it hanging us out to dry. Every Hitter on the planet just got a face to put on his revenge fantasies."

"Look on the sunny side," Lion said lightly, grinning. "They've only mentioned John by name so far. Stay out of his neighborhood, and we're all clear."

"Shut up!" Shark snarled good-naturedly, throwing a headlock around Lion's thick neck. Lion was still laughing as he struggled to get loose, mimicking the distinctive voice of news anchor Valerie Kine.

"*Leading this daring mission is senior Track and Pursuit operative Major John Shark, who enjoys long walks on the beaches of New Shilo, wearing no shoes or kevlar.*"

"*Shut up!*" Shark repeated, also laughing as Lion broke free and lifted the major high over his head. No one ever won a grappling match against Hussaff Lion.

"There it is," Gunner Alphonso Cheetah interrupted, gesturing toward the nose-view monitor.

It was the first time that any of them had flown directly to the port. Any approach to Continental

Yukon was usually amphibious or from the more exposed eastern coastline. It was a day of firsts.

The retaken military complex was a swarming hive. Technicians and sailors from the anchored offshore fleet were working overtime to ferry in the supporting Infantry units, in preparation for the rebuilding of the devastated port and the continental sweep. Massive CNE Liners were also bringing in more and more Canadian troops from every other continent. More than three thousand soldiers were now encamped around a base that had been the Bloodline stronghold only twenty-four hours before.

Colonel James Reynolds was waiting by the airstrip with Captain Ed Wallace when the deep green TAP Runner set down in front of them, the whirring hover plates raising a cloud of dust as the transport shuttle came to rest. The engine's roar idled slightly, being replaced with the sound of hydraulic rods extending, lowering the tail loading ramp. Six men in forest green combat gear emerged from the rear bay, blinking against the dazzling sunlight. Reynolds had always wondered what the Hunters would look like, and he was immediately surprised by how lightly armed they were. Aside from the distinctive knives each carried, most of the operatives only carried one weapon. The lean man who led them did not even carry a rifle, only a sidearm. He held out his hand as he quickly strode up to Reynolds.

"Major Shark, thank you for coming," Reynolds yelled over the Runner's engines, accepting the firm hand shake. "This way, please. This is CT4 Captain Ed Wallace, Bravo Team Six. He can get you up to speed on this whole fiasco." He led everyone toward the T-52 Mobile Comm Center.

"What do we know, Captain?" Shark asked, shaking Wallace's hand as they walked across the pavement.

"Not much, Major," the stocky captain replied. "Four Heir Defenders were posted around the perimeter, one in each lookout tower. We hit the towers pretty hard on our first pass, almost all the troops inside were KIA. Delta Team was securing the southwest tower when they were attacked. Heir Defender, playing dead. Corporal Wynette was stabbed in the stomach with a sword, and the target got into the forest."

"How's your man?" Shark asked.

"Not good, sir. We med-evac'd him to New Shilo, still critical. We sent Charlie Team in pursuit as soon as we had Kressel secured, but no luck. The guy's a ghost."

"Anything on thermals?"

"Sweeps are ongoing, sir, but nothing's showing. Everything's too small, coyotes and rabbits. Either he's already out of our search grid, or he's gone cold."

"What about canine units?" Lion asked, as they entered the comm center, a massive converted combat vehicle.

"Dogs are a no-go," Reynolds sighed. "We brought them into the southwest quad, and they couldn't find a thing. I ordered a spectral analysis of the area, and scanners picked up traces of some type of ammonia blended compound. We're running it now."

"Red Herring Mist," Shark ventured. "We've used it, it's good for throwing off search dogs, irritates and confuses the nasal cavities. How far out are your thermal sweeps?"

"We're holding at thirty-five k, west through southeast," Wallace replied, rolling out the contour map of the region over the briefing table. "Aside from the main to Lawrence, there's no roads. There's air traffic and goat trails. Nothing's moving on any of them."

Shark ran his finger from the location of Port Yellowknife to the nearest camp to the west.

"The coastal supply farm is the closest, but I'm betting he'll head for Camp 2-4, forty-two k southwest. He's going to be looking for troops, not just loyalists. Colonel, we're going to need you to extend your thermals another ten k. What's our time-frame?"

"Sixteen hours," Reynolds replied, folding his arms.

"Sixteen," Shark mused, rubbing his jaw. "Forty-two kilometers.... It's tough in that terrain, but it's doable. We need to move fast. He could be there already." Something was bothering Shark, and he had to ask, "Are you sure he only had a sword? Sidearm? Rifle?"

Reynolds shook his head.

"All witnesses say that he only had the Heir Defenders Blade, standard issue."

"Did anyone get a good look at him?"

"Caucasian or Latino male, shaved head, late thirties, early forties. Nothing definitive."

"This doesn't make sense," Tiger interjected. "He's in a lookout tower, gets bombed, loses his gun. The tower has no supply cache he can access, so he fights his way out with a sword. Two hours later, he's running cold, and dogs can't find him?"

"What's your point?" Shark asked.

Tiger shook his head. "You cannot tell me that he was carrying Red Herring Mist, and wearing a modulator, on a lookout assignment within the most secure fortress in the Bloodline possession."

"The Bloodline doesn't have modulators," Wallace stated. "They're way too new."

"Then he smuggled or bought it," Tiger said. "How else do you explain it? Three ways to run cold: Modulator, evacuation, or death. There's nothing for an evac on this continent, and, if he was dead, the dogs would have found him."

"Modulators aren't shielded," Reynolds pointed out. "The EMP would have disabled it."

"Unless it was stored in an emergency vault offsite," Shark commented. "Shielded, underground. Magnetic bunker maybe."

"They'd never have the funding to build something like that, or the necessary technology to maintain it," Reynolds was certain. "The Bloodline could hold this continent, but they were too contained to develop it. It took everything they had to keep Yellowknife and Lawrence operational."

"So, if there is a bunker, we put it there before '67," Shark realized. "Run the archive schematics."

"It's possible," Wallace admitted, turning to the file monitor. "Updates might have missed it, if it's overgrown. I'll get one of our Chops to start running a shielder sweep."

"Fall Point Bunker," Reynolds said, as the memory came back to him. "I remember it."

"Sir?" Shark said, raising an eyebrow.

"I was stationed here in '66," Reynolds replied grimly. "Transferred out to CNE two months before the attack. Fall Point Bunker was five kilometers due south of here. Emergency storage and bomb shelter, shielded against air displacement, nuclear pulse, and EMP."

Shark nodded. "That's where we'll start. Kressel may have discovered it, used it as an emergency cache. Colonel, we're going in dark. Our Cuffs will read as frequency K-109 on your monitors. Watch for Morse Code retrieval calls, we'll send them to you from the Runner."

"Very well," Reynolds agreed. "Major, Colonel Towers informed me that this was your op. Tell me what you need."

"Pull off all thermal sweeps," Shark instructed. "I don't want him tipped off by aircraft. Pull everything out, it's just us. Have six Chops on stand-by to evac my men back here when the target is acquired."

"On your coded signal," Reynolds acknowledged. "What happens if we only receive an unbroken signal?"

Shark smiled. "Then something very bad is happening. Initiate emergency thermal sweeps, and get my men out of there."

"Colonel," a comm lieutenant announced. "Rosewood Eight just reported in. Affirmative magnetic readings, five k south. The shielders are still operational."

"Fall back to the Runner," Shark said to his unit. "Colonel, we'll need you to upload the bunker's exact location and schematic to our bird. After that, break all contact with us."

"You're going in dark?" Wallace was confused. "No radios?"

"We always go dark," Shark assured him. "You use your eyes and ears a lot more when they're all you have."

Chapter Thirteen

January 3, 2191.
Fall Point Bunker,
5 km south of Port Yellowknife,
Continental Yukon,
Canadian Exodus.

The bunker was built into a washed out riverbank, and obviously had not been visited in years. The river had long since run dry, and the heavy vault entrance was all but invisible to the naked eye, heavily blanketed with protruding roots and driftwood. An untrained eye would never have spotted the door, and only those with Shark's powers of observation would have known that it had been opened only a few hours earlier.

Cobra had the door in the sights of his HK-80 Snipe from his position high in the treetops, his face painted green and black. Nothing was moving. Standing directly below the sniper, John Shark knew that no one was in the bunker. He knew that the only covert approach to the bunker was from behind it, on the southwest side of the bank. Any other approach was too exposed. Shark also knew that the temperature was sixteen degrees Celsius, the wind was blowing at a speed of seven kilometers per hour, and that his own position was one hundred ninety meters due north of the vault. Crossing the forest floor and dry riverbed with caution would take thirty-five to forty seconds. He would cross alone.

The four other operatives were spread out over five hundred meters along the north bank, all of them covering the vault entrance. Shark did not say a word as he drew his pistol, armed it, and cradled the weapon in both hands as he began his approach. His treadless combat boots made no sound on the cool black loam beneath them, and he never took his eyes off the vault door before him. His men were in charge of watching the forest. He was in charge of watching that door.

The sound of a hunt was silence. Shark's clothing did not rustle, his gear did not clack, and his feet did not thud. In the woods, Colonel Towers had often told him, people lived and died with the snap of a twig, and Shark did not intend to be one of them. He was a hunter, but he had rarely been as wary as he was on that day. For the first time in his career as a Track and Pursuit, Shark had no idea who he was hunting.

The riverbed was an exposed obstacle which Shark would have never considered attempting had he been alone, but the rules were now different. Five men were watching his back, and he had to trust them. After twenty years of working in solitude, there was nothing more difficult than trust.

Major Shark crossed the riverbed, barely disturbing the water-rounded stones, and stepped quickly to the east side of the vault door, pausing just long enough to click on his gun light. He touched the edge of the door, and it swung open easily and silently. A dark concrete staircase led down into the bank, deep underground. Whoever had been there had not even attempted to reseal the entrance.

There were size ten footprints around the doorway, but the patterns were curious. The Heir Defender had left a lot of tracks there, almost as though he had been waiting, pacing back and forth. The prints were unsmudged, close together, and deepest at the heel end, indicative of slow and deliberate movements. Shark had expected two sets of prints, one running in and another running out.

All of the tracks had been caused by the same pair of boots, with a tread pattern that matched the Heir Defenders combat footwear. Shark felt a cold lump forming in his stomach as he realized that the tracks leading back into the woods south of him were no more than four hours old.

Shark turned quickly to the northwest, knowing that he was staring into Sergeant Hussaff Lion's scope. He held up a forefinger. In seconds, he could see Lion's burly form rushing noiselessly toward him, doubled over and keeping low to the ground. He almost looked like a four-legged creature, yet he could still sprint as fast as any man standing erect.

Lion was at the vault in under thirty seconds, covering the opposite side of the door.

"What's wrong?" Lion whispered, in a voice that Shark would not have heard had he been only a foot farther away.

"Why did he hang around?" Shark muttered, glancing down at the footprints. "Why isn't he running?"

"Old tracks and fresh," Lion said with soft surprise. "He camped out here."

"He's not making sense," Shark growled. "I would've sworn he was long gone."

"And now you're not sure," Lion smiled. "Good heavens, Major. Is that a first?"

"Just watch my back. Let's clear."

Lion nodded, clicking the gunlight on his HK Ion-57 Assault Rifle.

Two light beams lit up the long staircase, and the two hunters began their slow descent into the concrete vault. By the time they reached the second vault door at the foot, and swept the huge underground room, Shark estimated that they were nearly two hundred fifty feet below the surface.

"Clear," he said. "No other exits."

The vault was large enough to house two hundred bodies in the event of crisis, and held enough food supplies to maintain that population for one month. Racks of weapons and survival equipment lined every wall, behind sliding glass locks.

"What are we looking for, John?" Lion asked, lowering his weapon. "He's not here."

"The supplies are electronically logged in with mag-locks," Shark said, turning on the inventory console by the base of the stairs. "Kressel would have kept this place fully stocked. We look for holes."

The screen lit up a pale green, a colour never seen on newer models. The system had not been updated since 2167, but that only made the operation simpler. Shark scrolled down the file banks and touched 'Opened

Locks.' There were only seven listings that had not been moved into archives.

"Unbelievable," he muttered, surprised. "Kressel never knew about this place! Nothing's been taken out between now and '67. Kressel might have left food supplies here, but they would have needed all these weapons. Half of the targets we ever took were on gun runs."

"What does that mean?" Lion demanded. "One Heir Defender finds this place, and keeps it for himself? Who is this guy?"

"Or, he knew about it before he ever came to the continent," Shark suggested. "Saff, I've got it. He reversed seven locks, fourteen hours ago."

"What's missing?" Lion asked, still looking in all directions, but mainly covering the staircase.

"Ion charger," Shark read aloud. "Survival pack. Ion-57 Assault Rifle, pulse puppy model. Ammo packs, seven ion clips. Webbing gear. Sniper rags. And a frequency. He's traveling light. Saff, this place is a weapons cache. Why would he just take one puppy?"

"He took a frequency?" Lion asked quickly. "Broadcast or two-way?"

Shark closed his eyes and sighed through his nose, lips pressed tightly together.

"Broadcast," he answered dully. "He's been listening to the news."

"Which we're all over," Lion finished, shaking his head. "He knows we're here."

"We landed in a Runner," Shark stated acceptantly. "If he's within ten kilometers, he knows we're here. Find those survival packs. Green racks, C-slots on the east wall, about halfway down. I'm opening the lock on the far north end. Tell me everything he's carrying."

"Found it," Lion called back, pulling the deep green backpack off the rack. "And there's one missing."

"Open it up," Shark muttered, closing the inventory window and touching 'Sanctum Surveillance.' The heading began flashing red, and the video did not appear.

"He deleted the surveillance tapes," Shark said, frustrated. "He's hiding his face, but not his trail."

"I know. I can't figure it out," Lion replied. "Okay, we've got a hooded forest cloak, tan and green, a hazard hood and gas mask, travel rations, med case, cooking utensils, folding shelter, thermal blanket, aluminum fire bag, phosphorous flares, compass, and.... Oh, here's a good one. Clean socks."

"So, how can he still be cold?" Shark wondered. "If there was a modulator here, it was the only one. There's no more here. If he had a modulator, why would he hide it here? It makes more sense to keep it with him. EMP strike was never even a threat."

"Could thermals penetrate this deep?" Lion was skeptical. "He could have been waiting in here the entire time they were sweeping."

"But he hasn't been here for at least four hours, and it's over an hour to get here on foot," Shark decided. "That's nearly six hours in the open, and Chops only just pulled back. He's gone cold, some way that we don't know about."

"John, I don't like this," Lion said honestly. "He's not doing anything. Fights out of Yellowknife, then just sits here? He knows that the famous Hidden Hunters are en route, yet he didn't touch the two-ways to try to contact other camps. He's not trying to escape, and he's not waiting for evac. The man is just waiting."

"An invisible enemy who prepares, listens, and waits," Shark mused. "Boy, who does that sound like?"

Lion thought about that, clearly bothered.

"John, he's hunting us."

Chapter Fourteen

January 3, 2191.
Northern Forests of Continental Yukon,
Canadian Exodus.

Track and Pursuit survived by knowing their prey. John Shark knew next to nothing about the man he was hunting, and what he did know both puzzled and troubled him. Every man Shark had ever hunted was dangerous, but he was now more reluctant than ever to embark on this particular mission without better intel. For the first time in his career, he used one of the two-ways from the bunker to contact Colonel Reynolds and request a fallback order from the Prime Minister's Office. The prime minister was not to be disturbed, but the Minister of Defense relayed Dee Robertson Stone's insistence that the Heir Defender be apprehended at any cost, and, by the way, CSIS Director Kage was getting impatient.

Shark regrouped with his unit at the Runner in a small clearing, and told them that the target was fully aware, and was most likely within a fifteen kilometer radius. In spite of the prime minister's directive, the major made it clear that any one of them was free to remain with the Runner. He was going to continue the pursuit, but would not order any of them to do so.

No one would consider falling back, and the hunt began.

The signs that led away from the bunker did not stay visible for long. More than anything else, that bothered Shark. The Heir Defender only left a trail where he wished for it to be found, so Track and Pursuit was not really hunting. They were being baited.

The dry riverbed and stone cliffs to the southeast were the most likely paths that the target would have taken, being largely rock and gravel. The bunker was built at the base of a horseshoe curve, which then ran several kilometers to the south and southeast. Shark assigned each operative a hunting area, covering a span of nearly thirty kilometers. The major deliberately assigned himself the southwest riverbank, in his opinion the most likely route the target would have taken.

Both suns were high over the leaves of the treetops as the six men fanned out into the woods, six predators all hunting the same prey. Shark was uneasy, concern for his unit making it harder to focus on the job. That was the advantage of working alone. When Shark could live and breathe nothing but the hunt, he was one of the most lethal men alive. Empathy and safety concerns were distractions he did not need.

Major John Shark would have been much more concerned had he known that the target was within one hundred feet of the TAP operatives, watching as each one diverged out of sight, the shadows of tall trees blacking out their elusive forms in seconds. They were soundless, and virtually invisible in the woods. TAP operatives were nothing short of the absolute best, a fact that the target was well aware of. He could tell where each one would be hunting, and knew that it would be double the challenge to find each one of them over such a wide search area. He was ready for the challenge. The target was possibly the only conscious being on the planet who knew exactly what Track and Pursuit was capable of, and yet had no desire to flee.

Cloaked and masked, he stepped into the clearing where his hunters had stood, and carefully read the signs each had left. He was preparing for the hunt as well, and knew that it would be unlike any other.

December 1, 2168.

An open letter to the volunteers of the Towers Program, and Track and Pursuit Unit.

All year, you have been told that the worst is yet to come, and it is called the 3-6-5. You will embark on it in one month, and many of you who choose to do so will not return alive. Now is the time for you to know what is being asked of you.

The 3-6-5. Three hundred sixty-five days, alone, in the woods of Continental Yukon, stronghold of the Bloodline, and long a collection point of its most radical followers. All you have to do is survive.

Each one of you will be issued the clothes on your back and a special wrist-worn transmitter, known informally as the 3-6-5 Cuff. That is all. You will be stealth-dropped into a preselected area of Bloodline territory at 06:00, January 1, 2169, and you will begin surviving.

Kill a sentry. Take his weapon. Kill another sentry. Take his rations. Dig a foxhole, barehanded if necessary. Take cover. Infiltrate. Eat. Sleep. Evade. Survive. That is the 3-6-5.

If you wander beyond the borders of your preselected area, the Cuff will self-activate. If the Cuff is removed, it will self-activate. If the Cuff is improperly removed, it will self-destruct. If your pulse stops, the Cuff will self-activate.

Whenever a Cuff activates under the above circumstances, an evac order will be issued, and you will be retrieved. You will then be taken directly to your original unit, or the Steele Hill Military Cemetery,

If you successfully complete the 3-6-5, at exactly 06:00, January 1, 2170, you will manually enter a preassigned Morse-Coded retrieval code into the Cuff, and evac will be dispatched to your location. If the retrieval code is entered at 05:59, you will be returned to your original unit. No exceptions.

The Cuff cannot be activated remotely. If you do not activate it, no one else will.

Go in, survive, and get out. Any volunteer who does not activate the Cuff by 07:00, January 1, 2170, will be pronounced dead.

I will not order any of you to do this. The 3-6-5 will be strictly voluntary, but successful completion is a prerequisite for admission into Track and Pursuit. I will think no less of any of you for instead choosing to return to your original units, where the training you have received here will be of great service to yourself and your country. But the choice is yours.

Go get'em.

Captain Maxmillan Towers,
CNE-CT4.

January 1, 2170.

3-6-5 final results.

Successful completion: 11 of 64.

Premature activation and live retrieval: 8 of 64.

Deceased: 45 of 64.

January 1, 2171.

3-6-5 revised results.

Successful completion: 12 of 64.

Premature activation and live retrieval: 8 of 64.

Deceased: 44 of 64.

Chapter Fifteen

January 5, 2191.

T-52 Mobile Communication Center,

Canadex retaken military airstrip,

Port Yellowknife, Continental Yukon,

Canadian Exodus.

There was no time to think about six men hunting one at Port Yellowknife. General Krunnion was on location, and his presence kept everyone busy. Transports were still arriving every few hours, and the troops were getting impatient to begin the continental sweep, which had been delayed due to an inexplicable desire by the CSIS Director to have the single missing Bloodline from Yellowknife apprehended before any further moves were made.

The military complex, once the pride of both the Canadex and the Bloodline, was too devastated to be saved. The Canadian flag had been removed from the shattered dome, and dusting crews were setting the charges that would drop what was left of the base in roaring clouds of fine grey powder.

Colonel James Reynolds stood in silence beside General Alvardo Krunnion, outside of the T-52 Comm Center, and they watched the final Ripple detonation sequence, the charges dusting what was left of the perimeter outposts. The last traces of Port Yellowknife dropped into grey clouds, as though smoking chasms had opened in the earth and swallowed the four towers whole.

Krunnion did not speak or flinch until the last wisps of dust had settled into the grey mat of powder and ash that had been Port Yellowknife.

"I was trained at this very base, James," the general said, his low voice a bit choked. Reynolds did not know if emotion or dust was to blame. "We got her back in time to say goodbye."

"I'm sorry she couldn't be saved, sir," Reynolds replied. "She was a fine base."

"Where were you trained, Colonel?" was Krunnion's next question, already knowing the answer.

"New Shilo basic, sir, then New Edmonton CNE, CT4 in polar Ontario."

Krunnion nodded. "Fine bases, all. James.... A soldier should never forget where he came from, Colonel. Our training camps should live on as monuments to the soldiers created there. A base should be a place of creation, not demolition and death."

"Canadian soldiers will be living monuments to this fallen base, sir," Reynolds said. "Many of them will live because Port Yellowknife died."

That made the general smile, just a little.

"Of course you're right, James. And we'll rebuild her. Her dome will rise higher than ever before. Built on the blood of men, Canadian and Bloodline, she'll rise higher."

"That she will, sir."

"James," the general sighed. "What this country owes you ... I cannot even explain it. On the Home Base, Canada was known globally for being synonymous with peace. We lost it when we came to a new world. Maybe, in some ironic way, this final slaughter has helped us to find it again."

"Perhaps, sir," Reynolds said tiredly. "Yet, I cannot believe that it's really over. General, I've lived the soldier's life, and I've seen the things that men do. I'm too old to hope for Utopia anymore."

"Understandable," Krunnion chuckled. "Just as long as you're not too old to have hope, of some kind. When you lose that, well, it's better to be dead."

Reynolds stood at attention and saluted, needing to return to Comm.

"O Canada, General Krunnion."

The general nodded and saluted in kind.

"O Canada, Colonel Reynolds. Report any word from Track and Pursuit to me immediately. We've already been delayed too long for this hunt."

"Sir." Reynolds turned on his heel and returned to the armored vehicle, his boots ringing on the corrugated steel ramp leading to the interior.

Captain Taylor Halak, Toronto Armored Division, was supervising the operations of the T-52, mostly a matter of coordinating and monitoring continual thermal sweeps over major Bloodline centers. Thus far, no one seemed to be attempting flight into the forests. Most were still baffled by their complete loss of power, and were futilely dedicating all resources and manpower to restoring electrical functions. For the moment, the only obstacle facing the impending continental sweep was the most under-equipped centers, where the occasional Bloodline troop would be armed with a manually or gas operated projectile weapon. Reynolds found it somewhat amusing that, in such a time of crisis, the most primitive of tools would prove to be the most valuable.

"Any movement, Captain?" Reynolds inquired.

Halak, a stocky, balding man with large glasses and an intense stare, shook his head.

"All I've seen is a few troops on the main trails, two at most. Messengers most likely, trying to reestablish contact with the other centers. Nobody's made destination yet, so they're still blind. As far as they know, they're the only ones who got hit."

"Excellent," Reynolds nodded. "Any word from our hunters? The general is very anxious to begin sweeping up."

"No, sir," Halak said, slightly disturbed. "Is two days a bit excessive?"

Reynolds sighed. "They have a lot of ground to cover. If we had thermal, it would be a different story, but somehow our man is alive and cold at the same time. We've just got to let them do what they do."

"It still amazes me, sir," Halak admitted, slightly awed. "Colonel Towers still alive, TAP is for real. We all thought it was a myth."

"I always suspected as much, but what amazes me is how impulsively the top of the food chain made them public," Reynolds muttered. "I knew Towers, and he will not be happy about losing his private slice of the pie. CSIS either thinks that TAP's day is past, or else they're just convinced that the war really is over."

"You aren't, sir?"

Reynolds shook his head, folding his arms as he watched the thermal monitors. "The Bloodline has a lot of supporters, Captain, and they're not all so neatly grouped into camps and strongholds. I look forward to a lot of uprisings in the next few years. It's going to be busy, and Track and Pursuit has been irreparably exposed."

"We are removing The Heir, sir," Halak reminded him. "The Bloodline can't last without a Kressel at its head. He's like a god in their eyes."

"They've lost Heirs before," Reynolds retorted. "And they found new ones. We *think* he's the last of his line, but who can know for sure? All I know is that any war that has survived one hundred years of negotiation and bloodshed will not end overnight. It's an historic impossibility."

It would be some time before Colonel Reynolds fully realized that the frequency which reached the comm tank at that very moment was a resounding verification of what he had just said.

"Sir!" a female comm lieutenant called. "Frequency K-109, 27 k southwest. Running Morse translation now."

"Track and Pursuit," Reynolds said, suddenly excited. "Captain Halak, get our stand-bys in the air, triangulate the exact location and move in for evac on my command."

"Aye, sir," Halak affirmed, touching the comm-link to the makeshift Chop hangar at the east end of the airstrip. "Rosewood One, this is Comm Center Peak. All Backbench birds stand by for Hunter evac, triangulate on transmission frequency Kansas dash one zero niner. Confirm."

"Roger that, Comm Center Peak. Confirmed triangulated, K-109."

The audio translation of the Cuff was a steady series of rapid, high-pitched clicks, which now filled the comm bay. Reynolds listened carefully, well aware of how rusty his own Morse Code was. He could not make out the coded message.

"I can't hear it," he admitted. "Lieutenant, what's the translation?"

The lieutenant was clearly confused as well.

"Nothing, sir. Translation reads no stops. It's unbroken frequency."

Reynolds could feel his face paling and chilling as he remembered Shark's warning.

"Captain Halak," he said slowly, "Send all stand-bys back into the triangulated zone now. If we do not receive a translated call-sign in the next thirty seconds, commence emergency thermal sweeps, holding radius at forty kilometers from the Fall Point Bunker. Do it *now.*"

"Aye, sir."

Before Halak could even touch the comm-link again, the lieutenant spoke up over a sudden increase in transmission chatter.

"Sir, I've got another transmission, K-109! Running Morse translation now."

"Another one?" Reynolds demanded. "From where?"

"Same sector, sir," the lieutenant replied, dumbfounded. "Triangulation puts it within six feet of the first!"

"*Translation!*" Halak barked.

The lieutenant's shoulders slumped, and she shook her head.

"Nothing, sir. Unbroken frequency."

"Central monitor!" Reynolds growled.

Two seconds later, a topographical holomap appeared across the central base projector, two green dots indicating the location of the 3-6-5 transmitters. As the colonel watched, two more green dots appeared, only a few seconds and feet apart.

"That's four readings, all unbroken," the lieutenant reported weakly. "All in an area of less than twenty square meters. Visual range of each other."

"Someone's switching on the transmitters!" Halak breathed. "How is that possible?"

"Activate emergency thermals!" Reynolds yelled, punching the comm-link himself. "Rosewood Backbench, this is Silver One! Launch all stand-bys immediately to search zone! Rosewoods One, Two, Four, and Five, converge on triangulations for evac! Rosewood Eight and Rosewood Ten, begin rote sweeps at a forty kilometer radius, east to west from the Fall Point Bunker! Locate all Hunters, and go for evac! *Get them out, now!*"

Chapter Sixteen

January 5, 2191.
Fall Point Creek riverbed,
31 km southwest of Port Yellowknife,
Northern forests of Continental Yukon,
Canadian Exodus.

John Shark had never experienced so much self-doubt. For two days, he had been hunting in circles, and now knew that he was being led by the nose. What tracks he did find meandered pointlessly, only to vanish before becoming a definitive trail. The Heir Defender was in the search zone, but was slipping past Shark at every turn. Shark was scared, and would have been the first to confess that.

Footprints were all that he had to go on. He had not heard a rustle of leaves, crunch of gravel, or snap of twigs. Nothing moved in the still air, not even the highest treetops. The forests were unflinching in their vast emptiness, almost painted in place. Shark had never felt such a void in an area so crowded with foliage. It made no sense, but he was still hunting, and he was hunting a ghost.

Shark had slept for three hours on the flight in from TAP HQ, and that had been over forty-eight hours earlier. That in itself was not unusual, as Shark was conditioned to hunting for even longer than that without sleep, but he had never been confused by a trail for so long. He could move without being seen or heard, but knew that would mean nothing if his prey was doing exactly the same thing.

Shark had been hunted. He had evaded entire search parties and skilled Bloodline trackers during the 3-6-5. In his subsequent Track and Pursuit years, Bloodline Hitters had been a constant threat, continually dedicating their assassin skills to finding and destroying the Hidden Hunters. Shark knew what it felt like to be both predator and prey, but this hunt was different. The target knew that he was a target, and was leading Shark somewhere he did not want to go. Being hunted was normal. Being toyed with was new and troubling.

Gripping the hilt of his sheathed knife, Shark whispered through the underbrush, barely stirring the leaves in his wake. Melting into every shadow, he continued deeper and deeper into the woods, a perpetual labyrinth of leaf and bark and tangled roots.

People died in Continental Yukon by wandering from the set paths, and most of the bodies were never found. The first portion of the water-bearing planet to be seeded had unexpectedly grown into the largest and densest forest known to mankind in a matter of years, and was also largely unbroken by topography. From the air, the treetops seemed to be an endless grass prairie, both flat and towering. The mystery of the wooded continent had grown into legend and mythology over the years. People said that monsters dwelt there. A few global maps from early colonization of the planet had even labeled the continent with the simple caption *Here Be The Monsters.*

John Shark had hunted in those woods for over twenty years, and the only monsters he had ever seen were artists depictions in galleries and museums. He recalled one enormous painting by the late artist Mallo Tompson, which had been on display at Tompson's personal gallery in New Shilo, along with hundreds of other works from the great naturalist painter's years of seclusion in the Yukon forests. *Sentry of the Yukon* was Tompson's most famous work, a portrait of one of the monsters which he claimed to have seen, and even interacted peacefully with, almost daily. Shark remembered the life-sized work with vivid detail, a bull-like creature that towered almost as high as the trees it stood guard over. With black scales, glistening as though oiled, and a shining black mane, the beast was an awe to all who saw its image frozen on canvas, an incomprehensible collage of light and darkness, ferocity and mercy.

Shark made no judgement on the existence of monsters. He had only visited the gallery to kill the renowned Bloodline Hitter Luke Morland, whose ability to evade capture was eventually crippled by his Achilles' heel of fine art appreciation.

Continental Yukon was the best kept secret in all of Canadian Exodus, and no amount of exploration and surveying would ever fully disclose that secret. However, for the time being, Shark's only concern was finding an Heir Defender, in his mind the vilest of all monsters imaginable. When the first Canadian troops were executed at Port Yellowknife, Heir Defenders had been the ones pulling triggers and slitting throats.

A shark is most dangerous when it smells blood, and John Shark could smell blood, a scent on the air like copper, mixed with the minty smell of the trees. Blood could mean injury or death, but it always meant danger.

Twenty meters to the south of him stood what must have been one of the original saplings planted by Lawrence Kressel himself, a full twelve feet across the base, and dwarfing all others around it. The massive snaking roots would not allow any smaller plant life to invade its space, so the giant stood alone in a small opening, a beam of light breaking the dimness of the forest.

Shark loved the woods, but could not allow his awe of the majestic living totem to distract him. That tree was the only thing in the immediate area which could conceal a human body, and it smelled of blood. The hunter did not enter the clearing. He remained on the outskirts, shielded from view by high green bush growth as he silently treaded around the perimeter, watching, listening, and smelling for any sign of life.

Sergeant Hussaff Lion showed no sign of life. His body was slumped against the west side of the enormous tree trunk, as though he had sat there to rest himself, and drifted into a peaceful sleep. But the massive Lion was not asleep. Blood from a stab wound to his abdomen had soaked through his protective vest and matted into his clothing. Hussaff Lion was dead, and years of training and field experience were scarcely able to prevent Shark from crying out and rushing to his friend's side.

Shark had tears in his eyes as he immediately dropped to a prone position and lay perfectly still. For almost ten minutes, he never flinched. He listened, and smelled, and watched, and wept, all in complete silence.

No Bloodline troop, Heir Defender or otherwise, should have been able to kill the mighty warrior Hussaff Lion. The Bloodline was just not good enough, and yet Lion's body was there, quiet and still at the base of a tree.

Shark could not fathom what was happening. A dozen thoughts churned through his grief-wracked mind, and none of them made any sense.

Heir Defenders could not outhunt Track and Pursuit. This one had.

An Heir Defenders Blade could not penetrate the TAP tactical body armor. This one had.

Lion's 3-6-5 Cuff was missing from his left wrist. The Cuff should have blown away any Heir Defender who tried to remove it, but Lion's obviously had not.

Finally, Lion's cleaver was still on his belt. That made less sense than all of the other impossibilities combined.

A soft breeze had finally begun to tease and tussle the tree leaves overhead when Major John Shark rose to his feet, his ion pistol in his hands. Although his eyes never stopped sweeping the trees, he strode directly from the west to his fallen friend, crossing the clearing with long strides. When he checked Lion's carotid artery for a pulse, he knew that he would never find one.

Deep footprints led from the southeast side of the clearing, directly to Lion's body, but no tracks led away. They were the same size ten treads, and were at least six hours old. Shark knew exactly what their unusual depth meant. Hussaff Lion's deadweight body had been carried to the base of that great tree, and there positioned peacefully, almost respectfully. From there, the ghost had vanished once more.

Shark's hands were quivering with sorrow and rage as he holstered his weapon and reached for his own Cuff. It was time to issue the abort codes. Whoever the Heir Defender was, he was a better hunter than Shark would ever be, and Shark was getting his men out of those woods. Notwithstanding the prime minister's orders, they were falling back. No Bloodline capture was worth this.

John Shark never had a chance to issue the abort code. Before his fingers could do more than activate the Cuff transmitter, a twig snapped.

Shark did not move for a long moment, and then slowly held his hands out from his sides, showing that they were empty. The twig had been no more than thirty feet directly behind him, placing it within the clearing. Sweat was on his brow, mixing with the camo paint as he very slowly drew in a long inhalation through his nose. Now he could smell salt and rubber, indicative of a long-worn hazard mask. The target was standing behind him.

Moving at a rate that could only have been measured in centimeters per second, Shark turned around, his hands remaining submissively raised. He was going to die, but he was going to see the man who killed him.

From the first glimpse, Shark was not even sure if what he was facing was a man. The target held no weapon, and showed no exposed skin. The empty hands were covered by dark gloves, and the expressionless face was veiled by an almost insect-like hazard mask, further shadowed by the hood of a forest cloak, the cape of which hung all the way to the loam floor. The bulky survival pack beneath the cloak made the target appear hunchbacked, a darkly shrouded beast that neither moved nor breathed. At that moment, Shark truly believed in monsters.

The man faced the beast, and the beast gazed right back with glassy black eyes. Shark slowly lowered his hands, still holding them out just away from his hips, unthreatening, yet on guard. His mouth was dry. Knowing that every movement could be his last, he carefully reached to his belt and lifted the water flask to his lips, drinking a long swig without breaking the unblinking gaze of his foe. Placing the canteen back at his side, Shark wiped his right hand down his face, removing what was left of the tear and sweat smeared paint. The beast would know exactly who it was facing.

The hunter stood up tall, his eyes dark and hard.

"My name is Major Shark," he said coldly. "You are under arrest."

As soon as the words escaped his lips, the beast was moving. With incredible speed, it dropped a gloved hand to the sheathed Heir Defenders Blade, and the sword rang out from beneath the billowing cloak. At the same instant, the beast was charging straight toward the hunter. Shark's teeth clenched as his own long, curved knife came into his hands, and he met the beast halfway.

Two blades crashed in the silence of the forest, once, and then again, and again. Shark and the beast were ravaging tornados, circling and clashing with a speed that was only matched by their ferocity and precision. Wielding the long hilt of his knife with both hands, Shark swiped and leaped and fell back, the beast matching his every move. Steel blades were flying relentlessly toward adversaries, each stroke evaded or parried at the last possible moment, death being held at bay by the raw skill of the two dark knights.

The beast's sword came arcing down from overhead, and Shark deflected it to one side with his own blade, following through with a full three hundred sixty degree spin, his knife coming within an inch of opening the target's throat, but the beast jerked back too quickly and fell on its back, sweeping Shark's legs out from under him with a kick on its way to the ground. Shark hit the dirt rolling, as the beast's sword hewed the earth that he had landed on. Unencumbered by the cloak, the beast bounded to its feet, and Shark, still on his back, could barely keep up with the smashing rain of vicious blows that followed. The two blades blurred together, faster and faster, sparks flying as steel struck cold steel with deafening resonance. Finally, Shark managed to parry a blow and thrust both swords into the ground by his head, his boot instantly lashing out and smashing into the side of the rubberized hazard mask. Roaring, the beast stumbled back, losing its grip on the sword, and Shark was on his feet a second later, now holding a blade in each hand. He closed the gap between himself and his foe with a single leap, both swords rushing down for the kill from above, but the beast was diving to one side, out of harm's way, and it held a six-foot section of tree branch when it rolled to its feet.

Shark attacked the staff with both blades, but the beast was evading now, ducking and spinning away from every stroke, protecting the staff from being hacked to pieces. Shark twirled around, sending one blade after the other toward the side of the beast's neck. Again, the hood ducked under the whistling blades just in time, but this time the bottom end of the staff was whipped upward into the wake of the blades, the splintered butt exploding onto Shark's left ear, driving him into the ground once more. His entire head was wracked with excruciating pain, but he managed to roll over onto his back in time to snare the descending staff between both blades like a giant pair of scissors, slicing the branch in two.

Dropping under the next sword stroke, the beast rolled to one side and smashed the remaining half of the branch over Shark's kneecap. Shark screamed, losing his grip on the longer Heir Defenders Blade, which went skittering across the protruding tree roots around them. Instantly, the beast pounced, rolling over top of Shark and grabbing his wrist, isolating the remaining blade. They grappled on the ground, driving fists, elbows, and knees into any exposed body area that presented itself. Knowing that the knife was merely a distraction at that point, Shark released it with a flick of his wrist, and whipped a forearm into his enemy's throat as the knife sailed away, clattering onto a patch of stones. The beast was choking and gagging, but still managed to seize

Shark by the throat with a gloved fist, pinning him to the ground. The second black glove immediately drove a palm across Shark's face, snapping his head to one side, blood flowing onto his teeth from the inside of his cheek. Gasping from the choke-hold, Shark knew that he had about three seconds before he blacked out, as the blood-flow to his brain was stopped. Using every ounce of strength that was left in him, Shark thrust his left knee up between his enemy's legs, sending the beast flying over his head.

This time, the adversaries stood up slowly and shakily, each still trying to draw breath. The beast recovered first, hitting Shark with a flying tackle as he was reaching for his pistol. Shark managed to deflect the tackle by seizing the beast's shoulders and twirling them away from him, using the momentum to Judo toss the beast hard against the tree trunk. However, as Shark drew his pistol and stepped toward the limp figure, a size ten boot lashed against his right leg, snapping his ankle bone. Holding a scream behind fiercely gritted teeth, Shark collapsed, agonizing pain shooting up his right leg when he tried to stand. Unable to move, Shark fell to his hands and knees, and raised the pistol up to fire.

The beast somersaulted around the tree trunk as Shark released the first volley, the silent flaming blue ion particles pelting into the tree and beginning to burn through the wood. Shark could not stand, but he could roll. He rolled over six times with lightning speed, coming to rest on his stomach, still firing at the diving cloak, which was trying to use the trunk as cover.

"Come out slowly!" Shark roared. "And don't even think about the bull-pup! You're not a dead man yet!"

There was no response, except the crackle of blue flames which were still grinding into the tree's flesh, the ion particles burning from the inside out. They had little chance of igniting the entire tree, but that was always a risk.

Shark began inching his way around the base of the tree on his stomach, the pistol ready in his hand. Ignoring the searing pain in his foot was impossible, but he forced himself to keep moving, covering the base of the tree he was circling. However, as the backside of the tree came into view, Shark knew that he had underestimated the target once again. The beast was gone, and Shark was alone with the body of Hussaff Lion.

Shark was suddenly enraged enough to be reckless. He fired his pistol again and again, sending a barrage of random shots fizzling into every area of the surrounding woods, praying that one would find the beast by pure luck.

"You're gonna run?!" he shouted. "I'm on the ground, crippled! *Show your face, you coward!*"

The bone-chilling reply came from the tree branches overhead.

"Gladly."

Before Shark could even whip his body over to face the sky, the beast dropped down on him like a stone, leaving the hunter breathless and coughing blood. Immediately on its feet, the shrouded nemesis kicked the pistol from Shark's hand, and then kicked him hard in the ribs. The armored vest prevented any fractures, but

124

the force was sufficient to send Shark rolling, groaning in pain. The beast had him by the collar, picking Shark up as though he were weightless, and then driving a heel onto the hunter's already broken ankle. Every bit of willpower in Shark's body could not keep him from screaming. Before he could even attempt to defend himself, the beast head-butted him. Shark fell flat on his back, seeing bright spots in front of his eyes. He could not move, his body made of lead weights. He was finished.

As suddenly as it had erupted into the cacophony of battle, the forest was silent again. The beast slowly approached John Shark and looked down at him. The Heir Defenders Blade was in one black glove, Shark's own knife in the other. Shark could barely wonder why the beast suddenly bent over him and replaced the knife in its own scabbard. Drawing the knife was impossible, let alone defending himself with it. Shark was armed and helpless. He simply could not move.

From behind the mask, the beast spoke a second time.

"I'm honoured, John," it said sincerely. "Bleed well."

The Heir Defenders Blade thrust down into the inner thigh of Shark's right leg. Blood sprayed over the blade as it was withdrawn from the wound. As the beast stepped back and sheathed its sword, Shark realized that his death blow had just been struck. He was being left to bleed out into the black soil covered with dead evergreen needles. His own blood was providing nutrients to the forest soil. The thought was almost amusing. The circle of life was getting a head start.

The beast casually slid its concealing hood back over its shoulders, revealing the full rubberized hood and hazard mask beneath. Shark stared straight into the tinted glass eyes, but still could not see what lay behind them. The black gloves were now loosening the straps which fastened the mask cowl to the modulator vest. The beast was removing its mask.

Before the mask could be lifted, two CNE Chops dropped down from the sky to circle the clearing. The beast was instantly on the run, serpentining away into the trees, evading the barrage of red plasma flares that the lead nosegunner fired after it, while the second Chop settled next to Shark's body, both the pilot and gunner leaping from the cockpit and rushing to his side.

At that moment, John Shark decided that he was not done hunting.

By the time the flyers reached him, his gunbelt was wrapped tightly around his upper thigh, just under the groin, momentarily pinching off the spraying wound.

"Sergeant Lion is dead!" he shouted, struggling to sit up. "I need an emergency arterial clamp, femoral is ruptured, most likely severed."

"Sir, I'm no medic," the young, pale-skinned pilot replied, looking squeamishly at the gushing injury. "We need to get you back to Port Yellowknife, to the medical corp."

"There's no time!" Shark grimaced. "I'm dead in a couple minutes, so get a clamp! My belt's not going to stop it. It's too close to the pelvis."

"Sir, I *can't!*" the pilot protested, fumbling to open the emergency aid kit on his vest. "I'm going to put more pressure on the wound, try to slow the bleeding."

"There's no time!" Shark rasped, shooting out his free hand to seize the pilot's Adam's apple with a vice-like thumb and forefinger. "All three of us live, or all three of us die! Twelve pounds of pressure crushes the human trachea, and I'm exerting *ten!*"

"Okay, we'll do it!" the burly black gunner snapped. "Lie down, and bite onto something. Hard." He pulled an emergency clamp from the kit, and gingerly inserted two fingers into the wound. Wincing, Shark released the pilot and slid his pistol holster off the end of the tourniquet, putting the leather between his clenched teeth. The pain was unbelievable, and he knew it would only get worse as the artery was pulled down from its retraction in his groin. The holster did little to muffle his screams.

"Hold him still!" the gunner yelled, as Shark thrashed about in agony, in spite of his best efforts to keep still. The pilot grabbed both of Shark's wrists and leaned hard onto his chest, pinning the major to the ground.

"I can't see anything!" the gunner barked, his face and uniform already covered with blood. "I need to get a hand in there! Wound's too small!"

"Hurry!" the pilot growled. "We're losing him!"

Shark spat out the holster, still whimpering with pain.

"Knife," he moaned, drawing it from the gunbelt. "Use it! Cut the wound wider, as wide as you need! *Do it!*"

"Oh, *crap!*" the pilot choked, reaching for the curved hilt.

The last thing Shark remembered was seeing the second Chop circling the clearing overhead. Then a fiery pain shot through his entire body as his thigh was slashed wide open, and two blood-soaked hands reached inside, seizing the spraying end of the severed artery. Shark's scream was cut off abruptly as he blacked out.

Chapter Seventeen

January 5, 2191.
T-52 Mobile Communication Center,
Canadex retaken military airstrip,
Port Yellowknife, Continental Yukon,
Canadian Exodus.

"What happened?!"

Colonel Reynolds slammed a palm down on the holo-console. He did not know what was going on, in a time when perfect order was supposedly being restored. He had expected more violence in the days to come, but not like this.

"Someone tell me what just happened!" he ordered, red-faced.

"Silver One, this is Rosewood Ten," the comm-link responded. "Hunter Six has been recovered, critical condition. I don't know if he'll make it back to base, ETA three minutes. Requesting EMS at LZ-145."

"Affirmative on EMS, Rosewood Ten," Captain Halak replied. "Where is target?"

"He was in visual, Silver One. Disappeared, heading south. Rosewood Eight is continuing sweeps, but he's still cold, no trail. Sir, Hunter Two is KIA. Found with Hunter Six, his Cuff removed, three k west of original triangulation. He knew exactly how to do this, and get away."

"Same wound pattern?" Reynolds inquired sharply.

"Identical, Silver One. Stab wounds, no ion burns. Close kills."

"Why didn't they design those transmitters with remote activation?" Halak snarled to no one in particular.

General Alvardo Krunnion's sonorous voice startled them all.

"Because TAP was created to be the most self-reliant unit in history," he replied from the entry ramp. "They had to understand that if they didn't get themselves out, no one else would. Ever."

"General, thank you for coming, sir," Reynolds sighed.

"Sit-rep," Krunnion ordered calmly.

"Sir...." Reynolds could only close his eyes and hang his head. "Sir, Hunter Team is down. We have five operatives confirmed dead, and Major Shark is seriously injured. The bodies are being brought back now."

"*What?!*" Krunnion's shock and disbelief was shared by all in the bay.

Reynolds shook his head, trying to believe it all himself. "The bodies were moved, sir. Killed sequentially, and used as bait. Unbelievably choreographed hunting scheme, sir. The target apparently activated four Cuffs before attacking Major Shark, three kilometers from the original kill zone, and he apparently escaped with

Sergeant Lion's Cuff. He's off the map.... We've got nothing, sir."

Krunnion had to sink into a command chair, appalled.

"How?" The word was mouthed with almost no volume.

"All six were stabbed with an Heir Defenders Blade, none of the wounds immediately fatal, sir," Captain Halak supplied wearily. "They all bled out, after being manually incapacitated."

"Manually ... incapacitated?" Krunnion demanded. "Someone physically took them down?"

"Definite signs of struggle," Halak answered. "We've got several blood samples, and we're running comparison analysis already. But footprints reveal only one assailant."

"General, please," Reynolds implored him. "You've got to help us here. It is my understanding that you have been Track and Pursuit's sole military contact all of these years. You know everything they do, and everyone they've ever faced. If they really are the absolute best, then who, on this planet or the Home Base, is good enough to kill five TAP operatives?"

Krunnion shook his head, feeling dead and defeated.

"In one word ... nobody."

Chapter Eighteen

January 5, 2191.
Holding cell of General Cole Dallas Kressel,
HMS Sovereignty,
Saskatchewan Ocean, off Yellowknife harbor,
Continental Yukon,
Canadian Exodus.

The Bloodline Heir had been shackled to a chair in a perpetual blackness for what seemed like an eternity. He felt as though he had no senses. He could not see, hear, taste or smell anything. All he could do was feel, and he felt like he was at the center of a black hole. Time did not exist for Cole Dallas Kressel.

Sometimes he sang, or talked to himself, just to remember what sound was, but even the words and lyrics seemed lost and hollow, swirling echolessly into space. He could not even remember what the cell looked like. For the first time in years, The Heir wanted to cry. He wanted to go home, and he still did not know where that was. Now, he feared that he never would.

His life suddenly seemed meaningless. He had fought battles his entire life, with a single goal in his mind and heart, to claim a throne that was his bloodright. Everything Kressel had ever done had been training him for a life of leadership, and he had faced every challenge as a soldier and a ruler. But, what did it all mean? What did it matter? Port Yellowknife, his palace of twenty years, was shattered to pieces, and his loyal troops were annihilated. The world he had tried to build for so long was gone, a wisp of mist caught in the sunlight. His life was in the hands of pirates, and he was afraid. Cole Dallas Kressel was the Bloodline. If he broke, all would break, as would his entire family legacy.

In his heart, Kressel believed that Major Bourgeouis had been right. The Bloodline would only have hope while their general and king lived. His existence was the thread holding what was left of his allegiant together. For their sakes alone, he forced himself to maintain composure.

"While you live," he muttered to himself, "hope lives. Kressel Mountain lives for hope."

The overhead light was blinding and frightening when it was abruptly switched on. The Heir cringed, closing his eyes against the glare. When he opened them again, General Krunnion was seated across the table from him. Krunnion had no pad and no coffee this time. He was just staring.

"Welcome back, Alvardo," Kressel smiled. "Now, assuming that your campaign is going smoothly, and my remaining forces are either neutralized or immobilized, you have no reason to be here. Interrogation borders on being pointless, as you are well aware, and I am also quite certain that Prime Minister Stone has ordered me to be returned intact and unharmed, which rules out the visceral satisfaction of torture. So, whatever it is that you wish to know, just ask me with kindness, and I will decide whether it is worth my time to respond. What do you want?"

"Truth," Krunnion growled.

"I despise lies," Kressel replied. "Your government is founded upon them. Mine will not be."

"Your mistress, Clarissa Yung, has been confirmed among the dead," Krunnion said. "Pity that you didn't shield her so well as yourself. But, as you wish, I will come to the point. Five of my own are dead."

"As are hundreds of mine," Kressel snapped. "What would you have me offer? Condolences?"

"Hidden Hunters," Krunnion said clearly. "Are you familiar with them?"

An uneasy light of recognition dawned in Kressel's eyes.

"Very much so, Alvardo. There are monsters in our woods. So, they truly exist."

"Your Heir Defenders Command Second killed them. Five Hidden Hunters, close range, hand to hand, over a span of nearly four kilometers, within minutes of each other. I want to know who this man is."

Kressel shook his head. "First answer the question which you so vulgarly ignored on our last visit. How is your wife?"

Krunnion glared in disgust. "You really think this is a game, don't you?"

"Alvardo, my destiny seems to be mummification in The Desert sands. All I have left is a game. Indulge me that much."

Krunnion's eyes were filled with a cold fire as he stonily replied, "Her cancer *was* in remission. Now, it's not. And I'm sure you already knew that."

"So, you promised her that she would live to see the end of the war," The Heir ventured. "And, now, one of my Defenders is hindering that. I can understand your frustration, Alvardo. We are all tired of the fighting. We all want peace. But we cannot have that until one of us gets what we desire the most. After nearly a century, there is no such thing as a suitable compromise. Annexation is not an option, nor is any form of coexistence. Quite simply, we win, or we lose."

"There can be honour in accepting defeat, Cole," Krunnion said tiredly. "To accept it, for the good of all.... That takes an amazing amount of courage, more than I believe I possess. What do you think? Are you brave enough to lose?"

Kressel shook his head with characteristic honesty. "Not at this time. Not now. Right now, I am afraid, and fear gives me the resolve to hang on. It is not about pride, General Krunnion. My pride is in the men and women who continue to fight for me. If just one of my Defenders will not accept the end of the war, then neither shall I. The Bloodline lives for hope. Now, you may not appreciate this in your deep-seeded bitterness, but I do extend my deepest sympathies in regards to your wife. I have never been married, cursed career soldier that I am. That would have to be my greatest personal regret. A man should have a family."

"Your Heir Defenders serve you as sons," Krunnion pointed out. "Do you think your Command Second will just be shrugged away if you don't help us find him? I will hold off on the continental sweep even longer, if I must, and I will send every available troop under my command into those woods, and someone *will* find him. It will be the largest manhunt in this planet's history, and it will almost certainly end in his death. I do not care. He killed five of the finest soldiers I have ever known, and every one of my boys will know that within a matter of hours. They will be bloodthirsty by the time the hunt starts. Furthermore, if they cannot find him, I will simply take advantage of the fact that nobody in the northern continents cares about Continental Yukon, and I will firebomb three thousand square kilometers of forest to the south of Port Yellowknife. I will burn it to the ground, and I will sift through the ashes until I find his skeletal remains. He will *not* escape, Kressel. If you want to reward his loyal service, tell me what you know about him, and he will be brought in alive. I give you my word on that."

Kressel paused to consider that, shifting his weight fitfully in his chair.

"He came to me, not long ago," he reminisced. "Three years ago, and change. He was a civilian, yet deadlier than any soldier I had ever met." He abruptly stopped talking, and sat in silent introspection.

"And?" Krunnion demanded, growing impatient.

"I would like to be unshackled when you leave," Kressel countered. "I am an old man, and this *is* a prison cell. Have some faith in your own security. I wish to stretch my legs, and lie down."

Krunnion sighed, but replied, "Done."

"Thank you," Kressel smiled. "He never spoke of where he came from, except to say that he had been born on the Home Base. He said that he had no family. The brotherhood of the Bloodline intrigued him."

"What's his name?"

"I want the light left on," Kressel's voice was firm. "And I want a glass of wine."

"Done."

"I will give you one name. The rest is up to you. You have to do some homework, Alvardo."

"Fine," Krunnion nodded. "One name."

"Ryan."

Krunnion touched his shoulder frequency. "Silver One, come in."

"Command Peak, this is Silver One," Colonel Reynolds voice replied.

"We have a name. Ryan, a private citizen, highly trained in deadly arts, mid thirties to mid forties, born on the Home Base."

"Roger that, Command Peak. We're running it now."

Krunnion leaned back in his chair, running a beefy palm through his short-cropped hair, tensely.

"How did he rise to the rank of Command Second so quickly?" he asked.

"By killing my previous Command Second," Kressel said simply. "Heir Defender positions are often won in duels to the death. Ryan killed his highly-elite predecessor very quickly. It was possibly the shortest and most awing battle that I have ever witnessed."

"And how did he become that good?" Krunnion wanted to know.

"No," Kressel chuckled, shaking his head. "Happy hunting, Alvardo. My preference runs toward Merlot, if any is available."

Chapter Nineteen

January 6, 2191.
Canadian Security and Intelligence
Service Complex,
Toronto Exodus, Ontario,
Canadian Exodus.

Jonathon Kage had never before heard an intercom message that filled his heart with such dread.

"Mr. Director, a Colonel Maxmillan Towers is requesting to see you. He says that it is quite necessary."

Kage had to swallow a hard lump in his throat before he could answer.

"Send him in," he said shakily, in spite of his best efforts at composure. Sweat droplets were forming on his brow.

Kage stood up from behind his desk as Colonel Towers strode into the office in full dress uniform. For some reason, Kage actually took comfort in the fact that Towers was a hair shorter than he was. However, the desperate comfort was short-lived.

"Colonel Towers," he said gallantly. "I wish to extend a nation's deepest sympathies toward you and your entire unit in this time~"

"Be silent, Mr. Director."

The colonel's voice was neither rude, nor commanding. It was soft, calm, and terrifying. Kage's mouth was shut in an instant. It was also dry, all of its previous moisture seemingly being transferred to his forehead.

Towers was actually smiling just a little, but his eyes revealed no humour.

"It is my understanding that Prime Minister Stone relied heavily on your advice to pointlessly send my boys out to the monsters," the colonel said simply. "When she inquired about the insufficient intelligence available for the planned operation, you were quoted as saying, 'Tell them to look for footprints, or broken grass, or whatever.' Mr. Director, I believe that it is unfortunate for you that Major Shark survived, and is expected to make a full recovery. As an indirectly involved third party, I hold you personally responsible for the outcome of this mission. As a man who just lost five of his brothers in the field, I am sure that Major Shark's feelings are much more personal. I trust that you will receive him into this office with the same courtesy and sincerity with which you have given me. I am quite certain that the major will be visiting you shortly. When he does, I would advise you to have Parliamentary Six news anchor Valerie Kine present. Witnesses are always useful."

Kage opened his mouth, but could not think of a word. Towers was shaking his hand, warmly and firmly, still smiling.

"Thank you for your time, Mr. Director. You seem to be a decent man, behind that nice suit. I do hope that all goes well for you, and that Major Shark does not realize that a man who is legally dead cannot be charged with murder. Good day."

Chapter Twenty

January 6, 2191.
Office of the Prime Minister,
New Shilo, Manitoba,
Canadian Exodus.

Prime Minister Stone had been in congratulatory holo and teleconferences for most of the week. In between the hourly progress reports from Continental Yukon, she had conferences with family, the media, military commanders, the continental premiers, fellow party members, and the Home Base diplomatic corp, and every call relayed an almost identical message.

"Madam Prime Minister, our sincerest congratulations on your victory at Port Yellowknife. This is truly a great day for Canadian Exodus."

Those words were spoken by the ghostly blue image of Montgomery Timmons, media mogul and one of Stone's chief campaign contributors. Stone knew that her entire office was in debt to this man, but she barely had time to do more than thank him and inquire after his family. She had more pressing calls to make.

Five of the country's most elite soldiers were dead, and a lot of people wanted to know why. Stone's entire staff had been scrambling to keep the story away from the media, but a few of the more tenacious journalists were not being satiated by updates on the planned continental sweep. They wanted to know why they had not been issued any follow-ups to that amazing story about the lone Heir Defender and the great pursuit by Canada's Hidden Hunters, who had suddenly emerged from a twenty year absence in the shadows. The world wanted answers, and so did Colonel Towers. Stone did not know what to do.

Her entire staff had given her the same recommendation: "Make it go away." The country was celebrating the end of a war, and no one wanted to hear that the Bloodline had managed to take one last, crippling swing. Let the people rejoice, dismiss previous reports as a hoax. Have Jonathon Kage appear on TV, with a face red from shame, and admit that he had been fooled by pranksters. Once again, Track and Pursuit did not exist. The nation would not mourn the loss. The nation would never know.

Even the deputy prime minister and the governor general had advised Stone to forget about the Heir Defender. No matter how lethal, one man alone in the woods was not worth anyone's time. The battle was won, which made the Heir Defender a mere distraction. Please, everyone had said, just let the whole thing go.

Stone would not let it go. She had run for the office of prime minister out of love for her country, and for the people who served it. No one had served her country with more diligence than Track and Pursuit, at the cost of everything that they had, including their own identities. No matter how many of her staff told her that ignorance was bliss, Dee Robertson Stone would not let the slaughter of such troops go unavenged. For the sake of the country, the story would not be told, but Stone was going to find that Heir Defender, a man known only as Ryan. She just did not know how she was going to do that.

The name supplied by Kressel had been of very little help to the search efforts. Only a handful of Canadian citizens had been born on the Home Base, and none of those still living were named Ryan. Stone knew that The Heir loved to speak in fluent riddles, but she also knew that he had lived his life in condemnation of lying. If he said that the Defender's name was Ryan, that was his name.

Stone was still pondering the riddle when her private line rang, startling her. It was considered a common courtesy for even private calls to be passed through reception.

"Stone," she answered, putting the red phone to her ear. The voice which spoke next was unfamiliar to her.

"I have an offer for you, Madam Prime Minister."

"Who is this?" Stone asked, immediately suspicious.

"My name is Captain Ridgely Falcon, Madam Prime Minister. I am an operative of Track and Pursuit, Alpha Unit, currently in command of the Towers Program, Charlie Unit selection. As such, I have a direct line to your office, to be used only in situations of urgency. You are trying to find a man in the forests of Continental Yukon. I can help."

"Captain Falcon, we have never met, but I am aware of your service to the Canadex. Are you saying that you can successfully hunt this man?"

"No, Madam Prime Minister. I cannot."

"You can't?"

"He is clearly better than me, Madam Prime Minister. He is better than any of my remaining operatives, and better than any man or woman in the entirety of the Canadian Armed Forces, or the RCMP. That much is obvious."

"Captain Falcon, you said you could help me. So far, all you are telling me is that the man cannnot be hunted at all."

"Everyone can be hunted, Madam Prime Minister, and I know the one man who could hunt us all. I might be able to acquire his services, but I will need your support first."

"Who is this person?" Stone demanded. "Why has he not been brought in already?"

Before Falcon could reply, Stone's intercom beeped, and the receptionist's voice crackled from the desktop.

"I apologize for the interruption, Prime Minister Stone, but I have CSIS Director Kage on hold. He says that he needs immediate security detail reinforcements to protect him from Track and Pursuit, I believe he said. He was somewhat incoherent."

"Hang up on him!" Stone snarled. "Redirect any further contact attempts to a Quebecois restaurant where no one speaks English. No more interruptions, please."

"Yes, Prime Minister."

"You were saying, Captain Falcon?" the prime minister said more calmly, turning her attention back to the phone.

"His name is Wolf."

Stone felt a slight shiver in her spine. She had not been prime minister for very long, but even she had heard the legend of the wolf.

"Captain Chester Wolf?" she clarified.

"Yes, Madam Prime Minister. He took the 3-6-5 twice, he killed more Bloodline than any of us, and I know where he is. No one else does. Would you like me to bring him in?"

The prime minister blinked, several times. She was holding her breath, and did not even know it.

"Madam Prime Minister?"

Stone slowly exhaled before replying.

"What do you need me to do, Captain?"

"I need a comm line to Patronage Aide Ronald Malcolm. Wolf made it very clear when he retired that he was not coming back. We need to be able to offer him what he wants."

"And what does he want?"

"Most likely reinstatement in the CNE, Comp Class License."

"You just said he wanted to get out of the military."

"He wanted to get out of killing, Madam Prime Minister, which brings me to the most important part. I need your assurance, in handwriting, that Wolf will be used only as a tracker on this assignment, not a hunter."

"I don't understand."

146

Falcon chuckled. "Madam Prime Minister, Captain Wolf is leading a peaceful life. I am not going to bring him in for one last mission that will put more blood on his hands."

"You have my word, Captain," the prime minister promised solemnly. "After all of the grief that this one Defender has caused for all of us, I want him brought in alive. I want to know who he is. The last thing this country needs is another Albert Johnson."

"Thank you, Madam Prime Minister. You may conference Mr. Malcolm to my office."

"First, I need an assurance from you, Captain," Stone countered. "And it is not one that can be put in handwriting. This Defender has demonstrated an almost superhuman ability to outhunt the hunters. Can you tell me that I am not just sending another good man to his death? I have heard, many times, that nothing hunts like a wolf, but Captain Wolf has been out of the hunt for five years."

"You aren't sending him anywhere, Madam Prime Minister," Falcon reminded her. "He will volunteer, or he will refuse. And Wolf will never be out of the hunt. I think he invented it."

Part Three

Wolver

December 7, 2183.
Track and Pursuit Mission.

Track and Pursuit Mission Class: Pre-emptive protection.

Operative No.: 12

Mission Code Name: Bonfire.

Mission Directive: Operative's discretion.

Mission Profile:

Captain Wolf,

The Bloodline wishes to remove from our ranks Canadian Defense Minister Gregory Marnell.

Your Target: Danielle West, Bloodline Hitter, female, aged 25 years.

Hazard Level: 8.

Psychological Analysis: Radicalized.

Proficiency: Close range weapons and unarmed termination.

Verified Hits: 6.

All intel points to a New Shilo hit, within the week. The Bloodline is troubled by Marnell's inspiration of Canadian youth, which has resulted in a considerable increase in military enlistment. This strike, if successful, would be more of a moral victory, as opposed to a strategic one, but I do not intend to give them any more to gloat about. Save Marnell, and acquire the target. Avoid publicity, to the extent possible. Media attention in itself is a Bloodline victory.

Mission Armaments and Gear: Operative's discretion.

Mission Boundaries: *Operative's discretion.*
Rules of Engagement: *Operative's discretion.*
Personal Notes: *She is beautiful, Chess. Shoot fast.*

Colonel Maxmillan Towers.
We're gonna get'em.

December 8, 2183.
Track and Pursuit Mission Report.

Operative Mission Report: Wolf.

Final Mission Status: Bonfire, successful completion, December 8, 2183.

Containment: 97.5%

Target Acquisition Status: Uneventful termination.

Mission Costs: 14 hunt hours, 0.5 kg consumed travel rations, 2 expended .45 caliber projectile rounds. Mission costs billed to Independent Manitoban Mining Research and Development Grants.

Captain Chester Wolf.

Chapter Twenty-One

January 7, 2191.
Stormy Coulee Ranch,
50 km west of White Rock, Alberta,
Canadian Exodus.

Chester Wolf did not see the world as others saw it. Most people looked at the world and saw life. Wolf had a difficult time looking at anything without seeing death.

Wolf had been gathering and herding cattle to the newly fenced north pasture all day, and had finally stopped in the shade of a small grove of deciduous trees to rest himself, and his black gelding, Spartan. The silver-bearded cowboy had kindled a small fire, just large enough to brew up a good cup of tea. He still had a long ride home, but, for the moment, he was at rest.

After twenty years of military service, the past five years of ranching had seemed like nothing but rest, and yet not a day went by that Chester Wolf did not see death. Looking at the campfire reminded him of charred bodies he had seen strewn across battlefields, like so many drifted ashes. Looking at Spartan reminded him of a target he had once chased down on horseback and then shot in the head. Even the spoon he was using to stir his tea with was death. Wolf had used many improvised weapons in his hunting days. He sometimes wondered how many other people had ever killed someone with a spoon.

Chester Wolf had lived a life of death, even more so than any of the other TAP operatives. One hundred thirty-seven men and women were dead because he had been assigned to acquire them. Death did not bother Wolf very much, even the thought of his own. In truth, one of the few things that bothered him at all was the fact that death did not bother him. He wished that death bothered him. That would have made him feel more alive, more human.

Wolf had to make deliberate changes in his life to remind himself that his hunt was over. Sometimes he talked to himself, or Spartan, or God. Five years earlier, a single spoken word in the woods of Continental Yukon would have sealed his fate. Even on the ranch, Wolf never spoke much, but, as he sat at the base of a sapling and sipped his tea, he did talk to the horse.

"You did good," he said, his naturally low voice soothing the tired old gelding. "We'll just rest now. You just rest. We did good. We got 'em all."

Alberta was not the urban collective that Manitoba and Ontario were. It was the farmland of Canadian Exodus, the largest continent on the planet, but with a scattered population. New Edmonton, on the eastern coast, was the only major city. Most of the other towns had populations under one thousand. Stormy Coulee Ranch was about as far west as anyone had ever settled, situated in the dense western forests, a true piece of the wild west. The nearest town, White Rock, was a farming community with a population of just under two hundred people. Wolf did not mind the seclusion and solitude, or the fact that many of his neighbors did not even have electricity in their homes. Wolf had moved there for the simplicity, and he embraced it.

Life was quiet on the ranch, even to Wolf's sharply-tuned ears. Any time that a foreign sound presented itself into the forest wind, he was the first one to know about it. Sitting under the shady green leaves of that small tree, he knew that there was one faint sound that did not belong in the air around him.

"Interesting," he muttered, standing. "What is a CNE Runner doing this far west? And why is it coming directly toward us?"

Spartan grumbled an unintelligible response, pawing the soil with a black hoof.

"It's moving slow," Wolf said, then downed the last of his tea. "It's hunting."

Spartan spread his four legs wide, and shook himself vigorously, sending a cloud of wind-blown dust into the air from his dark coat. Almost involuntarily, Wolf unbuttoned the holster that held his 1911 pistol by his side.

"Thanks be to God for this beautiful day," he said. It was the same simple prayer that he had offered up to heaven before every single hunt to which he had been assigned in TAP. He did not ask for blessings, or protection, or victory. He gave thanks for the moment he still had.

It was several minutes before the Runner appeared over the eastern horizon, flying low, straight toward Wolf. He began walking toward it, the pistol held in both hands, aimed at the cockpit.

The kilometers between man and machine were closed very quickly, and the forest green military transport shifted into hover mode as it sank to the wavy grass beneath its wings, looming in the open sights of the Colt. Wolf irritably gestured at the tinted cockpit, using a slashing motion across his throat. Obligingly, the whirring engines began to slow into silence.

"You're scaring my cows, Ridge," he said, glancing at the port-side surveillance camera as he holstered his weapon.

The hydraulics hissed as the tinted dome of the cockpit was first raised up, and then slid back over the hull, exposing the tall form of Captain Ridgely Falcon, his eyes and hair still as dark as the rarely seen occurrence known as night. He had a few more kilograms around his torso than when they had last met, but his body still exuded lethal power.

"Chess," he smiled, saluting both sharply and jokingly, as he unstrapped himself from the green flight chair.

"You're alone?" was Wolf's first inquiry.

"Of course," Falcon assured him, climbing down the port-side ladder. "Brass doesn't like anyone flying freighters without a co-pilot."

"But?"

"But I told them I'd have one on the way back. They cut us so much slack, don't they?"

"You're the best pilot on the planet," Wolf replied. "You couldn't crash if you wanted to."

"Someday, I might want to," Falcon laughed, and the two friends embraced each other.

"How long's it been?" Wolf asked, knowing the answer already.

"Almost three years," Falcon said. "Good to see you, Captain."

"It's good to see you," Wolf countered. "But the answer's no."

"I haven't asked anything," Falcon reminded his comrade, clapping him roughly on the shoulders. He could not help but notice that Wolf was stilling wearing his Cuff. "And I'm not going to."

"So, who is asking? The colonel?"

"The Prime Minister's Office," Falcon said dismissively. "The Right Honourable Dee Robertson Stone herself. Anyway, it wouldn't be the colonel's call anymore."

"Dead?"

"Retiring this year. I've got the Towers Program."

"They started another one?"

"It went annual as of last year. CSIS seems to think that more is always better, and Stone listens to them far too often. No 3-6-5, just mass production. At least we get to hand-pick them this time around. We're officially Alpha Unit. I'm training Charlie now, kicked off on New Year's."

"So why are you here?"

Falcon's face fell a little, and he had to steel himself before speaking.

"Five of us are dead, Wolf. Killed on the hunt, two days ago."

To a lesser-trained man, Wolf's face would have appeared frozen, but Falcon saw the flinch in those steely grey eyes.

"Cheetah," Falcon continued slowly. "Cobra. Tiger. Eagle. And Lion. They're all dead. Shark's down, wounded pretty bad."

"We got breached?"

"Nothing's that easy," Falcon sighed. "Have you been following the news out here?"

"Not since Christmas," Wolf said stoically, forcing his voice to remain level. "Buy a paper about once a month."

"Well, here's the short version," Falcon muttered. "We got Kressel, we got Yellowknife, and the war's over. All happened day after New Year's."

"Is Flaxton alive?" Wolf wanted to know.

Falcon's brow furrowed grimly. "Yes."

"I'm sorry," Wolf said. "How'd we get the port?"

"EMP'd the whole continent. CNE blew Yellowknife to bits, CT4 captured Kressel and his entire surviving staff, and one Heir Defender got out alive, running cold. Kage sent six of us in to get him."

"Six for one?" Wolf was confused. "Why?"

"Kage's call. He blew our cover on public media, and apparently wanted a grande finale to his little crusade."

"Who is Kage?" Wolf demanded. "Why's he calling shots?"

"Jonathon Kage," Falcon snorted. "Newly appointed director of CSIS, and the biggest riptide in Stone's political pool."

"So, they were waiting for us?"

"Chess ...." Falcon had to pause, barely able to believe the words he was about to say. "There was no they. There was one Heir Defender, and he knew exactly who was coming after him. He killed them all, he almost killed John, and he's still out there."

As expected, Wolf could not believe it either.

"One man took us out?" he clarified.

Falcon simply nodded.

"Ambushed them together?" Wolf speculated, raising a tense eyebrow.

Falcon shook his head miserably.

"Hunted them down, lured them to him one by one. Fought them face to face, killed them all. No possibility of thermal gear, sonar, incapacitants, or backup. He hunted us, Wolf. He's a hunter, and we have no clue where he is now."

"He's a butcher," was the only thing Wolf could think of to say. He did not notice himself sinking to his knees. Falcon knew that this was not a sign of breakdown. Wolf was thinking, and he thought better on his knees, staring vacantly into the horizon.

"Think aloud, Chess," Falcon requested.

"He's not running," Wolf said, almost in a hypnotic state. "He waited. He could have reached a camp before we arrived. This was personal. The Hidden Hunters were unveiled, and he wanted revenge for some loss. But he also needed closure. Five men, baited and killed.... That's unbelievable resolve. He needed to know something. Something about himself. He needed us to know."

"And now we know," Falcon finished, tiredly. "The prime minister wants him."

Wolf slowly rose from the grass, still watching the forested horizon bordering the field.

"They're calling me in." His voice was flat, but cold.

"I wouldn't let them," Falcon said firmly. "I told them that I could only think of one man, on this or any other planet, who could hunt like that. I told them I would present the situation to you, and hear your response."

Wolf closed his eyes for a long moment, listening to the soft breathing of the wind between the tall blades of grass.

"No," he finally said quietly.

"Chess, this is *us*," Falcon implored him. "He killed us, and he's still out there."

"We lived the job, Ridge. We die the job, just like any soldier. There's always someone better, and we just met him. If we're too arrogant to see that, we deserve to get taken down. Forty-four on the 3-6-5. No one screamed for revenge then. I don't see a difference."

"You're still the job," Falcon growled. "Don't try to deny that. You're Captain Chester Wolf, Track and Pursuit Operative 12, Alpha Unit. A unit without a team. We worked alone, but we were brothers still. Now, five brothers are dead, and you are the only man I know who might be able to do something about it."

"I don't kill people anymore. One thirty-seven. That was my limit."

"They want him alive."

Falcon's words actually stung Wolf a little.

"Alive?" Wolf was not used to hearing that.

Falcon nodded. "Yes."

"'Acquiring the target,'" Wolf quoted. "'Operative's discretion.' None of that applies?"

"Not this time. We all want to know who this man is. Everybody."

Wolf folded his arms, glancing back at Spartan, still grazing under the shade of the grove.

"In my last five years on the job, I put in five applications for reinstatement in the CNE. I received five rejections. Not even personalized, just a big blue 'Denied' stamp. They only wanted me for death. I'm not doing any favors."

Falcon began to smile again.

"I thought as much. I have documentation onboard, signed by the prime minister, and the Patronage Department. CNE reinstatement, New Edmonton Base, at the rank of captain, and a Comp Class. You can stay as long or short as you like, and you will not be required for combat ops. Just freight runs, troops transports, courier work. I'm getting you back in the sky. All that you have to do in return is capture the most skilled target we have ever hunted."

Wolf exhaled slowly, coming as close to a weary sigh as Falcon had ever heard from him.

"My cows have enough grazing in this pasture for three weeks," Wolf stated. "I need to be back here by then to arrange for their care. Aside from that, I want to talk to John."

"Saddle up, cowboy," Falcon grinned. "You're flying. I need some sleep."

163

Falcon lowered the tail ramp, and Wolf rode Spartan into the cargo hold. The half-day ride on horseback was retraced in a minute by the Runner, the log ranch house looking much different from the air. Wolf had not missed a beat for a man who had not flown in years, Falcon noted. The Runner landed smoothly, within two meters of the front door.

"Spiffy," Falcon commented from the co-pilot's chair.

"Don't let the rustic look fool," Wolf said, gesturing at the cabin. "There's a flight simulator in the bomb shelter."

"When was the last time the Bloodline even made an appearance in Alberta?" Falcon scoffed. "It's the most blindly patriotic population on the planet, and everyone carries a gun. The Hitters are spooked, even."

"The Bloodline is not my concern," Wolf muttered, unbelting himself. "Killing a hundred thirty-seven people on a planet with a fledgling populace, that's a lot of angry friends and loved ones."

"Are you afraid to die, Wolf?" Falcon inquired, lowering the tail ramp once more.

"I'm just not running toward it," the cowboy replied, returning to the cargo bay and stepping into the saddle again.

"You still wear a gun," Falcon stated the obvious.

"This is Alberta," Wolf snorted. "I'm blending."

He clucked his tongue, and Spartan plodded down the ramp. Falcon followed them to a ramshackle tack shed by the horse pasture, and watched as Wolf stripped off the saddle and blanket.

Falcon could only shake his head. "From driving a stake into the heart of the Bloodline to punching cows? That's pension quality living? I have a hard time seeing you as a cowboy."

"It's work," Wolf said, brushing the dust out of the horse's shoulders and flanks. "It keeps me moving."

"Is that all it does?" Falcon challenged mildly.

Wolf looked at him over the horse's back, running the brush along the barrel. "It's innocent. Our weapons shoot ion particles, our ships fly through wormholes, and, at the end of the day, somebody's still going to want to eat a steak."

"Fine," Falcon said. "Be honest. Do you ever miss the hunt?"

"Every day," Wolf nodded. "That's why I left."

Chapter Twenty-Two

January 7, 2191.
Stormy Coulee Ranch,
50 km west of White Rock, Alberta,
Canadian Exodus.

In the cabin, Wolf put a coffeepot on the gas stove, and then excused himself to the basement, which lay behind a heavy wooden door, locked with a deadbolt and padlock. Ridgely wandered through the single room, taking in the sparse furniture and appliances in a glance. There was no frequency of any kind, television, radio, or computer panel. Wolf had truly cut himself off from his beloved country.

Aside from an undecorated calendar, the only wall-hanging was beside a dusty mirror, just above the metal filing cabinet which stood alone against the west wall. It was not a portrait or photo, but an elegantly handwritten document, framed with a deep rose-coloured wood. Ridgely approached it and read the calligraphy.

A lone wolf fascinates the world, because it is anomalous in the animal kingdom. Wolves are, by nature, social animals. They mate for life, hunt in intricately coordinated packs, and live in a complex and orderly society, with amazing similarities to our own.

As a result, the lone wolf raises haunting questions by its very existence. Why does he roam alone? Has he been abandoned by his own kind? Did he choose to leave for the betterment and benefit of all? Or, like so many of us, did he simply get lost somewhere along the way?

The answers are never clear to those of us who dwell outside of the species, and it is rare for a lone wolf's story to be told. Most of the world is too busy to hear the whole story, anyway. But they still wonder.

"Who wrote this?" Falcon said loudly, hearing Wolf's soft footfalls coming back up the steps.

"Dr. Fenton Andelle," Wolf replied, returning with a brown duffel bag over his shoulder. "Famous visiting lecturer to my twelfth grade psychology class. It's an excerpt from his thesis on mankind's inherent codependence, and the crucial role of loneliness in the overall structuring of the human condition. Underlying theory was that society itself is a defensive reaction to our own natural fear of being alone. It was quite profound. I fell asleep in the back row."

"I hated psych," Falcon said. "I never wanted to understand the human head, or heart."

"It was so much easier to just put a bullet into one of them," Wolf muttered, setting the duffel on the kitchen table.

"Your old hunt gear?" Falcon queried.

"I couldn't throw it away. Hunt poncho, moccasins, fatigues. Guess I always knew I still needed them."

In the only outburst of temper Falcon had ever seen, Wolf abruptly spun around and drove a fist into the framed thesis, the glass cutting his knuckles as it shattered into the slab wall panel. Wolf's head was bowed, but he did not remove his hand from the smashed frame. Falcon put a consoling hand on his friend's sagging shoulder. He knew.

"Fifteen years," Wolf said slowly. "Eleven brothers. That's all I had."

"We're gonna get'em," Falcon said quietly. "You will."

Wolf looked up at his bleeding hand, and swallowed the slight lump in his throat.

"Let's hunt."

Chapter Twenty-Three

Januaury 8, 2191.

Infirmary and medical bay,

HMS Sovereignty,

Saskatchewan Ocean, off Yellowknife harbor,

Continental Yukon,

Canadian Exodus.

"He was lucky," the white-coated doctor asserted, as he led Falcon and Wolf to the recovery room where John Shark lay, slowly regaining strength. "A couple more minutes, no one could have saved him. He's a tough cookie."

"What's he said?" Falcon asked, as they approached the bedside.

The doctor smiled. "He said there's monsters in the woods. I'm not sure what you'll be able to get out of him. His artery had to be re-knit, but there was an infection and inflammation. Antibiotics are helping, but it's hard to keep him lucid. General Krunnion was going to talk to him later today. Does he know you're here?"

"He's been informed," Falcon assured him. "Just give us a few minutes."

The doctor nodded. "I'm right outside if you need anything."

After he left, Ridgely sat by the bed, and placed a hand gently on Shark's shoulder, shaking him lightly. Wolf looked at the sleeping major with pain in his cold eyes. He had not seen Shark in five years, and it was sickening to see him so pale and gant.

"Monsters...." Shark moaned. "Saw it...."

"John," Falcon said softly. "It's Ridge. Wolf's here too. We're here."

"Chess?" Shark whispered, one eye cracking open.

Wolf closed his hand over Shark's wrist, squeezing his arm reassuringly. Shark was running a dangerously high fever.

"I'm right here, John. Take it easy."

"Where's my knife?" Shark's voice struggled for volume.

"They're holding it for you," Falcon promised. "It's safe."

"Lion's...." Shark mumbled, then tried to focus his bleary eyes on Wolf, who was still adorned in civilian clothing. "Chess, why are you a cowboy?"

Wolf gave half a smile. "Change of pace, John."

"Lion's knife...."

"They have it, too," Falcon said. "No trophies, remember? They're all safe."

"Tried to kill the monster...." Shark's eyes could not stay open. "I hit him, and shot ... but he knew. He knew."

Ridgely leaned closer, trying to make out the increasingly shaky words.

"What did he know, John?"

"The hunt...."

"John, did you see his face?" Falcon asked clearly. "Did you see what he looked like?"

"Cowboy?" Shark muttered. "Why are you here? You left."

"I heard you got hurt," Wolf said simply. "I want to help."

"You're hunting?"

"Always," Wolf nodded. "John, think hard. What did he look like?"

"Cloak," Shark whispered. "Hood. Hazard mask. No face." His eyes were open now, momentarily alert, but still fighting heavy lids. "Lion's dead."

"We know," Falcon said. "But we're the job, remember? That's all we can think about right now. Can you remember anything else?"

"Blade ... Heir Defenders.... A vest."

"A vest?" Falcon said sharply. "What kind of a vest?"

Shark was drifting off again, eyes closed once more.

"John, was it a modulator?" Falcon persisted. "A modulator vest?"

Shark nodded, a barely discernable bob of the head. "He rigged it, Ridge. Mag shield.... Clever."

"What's a modulator?" Wolf asked.

"New stealth technology," Falcon said, perturbed. "It equalizes heat output to match the air around it, makes you invisible to thermals. We only got them a

171

year after you left. The Bloodline shouldn't be anywhere near them."

"Any stopping power?"

"No. They're strictly stealth ops."

"Could it have survived the EMP?" Wolf pressed.

Falcon shook his head. "Mag-shields are supposed to be too new for the Bloodline, too. But, if he did manage to rig one up, it does explain how he's running cold. We need to tell General Krunnion."

"Does that help?" Wolf asked.

"Thermal sweeps are still running over the forest. If the Chops can run simultaneous microwave sweeps with a frequency equal to that of the vest, they should be able to override the equalizer. That's the loophole. You can only find a modulator if you know to look for it, and the frequency. We'll need to run a sequence of common frequencies, but it's a start. Let's go."

He stood up straight, but squeezed Shark's hand before turning away.

"You get better, John. You just helped us find him."

Shark did not reply.

Falcon and Wolf had started to walk away, but Shark spoke just one more word. It was only two syllables, but it made both of them freeze in mid stride.

"Cougar...."

Falcon slowly looked over at Wolf, who did not move at all. After that, no one moved for almost a minute.

"Say that again, John." Wolf's voice was even quieter than usual, but very cold.

"Cougar." Shark's voice was strong with determination and conviction, rising above his weakened state.

Falcon turned around and looked back at the major. Wolf still did not flinch.

"It was Cougar," Shark said, his eyes wide open, staring at the ceiling.

"Cougar's dead," Falcon said.

"We're all dead," Shark muttered. "Yet, here we are."

"Cougar is dead," Falcon repeated emphatically. "I saw his body. I found it."

"You saw charred remains, and a 3-6-5 Cuff." Shark's voice was growing stronger with every word. "I fought Vance Cougar in those woods. I know I fought him."

"You never saw his face," Wolf said coolly. "Hazard mask, remember?"

"Besides, you saw footprints," Falcon reminded the major. "You would have known Cougar's tracks."

"And he would have known how to change them. I told him my name was Shark. He called me John."

"He had a frequency from the bunker," Falcon stated. "He probably heard your name when they declassified us."

"He stabbed me in the leg for a reason," Shark snarled. "He was taking off the mask when the Chops landed. He wanted me to see his face before I died .... As I died."

Wolf shook his head, his back still turned on Shark. "That means nothing."

"Then why couldn't I break his sword?"

That made Wolf turn around.

"What?"

Shark managed to smile. "He had a 57 Pulse Puppy under his cloak. He never even tried to pull it. My knife should have shattered that sword in two swipes. I couldn't break it. It was a chrystanium blade. I know, because I held it. Same weight and balance. Chrystanium. And that is the one thing we *know* the Bloodline doesn't have."

Wolf and Falcon turned to stare at each other for a long, expressionless moment. Then Falcon touched the frequency on the shoulder of his armored vest.

"Silver One, this is Hunter One. Come in."

"It was Vance Cougar," Shark said wearily, slipping back out of consciousness. Wolf watched the major's eyes fade shut.

"Hunter One, this is Silver One," the voice of Colonel Reynolds responded.

"Are you still running the name Ryan through Canadex?"

"We already did, Hunter One. No hits."

"Try again," Falcon said softly. "Narrow the search engine. Home Base nationals, Manitoba residentials .... Deceased."

"Dead? Why?"

"Just do it, please." Falcon's mind was far away from his quiet voice.

"Alright, hang on a sec, Hunter One.... Okay, it's searching.... Still searching.... Oh.... Hunter One, we've got a hit."

"What is it?" Now, Falcon's eyes were closed as well.

"Vance Ryan Coolidge. But he's been dead since 2170."

"Yeah," Falcon sighed, rubbing his brow. "I guess we have something in common."

"What?"

"Silver One, please tell Command Peak that we need to talk to him. Right away."

"Roger that, Hunter One."

"Hunter One out." Falcon had to lean against the wall. "So, Bishop wasn't as good as we thought. Vance killed him, torched the body, and left it with the Cuff for us to find. He hoodwinked us."

"It's not possible." Wolf's voice was grimly certain.

"What's not possible, Chess?" Falcon said, disgusted. "Vance being better than Bishop, or Vance defecting?"

Wolf shook his head.

"Ridge, it's just not possible. He was us. The job was everything."

"Just goes to show," Falcon growled, heading for the exit. "You can't trust a dead man."

Chapter Twenty-Four

January 8, 2191.
T-52 Mobile Communication Center,
Canadex retaken military airstrip,
Port Yellowknife, Continental Yukon,
Canadian Exodus.

"General Krunnion, we have reason to believe that the Heir Defenders Command Second is well known to us."

Falcon did not want to continue, but both Reynolds and Krunnion were staring hard at him in the empty silence of the enormous command bay. Wolf was standing silently by the main hatch, hands folded in front of himself. It was Falcon's place to speak. Wolf was a visitor in the vehicle.

"Who is he?" Krunnion asked calmly.

"We are speculating," Falcon answered. "We have only Major Shark's testimony, without any sort of visual or DNA verification.... We believe that the man we are looking for is Vance Ryan Coolidge, whom we knew as Vance Cougar, Operative 9, Track and Pursuit Alpha Unit. We were led to believe that he was KIA three years ago, on a hunt following the Shielders Corporation breach. We now believe that a body switch was made, and that Operative Cougar ... defected to the Bloodline."

"Why?" Reynolds demanded.

"Good question," Falcon replied. "He was one of our most devoted operatives ... and one of the most dangerous men I have ever met."

"You realize, Captain Falcon," Krunnion said icily, "that you have just called the loyalty of your entire unit into question."

"No, General, I do not realize that," Falcon replied. "If Operative Cougar did defect, it was wholly without our knowledge or consent. Please remember that Captain Wolf and myself are still here in offerance of our services to help you find him. You are aware of our service to the Exodus."

"And I am aware of Operative Cougar's service!" Krunnion barked. "He was untouchable. He lived and breathed the hunt, just like both of you! If you are here to dishonour his memory, you had better have something more than speculation and the delirious ramblings of a soldier who keeps speaking of monsters. Can you tell me what evidence you have that persuades you to turn against him so quickly?"

"His gear was inconsistent with that of the standard Heir Defender," Falcon said. "He wore a modulator vest, and his Heir Defenders Blade was forged of chrystanium alloy."

"How do you know that?" Reynolds growled.

"Major Shark recognized the balance of the sword, and he could not break it with his own knife," Falcon explained. "Operative Cougar had access to both of these items."

"Except Operative Cougar did not have a modulator vest in his possession on his final hunt," Krunnion countered. "Tracking Bishop was a largely urban hunt. Domestic uprooting, not infiltrating. He had no reason to fear thermal surveillance. Furthermore, his own knife was less than a third the size of an Heir Defenders Blade. He could not have reforged it into a sword."

"Cougar would never reforge his knife," Falcon was quick to point out. "But he was also our best at sidestepping computer security systems. He could have found a way to doctor our own inventory logs, and then smuggled out a modulator, and a small supply of alloy."

"Not good enough, Captain Falcon!" Krunnion snapped. "Less prominent traitors could have sold both the modulator technology and chrystanium formula to the Bloodline. It's not a pleasant thought, but it is just as likely a possibility, even more so knowing Operative Cougar as we did. I am *not* going to stand here and listen to slander! I want *proof!*"

"The proof is in five body bags," Wolf spoke, his low voice even and clear. "En route to an undisclosed location in the western forests of Manitoba."

The three others turned to look at him, standing motionless in the shadow of the hatch. He did not speak again.

"Captain Wolf," Krunnion said slowly. "You have lost half of your unit, and are you still willing to put the blame on one of your own?"

"General Krunnion," Wolf replied. "It is an honour to see you again. The only person good enough to kill us is us."

"The body I found three years ago was destroyed," Falcon said. "Charred beyond recognition, shot, stabbed, the entire skull smashed to pieces with a rock. We thought that was a warning to the rest of us. It was actually a cover. No positive identification was possible. Furthermore, Sergeant Lion's 3-6-5 Cuff was removed without detonation, which only a TAP operative would know how to do. And, finally, there is the matter of the knives. All were left with the bodies. General, the unbreakable knife of a Hidden Hunter would be the most spectacular battlefield trophy that any Bloodline could ever claim. Only someone who was attempting to leave Track and Pursuit out of sight and mind would ever leave them behind. He's running from the memory of himself, General."

Krunnion was scowling, but Falcon could read his eyes. The general knew the truth as well as he did.

"I want a reason," Krunnion said firmly. "I want to know why. Then, maybe, I'll believe you."

"I do not know why," Falcon said truthfully. "That is why you need to let us find him. If it really is Vance Cougar, we will find the why. If it is not him ... thank God."

"How will you find him?" Reynolds asked. "He has a week-long head start. He could be at any of the surrounding camps by now, spreading the warning. Our entire continental sweep has been put on hold for far too long because of this one man."

"Give me ten hours," Wolf said. "And a Chop. Then start the sweep. I'll have him back here by then."

"You're certain, Captain?" Krunnion snarled.

"Nothing's ever certain, General," Wolf answered. "I just said I'd get him."

"And now I'm supposed to trust any of you?!" Krunnion shouted.

Before Falcon or Wolf could reply, a comm signal sounded from frequency control.

"What is that?" Krunnion grumbled.

"Incoming transmission from the woods, General," Reynolds replied, switching the signal to audio translation. A familiar series of high-pitched clicks filled the bay.

"3-6-5." Falcon and Krunnion said it at the same time.

"Running Morse translation now," Reynolds said, busy at the comm panel. "Reading definite breaks."

Before the translation even appeared on the central monitor, Wolf had the answer.

"It says 'Wolver,'" he said.

"It must be incomplete," Reynolds said. "I'll try to wash out the atmospheric impedance. I'll have it in a minute. Location marked on central monitor."

"Opinion, Captain Falcon?" Krunnion asked. "Wolverine, maybe? I can't think of anything else. Is that what your Cougar would call himself now?"

"It's possible," Reynolds supplied. "Wolverines were small predators on the Home Base, noted for their ferocity, even against large numbers of dogs or bears. And they were only transplanted here recently."

"No," Falcon sighed, shaking his head. "Vance's pride was legendary. He loved being the cougar, a noble wild cat. That vanity would never allow him to take a name from the weasel family."

"Location tagged at forty-eight kilometers southwest, sir," Reynolds advised. "Near the coastal supply farm. It's on the move."

"I could have sworn he'd head for Camp 2-4," the general muttered. "Maybe there's more troops at the farm than we know about."

"Or, he's gathering troops as he goes," Reynolds suggested.

Falcon looked more troubled than ever before as he said, "I don't think he's looking out for Bloodline interests, General. And why would he give away his position? Vance isn't stupid."

"If it even is Vance," Krunnion growled. "He's taunting us. They may be better armed than we thought. Projectiles, perhaps."

"The message is complete," Wolf said. "There's no impedance."

"I'm still running diagnostic," Reynolds said impatiently. "Just wait."

"The message is 'Wolver,'" Wolf said simply.

"Wolver doesn't mean anything," Krunnion said irritably.

Wolf smiled at that. "Wolver. Noun. One who hunts wolves."

The general's broad shoulders fell. Even he could not argue anymore.

"He knew Captain Falcon would call me in," Wolf continued. "He's waiting for me."

"Why?" Krunnion was getting tired of asking that.

"Because he's arrogant," Wolf said. "Let us have a Chop."

"We are not going to play his game!" Krunnion was adamant. "You are not getting one of my Chops. Colonel Reynolds, scramble your Rosewoods. We'll lock down the entire area with Chops, then disembark the Silvers around the signal. Nothing gets out. Nobody."

"Aye sir," Reynolds replied, reaching for his frequency.

"Anticipate traps and ambushes," Krunnion continued. "Start running thermal and equalizer sweeps over the whole area, find anything with a heat signature or modulation. Saddle up your entire CT4, and two light infantry platoons, coordinating with Colonel Trafford. Let's get this guy, and whoever he's with."

As Reynolds began relaying the orders, Krunnion turned back to Wolf and Falcon, resting his palms wearily on the comm console.

"Forgive my manner," he sighed. "I believe you are right. It is your Operative Cougar, and I also apologize for questioning your loyalty. You, and Major Shark, have been an immense help in this matter, at no small conflict of conscience. We will proceed with the utmost of caution in light of your new information. And I promise you that you will be the first to interrogate Operative Cougar when he is in custody. Thank you for your time, gentlemen, and it is very good to see both of you well."

"General," Wolf nodded, turning to the door. Falcon followed him outside, the steel ramp resonating slightly under their soft footwear.

Once they were out in the open, the salty smell of the ocean filling their nostrils, Falcon lit a cigarette.

"That's bad for your sense of smell," Wolf said.

"You smell a lot of your enemies coming, Chess?"

"In the woods, about seventy percent."

"Well, that's why I'm a teacher now," Falcon snorted, taking a long drag. "And you know that Vance is nowhere near that Cuff."

"The code was a cycle," Wolf nodded. "Perfect overlap. No one is that precise, especially moving."

"Then it was programmed on a timer," Falcon guessed. "When they find whatever rabbit is wearing it, I hope they bring it back alive. My kid loves rabbits."

"How is Paisley?" Wolf asked.

"Eight. That was a good age. You were invincible when you were eight. So, do you think we should tell them?"

"No," Wolf said. "Let them chase rabbits. They'll live longer."

"So, it's old times, Chess. Me flying, you doing a stealth drop into the woods. The only question.... Where?"

Wolf shrugged. "Fort Lawrence."

Falcon blew a stream of smoke into the clear, salty air. "Chess, that's four hundred kilometers southeast."

"He's probably already there," Wolf stated. "Tagged the bunny right after he took out John, made a bee-line for Lake Vermillion. There's boats, and they run fast without electricity. Swift-flowing Vermillion River will take him to within twenty k of the fort. After that, it's just a pleasant half-day hike to the second most heavily fortified camp in the Bloodline possession."

"You said nothing's certain," Falcon pointed out, but then he shrugged too. "But, that's what I'd do. We can get there in the Runner, maybe even ahead of him. I'd rather have a Chop, though."

"You could ask Krunnion," Wolf said lightly. "Again."

"Forget that," Falcon growled, striding back toward the airstrip and TAP Runner. "This is our job."

March 17, 2187.
Track and Pursuit Mission.

Track and Pursuit Mission Class: Hunt and recovery.
Operative No.: 9
Mission Code Name: Mousetrap.
Mission Directive: Apprehension and termination.
Mission Profile:

Operative Cougar,

We are facing an extreme security breach. The chrystanium formula is truly our best kept secret in the war against the Bloodline, but its enormous development cost has crippled our efforts at mass production. Dr. Ramon Henlee, private defense contractor with New Edmonton Shielders Corporation, was our greatest hope for producing an improved alloy, one which would have matched the structural integrity of chrystanium at approximately one-twentieth of the production cost. We believe his new formula was almost complete, but we may never know for certain. An explosion devastated much of the Shielders laboratories at 24:08 hours, EPT. Dr. Henlee was among the ten dead, and his chief research assistant, Dr. Alger Broneau, is missing.

We believe that Broneau orchestrated the explosion to divert attention from his defection. We are certain that he would not have access to the new alloy formula, but he most certainly knows the original chrystanium formula by heart. Much more

185

disturbingly, we have since uncovered coded communications between Broneau and none other than Bloodline Colonel Milo Curtis. Broneau will be en route to a rendevous point on the southern coast of Alberta, most likely accompanied by a Bloodline Hitter. And, even better, the Hitter happens to be that wonderful Hazard Level 10 whom we know only as Bishop. Be under no illusion. He's the us of them.

Verified Hits: 48.

Psychological Analysis: Unknown, believed sociopath.

Proficiency: All inclusive.

Track Broneau to the rendevous point. Apprehend him, and terminate Bishop. You have a window of maybe twelve hours.

Mission Armaments and Gear: Civilian wear, concealed small arms.

Mission Boundaries: Do not let them leave Alberta.

Rules of Engagement: Avoid exposure. Hunt outside of urban limits to the extent possible. Do not allow Bishop to be cornered in a populated area.

Personal notes: CSIS is concerned with Broneau and chrystanium and alloy formulas. I want Bishop.

Colonel Maxmillan Towers.
We're gonna get'em.

March 19, 2187.
Track and Pursuit Mission Report.

Operative Mission Report: Falcon.

Final Mission Status: Mousetrap, partial completion, March 18, 2187.

Containment: Unknown.

Target Acquisition Status: Target Alger Broneau found dead. Target Bishop unacquired.

Mission Costs: Operative Vance Cougar MIA, incinerated remains and 3-6-5 Cuff found at scene. 9 hunt hours, urban hunt gear and rations, one chrystanium knife (.23 kg of alloy.) Mission costs billed to Independent Manitoban Mining Research and Development Grants.

Captain Ridgely Falcon.

Chapter Twenty-Five

January 8, 2191.
Fort Lawrence,
394 km southeast of Port Yellowknife,
Continental Yukon,
Canadian Exodus.

Six hours before Captain Wolf landed at Port Yellowknife, another former Bloodline stronghold received a mysterious visitor.

Prior to the 2167 Yellowknife Massacre, and the Bloodline claiming of Continental Yukon, Fort Lawrence was little more than a tiny farming and mining community. Its value as the central hub of the continents natural resources had made it the prime location for the Bloodline's secondary garrison. Although the mining camp had been rebuilt behind fortified walls, artillery stations, and missile silos, Fort Lawrence was the only true Bloodline city on the planet. While close to three hundred troops were stationed there at any given time, the majority of the one thousand residents were working-class Bloodline loyalists: Farmers, miners, tradespeople, fishermen, loggers, and trappers. Every one of them had chosen a side in the war for the planet, and every one of them would stand by their decision to the point of bearing arms against the Canadian government, if called upon to do so. Thus far, the call had never been given. Shielded by relocated weaponry from the Yellowknife air defense, and with all military facilities deliberately built into residential areas, Fort Lawrence was inarguable as the safest and most peaceful location in all of Continental Yukon.

The mood of the city was anything but peaceful when the visitor arrived, on foot, striding through the towering, wide open fort gates, which had started mass panic when they abruptly refused to close about a week earlier. Although accustomed to a simpler life, the citizens of Fort Lawrence knew what the repercussions of their complete power failure would mean. They had no air defense, no artillery, and ion small arms were little more than clubs in the hands of their militia bearers. All communication with Port Yellowknife had been lost, and what vehicles that were available, air or land, were inoperable, making SOS messages to allies impossible. Messengers had been sent out on horseback, or on foot, to try to reestablish contact with any neighboring forts and camps, but most of these were many days journey away, when only such primitive transportation was available. The few messengers who had returned all bore the same news. It was the same everywhere. The switch had officially been thrown on Continental Yukon.

The dirt streets were empty as the hooded and cloaked stranger walked down the center of them. The city had been all but abandoned, most of its residents assuming correctly that a Canadex invasion was now inevitable. Most had fled to the surrounding farms and mines, seeking refuge, food, and work. With the loss of all electrical operations, there was no shortage of demand for manual labour, to maintain some amount of food and natural resource production. Temporary camps had been set up to house the upsurged rural populace, while the excess had simply retreated into the deep woods to the south, beyond the bounds of all civilization, to carve out new lives from the forest. Most would never return.

The shrouded visitor could not help but smile at the irony. On his previous visits to this city, his greatest concern had been being seen. Now, there was no one left to see him. A few stray dogs roamed the streets, wandering in and out of vacated shops, searching for food. Aside from that, the air was the only thing that moved.

In the very heart of the city was the Bloodline Garrison Command Bunker, a massive stone complex, its four outer walls sloping in toward a flat roof, reminding the stranger of a cutoff Home Base Egyptian pyramid. To the naked eye, no sentries were visible, but the cloaked visitor knew where every one of them was concealed around the perimeter. He stopped in front of the heavy concrete doors, and held his hands out from his sides, showing that his gloved hands held no weapon, while at the same time revealing his sheathed Heir Defenders Blade.

"I am Heir Defenders Command Second Vance Ryan Coolidge," he announced, his voice distorted by the hazard mask he still wore. "It is my wish to speak to the Mountain Forces Commander, Colonel Redic Van

Belt. Security clearance code: Mountain Alpha 2581 Romeo. Admission password: Slings and Arrows ... which is quite fitting, as I am certain that you are armed with nothing more."

"Keep your hands raised, Command Second!" a quaking voice responded from one of the guard bunkers which flanked the main entrance. The sentries were doubtlessly terrified, the stranger knew, especially if their senior officer was sounding so intimidated.

A tall militia lieutenant stepped out of the bunker to the visitor's left, brandishing a semi-automatic crossbow, which had most likely been considered a novelty item the previous week. Sweat was on his prematurely balding head and brow, but his hands were steady enough. Within moments, five other sentries had emerged, three men and two women, armed with crudely designed spears and bows. The stranger could not help pitying them, allowing a brief foray into his emotions.

"Where did you come from?" the lieutenant demanded.

"It is my wish to speak with the Mountain Forces Commander, Colonel Redic Van Belt," the Heir Defender repeated coldly. "Stand down, and I will pass."

"Take off the mask, Command Second!" the lieutenant ordered shrilly, his knuckles tightening on the wooden stock of the crossbow.

"You have no need to see my face," was the distorted reply. "As you have no idea what the face of Heir Defenders Command Second Vance Ryan Coolidge looks like, unmasking myself would be redundant in giving you a positive identification. You are not very fit to lead, Lieutenant. You quake like an autumn leaf on a dried twig, and your orders are pointless. I have given my clearance code and password, and, as your computers died seven days ago, it is highly unlikely that new ones could have been issued, so stand down. You delay me, and that antagonizes me."

Awkwardly, the lieutenant lowered his crossbow, shameful blood filling his cheeks.

"I will announce you immediately, Command Second," he replied wearily, saluting and turning to the concrete doors behind him. The Heir Defender touched his own chest, returning the salute.

"Thank you, Lieutenant."

The other sentries shuffled their feet, uncomfortable with the prospect of being left alone under the glassy gaze of the hooded beast. The beast was disgusted with their apparent dependance on electrical power for any sense of order. He turned his attention to one of the female guards, a stocky black woman who had less fear in her eyes, stance, and breathing than any of the others.

"Sentry," he said to her.

"Sir," she replied, standing straighter and ordering her spear.

"Do you believe that you can kill me?" the Heir Defender asked simply.

The sentry stared for a moment. She was not afraid, but her eyes were cautious.

"No sir," she said. "I do not believe that I can."

"Then you never will," he stated. "Belief hinders you."

After a silent wait of several minutes, the lieutenant returned. He still looked tired.

"Colonel Van Belt welcomes you, Command Second. Please enter. You will be directed to his office."

The Heir Defender nodded appreciatively. "I would advise you all to remove your uniforms and relocate to the forests immediately. Become farmers. The war is over. We lost."

He ignored the flurry of questions that followed him into the stone complex, bolting the door behind him.

A narrow concrete corridor led the way to the main offices, lined with doors to various empty rooms. There was not another person in sight. Makeshift torches on tall metal stands lit the way through the windowless building, the overhead light bars dark and useless. The Heir Defender was much less unnerved by darkness than most of the inhabitants of Canadian Exodus. It reminded him of home.

The corridor opened into a large reception lobby, also empty and dark. A torch-lit map near the elevators told him that Colonel Van Belt's command center and office were on the lower levels. The elevators were not an option, several of them having been wedged open to rescue stranded passengers. A slight wind whistled from the black, empty shafts. The visitor took the emergency stairs, arriving in the massive underground command center without seeing another human. The entire complex seemed void of military personnel.

The command center was better lit than the rest of the complex, with torches and temporary neon rails strung along the walls and across the ceiling, but every console and monitor was no more than a black screen.

What had once been a bright and bustling center of tactical operations had become a fossil-filled cavern.

"The cowards ran when the lights went out."

The small voice startled the Heir Defender. In an instant, the Pulse Puppy which had been concealed under his cloak was in his hands and trained on....

... a child.

The pretty blonde girl in the black and red Bloodline uniform could not have been more than eleven or twelve years old, and yet she had accomplished what very few others had ever done. She had caught the Heir Defender off his guard. Standing silently in the corner, shadowed behind the burning torches, she gave a quiet smile as she stepped into the light.

"Some people are afraid of the dark," she said, stepping bravely into the gunsights without blinking. "It's new to me, but not scary. Actually, I find it fascinating."

The Heir Defender never blinked either, his sights trained on the child's forehead.

"You know stealth, child," he said. "Where did you learn it?"

"From my father," she said cheerily. "He trained Level 9 Hitters before taking over command here. Now that guy is sneaky. I'm Casey Van Belt. Are you looking for my father?"

"I was told that I would be directed to his office, little soldier. Are you the only other one here?"

"Most of the cowards fled," she replied, still smiling. "They say the Canadex is coming. Most of those who remained have been assigned to protect the new farm and mining camps. Do you think the Canadex is coming?"

He nodded, finally lowering his weapon. "Any time now. The war is over."

"That's too bad." Casey was disappointed. "I really wanted The Mountain to work out. Well, that's life, huh?"

"War is not about life, Casey Van Belt," the masked visitor replied. "It's about greatness. Thus, if we lose, we deserve to lose. Just remember that even if they are greater as an army, that does not make them greater as people. You can only determine that one at a time."

"I don't understand that," Casey said dismissively. "You're an Heir Defender, right? Take off your mask."

"And what would be the purpose of that?"

"Like, *hello!*" she scoffed. "Seeing your face!"

The Defender already respected this child more than any soldier or sentry that he had met in a very long time. He loosened the cowl straps, and pulled the mask back over his head, pushing it and his hood over his shoulders.

Vance Cougar was a handsome man, just entering his forties, with short-buzzed black hair and black eyes. His body was as tall and powerful as it had been in his teen years, standing three inches over six feet and weighing almost two hundred thirty pounds of muscle. His hands were large and powerful, and he knew, better than most, how to use them alone in combat.

"You don't look like a killer," the child remarked, after studying his face very carefully. "You look like a superhero."

"Maybe I'm both," he countered. "There's very little difference between heroes and murderers. They both fight for what they believe most strongly in, and they both will always believe that they're right. Belief is what separates and combines them, wasting everybody's time. Do you understand that?"

"I think so," Casey nodded. "You're one of those guys who stands on the outside, shaking his head at the pettiness of all the rest of humanity. Right?"

"You are a brilliant child," Vance Cougar said, quite impressed. "Perhaps you're great as well."

"Well, I don't know about *that*," Casey laughed. "I just can't get what all the fuss is about."

"Have you ever killed, child?" Cougar asked, looking her in the eye.

"Oh yeah, a couple of times," she nodded. "Daddy taught me to shoot. One time, we got ambushed by Canadex on the way to Port Yellowknife. A pirate tried to capture my father, so I shot him. I didn't really like it."

"But you did prove something," Cougar said solemnly. "You proved that you were greater than a highly-trained CNE-CT4. You're alive, and he's not, and in that is your proof of greatness. One day your number may even be low enough that you'll know what it is."

"What?" Casey was puzzled.

"Your number, Casey. We all have one, but we don't have to keep it. We can get a lower number, which is good, but it can be very hard and very painful. There are nineteen billion humans spread across eight planets in three galaxies, and every one of them has a number. None of them are equal. No two people are."

"What's your number?" Casey wanted to know.

Cougar crouched down in front of her, placing his large hands gently on her small shoulders.

"That is what I am here to find out," he said softly. "And I am so, *so*, close. In fact, I know the range that my number is in. Most people go through their entire lives and never even know that much. I am very lucky. Someday, maybe you will be, too."

"What's the range?" Casey asked, now quite curious.

Cougar's black eyes actually glinted with excitement. "It is between one and five, Casey. Maybe even between one and two. It might even be one."

"You seem happy with that," she commented.

Cougar placed one forefinger under her chin and replied, "I have searched my whole life, and the whole universe, to find that tiny little range. This is a very exciting time for me. But I can't stop searching, hunting. Not yet. Not until I know for sure."

"Is that your whole life?" Casey was skeptical. "Looking for a number?"

"We all look for something, Casey. As humans, we are driven to find out more about ourselves than we will ever have reason to know. Some look for dominion, riches, power, beauty, meaning, even death. Why should it seem so odd that some of us just hunt for a number? That is all I want out of life. Just to know."

"So ... what will you do when you know?" Casey asked.

Cougar thought for a moment, staring at Casey's blue eyes. There was such innocence in them. Such potential.

"It will not matter," he eventually answered. "There will be this short, bright moment of clarity, and, after that, I don't even know where I'll be. Alive or dead, it won't really matter. Because I'll know."

"Your number?"

"Exactly."

"But ... what *is* the number? Like, what does it mean?"

"*Everything*," Cougar said emphatically. "Who you are, where you stand, why you were born. It's greatness, and it's all mathematical. The essence of life is science, and the essence of science is math. Very simply, life is addition and subtraction, Casey. That's how we find out."

Casey looked slightly confused and troubled, yet also intrigued.

"I've never thought of life as math," she admitted. "I hate math. But it does sound kinda neat. How do I find my number?"

Cougar chuckled, standing up tall. "You've already started. You find it by living, living when no one else can. That will help you find your range. But to find that one specific number, the number that makes you who you are.... That's when you need to start hunting."

"I still don't understand," Casey sighed, scuffing a black shoe on the floor.

Cougar nodded. "Hunting."

"Why?"

"Answer this, Casey," Cougar offered. "Do you believe you could kill me?"

Casey looked him over intently before replying, "Yeah. I could."

Cougar smiled. "Then someday you will understand. Don't believe it. Know it."

"You don't talk to many people about this, do you?" Casey was perceptive, as well as clever.

Cougar shook his head. "There are some things in life that are so simple that only a child can really comprehend it. I don't waste my time with most people. A long life of study and work and experience usually just leaves them ignorant in the end, searching for more and more complexity. Most grown ups like confusing themselves. It makes them feel big."

"My father is always reading philosophy," Casey noted. "And theology. And a bunch of stuff written in Greek or Latin or something weird. If the meaning of life is that boring, I'm not even going to look for it."

"Oh, one thing is for certain about the math of greatness," Cougar assured her. "It will never, *ever*, be boring."

"Why do you need to see my father?" Casey asked suddenly. "Heir Defenders don't come here."

"I am going to tell him that it is pointless to hold this position," Cougar said honestly. "I'll tell him to take off his uniform and take you out to live quietly in the forest. If he cares about you, he'll probably do that."

Casey looked concerned as she inquired, "But what will you do?"

"I need to stay here for a while," he said quietly. "I need to hunt, and be hunted."

"Will you tell me when you find your number?" Casey asked, almost pleadingly.

"That depends," Cougar sighed. "If my number is between two and five, I won't be able to tell you. But ... if my number is one, you will be the first person I tell. I promise."

He sank down to his knees and gently placed his hands on the child's cheeks.

"I have a present for you, Casey."

Her eyes lit up instantly.

"What is it?" she asked eagerly.

Cougar smiled kindly. "Just something that I don't need anymore."

Chapter Twenty-Six

January 8, 2191.
Track and Pursuit CNE Runner,
En route to Fort Lawrence,
Northern forests of Continental Yukon,
Canadian Exodus.

Ridgely Falcon never tired of flying, but he knew that Wolf had an even greater passion for aviation than he did. He did not mind letting his friend take the controls, knowing that Wolf had spent too much time in Track and Pursuit being told that his skills as a pilot were not needed.

The Runner was flying high, at the nearly fifty kilometers of altitude required for a stealth drop, the forests below no more than an endless green ocean.

"Pity, isn't it?" Falcon remarked from the co-pilot flight chair. "How many years we've spent spilling blood over the most beautiful natural expanse I've ever seen. I'd love to settle in Continental Yukon. But it'll never happen."

"It's monster territory," Wolf said, having exchanged his rugged work clothes for a forest green tactical drop suit. "Reducing air velocity for a ten minute ETA. Console confirmation."

"Velocity reduction confirmed," Falcon replied, touching the flight console before him. "Switching to jet filters for stealth approach. Do you believe there's monsters in there, Chess?"

"Jet filters audibly confirmed," Wolf said, as the whistling engines faded to an almost inaudible whisper. "Auto pilot engaged for stealth drop. We're human, Ridge. We don't need monsters."

"Cougar was no monster," Falcon sighed. "What went wrong, us or him? He was no psycho, no sociopath. He was us. The job."

"Being the job might have been enough," Wolf said.

"I guess TAP finally pays for being closed door," Falcon growled. "Independent Manitoban Mining Research and Development Grants should have covered such necessities as quarterly psychiatric evaluations. Vance must have been sliding away for years. We should have seen it."

Wolf shook his head. "The job was killing bad people. To do that, we had to believe that we were good people, all of us. Cougar knows we're coming."

Falcon looked over at him. "Are you sure?"

"He knew you'd call me in. He's waiting for me."

"Chess...."

Before Falcon could think of anything else to say, the console frequency began to speak.

"Hunter One, this is Silver One," Colonel Reynolds voice announced, clearly annoyed. "What do you think you're doing?"

Falcon chuckled. "Let me guess, Silver One. Acquiring the target turned into following the white rabbit?"

"Hunter One, you are not helping the question of your unit's loyalty by withholding information from us. Especially if you are heading for where it really looked like you were heading just before you went dark."

"Now, don't be jealous that Colonel Towers made the stealth prototype just for us," Falcon admonished. "And I only withheld speculation, not information. Hunter Twelve requested ten hours, but apparently that was too much to consider. And contact Hunter Six if you need help disarming the bunny. It is a bunny, isn't it?"

"Command Peak will not be pleased, Hunter One," Reynolds growled through the static. "You will answer for this."

"I'm dead," Falcon snapped. "You'd be amazed at what I can legally get away with. CSIS should have considered that before declassifying me on national television. They just lost whatever leash they thought I was on. We're acquiring the target. Over and out."

"Acquiring the target...." Wolf mused.

Falcon nodded. "Intact. How good are we, Wolf? Really? We were the best, and he hunted us down, six of us. But we know him better than anyone. We have to be able to use that."

Wolf thought for a moment before replying, "Eyes." Without another word, he unstrapped himself from the flight chair, and began buckling on his pressurized drop gear.

"Eyes?" Falcon did not understand.

"Cougar told me about the eyes of the people he killed," Wolf said. "He saw them in his sleep."

Falcon snorted, disgusted. "He should have taken them from behind. Everyone knows that. Eyes are the final curse."

"I told him that. He said he had to see their eyes. Always."

"Adaptation," Falcon guessed. "He tried to face his fear, desensitize himself."

"That's what I thought, first. Later, I knew they didn't bother him anymore. I think he found pleasure in seeing them."

"Pleasure?"

"Knowing that they knew."

"We knew he was arrogant. We all did. And we loved that about him. Can we use that?"

"We have to."

Falcon rubbed his jaw, unnerved by the predicament. "Be under no illusion, the colonel would say. Cougar knows everything there is to know about being the best and the worst. He can't play by standard bad guy rules. Chess, I have no idea where he's coming from, physically or mentally. Heck, I don't think we can even blame this on the war, on picking sides. Somehow, this has to be personal. What did we do wrong? It's one thing to run from your unit, hoping to never see them again, to swap allegiances. People can change politics and beliefs like they can change their socks, but Vance.... I've never seen evil like this, Wolf. Killing people you loved, without a reason. I mean, he must have known it was over. He could have disappeared, recreated himself, shot himself, but he just stayed. He waited. And then he looked in the eyes of the only family he's ever known. Close range wounds. He watched every one of them die. He saw their eyes.

"Strange, the things that hunt you back in a war. Cougar sees eyes. Shark still smells blood, all the time. Sometimes, I pass someone on the street with a respiratory disorder. I hear that rattling, wheezy gasp for breath, and I'd swear my knife just went through another throat. What about you? The things we never talked about when we were the job. What haunted you? Be true, come on. Even the great Captain Chester Wolf is hunted by something. Eyes. Blood. Widow's tears. There's always something."

Wolf drew his 1911 pistol, pulling back the slide and watching the lone brass round slide into the chamber.

"I gave up trying to understand years ago," he said, staring across the gunsight at the open sky beyond the canopy. "How, why, whose fault. We take the order and shoot the gun. We judge the outcome. It's up to God to judge the means."

"Answer the question, Chess."

Wolf slowly holstered the pistol, still watching the clouds far beneath the Runner's belly.

"I used to get blood on my hands," he said. "Didn't have time to wash, and it dried, tightened. My hands felt like they were being choked."

Falcon gave a quiet, understanding nod, knowing that Wolf had just shared as much as his silent nature would allow.

After twenty years of friendship, including fifteen years of service together, Wolf was still a mystery. His entire existence seemed to be based in oblivion.

Describing the man to others was difficult for Falcon. Wolf was not tall or short, fat or thin, old or young. He did not wear anything out on his sleeve, even his age. Wolf was not average. He was invisible.

"Are you sure that's all you'll need?" Falcon asked, trying not to sound overly concerned.

"No. I never am." Wolf replied, strapping his knife sheath to his left forearm, the black rubber hilt extending over the back of his hand.

"Rifle?"

"I'm catching live fish."

Falcon shook his head, amused. "A man and his antiques. The rest of the world is in love with ion particles, and you're still packing projectiles."

"I don't like weapons that can be taken down by magnets," Wolf said. "TAP was about winning a modern war with stone tools."

"And the war was won by a magnet," Falcon pointed out.

"And a new war started in less than an hour." Wolf cinched up the drop harness around his chest, waist, and thighs. "I'm on your mark. Drop me in 5 k east of the city, right below the cliffs."

"Five? Cutting it pretty close?"

"Closer if I could," Wolf said, strapping on his helmet. "Krunnion knows where we're going, and he's saddling up for Lawrence right now. If we don't get to Vance before they get here, a lot more people are going to die."

Falcon rubbed his brow, suddenly feeling very tired and old. "Chess ... say the word, and I'll drop in with you. Forget the Runner if you don't want to hunt this one alone."

Wolf could only shake his head. "Ridge, this isn't going to be a hunt. I'm going to walk in, and he'll either find me, or be waiting."

Falcon closed his eyes for longer than a blink required. "You're willing to bet your life on the belief that he will face you before he tries to kill you?"

"I can't hunt him," Wolf stated plainly. "All I can do is hunt his mind. You said it, arrogance. It's all we've got." He zipped up the thermalized pressure breastplate, and placed the clear respiration mask over his face and throat.

"Good luck," Falcon ventured.

"Listen for my call," Wolf replied, his voice hollow and raspy behind the plastic screen as he walked to the drop chamber, a vertical, transparent tube which would open over the blue sky below. The clear door hissed open at Wolf's approach, and he stepped inside. Falcon rose from his chair to give his friend one last thumbs up.

"We're gonna get'em," he said, forcing a grin.

"I want you to come with me," Wolf quietly confessed. "That's why you can't. Listen for my call."

With another hydraulic buzz, the chamber was sealed and pressurized. Falcon touched the drop command on the nearby console, and Wolf felt a blast of cold, thin air, crossing his arms over his chest as the floor beneath his feet opened up.

Wolf was dropped into a motionless world of silent blue. From that height, nothing seemed to move at first, a frozen ocean with Wolf suspended in the heart of it. His last stealth drop had been over six years earlier, but he had never lost his dislike for that first long moment of suspended animation. He felt like a sitting duck, although he knew that his plummet speed was increasing exponentially with each passing second, pulling him down toward the clouds below.

Wolf fell feet first, his arms still folded, unconsciously making himself a small, motionless target to anyone who may have been watching from the ground. The odds of anyone spotting a lone falling man fifty kilometers above the surface were virtually nil, but Track and Pursuit had survived by largely ignoring such things as the theory of odds.

At that altitude, Wolf would have frozen, passed out, and asphyxiated in moments without the thermal suit and oxygen cannisters. Even in his gear, every breath still felt cold in his lungs, and he was thoroughly chilled after the first minute, but he knew that could not be helped. He still had a long way to fall.

Wolf had heard many people speak excitedly about the thrill of skydiving. To him, a stealth drop was an almost unimaginable bore. After living a controlled and largely agoraphobic existence, the sky always made him irritable when he did not have a plane between it and himself. The vastness of the sky was the only thing to hide in, and that was simply not good enough.

Falling through clouds was always a relief, a short reminder that even the sky could offer some camouflage, but then there was the dampness in addition to the cold. Well, nothing about hunting a human being was meant to be pleasant. Blinded by white, Wolf was able to briefly relax, the calm before the storm of land rushing toward him once he burst through the cloud cover. After that, he would be exposed.

Colonel Maxmillan Towers used to tell Wolf that stage fright was the most rational of all fears. It traced back to mankind's most primitive roots, to days when survival was based almost entirely on one's ability to remain unseen.

"That is why Track and Pursuit will never have glory," the colonel had told the unit, many years earlier. "Glory is to stand in the spotlight, in stupid adoration of adulation. What the world calls glory, I call skylining. Men who think they're great seek glory. Men who know it have nothing to prove."

Wolf had nothing to prove, and never had. He had been a government-funded hunter for fifteen years, and he had been comfortable with his life in oblivion. The only aspect that ever made him uncomfortable was the initial warning of Towers. Wolf's life was death, and he had finally left that life in order to find life. Five years later, death had called him back into its icy grip, allowing him to live and breathe and kill.

Wolf was under no illusion. He knew that the Prime Minister's Office and military wanted the Heir Defender brought back alive, but would not lose sleep if he was brought back in a bag. Furthermore, Wolf knew that Vance Cougar would be nearly impossible to bring in alive. Cougar would do anything in his power to force Wolf's hand, and to hesitate was to die. All of this was brilliantly clear. There was no illusion.

Chester Wolf did not want to kill, but he did not want to die, either. He did not fear death, as many others did, but he believed that his life had more purpose than just hunting and acquiring targets. He wanted to live long enough to find that purpose.

When his bulky drop boots punched through the final layer of clouds, he was no more than two kilometers above the forest, and Fort Lawrence was clearly visible to the west of him, but he still did not deploy his gliding chute. He was still too high.

"Thanks be to God for this beautiful day," he said, as the forest began rushing up toward him.

Chapter Twenty-Seven

January 8, 2191.
Bloodline Garrison Command Bunker,
Fort Lawrence, Continental Yukon,
Canadian Exodus.

Vance Cougar was a man alone.

They had taken his advice, and they had taken off their uniforms. Their war was over. Cougar had watched from the entrance to the bunker as Colonel Redic Van Belt took the hand of Casey, and began the long walk down the dusty road, with nothing ahead of them but the woods. Everyone except Casey had urged Cougar to come away with them before the Canadex arrived, and nobody except Casey had looked back after he refused. She was still looking at him over her shoulder as her father silently led her away. Cougar gave her a brave smile, and raised his hand. She waved back, just before the curve of the road carried her out of his line of sight. He already missed the child. Of all the people he had ever met, he believed that she was the only one who really understood.

He stood alone, the only human left in the city. The stillness made the abandoned settlement seem absolutely vast. He looked up at the sky, noting enough cloud cover to mask the arrival of any intruders. That did not bother him. He knew exactly who was coming, and he did not expect to see him arrive. Truthfully, that would have been very disappointing.

Vance Cougar had been very patiently running for days, but he knew that his patience would soon be rewarded. His estimates placed the reward's arrival between fifty minutes and three hours away. That gave him very little time to prepare for the greatest and simplest hunt of his life. He turned back to the bunker and closed the door behind him, but left it unlocked. The lone manual deadbolt would scarcely have slowed the arrival, anyway.

In Colonel Van Belt's quarters, Cougar found a clean uniform and a working shower, and he allowed himself ten beautiful minutes under the rain of hot water. Shaving seemed like an appropriate next step for this special occasion. He shaved both his face and head, then suited up in the pressed uniform and a fresh hooded cloak. His pulse puppy was fully charged, and the Heir Defenders Blade was polished, along with its black leather scabbard and belt. Dressed as he was, Cougar was fit to meet a king, but there was no king coming to meet him. There was someone better than that.

Almost one hundred people had died at the hand of Vance Cougar, both on Canadian Exodus and the Home Base, but less than forty of those had been targets of Track and Pursuit. Unlike his brother operatives, and unbeknownst to them, Vance Cougar had hunted in his personal time. To hunt greatness was a personal challenge.

He was anxious, but knew that he could not allow himself to be impatient. He had hunted for too many years to get careless now, when he was so close. Greatness could not coexist with impatience. They were oil and water.

A wolf was en route to him, and he knew it. The wolf would hunt him in this command bunker, and then, only then, would Vance Cougar have the answer that he had sought for the majority of his life. He would have his number.

How could he not be excited? Everyone sought their own private meaning of life, but Vance Cougar was not like anyone else. He had realized his meaning of life shortly after his first kill, but the meaning required the achievement of a goal. In that, his greatest challenge awaited. Finding the meaning of life was hard, harder now than he could have ever imagined.

Greatness required sacrifice. This included the sacrifice of traditional values, personal dreams, ambitions, emotions, and even the lives of loved ones. It was a painful road to follow, but Vance Cougar was not one to lose sight of a trail once he had found it. What he was hunting was so much more than any one man. Sorrow and regret were necessary burdens, but he knew that the joy of finally knowing would make all of it worthwhile, very soon.

This hunt would be different. He had no intention of evasion, ambush, or traps. His own role in this hunt was simply patience. He would let the wolf come to him, and greatness would decide the rest.

Maybe he would die, and maybe the wolf would die. Vance Cougar did not care. The meaning of life was not even about victory. It was about a final knowledge. The best man would win, and Cougar would know, win or lose. Either way, his mind would finally have peace, even if just for one instant, the time that it took for his death blow to be delivered. He hoped that he would have time for last words, even if they were as simple as saying, "You win." Greatness deserved that much tribute.

The bunker's gymnasium was the ideal location. The low-level white brick room was massive, open, and empty, with no windows and only two doors leading into it. That was where the hunt would end, the culmination of Chester Wolf's search for Vance Cougar.

The Heir Defender set his overwatch position in the center of the vacant arena. He set his pack on the floor by his feet, snacking on dried travel rations to renew his strength. Then he sat down on a chair, and he waited.

Time passed in absolute silence and stillness, first minutes, and then hours. Vance Cougar sat, his grey hood over his head, the cape wrapped tightly about his chest. His ears were his primary sense for the time being, listening for any sign of his wolf, whether a hollow footfall or a creaking door. The silence was unbroken for three hours, which seemed like three days.

And then a twig snapped.

The snap was sharp and crisp, made from a long dead leaf stem. The sound came from between six and eight inches directly behind Cougar's head, sending a sickening involuntary jolt through his entire body.

His overwatch of the entrances had been to no avail. Chester Wolf was standing three feet away from him, and Vance Cougar was hunted.

Cougar turned his head upward, looking at the neon rails that cast a dim glow over the room. He smiled.

"*We live and die at the snap of a twig....*" he mused. "Hi, Chess."

Wolf wore his old hunt gear. Taking a few short whiffs, Cougar smelled the familiar scent of those grey leather moccasins and forest green hooded poncho, the legendary huntwear that never had a chance to become a legend. Except for Vance Cougar, no living Bloodline had ever seen them.

Cougar did not dare turn around, but he stood up very slowly, being careful not to move his folded arms at all.

Wolf's voice betrayed no emotion whatsoever.

"I respected you when you were dead."

"How are you?" Cougar inquired sincerely.

"Dead. I want your knife."

Cougar moved one hand slowly to his belt, drawing the chrystanium bladed dagger from its sheath, rubbing the hilt-end cougar's head with his thumb one last time as he held the knife out passively from his hip.

"You hunted me. I owe you that much."

The dagger was taken silently from his hand, the first time that it had left his possession since the day it was forged.

"You want the sword too, Chess? The puppy?"

"Keep them."

Cougar actually chuckled a bit. "Go ahead and ask."

"Why?"

"It wasn't revenge," Cougar assured the voice behind him. "I don't believe in revenge anymore."

"You enjoy killing family."

"There is a certain thrill to it," Cougar admitted. "But adrenaline, bloodlust, that's for kids, infants. That is not the reason. Are you even holding a weapon?"

"What do you think?"

"Very good, Captain! Question for question. What did the colonel tell us? *'Ask a question of your opponent, but don't care about the answer. You want him to care about it. He distracts himself by forming an answer.'* Do you think that'll work on me?"

"What do you think?"

"That's why we're the best, Chess. But, now, I really am intrigued. Are you holding a weapon? Don't tell me, I want to figure this out. One hand says that you know what I'm capable of, or at least think you do, so approaching me empty-handed would be deemed foolish. Now, what contradiction would be on the other hand?"

"A weapon can be a distraction. It requires a focus of its own."

"A focus that would be wiser to keep trained on such a dangerous target," Cougar agreed. "To get the drop on someone is a risk in itself. Overconfidence can result."

"And blindness," Wolf's voice quietly added.

"Stand-offs," Cougar muttered. "It's all about the distractions. That's what tips the scales. Remember what else the colonel would say? The risk we take every time we open our mouths."

"'*The only thing more distracting than a beautiful woman is the sound of your own voice.*'"

"So, ideally, even if your target has the drop on you, if you can get him to breathe one word, you can still kill him. Distraction. But we're both too good for that, aren't we, Chess? Our minds are working twelve ways at once right now, so you could easily keep focus on myself, your weapon, and your complete overwatch. No challenge there."

"You sound confident."

"Confidence is a distraction. It is possibly the hardest one to overcome. It's very dangerous."

"The secret of survival, Vance. Know everything, without believing anything."

"But you couldn't buy into that anymore, could you? That's why you left, Chess. You started believing in things besides the job. Your distraction was your conscience. And you don't have a weapon."

"Not in my hand."

Cougar smiled at that. "Still fixed on projectiles, Wolf? Let me guess. No rifle. Forty-five caliber gas-blowback slide action pistol, semi-automatic M-1911 Colt model, seven hollow point lead rounds, grip insert clip magazine, blued metal frame and open sights, with an under-barrel accessory rail for the laser sight you never carry. No backup firearm. Just a tanto-point chrystanium knife, single edged, black rubber hilt with a wolf engraved in it. Blued, anti-glare blade finish prevents unnecessary light refraction."

"A lesson your nickel-plated shiv never learned," Wolf replied. "1911's don't have accessory rails."

"I missed you, Chess. I defected, but I really missed you. I had friends in the Bloodline, sure, but none of them awed me the way you did. I mean, they tried. Two years ago, this scientist whack-job sold out to us, with this genetic enhancement surgery that was supposed to revolutionize the art of hunting. Eight troops, all good Hitters, were subjected to the experiment, a gene-splicing operation that gave them a sense of smell almost equivalent to that of a bloodhound. I volunteered to be the crash dummy they were supposed to hunt down. I guess terrorists and mad scientists really do go hand-in-hand, huh?"

"How long did it take you to kill them all?" Wolf's voice inquired.

"Five hours, twenty-three minutes. They could smell me, but they couldn't see, hear, sense, hunt. They put their entire being into their nostrils."

"Unbalanced focus," Wolf said.

"May I turn around?"

"What do you think?"

Cougar turned around, and he looked on the face of Chester Wolf for the first time in five years. The hunter held no weapon, only the twig he had snapped over his thumb. He looked older than he should have.

"I like the beard," Cougar commented. "What is it? A change, or a mask?"

"Me." Wolf's grey eyes had not changed at all. They saw everything, and revealed absolutely nothing. They rarely blinked, glanced, or darted about. They just saw.

"Non-regulation hair length," Cougar noted. "Where did they find you? Behind a plough? Sawmill?"

"The north pasture. Spring grazing yards."

Cougar snorted. "You always were a bloody cowboy."

"No, you were," Wolf said. "Rancher. Big difference."

"Tell that to the wild west," Cougar laughed. "Here, Alberta, it's all the same. Unbroke, uncivilized. The only difference is that here's the Bloodline, there's the Canadex. Geography decides it all. Sad, isn't it?"

"The war's over, Vance. You should have let it end."

"I did, Chess. I've started a new one. New war, same hunting grounds. This continent was your home, once. For me, it always will be. I can breathe easy in these woods."

"Don't try to tell me that you were defending a home," Wolf said. "All you had to do was walk. The deeps were yours. Why?"

Cougar smiled and shook his head, admiringly. "*'The great Captain Chester Wolf.... The deadliest man alive.'* I overheard the colonel saying that on a holoconference to Krunnion, just after you got out."

"Why?" Wolf repeated. "Tell me why."

"I just did."

"What?"

A tear glittered in Cougar's shining black eyes, and he continued to slowly shake his head, barely able to believe that this moment had finally come.

"I've missed you, Chess. I missed all of you. It hurt so much to do what I did, trying to listen to my mind without my heart. But I had to. I did it, and it's done. We're one step closer. We're so close now."

Wolf's impatience would have been imperceptible to anyone else as he asked, "Close to what?"

Cougar was still smiling as the tear rolled down his tanned cheek.

"Knowing."

"Knowing what? Vance? Knowing what?"

Cougar snorted. "Eyes, Captain. You're not playing poker anymore. You're letting emotion in. Why do you hate me? You should be happy."

"Happy." Wolf's voice was slow. "You killed us."

Cougar took a huge risk as he waved a dismissive hand. "Canadex and the 3-6-5 killed us. Then Bishop killed me again, right? We all died once, I died twice, now they've died twice. What's one more? Track and Pursuit. You live your entire life with a self-destruct device on your arm. *'Your life will be death.'* In the Bloodline Hitters, they say, *'Death til we die.'* It's all we've ever known. Dying, killing, being dead. Why does it even bother you? Why weren't you prepared?"

"The job wasn't betrayal."

"Oh, I see," Cougar retorted. "I'm evil for betraying a mind-set, not for killing six brothers. Is that it?"

"Five. John survived."

"Ah," Cougar said, with dawning realization. "So, you're not as good as I thought. John made the ID. I'm glad that he made it. Maybe he's greater than I thought."

"He's strong."

"Lion was strong. Shark got lucky. And you should be happy."

"Why do you say that? This is not a reunion. I don't know you."

Cougar grinned wider. "You are me, or pretty close to it."

"I'm not a murderer."

"So, every single target of your hunt was armed and facing you? Don't even try to answer that. One hundred thirty-seven clean conscience kills does not happen, Chess."

"Enemies of my country."

"Hide behind that if you like. And you're just a humble executioner?"

Wolf stared into Cougar's dark eyes for a hard moment.

"What is this about?" he asked.

Cougar's smile was gone, his face a carved rock.

"It's about our limit. It's about the job. It's about what murder really is, or isn't. It is about the very essence of man. What are we, Captain Wolf? All the questions that haunt the mind of a soldier, that no one answer seems to satisfy. It took a lot of years, and tears, but I finally found an answer. Just one. What are we? One answer. We're ... *great.* And I'm happy. We'll know."

Wolf blinked, slowly and deliberately.

"That is your answer? We are great?"

"Tiger was happy. He smiled at me."

"Happy to be murdered by a friend? No."

"*How am I a murderer?!*" Cougar shouted, his face contorting. "I face the men I kill! I let them raise their weapons. I let them be defeated, and I let them know what's coming. You sneak up on sentries with a knife, and you'll blame me for killing us? Why? Because you think I hated them? Death has to be personal, Chess! It's the one thing we don't come back from. Not when

222

it's real. How are you better than me? What could be better? I killed brothers I once loved. You just killed men and women that the Canadex hated, so you're either a tool or a murderer. Either way, you cannot stand in judgement of me. Your life will be death, your life will always be death! Do you know the only real difference between us, Wolf? I learned to be happy with the life I chose. I loved my job. Your lack of ambiguity held you back.

"My life is death, too. Did you know that I killed on the Home Base? I was fourteen the first time. When I was sixteen, just before I migrated to the Exodus, I angered a man that the people said no one could anger. Touched the right nerve, I guess. But this time, he was a masterful killer, a kung-fu master. He was an *artist*, Chess, an old and wise sensai who taught death to hundreds. I fought this great man ... and I killed him.

"That's when it really first occurred to me, even as his body was falling to the ground, his eyes still staring at mine. If that great man was not greater than me, then ... who was? Was anybody? I realized then that there is a number for everyone of us. That means that there is a human being out there who has the number one. Chess, I hunted all over both planets, and I've realized that number one is not out there. I think it's in here. This room. You or me."

"That's it?" Wolf let some of his incredulousness slip into his voice. "You killed us for a metaphorical number?"

"The number is real, Wolf," Cougar quietly insisted. "Did you think this was about the Bloodline? The Mountain? Did you think I turned on us because the

Canadex shut the lights off? I love darkness. It is the only thing about the Home Base that I miss. Strange, isn't it? A nation came to this planet for a better life, and the first thing they do is try to make it just like home. Blackouts are not my problem. Throwing the switch on Continental Yukon is the biggest favor the pirates ever did. People need to remember what their hands are for."

"Depends on what you've done with them," Wolf said. "You refer to pirates, and us. Are you still undecided?"

Cougar laughed again. "You still don't see, do you? Canadex, pirates, Kressel Mountain, the Bloodline, the war, the peace that's supposedly coming. None of it is real. It's just politics. None of it is about the status, the mind, of man. Who we are is all that matters. Collective thought, society, religion, politics. All fabricated, all equally pointless. We're a bunch of animals who have mastered verbal communication, climatic resistance, and the power of hydrogen. That's the species, Chess. Overgrown bacteria with laser guns. Hamsters on a wheel.

"Then, there's us. You and me. Bishop. John and Ridge. Every species has alpha members. Mankind is the only species that forgets how to identify them. Lion's take over prides with the only thing that matters. Power, greatness, killing. That's how the animal kingdom decides things. I'm just going back to the tried and true."

"What about love?"

Wolf's words actually made Cougar fall silent, his lips parted and still.

"Mercy," Wolf continued. "Empathy. Justice. Forgiveness. Hope. Is that all fabricated?"

Cougar forced a nod. "It's like confidence. It's hard to shrug off, but ... yes."

"Honour," Wolf said. "You can't believe in greatness without honour. If you do, you're insane."

"Greatness is what's taken," Cougar said. "Honour is respect, given to the great by the lesser. Only the greatest can share it."

"Honour is in your heart," Wolf replied. "Or it isn't. It's not currency."

"Do you believe that you could kill me?"

Wolf blinked again, and shook his head. "I don't kill people anymore."

"Don't is very definite," Cougar retorted. "If I forced your hand...."

"You can't," Wolf interrupted. "That's definite."

"Don't you have anything to prove?" Cougar was disgusted. "Apathy! What happened to you? Chess, you have to know, better than anyone, that we are not part of the world we live on. We are no longer part of our species! *Greatness, Wolf!* It binds us, just as it separates us. We are so much more than just elite training and sharpened reflexes. We have passed the limit of best, of elite. We have reached a level that no human has reached before! *The Titans have nothing on us!*"

"What are you talking about?" Wolf demanded. "Look at yourself, killing for a pointless point. That is not greatness. It's pathetic."

Cougar's sword was in his hand before the last sentence was out of Wolf's mouth, and the shining chrystanium blade screamed as it sliced air, flying toward the side of Wolf's neck. Cougar's eyes were on fire as the blade met the skin ... and stopped.

Wolf never blinked, or moved. The blade was cold on his neck, but had stopped short of even drawing blood. Cougar was shaking with rage and disbelief as he slowly lowered the sword until the point touched the concrete floor.

"How do you do that?" he had to snap, irritably.

Wolf smiled for the first time, albeit no more than a slight tightening of his mouth.

"Eyes, Vance. You weren't ready."

"Just proving everything I've said," Cougar snarled. "You and me."

"You can't force my hand. All your purported greatness, and you can't even make me kill you. I'm arresting you now."

Cougar raised the sword again, but this time his hand opened as his arm lashed out from his side. The blade flew across the room like an arrow, burying itself ten centimeters into the brick wall.

"Only one of us leaves this room alive!" Cougar snapped. "You're not taking that away from me."

"I haven't even shifted my weight. I've already disarmed you two out of three weapons."

"I don't even need the puppy!"

"You've been hunted. Let's go."

Cougar gave Wolf a long, almost puzzled look before replying.

"I'll tell you how they died," he offered, smiling.

"You're under arrest."

"Everyone needs proof, and I gave it to them. They knew."

"You killed five men who loved you, and honoured your memory. I know what I need to."

"If they had been greater than me, I would be dead. Dead, with no regrets. You speak of honour. Why can people never see the honour in being killed? Everyone I've ever killed, on my own or on the job, was selected, chosen for their importance and controversy. Their end had purpose, the purpose of finding one. I honoured them. I respected my brothers, even as I stabbed them and watched them die. I honoured them by letting them see my face at the end. Shame on you for not honouring me now."

"Shame," Wolf said. "Only that I mourned you as long as I did."

"I outhunted every one of them, Chess! Don't you understand that?"

"Get on your knees, Vance. Put your hands on your head, interlace your fingers, and cross your ankles."

"Are you listening? I had the puppy the whole time! Why do you think I even had it? So that they would know how differently I could have done things. I could have ended each one of them with an ion flare through the back of the skull. Quick and over. Why do you think I didn't?"

"Arrogance," Wolf said plainly.

"*Respect!* Honour! They were great, just like us. For that reason, I gave them what every one of us secretly wants. I gave them time to die. Honour in death. A perfect death! I allowed them to face a worthy adversary and fight valiantly, knights and dragons. Then, I let them see it coming. Isn't that what we all want? A death we can be proud of?

"Think about a fast death. A sniper, who you don't even know exists, fires a single round, twitch of a trigger finger, and you die before you even hear or feel the shot. Silence. Blackness. That's it. That's not an end. That's just over."

"You still have a soul, Vance. Hide from it all you want."

"We died proud, Chess!" Cougar's voice was beginning to quaver. "Every one of them. Lion actually laughed, just before he fell asleep. He said 'Guess we both died twice, huh, Vance?' He laughed. He was happy. Tiger saw my face, and he just reached out his arm to me. It was an honour to hold his hand as he died. Great men, honoured with a great death.

"Then, there was Eagle. Stabbed through his kidney, he asked me for one favour."

Cougar reached under the cloak and produced a crumpled yellow paper from his pocket. Carefully straightening out the creases, he held it up in front of Wolf's frozen grey eyes.

"He wrote this," Cougar sighed, his eyes misting up just a little. "'*Leslie Hope Miller, Toronto Exodus. I lied to you once. We had coffee before I enlisted, and I told you that I'd had a crush on you in college. That was a lie. I love you. I'm sorry. Gerald Grimms.*' Isn't that a beautiful way to die, Chess? He trusted me with this, and I gave him my word that she would receive it. If I am greater than you, I intend to keep that word. If you are greater, I hope that you will carry out his final wish." He watched Wolf carefully while refolding and pocketing the note.

"Eyes, Chess. Again. You're confused. Why am I not behaving as an evil man should? That is what really surprises you. Well, I'll tell you exactly why. Because you are starting to realize what I realized years ago. There is no set morality, just more fabrication. Evil does not exist. Good does not exist. It's all more politics and theologies. One thing does exist, and that is mathematical greatness. The rest is all theoretical, and the theory doesn't work. Show me your God!"

For the first time, Wolf had to swallow a lump in his throat before he could answer.

"You're insane. Vance Cougar."

"My words don't convince you. Maybe history will. Thousands of years of human society, and it's all been nothing but a quest for greatness. Heroes and mass murderers all come from exactly the same place. Long, bloody wakes. Alexander, the Crusaders, Towers. They're all from the same place as Hitler, Pol Pot, Kressel. The more you kill, the greater or more evil you are considered. I needed you to understand that. It's arbitrary. Your intricately evolved society makes the only distinction. Basically, good and evil are determined by climate and topography."

"Vance ... if this is where a lifetime of atheism has brought you.... Sad."

"To be able to touch death, to hold it in the palm of your hand, without being afflicted by it. That's what it is. That's everything."

"Kill everyone," Wolf paraphrased. "The last man standing gets to say, 'Hey, look at me.'"

Cougar smiled broadly. "So you do understand."

"You are insane."

"Careful, Captain Wolf," Cougar admonished. "You've killed more people than I have. If you do believe in evil, what does the math make you? Is that why you got out? Because you were afraid?"

"I got bored," Wolf said. "I'm trying to cherish life."

"I know I can kill you."

Wolf nodded. "So do I."

"You think I won't?"

"I think you won't."

"How many martial arts does John know? Karate, kung-fu, judo, greco-wrestling, kalaripayattu, katana and bo staff combat. None of it saved him."

"You were always a step behind me," Wolf sighed. "Wasting time. You fight, defeat, and kill. A soldier skips the first two steps."

"Then kill me, soldier!"

"I'm retired."

"I am not going anywhere until we both know."

"Vance, in the eyes of God, I may be the greatest or the absolute least. I don't care."

Cougar turned and spat on the floor in disgust.

"If you can live like that, you don't even deserve an honourable death! Billions of lesser people will never face the choice we're facing right now, and you're willing to let it pass you by. This is a glorious moment, for one of us! Can't you see?"

"I don't fight."

"You'll fight me," Cougar rasped, beginning to tremble again, the rage rising within him once more.

"No." Wolf shook his head, and smiled a small, sad smile.

They both knew.

"Jesus loves you, Vance," Wolf said.

Wolf's hand was closing over the butt of the 1911, as Cougar grabbed for the pulse puppy slung under his cloak. Both weapons were brought up to eye level in the blink of an eye, although neither man blinked once. Time froze for a fraction of a second, and then a single shot roared in the hollowness of the vast room.

The round caught Vance Cougar in the throat, and he flinched involuntarily, his weapon clattering to the floor. Staggering back and gurgling, his hands closed over his own Adam's apple, trying to stem the blood. His black eyes were wide as he stared into the grey eyes of a wolf. His legs gave out, and he collapsed onto his back, trying to speak. No words came out.

"Relax, Vance," Wolf said coldly.

Cougar blinked, gagging. His hands were wet, but only with perspiration. There was no blood on them. There should have been blood.

"Bovinic sleeper," Wolf explained, taking a slow first step toward Cougar, the 1911 still held firmly in both hands. "Controls sick or injured cattle for treatment. Based on your body weight, you'll wake up in twenty-eight hours."

Cougar still could not breathe. He could not speak or blink, or even form a thought. His eyes were clouding over into darkness, but would not even close, and his twitching head slowly lolled back onto the cold concrete. He could not even feel it on the back of his scalp.

The last thing he saw was Chester Wolf standing over him, lowering the pistol.

"I don't kill people anymore."

* * *

The TAP Runner, in a holding pattern fifty kilometers overhead, was a circling bird of prey, waiting for the moment of descent. The moment came when the comm panel lit up with a flashing Morse Code translation.

CHECKMATE

Chapter Twenty-Eight

January 8, 2191.
Mountain Wheatfield,
2 km south of Fort Lawrence,
Continental Yukon,
Canadian Exodus.

Wolf did not look like a man who had just carried a large deadweight man for a distance of nearly three kilometers. When Falcon set the Runner down in the waving wheat, Wolf was standing straight, the only sign of weariness in his eyes. The still form of Vance Cougar lay at his feet.

Falcon rose from the flight chair as the tail ramp was lowered to the earth. He stood in the cargo bay and watched his friend slowly make his way up the ramp, weighed down by the body of a man they had once loved as a brother. Only after Wolf rolled Cougar's body to the steel floor did his exhaustion catch up with him. His stiff left leg buckled, and Falcon had to catch him by his shoulders as he sank to his knees.

"It's okay, Chess," Falcon said, trying to help Wolf stand.

Wolf held up a weary hand. "Let me kneel, Ridge. Just a minute. Vance."

"Where's his knife?"

"It's safe."

Cougar was lying on his side. Falcon nudged him with a moccasin, rolling him onto his back and exposing his face. It was a face that Falcon had thought he would never see again. The face did not look alive.

"Is he dead?" he asked quietly.

Wolf did not look back, but slowly shook his hanging head, still shrouded by the hood of his poncho.

"He's resting."

Falcon had to rub his own tired eyes. "There was so much of me that was still hoping it would be someone else. Some nameless thug who got lucky. Hi, Vance. It's been awhile."

"We should kill him," Wolf said. "Tranqs are too good. There's so much evil, Ridge. Peace can't exist with evil. That's not peace."

"You're a brave man, Chester Wolf. It took all of the courage in this world to *not* kill this man. That's why you're still a good man. Before the drop, when you chambered the Colt, I saw brass go up the pipe, not a dart. Somewhere between the drop and Cougar, you made a very conscious decision to reload that gun. You decided that you were not going to let your hand be forced. The first step in getting rid of all that evil is deciding not to play by its rules."

"Good men," Wolf muttered, standing tiredly.

"And the short of it is that I want to kill him, too," Falcon replied. "Let's put him in the drop."

"He keeps nothing," Wolf said firmly. "The man could kill with a pair of socks."

When Cougar's stripped body was secured in the chamber, Wolf began sifting through the pile of clothing and captured weapons on the cargo bay floor. Falcon raised a curious eyebrow, but reached for his shoulder frequency.

"Silver One, this is Hunter One. Come in."

"Reading you, Hunter One. Where are you?"

"The target is acquired. Returning to base."

"Hunter One, repeat your last."

"The target is acquired. Begin the sweep." Turning to Wolf, Falcon asked, "Are you hoping to find anything specific?"

"He had a letter from Eagle," Wolf sighed. "I'd rather it didn't go through evidence. It's none of their business."

"Family?"

"A girl. Every man's last thought. That one girl who gave him something to hope for."

He found a paper in the Bloodline tunic, and carefully unfolded it. Falcon watched him read.

"What does it say?"

Wolf looked up, but said nothing. His eyes were always hard to read, but Falcon was surprised by what he saw.

"Chess?" he said cautiously.

He had never before seen Wolf's hands tremble, but they did as the paper was slowly held out for him to take. Falcon was suddenly afraid to take it, but he did not know why. All he knew was that Wolf was afraid, and Wolf was never afraid.

"This isn't it," Wolf whispered, as Falcon took the paper. He began reading, then looked back at Wolf. Without another word, he reached for the frequency again.

"Silver One, this is Hunter One. Come back."

"Go ahead, Hunter One. ETA?"

"Holding on that. Tell me about the rabbit."

"What about the rabbit?"

"How did you disarm it?"

"Hunter One, I'm not following."

"The transmitter. How did you disarm the charge?"

"What charge?"

"What ... was on ... the bunny?" Falcon said emphatically.

"A standard one-way board, lashed on with a leather strap. There was no charge."

"You didn't find the rest of the Cuff?"

"No. Target must have dismantled it."

Falcon turned the frequency off, then read the paper aloud. He needed to hear the words.

"'Following the white rabbit doesn't lead to full answers, Wolf. In the case of our rabbit, it only led to a transmitter board. So, where is the pretty little bracelet that carried it? And where is the charge that kept it from falling into enemy hands? The Cuff is not child's play, Captain. It is a tragedy, albeit one that is not yet written in stone. Forgive me this relapse, Chess. Although revenge is a cause I no longer believe in, it remains a bad habit that is hard to shake. But don't be afraid. You believe in heroism, and I am giving you one last chance to be that hero, in the eyes of both enemies and allies. Be honest. You knew, deep down, that this hunt was too easy,

so here's a harder one for you. Be a hero, if it is what you're supposed to be good at. I did miss you. Vance.'"

Wolf's eyes were closed.

"Someone's wearing it. Someone who doesn't know."

"Can we wake him up?"

"He'd never tell us."

"Then think, Chess! *'...in the eyes of both enemies and allies.'* How would you do that?"

Wolf's mind was racing. "I have to save someone innocent, to both sides."

"It's a war. No one's innocent!"

"Except the children."

"No...." Falcon felt sick. "Please not that...."

"Child's play, Ridge. He gave it to a child."

"That sick...! How could he get to this?!"

"I don't know."

"He called it a pretty little bracelet, Chess. We're looking for a girl."

"The city was empty. There were fresh tracks, but his were the only ones going in, and they went straight to the bunker. Everyone else was leaving."

"Then we start at the bunker. Winds low, but the streets are dust. How fresh were the tracks?"

"His were six hours, ten at the most. We've got a couple hours before we lose all tracks."

"Belt in. We're flying now!"

The Runner took only moments to reach the command bunker, Falcon landing the craft expertly in the narrow road between two adobe residences.

"I'm going back in," Wolf said, tightening the leather straps of the knife sheathed on his forearm.

"Get Reynolds, see if they can send some backup. We need to hunt fast."

Chester Wolf saw death everywhere, and sometimes he hated his own eyes for that. The only thing that made it tolerable was that he could also see the traces of life behind the death. Every smudge on a dusty windowsill told a story of life. A quick look in the guard bunker told him that no child had been there for several weeks, at least. The main entrance to the command bunker told a different story. Nearly lost in a river of soldier's prints were the tracks of a child, both going in and coming out. Some of the tracks were shod, others barefoot. The doorframe provided a windbreak, preserving old and new prints, all clearly belonging to the same girl, one between ten and thirteen years of age. Her tracks were distinctive, either from a minor ankle deformity or a previous injury. No child would be permitted to visit a command bunker so freely. This child lived there.

Even inside the bunker, where the floors were smooth and quite clean, Wolf could read the empty rooms as if they were pages of a children's book. The girl had been curious about, and familiar with, military operations, evident by her lingering presence around the consoles and conference tables. In his mind's eye, Wolf could see her hovering around busy elbows, asking questions.

Wolf was rapidly putting together a picture of a child he had never met. She was advanced for her age, spending most of her life around tactical, calculating soldiers, rather than other children. Each room told him more. She was stealthy, her prints light and deliberate. More importantly, Wolf realized that she had met and talked for some time with Vance Cougar in the command center. Their feet told the only story Wolf needed. Now, he needed a face.

He found the face in the office of the Mountain Forces Commander, Colonel Redic Van Belt. On the dusty desk was a portrait of the Bloodline colonel, a heavyset balding man in his late forties, hugging a blonde girl seated in his lap, obviously his daughter. The portrait was one of many treasures left behind in the garrison's wake. Another treasure was a blue leather-bound book, one that Wolf knew well. *Echoes of a Mountain* was a children's book, written by the late Bloodline historian Marcus Levinson. It had long been used to educate the children of Continental Yukon in the history of the Bloodline, albeit from a decidedly anti-Canadex perspective. Years before, Wolf had been amused to find confused references to Track and Pursuit in a cautionary chapter entitled *To Venture in the Trees*.

Today, Wolf's only interest was the inside cover. Colonel Van Belt had inscribed it, *"To my beloved Casey. The past is never gone. The past is the stones, and our experiences the mortar, which build us into the future. Merry Christmas from your father, Redic Van Belt. December 25th, 2189."*

Wolf rarely ran on his past hunts, even when he suspected that he was being pursued. As he returned to the Runner, he ran as fast as his stiff left leg would allow him. The seized joint felt as though it would tear in half, but he did not slow as he ran up the tail ramp, holding the book and portrait, his gritted teeth and tearing eyes fighting back the pain. This hunt was not about the slow and deliberate tracking of a target. This hunt was a race to save the child of an enemy.

"Her name is Casey," he wheezed as he limped heavily into the cockpit, tossing the picture at Falcon. "She talked to Vance for at least ten minutes. She's got Lion's Cuff."

Falcon looked over the photo, his eyes memorizing every detail of both father and daughter in a moment.

"That's Van Belt," he said, quickly recognizing the man's face. "He's the Mountain Forces Commander!"

"What do we know about him?" Wolf demanded.

"Not a front line man, but one amazing tactician. He was too moderate for Kressel's personal staff, so they assigned him here to command the home guard militia. He was still a major advisor to Kressel."

"How moderate?"

"Reportedly, he screamed at Kressel after Port Yellowknife was taken. He wanted to keep the prisoners alive, to barter for Bloodline captives. Kressel respected his defiance, rather than just shooting him like most insubordinates. The man has a conscience."

"And a daughter, with a bomb strapped to her wrist," Wolf muttered. "Are we getting support?"

"Krunnion's orders were to patch me through to Kage. He says the op's over, get Cougar back there now. They think the note's probably just a stall tactic."

"They didn't read that command bunker," Wolf snapped. "I just did, and she's out there."

"Do you want to talk to Kage?"

"Let's hunt."

"No vehicles," Falcon pondered, firing the hover jets. The Runner vibrated slightly as it lifted off the ground. "They can't have gone far on foot. So, the first thing they look for...."

"Horses," Wolf supplied. "A ranch or supply farm."

"There's half a dozen of them around the city," Falcon pointed out. "They could have gone to any one."

"Fly low, follow me," Wolf instructed, rushing back through the cargo bay. "I'll find them."

It was a six foot drop from the tail ramp to the ground, but Wolf landed lightly on his feet, his eyes reading the dusty streets. Casey's tracks were one set in the midst of thousands, but they were fresher than any of the others, and they remained close beside one set of size eight boot tracks, matching them step for step. With the hand-in-hand tracks of Van Belt and his daughter etched permanently into Wolf's memory, the hunt was now a running game.

"Heading south!" Wolf shouted into his shoulder frequency, jogging about twenty feet ahead of the Runner's nose cone. "South gate, the girl, Van Belt, entourage of eleven, four of them female. There's a ranch south?"

"18 k due," Falcon's voice answered. "And a mining camp near that."

Wolf ran up to the side of the cockpit, leaping up and catching the side ladder.

"Go there!" he barked over the screaming engines. "Stay low enough for me to read!"

"Jet filters on," Falcon answered, as the engine's roar softened to a low whirring. "Hang on."

Continental Yukon was a world with no roads, only dusty foot paths and rugged trails through the forests, which gave Wolf a considerable edge in hunting. In the concrete cities of Ontario and Manitoba, tracks were lost as quickly as they were made. Wolf liked the parts of the world where his eyes could read history in the dirt. Today was a challenge, though, as his eyes had to follow a story which was rapidly becoming a blur beneath the speeding Runner, whistling down the forested trail, needled green branches slapping against the wedge-shaped wings.

Eighteen kilometers later, the ranch yard told Wolf most of what he needed to know, and the lone rancher willingly filled in the blanks.

"Yes," the young man quavered, swallowing the tightness in his dry throat. "I knew it was Van Belt, so I gave them six of my horses. He's been good to us."

"The girl," Wolf said quietly, his finger on the trigger, his other hand holding up the photo. "This girl."

The rancher nodded, closing his eyes so that he would not have to see the muzzle of the 1911 pressed between them.

"His daughter. She was with him. I gave her my best mare. Please don't hurt me."

"Do not lie, and I won't."

"Chess!" Falcon called, studying the ground around the corrals, near where the Runner had set down.

Wolf never looked away from the trembling young man.

"Have you ever been hunted, son?" he asked softly.

The rancher cracked one terrified eye open.

"What?"

242

"Chess!" Falcon repeated. "She mounted up right here. Tall horse, no shoes. Two hours, tops."

"Listen," Wolf said ominously. "Did the girl have a green band around her wrist? A green band."

"I don't know."

Wolf pressed the gun barrel harder between the clenched eyebrows. "A green ... band."

"I don't know! I don't remember!"

"Projectiles," Wolf reminded him irritably. "Can't be neutralized."

"I don't know, *I don't know!*"

"Why was she your best mare? Best in what way?"

"She walks out, fast and smooth. Her walk keeps up with most trots, and she keeps it up all day. What do you want?"

"She's a long walker?" Wolf clarified.

"I just said that!"

"Where were they going?"

"They didn't tell me. They said they'd send the horses back in four days."

"It doesn't take two days to get to the mines. What settlement is that far away?"

"I don't know!"

"Then think!" Wolf roared, making Falcon flinch. He could not remember the last time he had heard such fury in Wolf's voice, let alone such volume.

"Don't shoot!" the man wailed. "I'm thinking! I'm thinking!"

"You're being hunted right now," Wolf said.

"A brother! Colonel Van Belt had a brother. A cabin near the deeps. He traps, spends most of his life there."

243

"How far?"

"Maybe sixty kilometers south. Nobody else goes in there. That's the interior, there's nothing else after that. Canadex or The Mountain, that's as far as they go."

"How do you know him?" Wolf ordered. "Do not lie."

"He comes through here with his furs twice a year. I always buy a couple from him. The best furs on this planet are in the deeps."

"His brother is the Mountain Forces Commander, and he's a wolver? Explain that."

"I have no idea. I barely know them."

"You just lied to me," Wolf pointed out. "But not to protect your own interests, so I won't blow your kneecap off from behind this time. Who are you protecting?"

The young man sighed. "I think.... I think he's a Canadex loyalist. He stays out of sight. They aren't shown any mercy around Fort Lawrence. There's rewards for their eyeballs. Van Belt hates it, but it's a huge black market."

"But you think he would go to his brother?"

"They're brothers."

Wolf's unblinking eyes, and the pistol, were very unnerving. The young rancher had to look down at his own feet, while trying not to make a threatening move.

"How many acres?"

"What?"

"Your ranch."

It was a strange question for the rancher to hear from a man holding a gun to his head, but he replied, "Four thousand."

"Head?"

"Thirty-five, plus foals. I'm just starting."

"Thoroughbreds?"

"Quarters."

"Good choice," Wolf stated. "It's well kept. Let your southeast grazing quarter go fallow next season. It's an investment."

"Um ... thanks."

"One more question, and do not lie. Where is the nearest doctor?"

Chapter Twenty-Nine

January 8, 2191.
53 km north of the deep woods,
Continental Yukon,
Canadian Exodus.

"We're hunters, Wolf."

"Yes."

Falcon raised his binoculars to cautiously peer over the wooded slope at the small Bloodline encampment below. He and Wolf had been prone on that peak for nearly fifteen minutes, observing Van Belt's entourage setting up tents and lighting campfires. None wore a uniform, but it was fairly obvious which of them had been troops.

"We trained to hunt men, not take on armies."

Wolf nodded. "I know."

"I'm counting nine troops, two assistant-looking types, Van Belt, and his daughter. That tall woman looks like she's Casey's detail. She's never more than two feet away from her. These Bloodline kids can be more ballistic than their parents, so we're two on a baker's dozen, and they will not understand. They all have spears, knives, and I've seen four bows and a crossbow."

"What cross?"

"Semi-auto, gas operated. That's as many as forty bolts."

"Any sign of the Cuff?"

Falcon shook his head, lowering the binoculars. "The girl's got a riding cloak on. I can't see her hands."

"The possibility of innocence, Ridge," Wolf said, raising his hood over his head. "We're trying to save someone who will probably try to kill us."

"Smash and grab?"

"No."

"Then what?"

"I'm going to skyline. You're going to cover me."

"Chess, we could infiltrate. We can get close."

Wolf sighed. "Until they're all down, there's too much risk of interruption. Boom. I'm skylining."

"And if they kill you?"

Wolf pulled a small satchel of bovinic sleeper darts from beneath his poncho, and passed it to Falcon.

"They're compatible with a 57," he said, then stood tall at the top of the rise, slipping a micro-frequency into his left ear. "No one dies except me. Don't shoot anyone twice. Comm check."

"O Canada, Captain Wolf," Falcon muttered, lining up the crossbow man in his crosshairs. The voice was clearly passed into Wolf's ear.

"God willing," Wolf said, beginning to walk down the grassy slope.

"Girl's in the center tent, next to Van Belt's. No one's looking at you yet."

"People rarely look at me."

The slope seemed kilometers long, although Wolf's calculating eyes measured the distance at just over two hundred fifty meters. He could see eight soldiers and one aide. They were not watching their perimeter at all. Their war was over, they had been told.

Falcon's voice was amused. "Yellowknife really was their only solid rock. You're fifty yards off, and they haven't even looked up."

"It's the deeps," was Wolf's barely audible response.

"Forty yards."

"Forty-six," Wolf said.

"They're not going to listen."

"I know."

"You're going to have to go out of your way not to kill anyone."

"First time."

"The end of the war doesn't make them good people. You've seen the news. Reasonable doubt?"

"Pure ignorance. We don't see their hearts."

"Okay, they're looking at you now."

A sentry had been raising his canteen to his lips when Wolf stepped into his line of vision, only twenty yards away. The canteen was dropped, and an arrow was notched an instant later, the bow at full draw.

"BREACH!"

Wolf stopped walking, his empty hands held out, the poncho hanging down from his outstretched arms.

"Forgive me," he said. "I'm lost."

Other sentries were rushing toward him, bows drawn, spears hoisted. It occurred to Wolf that this was

248

the first time that Bloodline troops had seen his face without dying.

"Keep your hands raised!" the crossbow man roared, still advancing.

"Easy," Wolf admonished. "I'm just fishing."

"Tell them you're here to help the girl!" Falcon's voice hissed in his ear. "Preferably before they shoot you."

"Colonel, we've got a breach!" announced another voice that Wolf could not see.

"You've got a fisher!" Wolf snapped. "Is this Lake Mayerthorpe or not?"

"Do you see a *lake?*" the crossbow man snarled.

Colonel Van Belt had stepped out of his large tent, holding a saber in his right hand.

"Colonel?" Wolf inquired, squinting anxiously. "Can you tell these bad guys to back off? This is supposed to be a vacation."

"Hold your fire," Van Belt ordered. The sentries had fanned out, forming a semi-circle in front of Wolf. Colonel Van Belt approached, carefully examining Wolf's face and clothing. "Who are you?"

"My name's Chester, and I've been lost for a long time. I saw your camp, thought I could help."

"This is a dangerous time to sneak up on people," Van Belt growled.

"You need help," Wolf repeated.

"What?"

"Your daughter's in trouble."

"*On your knees, now!*" Van Belt shouted, raising the tip of the blade to Wolf's throat. The crossbow man stepped in quickly to place the point of the bolt against the left side of Wolf's neck. The hunter slowly sank to his knees.

"Don't do anything," Wolf said, his words meant for Falcon.

"Tell me!" Van Belt rasped, lifting Wolf's chin with the flat of the blade. "What do you know about my daughter?"

"I know that's her," Wolf said, gesturing behind the colonel with a nod of his head. Casey had stepped from her tent, looking at the assembly with puzzled eyes.

Van Belt's head turned, and Wolf was already moving. In a single instant, he had knocked the crossbow aside and dropped onto his back, the Colt coming into his right hand and lining up on Casey's chest. Van Belt realized what was happening, and did not even blink as he stepped in front of the pistol, just as Wolf squeezed off the first round.

Two guns roared, and two tranq rounds burst from steel muzzles. Wolf's round caught van Belt in the abdomen, while Falcon's slammed into the neck of the crossbow man. The sleeper darts incapacitated both men almost instantly, their buckling knees dropping them to the ground. Wolf lashed out his moccasin into Van Belt's knee, causing the stocky man to topple right on top of him, creating a human shield as the 1911 fired a second round into the nearest sentry, her arrow flying wild. Falcon was firing rapidly from the hilltop. Three shots took down three more troops.

"*Sniper!*" someone bellowed. "Cover!"

The troops were diving for the cover of the tents, but Wolf managed to fire another tranq into the calf of one of the female guards. Van Belt was still conscious, but drifting quickly, unable to rise. Wolf wrapped his left forearm around the colonel's head, preventing him from struggling.

"Casey, *run!*" Van Belt managed to shout, his words thick and slow. Wolf could hear a child screaming for her father, but could not see her.

"Take the girl, Ridge!" Wolf wheezed, scrambling out from under Van Belt, and rolling to cover behind a nearby log. Arrows thudded into it.

"No shot," Falcon answered. "Stay down."

"Give me a count."

"Seven down, six covered. I'm relocating, coming to you."

"No! Lock on the girl!"

"No shot on the girl. Five covered, waiting for visual. Move west, stay low, we'll flank. I'm coming down."

"No, we need the high ground. We need the shot on the girl."

Another shot rang out from Falcon's position.

"Eight down."

"Twenty on girl's last position."

"She ducked behind central tent, south side. Three targets behind northwest tent, one on northeast, west side. Check your two o'clock."

"I got him."

Peering carefully over the log, Wolf could see a lone troop crouched beside the northwest tent, bow and arrow ready. Wolf ducked as the arrow whistled over his head, then rose up on one knee, the 1911 in both hands, and fired again. The sleeper pierced the man's shoulder, and he flinched as he stumbled back against the tent, still trying to notch another arrow.

"Nine down," Wolf said, dropping the sleeper clip and ejecting the chambered round. "Stand by for northeast shots."

Slapping a clip of live rounds into the pistol, Wolf began sighting in on the center of the target tent, just above ground level.

Two .45 caliber hollow points blew the tent's main mast apart, and Wolf could hear the three Bloodline troops cursing as the canvas slowly fluttered to the ground. Falcon engaged each one as they appeared, all three falling as they scrambled for new cover.

"Twelve down," Wolf said. "Moving on the girl."

Wolf was still on one knee as he spoke, reloading the sleeper into his pistol. The words were barely out of his mouth when Casey stepped out from behind the central tent. Their eyes met for a frozen second.

"Ridge...." Wolf whispered.

Casey was running south, heading toward the picketed horses.

"Ridge, take the shot. My gun's still hot."

"No shot, Wolf. Moving to you."

Wolf could see Falcon running down the slope toward him as he lunged to his feet and began limping after Casey as fast as he could.

"Casey, stop!" he shouted. "We don't want to hurt you!"

The girl was too scared to listen, and Wolf could not blame her. Coming around the southernmost tent, he pulled the slide on the 1911 to eject the final live round, putting a sleeper up the pipe. Casey was running fifty-two feet away from him when he shot her in the back.

Wolf had never hated himself as much as he did the moment that Casey toppled to the ground, still crying as she fell asleep.

"She's down, move in!" he called to Falcon.

Casey was lying face down, her riding cloak covering most of her small body. Her right hand was weakly clawing at the dirt, and Wolf could see her wrist. A green canvas Cuff was strapped around it.

"Lion's Cuff," Falcon wheezed, rushing up behind Wolf. "Let's get it off."

"Get the doctor first," Wolf advised. "God help us if Cougar rigged it."

"What are you thinking?" Falcon ventured, keeping a careful eye on the unconscious bodies north of them.

Wolf holstered the 1911 and hunkered down next to the girl. She still had dirty tears on her cheeks.

"I'm thinking that no one noticed missing chrystanium, or your so-called modulator. If he can steal from TAP, he can rig a Cuff. Get the doctor."

He gingerly pulled the blue cloak back from the Cuff, inwardly cringing at the blast premonition. Aside from the missing transmitter, the canvas band was identical to his own.

"Strange," he mused absently.

"What?" Falcon asked.

Wolf started back to his senses. "Nothing."

"Chess...." Falcon raised an eyebrow curiously. "You never say nothing. Ever."

"It doesn't look tampered."

"I know. It's green canvas that blows up."

"Maybe he rerouted the ground through...." Wolf could not concentrate. He was blinking a lot more than usual, Falcon noted.

"Chess?" Falcon was becoming concerned. "You have the job, right?"

Wolf rubbed his brow tensely.

"Van Belt had no time," he muttered.

"What?"

"Van Belt. There was half a second between seeing his daughter and seeing the Colt. He had no thought process. He didn't have time to be afraid for her safety. He didn't even have time to think about saving her life. Casey. Gun. Two images, and then it was instinct to step in front of a .45. What kind of man did I just shoot?"

"He's asleep, Chess."

Wolf immediately had his focus back. "The ground could have been rerouted through the canvas, creating a complete circuit through the decoy buckle and the coded seal, so it blows either way when you take it off. Or, he could have separated the charge and put a second ground in, so it's two bombs on one strap, and it blows unless we cut both at the same instant, which is impossible because they're light lines, not electrical. Or, he might have done absolutely nothing, just to mess with our minds, but we can't afford to believe that. I miss my cows."

"I'll bring the kit, too," Falcon soothed him, rushing back toward the hilltop.

Wolf knew that it would take Falcon fourteen minutes to return to the Runner, retrieve the kit and nice old doctor whom they had kidnapped, and return to the camp. Wolf always knew things like that, but, as he stood guard over the sleeping child in the dirt, he did not know why waiting for those fourteen minutes to pass was so frightening. It scared him to stand there, just as reading Cougar's letter had scared him. It scared him to watch the tears on Casey's cheeks dry into rivers of smudged dust. Someone should have been there to wipe those tears away, and hug her, and tell her that everything would be okay. That was a father's job, and her father was sleeping.

Wolf's war had begun when everyone else's had ended. The fallen enemies around him were not even a part of it. This new war was between two men only, and Wolf was not going to let Cougar win this last battle. The rules of war were different today. If Wolf killed anyone, he would lose. War had been easier when it had been about acquiring targets. Wolf had been forced to leave five years earlier, when war had become about killing people. To a civilian, the terms "acquiring the target," and "killing people" may have seemed ambiguous, or even arbitrary, but a hunter knew the difference. To acquire a target, one only had to aim for the center of mass. To kill a person, you had to look in their eyes. Wolf could only wonder if such eye contact had driven Cougar to this madness.

Wolf had joined the army to do what he was only doing now, nearly twenty-six years later. A child's life was in danger, and he was saving her. Protecting the innocent was the dream of any good soldier, but Wolf had never dreamed of saving a life the way he was being forced to now.

Falcon was running back down the hill, escorting the handcuffed doctor ahead of him. He was forty-three seconds away.

Wolf used the side of his fist to lightly rub Casey's dirty cheek, wiping away the trails left by her tears.

"Don't cry, Casey Van Belt," he whispered to the motionless body. "My name is Captain Chester Wolf. I'm here to save you. And I never save anyone."

He took off his gunbelt and wrapped it snugly around Casey's upper forearm, cinching it tightly.

"Chess!" Falcon was calling. "I've even got a scanner. Should show us anything he did."

Wolf did not reply as he pulled even harder on the belt, buckling it only when it was as tight as he could make it.

"What are you doing?" Falcon asked, now only a few meters away.

Wolf's eyes were closed. He was praying.

"Chess, take that belt off! It'll make her arm swell! Chess!"

"God forgive me," Wolf rasped, his right hand closing over his knife hilt.

Falcon's eyes widened involuntarily.

"Chess, *no!*"

The knife flashed into Wolf's hand, freeing Casey from the bomb with a single overhand strike.

Chapter Thirty

January 10, 2191.
Office of the Prime Minister,
New Shilo, Manitoba,
Canadian Exodus.

Colonel Maxmillan Towers had not been in the prime minister's office very often over the past twenty years, while attempting to keep most of the world convinced that he was dead. Even so, he wondered if this would be his final visit. For the first time, he sincerely hoped so.

The colonel was sitting in the marble hall outside of the office, having been forewarned by General Krunnion that Prime Minister Stone enjoyed making people wait. The prime minister must have had him on a timer, because Towers knew that he had been waiting for exactly fifteen minutes when Stone summoned him in via the intercom. Entering the office, Towers first saluted General Krunnion, who stood from the sofa to return the salute, and then gravely shook his hand. Then the colonel stood at attention, facing the desk of Prime Minister Dee Robertson Stone.

Stone did not stand from behind the desk, but motioned for Towers to be seated. He sat on the sofa opposite the general.

"Colonel Towers," Stone said quietly. "Please accept my condolences on the horrendous loss to your unit. Few men in history have ever served a nation so well as your operatives. They will not be forgotten."

"Madam Prime Minister," Towers replied, without allowing any of the ice in his heart to reach his voice. "My men were forgotten as soon as they were accepted into Track and Pursuit. They joined so that a great nation would be remembered. Yourself and General Krunnion will be in the history books, and a few of us, for a few more years, will remember the role that my boys played between the lines. People who want to be remembered should not be soldiers. But I thank you."

"At the same time," Krunnion said, "congratulations are in order. Major Shark, Captain Falcon, and Captain Wolf did an incredible job. You must be proud. They ended the day with the utmost skill and professionalism. They're a credit to your leadership."

"With all respect, sir," Towers said irritably, "a man named Vance Ryan Coolidge was once a credit to my leadership. Pride is mixing with shame at the moment, and anger and confusion. The rest of the planet is feeling only relief, and I sincerely wish that I was one of them. May we please discuss the Hamelin Mission?"

"Ah, yes," Krunnion said reluctantly. "Max, you know I have never questioned your judgement before, but I do have reservations."

"Reservations?" Towers said slowly. "We have, in custody, scum who kill people, and we need to move them."

Krunnion almost had to bite his lip, reminding himself that Towers was officially a private contractor, not even required to address higher ranks as "sir."

"Colonel, I reinstated Captain Wolf in the CNE as a favor to you, and as a reward for his outstanding service. He is technically unfit for pilot duties. That leg should be an automatic disqualification. If something goes wrong while he's in the air, it's on me."

"He's as good a pilot as he is a hunter," Towers assured them. "His idea of investment options for his pension was a flight simulator in his basement. He has more simulated air time than most career pilots."

"Let's cut to the point," Stone interjected. "Colonel, the man who killed half of your TAP Alpha Unit is going to be on that plane. Your operatives should not be anywhere near him."

"Well, as the crew of a CNE Orbit Runner, they would all have to be provisionally reinstated in the Canadian Northern Eagles," Towers pointed out. "They would no longer be my operatives. They would be soldiers, yours and the general's."

"We have soldiers," Stone replied. "A lot of them. Why do we need yours?"

"Because this is not a prison transport," Towers snapped. "This is the Bloodline, the most deadly and highly trained terrorists to ever face this nation. We cannot risk sending them to their banishment with supermarket rent-a-cops."

"Reynolds is no rent-a-cop," Krunnion sighed. "And most of CT4 would resent the implication. They're my best."

"And your best come to me," Towers said. "And I make them better. Most of TAP Bravo was selected from CT4. They all know how to fly and kill."

"And what about Captain Wolf?" Stone inquired.

"If he wanted revenge, he would have taken it at Lawrence." Towers was adamant. "No one would have cared, and yet he brought Cougar in alive and unharmed."

"All that suggests to me is that he may be hesitant," Stone said, unconvinced.

Towers could not help smiling. "Madam Prime Minister, that only suggests to me that Captain Wolf is still scary. If Cougar had sensed the slightest hesitation, the most indiscernible flicker of an eye... Wolf would be dead. He's not."

"But, would he be willing to take this assignment?" Krunnion wanted to know.

"He will take orders, like any good soldier," Towers assured the general. "Let me speak to him, first. He may not like it, but believe me when I say that he will do it."

"I still consider him a risk," Stone said, shaking her head. "And I thought risks were not something we could risk. Not now."

"Then allow me to be blunt, Madam Prime Minister," Towers said crossly. "Chester Conrad Bradley grew up as a hunter, and he became a soldier. Then he became a hunter for me, and now he is a soldier again. He will always be both, which is exactly what this mission must have at its head. We need a soldier who can operate with incomprehensible restraint and discipline, and we need a hunter who can kill everybody on that ship if something goes wrong."

"I'm taking it under advisement, Colonel," Stone said cautiously, "but only if General Krunnion agrees that it's the best course."

Krunnion groaned. "Max, you're the smartest soldier I've ever known. I think Reynolds could handle this assignment ably, but I recognize that you understand the Bloodline better than I ever will. For that reason alone, I will reinstate select TAP Bravo into the Eagles to crew the shuttle, and Captain Wolf will take the lead. But, for the record, he concerns me."

"And Cougar concerns me," Towers admitted. "Which is why we need Wolf now more than ever. Cole Dallas Kressel and the entire Bloodline force do not bother me. Heir Defenders Command Second Vance Ryan Coolidge is now the single greatest threat to this planet. And, considering that he is already in prison, that is impressive."

March 20, 2187.

From the eulogy of Operative Vance Cougar,
Delivered by Captain John Shark.

"When one is trained to be the best of the best, it is very easy, and very dangerous, to forget that there might be someone out there who is better than you. We measure our own greatness by how much we know, and by what we have accomplished. We are limited by the fact that we only know so much, and can only learn so much in a lifetime. Even if we knew every living human being, we would only know their name, face, and training. We can never know the strength of heart that is hidden within each one of us. We're limited. We can only be so strong.

"After so many years without a loss, I had almost begun to think that I was invincible, the best. When I heard that Vance was dead, it scared me. Because it shouldn't have happened. No one man should have been able to take him down. No one can be better than the best. But Bishop was.

"I don't think Vance ever made my mistake. He was more aware of his own mortality than any one of us. He knew that life and death were all just a matter of chance. The most highly skilled soldier alive can still be killed by simple sticks and stones. We all cough. We all step on twigs.

"Every one of us has a limit, in our minds, hearts, and bodies. Whether you are a good soldier, or just a good man, there is only so far you can go."

Part Four

Banishment One

January 15, 2171.
From the diary of Chester Wolf.

My Dearest Rachel,

Have you ever been hunted?

You always knew that you loved a hunter. I grew up with hunters, and I learned so much from them. There was always one difference between me and them. They cheer out loud and hold their weapons aloft when the deer falls into the rustling leaves of the forest floor. Their joy, their thrill, is in the conquest and the kill. What joy I have is never in the kill. It is in the hunt.

Every hunt is a test. One hunter is always greater than the other, even by an amount so small as to be unmeasurable. The hunt is what determines our value. It is as old as humanity itself, and yet it constantly evolves, as the hunters themselves evolve with the times. Our most primitive instincts, those of survival and dominance, are combined with centuries of passed down knowledge, but as long as there is the possibility of a greater hunter being out in the world, somewhere that I can't see, the hunt will never be complete.

My life is the hunt. To hunt and be hunted is what I am. It has been a long time since I killed for food. It is illegal for me to eat what I kill, and repulsive. I am not a killer, but I am no longer a soldier.

What is my life, Rachel? What does the job force me to be? The men I have killed, during my two years of survival, were self-declared enemies of my country, men sworn to kill me because of the uniform I wore. So I killed them because of the uniforms they wore, and my leaders praised me for it, while training me at a hidden base and calling me by a name that was not my own. They call me Wolf, and they look at me and say, "Nothing hunts like a wolf." If they are right, then maybe I could one day end the question of who the greatest hunter is, but I doubt that a contest that has been waged since the dawn of our very species can possibly end with me. Someday, even I will be hunted by one greater than myself, and then I will finally know if I am a soldier or a murderer. God alone can make that distinction. To be a man of God is all that I can hope to be at the end of the day, but, while the suns still shine, my country has given me only one duty to perform.

Hunting.

Your loving husband,
Corporal Chester Wolf.

Chapter Thirty-One

February 25, 2191.
CNE Chop Hangar Eight,
Canadian Northern Eagles Garrison,
New Edmonton, Alberta,
Canadian Exodus.

It had been a long time since Chester Wolf had felt the cool controls of a CF-48 CNE Chop, but his hours and hours of simulator training had helped him to surpass the skills of his younger pilot years. The new CF-50s, however, were completely unfamiliar to him. The principle fighter of the Canadian Air Force had many new automated features, including voice recognition software that allowed the jet to follow vocal commands issued by the registered pilot. Wolf was looking forward to his first flight in the plane that carried his own name on the hull.

Officially reinstated as CNE Captain Chester Wolf two weeks earlier, he was still realizing how much he had missed this airborne life which had been his for a few short years before TAP, even if it had meant turning his ranch over to a new manager. To Wolf, the most important thing was that he was a pilot, and nothing more. His new superiors, including Colonel Reynolds, were well aware of who he was, and the conditions of his reinstatement. He had flown freight and transport runs, and was preparing for Chop aerial recons over suspected Bloodline holdout camps in southern Manitoba and Ontario. He would radio in positions, and CT4 would handle the rest.

The month of peace following the sweep of Continental Yukon had not lulled him into any sense of security, however. Wolf knew his own value to the military, and he was not going to be forced into any direct military actions. His ranch was his fallback. No one knew about Stormy Coulee, and he let most of those around him know little more than his name. If pressure was ever put on him to get back in the job, he would simply resign his commission, and disappear for good.

"Good day, Captain Wolf," he was greeted by Eddie Devane, the portly hangar maintenance supervisor, as he strode into the domed metal bay, attired in the dark green flight suit of the CNE. "First flight in the 50?"

"Indeed, Eddie," Wolf nodded, smiling at the silver jet before them, the hover plates humming quietly as they held the craft's belly a foot above the concrete. "How is she?"

"You'll love'er, Captain, she's amazing. And she's personalized." Eddie gestured to the golden title just below the forward tandem canopy.

SPARTAN II

Cpt. Chester Wolf

"Hunter Twelve"

"Good enough?" Eddie was grinning broadly. "Finished it yesterday."

"Perfect," Wolf said. He had not been so content in a long time.

"A few of the boys been wondering," Eddie commented, handing Wolf the release form. "Spartan. What's that from?"

Wolf smiled dismissively, quickly signing the sheet. "Just a name, Eddie. How's the family?"

"Doing good, Captain. Strange, though. What with the war over, I need to find new scare tactics. The Bloodline used to be the boogeyman, kept the kids in line. What do I tell them happens to bad kids now?"

"Monsters, Eddie," Wolf replied. "There's always monsters in the woods."

They shook hands, and Wolf turned toward the Chop, stopping at the cockpit.

"Hunter Twelve," he said clearly. Obediently, the forward canopy was raised up, and he climbed over the silver hull into the flight chair, belting himself in securely.

"Take-off containment," he continued, and the canopy was closed again.

"*Good morning, Captain Wolf,*" the garbled console greeted him. "*Spartan II, standing by.*"

"Full operational diagnostic and system check," Wolf instructed, fastening his flight helmet.

"*All systems go,*" the console confirmed.

"Comm, tower."

"*Comm to Flight Tower One Eight. Line open.*"

"Tower One Eight, repeat Tower One Eight, this is Rosewood Eight-Nine, requesting clearance for scheduled inaugural test run of Spartan II. Flight plan uploaded, clearance code: Mercury 2 5 Bravo Bravo."

"Roger that, Rosewood Eight-Nine. Runway's all yours."

"Thank you. How's my meteorology?"

"Playing with a full deck, Rosewood Eight-Nine. It's bright, beautiful, and, if I wasn't behind several inches of blast glass, I'm sure I'd hear birds singing. And I hate birds."

Wolf grinned. "Flying was their idea first, Tower One Eight. Now, if we could steal their songs, the world might actually be happy."

"Well, talking was our idea, and parrots stole that before the Wrights ever lifted off. They started it. Happy sailing."

"Roger that, Tower One Eight."

The bay doors slid open, letting in the blinding light of both suns.

"Spartan II, liftoff," Wolf directed. "Initiate takeoff alignment. Due west, fifteen degree ascent. Activate manual controls at level elevation two hundred meters."

The jet rails fired on cue, and the craft rose to a six feet hover clearance before slowly advancing out of the hangar, then turning westward. Once over the tarmac, the Chop halted, awaiting one last command.

"Spartan II standing by for final execution command."

"Tower One Eight, this is Rosewood Eight-Nine. Requesting final clearance."

The comm was silent.

"Tower One Eight, repeat, this is Rosewood Eight-Nine, requesting final clearance for Spartan II test run. Are we a go?"

"Stand by, Rosewood Eight-Nine."

"Tower One Eight?"

Silence.

"Tower One Eight, are we obstructed?"

"Rosewood Eight-Nine, this is Tower One Eight. Priority message. Stand down, repeat, stand down. Return to hangar bay, and report to command. Be advised, priority visitor is on site."

"Roger that," Wolf sighed. "Returning to bay."

Twenty minutes later, Wolf arrived at the massive, silver command complex. Shaped like a twenty storey soup can, the CNE HQ was a sight he never grew weary of, and had missed dearly during his hunting years. Today, however, he was wary. "Priority visitor," usually meant someone of higher rank, which, in turn, usually meant yet another request for services he was trying to leave buried in the past.

"Good morning, sir!" the two posted sentries greeted him at the main entrance, saluting sharply. Wolf returned the salute as he entered, still feeling unfamiliar with the concept of being saluted. Ranks had been meaningless in Track and Pursuit, and he had been only a corporal before volunteering from the CNE. For the next twenty years, salutes had been reserved for Colonel Towers.

From the reception area, Wolf was directed to Colonel Reynolds office, and took the elevator to the fifteenth floor, taking a brief moment to be amused by the fact that one reception area usually led to another. He did not mind, though. Reynolds personal receptionist was one of the more attractive women on the base.

"Good day, Alice," he greeted the tall, black woman in her early thirties, as he entered the posh foyer outside of Reynolds office.

Her smile was as refreshing as ever. "Captain Wolf, good day. Please go right in. The colonel is expecting you."

"Thank you."

Reynolds office was a dark, cylindrical room, rather ornately decorated with hanging antiques, chiefly old weapons such as swords, battleaxes, muskets, and even a medieval suit of armor which his ancestors had brought as an heirloom of the Home Base. Wolf's bomb shelter beneath his ranch house was cached with enough modern weaponry to outfit a platoon, and yet he always wished that his collection was more like that of Reynolds, weapons admired more for their beauty and legacy than for their stopping power.

Reynolds was seated behind his desk, talking to a white-haired man in civilian clothes, sitting with his back to Wolf. Wolf did not need to see a face to know who it was.

Reynolds rose to his feet, but the seated visitor did not turn around. Wolf stood at attention.

"Captain Wolf, reporting as ordered, Colonel."

"Thank you for coming, Captain," Colonel James Reynolds nodded at the vacant seat across from his desk. "Please, be seated."

"Thank you for the offer, sir."

Reynolds chuckled. "I will never get used to giving a man like you orders, Captain Wolf, so I won't even try. I'll leave you gentlemen now. I'm sure you have a lot to discuss."

Wolf saluted Reynolds as the colonel left the room. It was almost a relief to have a salute returned, instead of always returning them himself.

Wolf could not remember the last time that he had seen Colonel Maxmillan Towers out of uniform, but that made no difference. He was saluting again as the old man stood from his chair and turned to face him.

"I'm retiring, Captain," Towers said simply. "And I was a private contractor. Salutes are long a thing of the past."

"You're the colonel, sir," was Wolf's reply.

Towers saluted, smiling. Wolf stood at attention once more.

"You know how to disappear, Chess. Oblivion always was your gift. Still ... why didn't you come to see me? Or any of the others?"

"Sir, I came back for one hunt, for my own reasons. Track and Pursuit is no longer my life."

Towers was not smiling anymore. "You didn't even come for the funerals. The memorial."

"Twenty years ago, sir, I didn't even attend my own funeral. Or Cougar's, three years ago. I don't like funerals."

"You are still the best soldier alive," Towers stated. "I do not often question you, because you never once questioned me, but ... I admit, I was surprised."

"Have you seen him, sir?"

"I was one of the first to interrogate him. I understand that you and Ridge both declined General Krunnion's invitation to take the first shot at him. Again, an odd decision, don't you think?"

"I had nothing left to say to Vance Cougar, sir."

"At least he talked to you, then. He wouldn't say a word to me. May I ask what he said to you?"

"Nothing of consequence, sir."

"You wouldn't even file a report. Little outside of standard mission OP, isn't it?"

"I was under no obligation to the military, sir. I had all of the documentation for my conditional reinstatement, and I did not sign any of it until Cougar was transferred to Beaumont. I hunted him as a civilian. Not Track and Pursuit, not CNE."

"Very wise, Captain."

"Thank you, sir."

"Your last transmission before your return mentioned a possible child in jeopardy situation. What became of that?"

"Nothing pleasant, sir."

"Our job is to commit borderline atrocities on openly atrocious people, so that average people can be happy. We never expect to find our own happiness. Our misery is our sacrifice."

"I am not the job anymore, sir."

"Well, let's talk about that. Colonel Reynolds and I were just discussing your next assignment here."

"I have not been informed of my next assignment, sir."

"That's why I'm here."

"Sir?" Wolf knew he would not like the assignment.

"Chess, they want you to take the banishment mission."

Wolf did not reply.

"You should know that it was my initial suggestion," Towers continued. "Right after I heard that Ridgley had brought you in. For the good of the nation, I recommended you. I would trust no one else with it. Not Falcon, Shark, CT4. For the good, for the security of the nation, Chess."

It was another long moment before Wolf's cold voice was heard.

"Conditional reinstatement, sir. Three conditions. No questions. No mandatory commission period. No combat ops."

"It is a prison transport, Captain Wolf. It is one of the basic principles of our system of law that a prison transport is in no way a combat op."

"No semantics please, sir. You want me there for when something goes wrong."

"That is exactly why I want you there!" Towers voice was hard. "Track and Pursuit was not the stake driven into the heart of the Bloodline. *You were*. You took out more of them than any one of us. I serve my country to the last, and I will *not* entrust the Bloodline's final destruction to anyone except the most deadly man alive! Do you understand that, soldier?"

"You are retired, sir," Wolf said. "I am retired from killing."

"We both serve, and we always will! If I had a choice, I would go to Beaumont myself and slit the throat of every Bloodline prisoner! Kressel, Flaxton, Whitefeather, Cougar. All dead in a spreading pool of their own blood for once. But our country has decided to grant them further historical recognition in the form of a meaningless and ridiculous banishment. We serve the country, Chess, out of our love for it, regardless of the stupidity factor. We protect the country, and this is the only way they're going to let us do that. Now, they are going to give you the assignment the moment I walk out that door. Under the terms of your reinstatement, you are free to take the walk, back to oblivion. No one could say anything about it, because you have already served as few soldiers in history have ever served. You are the great Captain Chester Wolf... and I am *asking* you to do this thing. Please."

Wolf blinked. "You're asking me to kill again, sir."

"I am asking you to kill everyone on that plane if they force your hand," Towers said plainly. "I pray that the mission will be uneventful, and that the Desert sands will be the final executioner. But I am asking you to be ready to do whatever is needed, because, if you are not and something goes wrong, the Bloodline will come back. They're not gone yet, and the war is not over. It's over when they're dead."

"Aren't we all dead, sir?"

For the first time, Towers could read some of the pain in Wolf's eyes as he spoke.

"Your life will be death," Wolf said. "Can you not let me get away from that, sir?"

Towers folded his arms and leaned against the desk.

"I have no power to stop you, Captain," he slowly replied, sounding tired. "A country will always need the best soldier it has. As you get older, slower, one better will take your place. But he hasn't shown up yet. For now, he's still you. I don't want you to have to kill again, Chess. I don't want to kill anymore, and I've done it longer than you have. There is always a price to pay for being the best at what you do. You have to do it. If you didn't want to do it, you never should have learned. Hey, you didn't even learn. It's your gift. We use our gifts to help those we love. We can never choose what we're born with, but we have to choose what we do with it. It's your choice."

"It's my choice now, sir."

"I know. So make it. I'm walking out now, and they're walking in with the papers. Good day, Captain…. You should have come to see me."

"Tell me one thing, Colonel," Wolf requested. "If I had not come back, what would they have done?"

"They would have found a soldier," Towers replied, walking back to the door. "For Vance, and the banishment mission."

"Would they have found one, sir? One good enough?"

Towers had to stop in front of the door. "Chess … it has been far too long. It is very good to see you again."

"Godspeed, sir."

Towers opened the door and stepped silently into the outer office. Colonel Reynolds was standing by Alice's desk, holding Wolf's next assignment in a beige file folder, marked *Classified*.

"He's all yours, Jim."

Reynolds seemed strangely reluctant as he slowly walked past Towers, and disappeared into the dim office. Towers was smiling, but not at the pretty lady behind the desk. He was mentally counting down.

5...4...3...2....

He turned around just as Reynolds returned from the office, confusion in his eyes.

"Colonel Towers ... he's not in there."

Towers could only chuckle and shake his head as he pulled on his overcoat. He had a flight home waiting.

"Sorry, Jim. Even I don't know how he does that."

Chapter Thirty-Two

February 25, 2191.
Holding cell of Major Powers Bourgeouis,
Beaumont Maximum Security Prison,
Northern polar region, Ontario,
Canadian Exodus.

General Alvardo Krunnion had never before been saluted by a Bloodline of any rank, but Major Powers Bourgeouis had been a puzzle to him for over thirty years. Clad in navy blue prison coveralls, the old soldier was still as imposing as he had been in his earlier years, when he had been Heir Defenders Commander. Although his shackled hands were on a short chain to his belt, Bourgeouis managed to raise them high enough to touch his chest with the fingertips of his right hand, as the posted guards opened the cell door to allow the entry of the Canadex general.

Krunnion returned the salute, and both men stood tall, facing each other until the door was closed.

"I will break Kressel's self-assurance before I ever break your loyalty, Major."

"General." Bourgeouis nodded his agreement.

"And yet you salute me."

"You defeated a great army, under a greater leader, fortified within an impenetrable fortress. That deserves respect, at the very least. The general always spoke very highly of you. Has a day been set for our banishment?"

"Yes."

"When?"

Krunnion smiled. "Soon."

"So, are you here to be praised, or to petition me?"

"Major Bourgeouis, how long have you served Cole Dallas Kressel?"

"The Heir was assigned as my principle on my seventeenth birthday. He was six at the time."

"He's been your entire life."

"He's The Heir. He deserves more than one life, his or mine."

"You have no family, wife, children. Your devotion to your leader defies anything I have ever seen."

"The Bloodline has been called terrorists, General. I have seen my men behave as such. To survive, they had to be savage. We were outnumbered, outgunned, and slandered. I did not agree with every action taken, but a soldier's job is to obey, at the cost of his own life, or the lives of others."

"At the cost of his conscience?"

"The Heir is not a god. He is a man, flawed, prone to error, but still a leader, with a blood claim to this world. I do not revere him as a deity, but I served a general."

"For which service your position was handed over to a confessed serial rapist," Krunnion reminded him.

"I hate Robert Flaxton," Bourgeouis seethed. "I would have killed him myself, years ago, if his life was not held so dear by The Heir. We may not lose love for one another, but we serve the same cause."

"Flaxton will die," Krunnion stated. "You do not have to."

"Ah ... so you do want something from me. I understood that my fate was written in stone."

"Stones break, Major. We know that there are Bloodline cells and hit squads operating in southern Ontario, working comm-free ops, who missed your recall. Where are they? What are there missions? Where are their fallback points?"

"Haven't you read the papers, General? You won."

"You know where they are."

"But what is my incentive?"

Krunnion chuckled. "You will be banished, Major, but you don't have to die. You give us the locations, present, potential, and fallbacks, and you will not be banished to The Desert's equatorial region."

"So I can die from starvation, rather than exposure. Tempting offer to be sure, especially at my age."

"Hear me, Major. You will be banished to the polar lake. The water is pure, and the ground is good. The temperature is stable. You would have a chance. Give us the cells, and I will leave you with food, seeds, fertilizer, and the makings of shelter."

"No one has been to The Desert in over eighty years," Bourgeouis sourly reminded him. "You cannot be certain that the polar lake is still pure, or even still there. You can offer me freedom and riches, General. The cells you speak of are still fighting for a cause that I believe in. Forgive me, but I have always hated the idea of being a vegetarian, or a hermit. I stand proudly guilty of what you call war crimes. I will take the equator."

Chapter Thirty-Three

February 25, 2191.
Our Lady of Mercy Chapel,
Canadian Northern Eagles Garrison,
New Edmonton, Alberta,
Canadian Exodus.

"Forgive me, Father, for I have sinned."

Lieutenant Amanda Lewis believed in the crucifix that hung from a brass chain around her neck. Very few TAP operatives did not. Living a life of death made God seem very close, for some reason.

"It has been one month since my last confession. These are my sins."

Amanda Lewis was an operative of TAP Bravo Unit, following on the revered heels of TAP Alpha. Trained by Colonel Towers himself, the attractive thirty-three-year-old with short black hair had successfully completed four hunts since her admission into the unit on December 31, 2190. Most of the hunts had been mop up work, tracking down fleeing terror cells in Ontario and Manitoba, now that Yellowknife had finally been retaken. She had never even been to Continental Yukon, and could not help wondering if Track and Pursuit would even be continued. Annual recruitment had been an impulsive decision, according to Colonel Towers, and now seemed even more pointless than before. The war they were training to wage was over.

"I was careless on my last hunt. I should have taken greater strides to capture my target. Three more of God's holy creations died at my hand, Father."

"My daughter, you did not commit murder."

She did not know if the words were statement or question, but replied, "No, Father. They would have killed me. Yet, I feel remorse. They should not have died. They should have faced justice, according to the laws of man and God. The war is supposed to be over."

"Some wars can only begin when another ends," the priest said quietly from behind the dark screen. "Insurgents are just as much a war to you as an entire army of evil-doers."

"I am a hunter, Father. Jesus told Peter that he would be a fisher of men. I am a hunter of men. I hunt lives, not souls."

"King David was a hunter of men, too," the priest replied. "Tens of thousands were said to have died at his hand. He committed cold-blooded murder, taking the life of Uriah in order to steal his wife. And, yet, his heart was set right in the sight of God. His penitence made him a great king, not his battlefield triumphs. Our actions may haunt us, but our repentance, true repentance, separates us from the evil men we may strike down."

"Forgive me, Father."

"Do you believe you need forgiveness?"

"Hearing the words aloud is a beautiful sound."

"Christ forgives you. His words to the sinful woman remind you. Go, and sin no more."

"My life is death, Father."

"God knows when your hand is forced. Two men may simultaneously stab one another, with identical knives. God sees the righteousness of the heart. He sees *why* the knife was driven, not just how."

"And what if two righteous men, through an error of judgement, stab each other?"

"You fear that situation, don't you?"

"God sees the heart. I can only see the uniform. If I have ended the life of just one righteous man ... then what am I?"

"A soldier, my daughter," the priest sighed. "You have one second on the battlefield to make a choice. You have years to plague yourself with the memory. To be a soldier is to live with pain, and it is a cross we bear out of love. By defending our lives, we defend our country. By defending our country, we defend our family. Evil men and good men will die. Peace can only exist in the kingdom of God, but, until then, we have to survive in the world of man. You help people to survive, giving them more time to find the right path."

"I once killed an evil man," Lewis said, "to save the life of a man whom I now believe to be more evil than the first."

"Then you gave him a second chance," the priest answered. "You have to trust that God will help him to make the most of it. That ... is faith."

Lieutenant Lewis prayed daily, but felt closest to God when kneeling at the front of an empty church. Stepping from the confessional, she softly entered the dim sanctuary, passing the rows of pews, her eyes fixed on the tall crucifix behind the alter, silhouetted by the shining stain glass murals behind it. Crossing herself, she knelt and bowed her head, her palms resting on her knees.

"A Track and Pursuit should know better."

The low voice to her left made her start and look up. She had not even seen the cloaked man kneeling beside her, no more than six feet away, his face hidden by a hood.

"Who are you?" she demanded. She was not used to being surprised. Her life was based on seeing others first.

"Even in a moment of reverent awe, never look directly at a lit-up window, stained or not. You blind yourself, see spots."

"I don't hunt in church."

"I'm sure God would understand."

"Who are you?"

"Someone who knows your pain. King David has been my inspiration as well. Sins and redemption."

"You eavesdrop on confessions, too?"

"No. I just have good hearing, and the confessional is only sixty-four feet away in a resonant room. Do you believe you killed a righteous man?"

"I don't know," Lewis said, annoyed. "Have you?"

"It is very probable."

"Is that why you're here?"

"No. I'm here to pray."

"So am I. I'm praying for the souls of the three men I killed. Who do you pray for?"

"Me."

"Why?"

"Because I have prayed for too many souls."

"Who are you?"

"My name is Wolf. You have heard it before."

"Captain Wolf?!"

"Do *not* stand, do not salute. This is church."

"Sir...."

"I have been reinstated in the CNE. You are not required to call me 'sir.' You're dead, remember?"

"So are you."

"Well, since Kage's declassification, who knows how long we'll enjoy that luxury. I think I'd miss being dead. Nobody bothers you as much."

Wolf pushed his hood back over his shoulders, and looked up at the crucifix. He could feel Lewis's dark eyes examining his bearded face.

"I'm surprised to meet a Track and Pursuit here, Lieutenant. I can only assume that you are being assigned to the Hamelin Mission. Welcome to the CNE."

"Welcome back, actually," Lewis smiled. "I was selected for TAP from CT4."

"What is your banishment assignment?"

"Transport security."

"Are you happy with that?"

"It feels strange to feel happy about leaving men to their deaths. How do you even know about the Hamelin Mission? The details were classified, last I heard."

"They want me to command it."

"You've been assigned?"

"I've been requested."

"Sir.... Captain Wolf, I have only heard your legend, and it was just that, even in the job. If I may ... who is Captain Chester Wolf?"

Wolf stood and looked down at her. She had expected that he would be taller.

"Lewis?"

"Yes, sir."

"I walk through the door, and I kill you. Sometimes, I have to leave through a different door. Once it's over, no one can figure out how I even got the first door open. A few steps, two shots, chaos, oblivion. And I enjoy horseback riding."

"And will you accept the request?"

"That is what I was praying about."

"Did you get an answer?"

"I did now. Good day, Lieutenant."

"Christ be with you, Captain."

"Risen, indeed."

Chapter Thirty-Four

February 25, 2191.
Office of Colonel James Reynolds, CNE-CT4,
Canadian Northern Eagles Garrison,
New Edmonton, Alberta,
Canadian Exodus.

When Colonel Reynolds returned to his office after six hours of absence, Wolf was standing at attention, waiting for him. Reynolds smile was a tired one, more acceptant than amused.

"I'm not even going to ask how you got back in here," he grumbled, taking off his cap and hanging it on a coat rack.

Wolf saluted. "Who said I ever left, sir?"

"You are not required to salute."

"A privilege, sir. All I'm used to."

"At ease, soldier. For crying out loud, Wolf, stop acting PFC."

"I barely know how to act like a captain, sir."

"The point is taken. The assignment stands. Your commission is still your decision."

"I am accepting the mission, sir."

"Surprised, Captain, but glad to hear it."

"Conditionally." Wolf's voice was firm.

Reynolds sighed. "I might have guessed. How much leeway do you think they're going to give you?"

"I hate leeway. I'm upgrading the mission, in the national interest. My place is with the bird, so who's got the lunar?"

"Lieutenant Jessica Arnett, TAP Bravo. Towers recommended her, just like he did you. She was my best pilot to come out of CT4. She's off the charts."

"Did Falcon train her for TAP missions?"

Reynolds shook his head. "I'm still not in the loop on TAP, but I would assume Captain Falcon was at least involved with last year's class. Haven't you talked with him?"

"Not since Beaumont. Can you trust Jessica Arnett?"

"With my life, Wolf. She's my best."

"Sir, I don't have time to have my trust earned. I need someone who already has it."

"You can trust her. Believe me."

"As a copilot, maybe. What's her combat experience?"

"CT4! Are you going to have a hard time working with women, or what?"

"I'd ask the same question of anyone I don't know. I can trust a lot of people. I just don't."

"Captain, we gave this mission to TAP, and a lot of my kids were not happy about it. What more do you want?"

"Falcon."

Reynolds leaned back against his desk, letting his head sag just a little.

"Captain Wolf ... I cannot shut down the Towers Program."

"We can't disclose the Towers Program, either. Didn't stop Kage."

"If Kage wasn't on top of the world, and the prime minister's nephew-in-law, I would have arrested him myself. I can't bring them back, Captain."

"I'm not asking you to. I'm asking for easy stuff. Help me save the world."

"You want me to shut down your own unit?"

"No. TAP missions are already down eighty-eight percent since Yellowknife. We can give the Towers to Shark and Hawk. Shark's mostly recovered, and Hawk knows it inside out. They can handle it."

"Handle it?" Reynolds scoffed. "Good enough? Fair to middlin'? Proficient? Elite? Falcon is in command because he's the best! No one else can 'handle it.'"

"Be honest, Colonel," Wolf said flatly. "Track and Pursuit died with disclosure. The entire unit will be disbanded before Charlie ever reaches final selection. It's already over. But between Hamelin and The Desert, there is a long stretch of empty space that can only be closed by a lunar module. I need the best soldier and pilot there. I'm not banishing the Bloodline, the module is. The question you need to answer right now, are you going to trust the ultimate disposal of the greatest single threat to the peace of this planet to a first year TAP graduate, or a twenty year TAP veteran? Can you answer that right now?"

"Captain ... our authorization in this mission is just the mission. People bigger than us are writing the script."

"That's why I need you to make it happen. Get Krunnion on your side, and I'll make the request to Falcon personally. I need the best team I can possibly put together, but, without operational command, I need your support."

"Do you expect peace, Captain Wolf?"

"Sir?"

"The war is over. Do you expect peace?"

Wolf paused for a moment. "Sir, I have heard that the secret to making God laugh is to tell Him what you're doing tomorrow."

"Do you believe that?"

"I don't think war makes God laugh, sir, or the aftermath. We're taking them out to die. I don't consider the war over."

Reynolds smiled. "Me neither. I hope that the rest of the world has more hope than we do. That's where real lasting peace starts. With hope."

"No one has ever seen lasting peace. The history of mankind, we just remove immediate threats. National interest. The country writes a bloody, violent script, soldier's take the stage. Only the best of us never get a curtain call."

"Well, I know that you would write better than any bureaucrat, Captain. I'll back whatever calls you make, but I can't guarantee anything."

"Kage is terrified that Major Shark is coming to kill him, sir. I think he'll cooperate. Shark might kill him anyway."

"What happened in the deeps, Captain?"

Wolf blinked. "Sir?"

"Captain Falcon brought you back, and got you back in the sky. He was the only man you trusted with your residential location, and you haven't spoken to him since. What happened?"

"It wasn't quite the deeps, sir. Ways north."

"Did someone die?"

"No, sir."

"But the legend of the Hidden Hunters is not going away?"

"No, sir. I wish it was."

"Will he accept your offer?"

"Have you read his file, sir?"

"You're TAP. You don't have files."

"The Bloodline killed his father and sister. Flaxton killed his sister at Yellowknife. We all know what that means. He'll accept."

Reynolds nodded slowly. "I see. Very well, Captain. I'll put in the calls to General Krunnion and Colonel Towers. That will be all. Don't salute."

"Colonel Reynolds, if I may...."

"Say what you will, Captain."

"Sir, you took down Yellowknife, and you took down the Bloodline. The Hamelin Mission was rightfully yours."

"But I am still not the soldier or hunter that you are, Captain. We cannot risk anything but the best. You'll meet your team tomorrow."

"Good day, sir."

Chapter Thirty-Five

February 28, 2191.

Somewhere in the northern tundra, Alberta, Canadian Exodus.

Eddie Devane was more than just an aircraft maintenance supervisor, and he was going to prove it. He was going to show the Canadex what a sleeper really was.

The binary suns made snow a rarity on Canadian Exodus, even in the polar regions. Eddie Devane had never driven through snow before, and he did not like it. A beautiful annoyance was all it was, and slippery, especially on the dirt trail he was following. Snow was falling thickly as his car slid and skidded toward the old prospecting cabin ahead, a sole man-made structure in the wide open barrenness of northern Alberta.

"I thought The Mountain had no presence in Alberta."

Roger Craven had never seen snow before. It was almost frightening, so bright and blinding.

Devane smiled as he parked the off-road vehicle in front of the cabin.

"That's why he's so safe here," he answered his friend.

"Is he reliable?" Craven did not like going into foreign territory without information. He reached into his jacket and flipped the safety off his ion pistol.

"Kressel himself utilized him, many times," Devane assured him. "He's a loner, but all the best are."

"Loners don't have corporate resources. We have enough supporters in industries around the globe. We should have utilized them."

"Industries are tied deep into the entire Bloodline infrastructure," Devane said, stepping out into the snow, and slinging a brown canvas shoulder bag over his back. "Which the Canadex now has full access to. Who knows how many of them have been compromised, or just given up. He has no ties to cut, which means no strings to follow."

"Fine," Craven snorted, eyeing the cabin cautiously. "Just a man who doesn't have a name...."

"Smart," Devane replied. "Names are strings."

Devane's undercover assignment had been nothing short of a joke. Other Bloodline sleepers, radicalized from an early age like himself, had worked their way into key positions for assassinations and high-profile acts of sabotage against centers of Canadex military industry. Meanwhile, Devane had been ordered to utilize his mechanical expertise for the eye-rolling purpose of reporting the newest advances in military aircraft technology, in a rather feeble attempt to ensure that what had just happened at Port Yellowknife could not happen. Unfortunately for the Bloodline, Chimney Sweep had been designed by the Shielders Corporation, a private defense contractor which Devane had absolutely no access to. Even so, Eddie was more than aware that many of his own people would be looking for a donkey to pin the blame on, and he was a very easy target in that regard. But he was going to show them what he was made of, along with the Canadex. It was no coincidence that he was the chief maintenance technician of a certain CNE Runner, and he knew that his placement as such was going to turn the war back around for the Bloodline. In fact, it was going to do much more than that. Eddie Devane was about to single-handedly save the Bloodline.

But first he had to see a man about a bomb.

The door opened before Devane could even knock. The man in the doorway did not look like a soldier, or a mercenary, or a killer of any kind. He was tall, lean, and plain, an average man alone in the tundra. His clothes were rugged, seemingly handmade from animal hides, his unshaven face and shoulder-length brown hair shaded by a wide-brimmed hat.

"You're The Freelancer?" Devane ventured, feeling more chilled than the weather should have been responsible for.

The man in the doorway nodded, but said nothing.

"I'm Eddie Devane. I have the money."

"I said to come alone," the man said.

"The entire continent is armed and hostile," Devane said coolly. "It pays to have backup. This is Roger Craven. He's one of us. Do you have my bomb?"

The Freelancer turned inside, silently.

Craven looked over at Eddie, nervously. Eddie nodded, then walked into the unlit cabin.

"As I understand it," Eddie said, "the device will maintain a continuous charge from the ship's...."

Three ion charges slammed into Craven's chest before he had even passed through the wooden doorway. His body was lifted from the ground, and hurled back into the snow, smoke rising from the three burning holes in his heart. He was dead before his body hit the ground.

The Freelancer holstered his pistol, then looked down at Devane, cowering behind the door.

"I said to come alone," the man said quietly.

Devane swallowed the knot in his throat as he slowly stood up.

"I create chaos, Mr. Devane," The Freelancer explained. "It's what I'm best at. But I do not like confusion."

"He was one of us," Devane managed to whisper, shaking with rage and fear.

"He was one of you," The Freelancer said. "And, no doubt, he had a wife, children, friends, loved ones, cherished memories, secret dreams, ambitions, a personal legacy. Your defiance cost him all of that. Do not confuse me again. Do you want your bomb?"

Devane nodded.

"You are unaccustomed to death," The Freelancer noted, picking up a small wooden crate, and setting it on the dusty slab table. "The problem with being a sleeper is that you sometimes fall asleep. You remember what you have to do, but sometimes you forget what you may have to do in order to achieve it. Set the money on the table."

Devane slowly removed the shoulder bag, and set it next to the crate.

"You can install it directly into the main charge coupler of the aft light rails," The Freelancer stated. "Security scans will not even pick it up. By the time the signature overrides the charge, it will be too late."

"Who are you?" Devane could not help asking.

The Freelancer smiled. "I was one of you, once. A doctor eventually told me that I was a sociopath. After that, I decided to just create chaos. The money is good."

He flipped the lid of the crate, revealing the small plastic bomb inside.

"Well, I do believe in causes," Devane said slowly, gazing into the box. "And I will risk all to accomplish them. Great risks. They say the Hidden Hunters themselves will helm the mission. I even spoke with the commander a few days ago."

The Freelancer's eyes actually lit up with excitement.

"You have met the wolf?" he said, awed.

Devane was surprised, but replied, "Captain Wolf, yes."

The Freelancer grabbed him by the shoulders, delighted by this unexpected news.

"Tell me about him!" he implored eagerly.

Chapter Thirty-Six

February 28, 2191.

Primary Briefing Room, Command Complex,

Canadian Northern Eagles Garrison,

New Edmonton, Alberta,

Canadian Exodus.

Wolf understood that this briefing was quite possibly the most important of his career, but his concentration was elsewhere. General Krunnion was a man he had known and worked with for twenty years, a man whose very presence demanded attention and respect, but Wolf knew the rundown already. He was more preoccupied with his team, spread out amongst the rows of seats surrounding him.

"Well, one war's end always sparks the real storm," Krunnion was saying. "Public outrage."

The Hamelin Mission had a crew count of eight, six from TAP Bravo, two from TAP Alpha. All were gathered in that room, and all but one of them was completely attentive.

"The people who never did a thing finally have the guts, and, amazingly enough, the obligation to tell us what we did wrong, and why. Because they know."

Wolf had met his crew only three days earlier, but simulation runs had told him a lot more than responses to disaster scenarios. He could read people as easily as he could read their footprints. The only thing he was unsure of was whether or not he liked what he was reading.

"Apparently, this week we're a toss-up between mass murderers, and flat out genocide. Bombing Yellowknife was the wrong call. We should have anticipated the whim of our noncombatant protectees, and utilized our arsenal of tranqs and water guns."

Wolf's eyes were sweeping the room, studying the faces of each member under his command.

Lieutenant Jessica Arnett was a highly qualified pilot, and her training scores had been the highest in TAP Bravo. Although not yet thirty years old, Arnett had seen more combat than any member of the second class. She had hunted Colonel Towers in the Towers Program final selection, a feat that had only been previously accomplished by Wolf and Vance Cougar. She was as cold a killer as Wolf had ever seen. Only Wolf's absolute trust in Falcon's piloting skills prevented him from second-guessing his decision to reassign Arnett as the ship's copilot.

Wolf noticed people's eyes, and Jessica Arnett's were intriguing for two reasons. One was the beauty factor, blue and brilliant. The second was that they were constantly glancing over at Captain Ridgely Falcon, seated two rows ahead of her.

"Here's what it comes down to, the cost of ending a war," Krunnion continued. "The University of New Toronto is rallying in the coliseum, calling for the court-martial, and a few calls for the public executions of ... well, pretty much the entire CNE and CT4. Oh yes, and they want all Bloodline prisoners returned to Yellowknife, to 'rebuild.' Unquote."

Wolf's eyes were still roaming.

Sergeant-Major Donavan Cardinal was a comm operator and technician, as skilled in aircraft and spacecraft maintenance as he was in combat. Arguably the smartest member of the crew, Cardinal also presented a problem. Wolf could see something in the young soldier's eyes that he did not like. It looked a lot like fear, albeit veiled behind an indifferent veneer.

"'67 doesn't matter anymore," Krunnion stated. "We're the bad guys now, since the Bloodline is no longer scary enough. The students have decreed it."

Privates Reginald Connors and Staton Hanley had been given the guard postings in the lunar module. Both seemed more than capable, and had proven their eliteness in several covert assaults on Bloodline insertion camps in Ontario. Wolf's only concern in regards to either one was how they would react without a superior officer in command, should anything go wrong in the lunar. Despite TAP's emphasis on being alone in the woods, Connors and Hanley were still followers. "Clearance" was an issue which they had raised more than any of the other members in the past days.

"We fight for security," Krunnion sighed. "Never for gratitude. Free country. We die so that they can have the right to complain. But, in the meantime, our evil knows no bounds, and we're not done. Hamelin is our end-game, and here's how it plays out."

The shuttle guard posts had been given to Corporal Amed Ustaf and Lieutenant Amanda Lewis. Of the two, Lewis was the only one who gave Wolf any concern, and that was because she reminded him of himself. She thought about people, not targets. What he had overheard in the chapel had told him that. She could kill, but she could not forgive herself for it.

"The easiest way for Bloodline supporters to attempt a rescue is during transit, between Beaumont and the launch site on Vancouver Island. We can use air or ground convoy, but we're still most vulnerable then, armored or not. I apologize for keeping you all in the dark until now, but it was for all of our security. Admit it. Every one of you prefers to take the order and shoot the gun, no questions, no thought time.

"There isn't going to be a transit. We're bringing the launch to Beaumont. As Captain Wolf and Lieutenant Arnett are already aware, Banishment One is a modified Kressel Liner. By modified, I mean ... it's not really a Kressel Liner, as the media has been told, again for our security. Banishment One is an Orbit Runner, short range solar, modified with Liner light rails. It can operate in deep space, well beyond its standard solar-charge range. However, the added mass has rendered the hover-mode inoperable. You can have a horizontal liftoff, but you can only land on a suitable runway, or water. Bottom line: Don't land. The sand would snap the landing gear right off, and you are all aware of the difficulties of a water takeoff, not that The Desert has a whole lot of that. We stay in orbit, just like a Liner would. Yes, Captain Falcon?"

Falcon, seated in the front row, lowered his hand.

"Field-tested, sir?"

"Orbital runs, no solars. No hitches."

"No deep space runs?"

"No."

Falcon's jaw tensed. "So, it's another prototype."

"Even worse," Krunnion smiled. "It's a jerry-rigged modification, successful on short-range tests. Bring an extra airtank, Captain."

The joke almost made Wolf smile. Falcon was not even tempted.

Krunnion was no longer smiling. "You all know The Desert for what it is. The Home Base's only other atmospheric match, and if you actually dropped a match at the equator in mid-summer, it would just about light itself. Right now, though, it is coming to the outer reaches of a very long elliptical, which is why we have to go now. I'm not getting you any closer to our binaries than I have to.

"We have four Bloodline Seconds, fourteen Heir Defenders, and one Heir to banish. Nineteen bad guys. The lunar module can only transport three prisoners at once, so Captain Falcon is going to be making seven descents. Six of those descents will be made at Captain Wolf's discretion, in regards to who's going when. But the first descent is my discretion, and I'm putting it into two words. Kressel first."

The assembled crew nodded solemnly.

"I'm seriously growing weary of hearing what a great day it is for Canadian Exodus, every single time I watch the news. For me, the only great day will be when you return, and they don't.

"I am very, very proud to know every one of you. No matter what anyone says about the war being over, I say that you are the final hope for this nation. There is no such thing as a guarantee, and peace is not the exception. If I had to guess, I'd say a person wants peace. People don't. I don't see a lot of hope in the world, war or no war. If any of you do still have some ... cling to it. We may never have a world filled with hope, but we can still have our own. Maybe that's all we need."

Wolf had never seen Krunnion get even this emotional during a briefing, or anywhere else. The old soldier was holding the edges of the podium tightly, his body looking tired and teetering. The general was on the brink of tears.

"Your mission specs are on your terminals," he said shakily. "That will be all. O Canada."

The general left the room without even acknowledging the assembly rising to salute him. Silence followed, as Wolf stepped up to the podium.

"Report to Banishment Hangar, 06:00 tomorrow," he said quietly. "No one leaves the base. Crew dismissed."

Everyone stood to exit, but Wolf nodded slightly in Falcon's direction, telling him to remain seated. Falcon's scowl was intimidating, but expected.

"Krunnion's wife," Wolf explained. "They don't think she'll last the week."

"He'd want her to see this," Falcon said, crossing his arms. "But it's hard. We can only explain away loved ones killed by enemies. Nature's supposed to be objective."

"Vance told me that we have our entire lives to prepare for death, but none of us ever do," Wolf commented.

"I'm ready," Falcon grumbled, standing to leave. "Maybe Vance is the one who should be."

"Ridge...."

"We're banishing the Bloodline, Chess. Tomorrow. Do we really need to talk about anything else?"

"I was just saying that you've had more space time than anyone here. We can sidestep the quarantine if you want to see Paisley before we leave."

"I'll see her when I get back," Falcon said shortly. "Don't call her." He began walking to the corridor.

"I'm not apologizing for anything," Wolf stated. "Vance lost. She's alive."

Falcon turned on his heel, striding back toward Wolf, his eyes angrier.

"We should have disarmed the bomb, not the child! That is *not* the job!"

"The job is killing people," Wolf retorted, "and no one died, so this wasn't the job."

"I took this one for the sake of my own child!" Falcon snapped. "Innocence! Just like Casey."

"I made a call to save a life."

"You threw the hand, and detonated the Cuff! The doctor could have saved it!"

"He saved her life. Sometimes, that has to be good enough."

"It's not good enough!"

"Fine," Wolf said. "You're a father. So is Van Belt. What do you think he'd rather wake up to? Scattered fragments that used to be his daughter, or his wounded daughter being treated by a doctor?"

"I had a full bomb kit! I have been disarming bombs and security systems, overriding secure computer files.... I know the Cuff!"

"It's about trust, Ridge. I trust Vance's ability to rig a bomb more than your ability to disarm. Or mine, or anyone else I know. We could have saved her hand, or we could have all died trying. I don't take risks anymore."

"You told me once '*I don't hurt people. I kill them, or I leave them alone.*'"

"Neither of those seemed like legitimate options this time."

"I trust myself," Falcon growled. "What you think should not have mattered."

Wolf squinted curiously. "You're not hiding well. You don't care about that kid. Is this Flaxton? He'll die soon enough."

"Should have died years ago!" Falcon barked, storming out of the room. "Like the day he hit puberty!"

"*Captain Falcon!*" Wolf said, his voice resonating with unexpected power. Falcon stopped in the doorway, not looking back.

"I don't care if the launch countdown has already started," Wolf said with slow clarity. "These prisoners are under my protection, and regulations specify that I kill you if you try to kill them. I asked for the best pilot available, but I will replace you if you threaten my mission in any way."

"Yours?"

"They asked for me. I asked for you. It's mine. You're under my command, and I need you to work with that."

Falcon glared. "Captain Wolf, I am going to banish Robert Flaxton, and it will haunt me to know that I will be the last person to see him, and he'll still be alive. But I serve the country before myself. He'll die without anymore help from me than the opening of the drop chute. You wanted me on this, Chess, but do not question me!"

"Wouldn't dream of it," Wolf sighed.

Falcon slumped against the doorframe, his eyes sliding shut.

"Crap.... I'm sorry, Chess."

Wolf said nothing.

"I'm getting tired of the job," Falcon said wearily. "I want my daughter to know about me, something besides being a traveling insurance investigator. And I know that she'd be scared of me if she ever knew the truth. If I told her that someone just like me murdered five men just like me ... she'd be afraid. I don't know if she even trusts me now, but she'd never trust me after that. She'd spend her life wondering if her daddy was going to snap someday, and come after her. And that scares me, too. Vance had a point of no return. What's mine? Is it how many people I kill? How many missions I run? Where is the line that separates me from the man who used to be my brother?"

Wolf placed his hands in his pockets. He had no answer.

"You're still a good man, Chess. You did make the right call. You always make the right call. I guess I was just hoping that we could get through one op without ... blood spatter.... Do you really think Vance just snapped?"

Wolf gave his head one slow shake. "He's too categorical. He's evil. And he's working at it."

"You called him insane."

"Insanity is something *I* can explain away. It made everything make sense."

"But does he really believe what he says? About greatness, math, the numbers.... Does he believe that?"

"No," Wolf said. "Vance doesn't believe. He knows. He considers belief a weakness. That's his only insanity."

Falcon heaved a deep sigh. "I've got your back, Chess. I'm sorry. I just get frustrated."

"Do you know what scares me, Ridge?"

Falcon looked up in surprise, unconsciously realizing how rare it was for Wolf to introduce a topic.

"No," he slowly answered.

"I've never killed in anger."

Falcon's brow furrowed curiously. "That scares you?"

Wolf nodded. "That terrifies me."

"I know a lot of people who killed in anger, Chess. Some are dead, some are in jail, most of the rest should be. There's better ways to prove your humanity. The fact that you got out says enough."

"And the fact that I came back?"

"You just love the sky."

"Something's going to go wrong, Ridge," Wolf said plainly. "I know it. People are going to die."

"No one can force your hand," Falcon said calmly. "Everyone's scared, everyone thinks something's going wrong. That's why they wanted TAP. We're not supposed to be scared."

"Cardinal's scared," Wolf pointed out. "Can you see it?"

Falcon nodded. "I trained most of them, and I'll vouch for them, but facing the entire soul of the Bloodline.... That's intimidating. I still think he'll hold up."

"Then tell me about Arnett."

Falcon raised an eyebrow. "Too young for you, Chess."

"What about you?" Wolf asked mildly.

"What?"

"She looks at you. And it's not angry looks."

"She looks at me?"

"Through the briefing, the scenario runs. I want the why."

"She's a great pilot," Falcon replied simply, not flinching.

"So are you. Your prize pupil. Best pilot in Alpha, best pilot in Bravo."

"Say what you're going to say, Chess."

"If you're having any kind of romantic involvement with a member of this team, I need to know now."

"I don't compromise missions. You know that. Yes, we worked together a lot last year. I was her primary.

311

Maybe we got too close, I'll admit that. She's a good friend. Maybe I've just been divorced too long."

"But she looks at you."

"Yes."

"Has she met Paisley?"

"Yes. And they love each other. Paisley still misses you, you know."

Wolf smiled slightly. "I'm surprised she still remembers."

Falcon sat back down in the front row of seats, briefly rubbing his face with his rough hands.

"Why did you say that, Chess? That people are going to die?"

Wolf hunkered down beside the podium, leaning his shoulder against it. "Because I'm TAP."

"Know everything, without believing anything. I know."

Wolf shook his head. "More than that. In '67, June 27, I looked at Rachel and I said, 'Something bad's going to happen.' I knew."

"Really?" Falcon's eyebrows raised a bit. "I didn't know that."

"Bad things haven't stopped happening since. Next time, I'll keep my mouth shut."

312

Chapter Thirty-Seven

February 29, 2191.
Somewhere in the northern tundra, Alberta,
Canadian Exodus.

The wind was howling outside, but the woodstove kept the cold and swirling snow safely outside of The Freelancer's cabin. He sat in a handmade rocking chair, his legs crossed, sipping a tin mug of tea, hot from the stovetop. He smiled contentedly, his eyes closed.

The old radio was turned on, and the prime minister was making yet another speech about how the following day would be remembered amongst the greatest in Canadian history. She was talking about the launch site on Vancouver, and the great Kressel Liner christened Banishment One. She answered questions about the transport from Beaumont Prison, and the heavily armored convoy that would escort it, including an entire CNE Chop squadron and mobile artillery.

The Freelancer wanted to laugh out loud. Even if he had not already known the true identity of Banishment One, the prime minister's ramblings would have given it away. No doubt there would be a convoy, possibly even a launch, but it would all be a ruse to divert attention from the real Hamelin Mission, which would launch directly from Beaumont in Polar Ontario. The prime minister was not a good liar, even when the lives of her own soldiers depended on it.

Chuckling, The Freelancer took another sip of his tea, blowing on the hot tin rim, and then rose to throw another clump of peat into the fire. At that very moment, he knew, the hangar maintenance supervisor would be almost finished installing the device into the makeshift light rail, ensuring that no part of the Hamelin Mission would go as planned.

The Freelancer topped up the fire, then squatted down in front of the stove, holding his hands out to soak in the warmth. He was still chuckling, because he knew something that Eddie Devane did not. He knew about the single drop of neuro-toxin that had been carefully applied to the device's charge coupler, moments before Devane had picked it up with his bare hands. The Freelancer knew something else that Eddie Devane did not. He knew exactly how many hours Devane had left to live.

He knew that the sudden death of Banishment One's primary technician would cause panic in the Canadex government and military, but it would be too late. Banishment One would be in deep space, far beyond comm range, flying to her own fate.

Walking to a small window, The Freelancer rubbed the frost away with his fist, peering out at the raging blizzard beyond. He smiled, loving the swirling sight.

"Chaos," he murmured.

Chapter Twenty-Eight

February 29, 2191.

Garrison residence of Captain Ridgely Falcon,

Canadian Northern Eagles Garrison,

New Edmonton, Alberta,

Canadian Exodus.

"I told a lie today."

Falcon leaned back into his sofa, taking a long inhalation on his cigarette, then passing it to the woman beside him. Falcon was still in uniform, but his collar was loosened. He was tired.

"About us?" Jessica Arnett was not a smoker, but took an obligatory draw.

"I have nothing else to lie about," Falcon sighed. "I lied to a man who trusts me, and who I trust. My word to him is supposed to mean something. So, what does that tell you?"

"We mean something more," Arnett said quietly.

"I want to tell him."

"But one of us would have to leave."

"So, the question becomes what do we love more? Us ... or us?"

Arnett slid slowly off the couch, kneeling down in front of Falcon, her palms resting on his knees.

"I love the job, Ridge."

"And you're better at it than me. I want to tell him. He probably already knows."

"I love you, Ridge," Arnett whispered. "More than the job. And I love Paisley. I want to be your wife. I want your child to be my child. Even if that means losing the job."

"What do we have if we don't have the job? Two cold-blooded hunter assassins, just trying to build a doghouse, paint the picket fence? Jess, do you really think we could do that?"

"I think we could try."

Falcon took her hands in his, raising them up to kiss her knuckles.

"I tried before. The job does not make marriage any easier."

Arnett smiled. "That's why you need a wife who truly understands it. And you."

"I loved Larissa, more than my own life, more than any other person in this universe, and serving my country lost that. I do not want to make a mistake with the one woman I have come to love even more."

"Everyone I have ever loved was lost, serving my country," Arnett stated. "Father, brother, a boyfriend, a fiancé, and I still believe in love in this world. They all showed me love, and taught me to love what I serve. Be under no illusion. I love you, knowing that I could lose you at any time. Real love is willing to take that risk."

"Risks come from not knowing everything. That goes against everything that TAP survives on."

316

"TAP does not hold the answers to the world. No army does. Sometimes, the answer to saving the world comes from just one person. The job is not worth taking risks for. Only love is."

Falcon leaned forward to gently kiss her.

"Wolf knows," he said softly. "Not many people could ever lie to him. He knows, but he trusts my judgement, at least for this one last mission. But I still want to tell him."

"Then we'll both tell him, and anyone else," Arnett decided. "I'm tired of hiding it. If we lose the job, we have each other. What can they do? We're dead."

"Sometimes I almost start to believe that," Falcon replied, brushing Arnett's hair back from her forehead with his fingertips. "I feel like a vampire, roaming around lost, my entire existence based on death. I don't want you to have that. I want you to have a life that's about life. I don't want you with me on this mission."

Arnett's lips parted in surprise, pain in her eyes.

"Why not?"

Falcon almost smiled. "Because Wolf said people were going to die."

"Wolf is not always right," Arnett said crossly.

"Except in his predictions."

Arnett shook her head. "We love together, and we fight together. We. Together. No matter what. If one of us dies, there's no place the other should be but right there."

"This won't be like hunting," Falcon reminded her. "If something goes wrong, we watch our own die. We're too used to working alone. It's easier when you only think about yourself. People you care about are

317

distractions, and we cannot afford that. Not with the Bloodline right there, anticipating."

"I know how to focus. So do you. The job is always first. That's what we trained for."

"I do love you," Falcon whispered, kissing her one more time. "And I will marry you, if we survive this. Maybe this will be the last job. Wolf got out. After this year, maybe I will too. Shark always wanted the Towers. He can have it."

"What about the rest of us?" Arnett wondered. "Rumors are flying. They say TAP is already over."

"Hey," Falcon soothed her, pressing a finger against her lips. "It's not over. Maybe it will be, but it's not yet. Right now, they still need us, maybe a lot more than they think they do."

"You always said the world needs wolves," Arnett said. "The Towers Program mantra. Why doesn't anyone else believe that?"

"People see, hear, and believe whatever they want. In that is the importance of knowledge. It's something definite, or, at least, it's supposed to be. Most people can't get by on nothing but knowledge. We need to hope for something better. Soldiers are supposed to have an off switch for that."

"My uncle used to tell me '*Hope is a pursuit of mist, trying to catch it in your hand,*'" Arnett said reflectively, resting her head on Falcon's knee. "I never wanted to believe that. All the things I hoped for, I wanted them to be real, definite. Peace, love, courage. I wanted them to be something that I could reach out and touch, at least when I was a child. Now ... I'm starting to wish for that again. I want to see them."

Falcon nodded. "So do I."

"But that's my humanity," Arnett softly decided. "The soldier in me is not done yet. I want death. I want to kill them all, every prisoner at Beaumont, every rat still hiding in the deeps. Their blood on my chrystanium."

Falcon's eyes closed, his head bowing. "So do I."

"Can God forgive us for enjoying it?" Arnett murmured. "The thrill of destroying an enemy.... You know what I'm talking about, Captain Falcon. There is no greater passion than to kill close, with a knife, hands. The thrill of love doesn't even come close. Your blood runs hot and turns to ice at the same time. Sometimes ... I can almost *taste* death. And it's not foul. It's rich. But not filling."

"Never filling," Falcon admitted, stroking her hair. "Actually, it makes me want more. Our life is death. I suppose that's our way of showing that we can appreciate what we've chosen."

"But do the nightmares ever stop?" Arnett whispered.

Falcon lowered himself from the sofa to sit beside her, drawing her into his arms.

"Never," he said acceptantly, kissing her light hair. "They just stop scaring you."

Chapter Thirty-Nine

February 29, 2191.
Archives Office, Northern Eagles Library,
Canadian Northern Eagles Garrison,
New Edmonton, Alberta,
Canadian Exodus.

Wolf disliked computers, but he was often most proficient with the skills which he most hated.

The office was unlit, but for the cold blue light from the terminal Wolf sat in front of. The screen was scrolling an endless list of open cases from police and military databases, a chronological tide of unsolved murders from both Canadian Exodus and the Home Base.

Vance Ryan Coolidge was born April 9, 2150, on the Home Base, or at least that was what TAP had been told. Wolf could only guess how much of his friend's life had been a lie, but he had nothing else to go on. What he did know was what the colonel had taught both of them. The best lies are smoothly mixed with truth.

Cougar had said that his first kill had been accomplished at age fourteen, so Wolf searched from

April, 2164 and beyond. He narrowed the search to Washington Island, where Vance was reportedly raised.

Between the Aprils of '64 and '65, there had been more than two hundred murders on Washington alone, and less than forty percent had been closed. Wolf narrowed the search further. He was not looking for a professional hit, but for a clumsy first time, a virgin kill.

He scanned several unrelated reports before one caught his eye, from a Washington newsreel, dated June 18, 2164.

Local businessman killed in bar fight,

Juvenile arrested on manslaughter charges.

According to the article, Rayton Carlinni, a successful dry goods manufacturer, had been stabbed twice with a pair of scissors, in a bar brawl which he had apparently instigated. He had bled to death before the paramedics could treat him. A fourteen-year-old male had been arrested at the scene.

In order for paramedics to have even witnessed the death, the man would have to have been injured between five and fifteen minutes before their arrival. That meant the injuries were steady bleeders, but not immediately fatal, not quick kills. They were most likely chest or abdominal injuries, nicking an artery or major organ.

The fourteen-year-old had apparently been weeping uncontrollably when he was taken into custody.

Wolf opened a second window, this one an archive of Washington Island Police Department arrest reports, dated June 18, 2164. Two juveniles had been arrested that day on manslaughter charges. One was a fifteen-year-old girl who had shot a drunk ex-boyfriend who was allegedly trying to rape her. The second was fourteen-year-old Ryan Roland Meldt. The mug shots told Wolf all that he needed to know.

It was obvious that the young Vance Cougar had been crying.

One more thing caught Wolf's attention. The report contained a snapshot of the weapon used in Carlinni's death. Although the scissor blades were bloody, they were familiar. They were exactly the same shape as the blade of Cougar's TAP knife.

A genealogical registry search brought forth one final surprise. Although Ryan Roland Meldt had been orphaned at a young age, as Vance had always claimed, he had not been orphaned alone. He and his younger brother, Jeffrey Taylor Meldt, had both disappeared from all Home Base records in late 2166, the same year that a Vance Ryan Coolidge had immigrated to Canadian Exodus.

Wolf did not often talk to himself, but surprise overcame caution as he stared at the immigration records.

"Jeffrey," he muttered. "Where are you?"

Chapter Forty

March 1, 2191, Day of Banishment.
Banishment One, CNE Orbit Runner,
En route to Beaumont Prison,
Northern polar region, Ontario,
Canadian Exodus.

Even on a day such as this, Wolf could not think of a newer or better prayer. It ran through his head in an unending cycle.

Thanks be to God for this beautiful day.

Thanks be to God for this beautiful day....

The rest of the world was not so appreciative. Crowds of protesters had gathered at the Vancouver launch site, where the dummy launch was being prepared. Similar protests were being held on campuses and in churches in most major cities throughout Ontario and Manitoba. Peace and forgiveness were being demanded so loudly that violence had erupted in some cities. Two fatalities had already been reported. Home Guard militia units in Toronto Exodus had been ordered to reinforce the most riotous protest stemming from the university. Three student leaders had already been arrested for inciting insurrection in the name of the Bloodline. The war was over.

"Beaumont Tower, this is Banishment One. ETA, four minutes."

"Banishment One, this is Beaumont Tower. Clear for landing in northeast courtyard. All cargo is packaged, standing by to embark."

"You're looking at me, Captain Wolf," Lieutenant Arnett stated, sitting next to him in the cockpit.

"Forgive me," Wolf said. "I was reading."

"You've been reading all week, over and over, sir. What part don't you understand?"

Wolf shrugged. "I keep reading myself. I understand that perfectly."

"You understand it, but can you accept it?"

"You're accustomed to being in charge, Lieutenant. Commanding Point Squadron for two years? CT4's finest, they say."

"People say a lot of things, sir. I worked my way to the top, and I will keep working."

"Direct translation, Lieutenant: You're bitter because I pulled you from the lunar. Some calls I do have to make. I'm not questioning your job, or your abilities, or your ice. I'm questioning your time, simply because Captain Falcon has more."

"More is not always more, sir."

"Except with time. How many targets have you acquired?"

"Live or dead?"

"Unless the job changed, live targets are captured, not acquired."

"Fifty-eight, Captain Wolf. Eighteen long-range, twenty-five short-range, four unarmed, three improvised, nine by timed device, and unknown numbers by airstrike, artillery barrage, strafing runs, mortar rounds, and airborne agents. May I inquire if you would ask any woman the same question?"

"No. I wouldn't."

"I think I can take that as a compliment, sir." She held out her hand. "Bad start. Lieutenant Jessica Arnett, TAP Bravo, formerly CNE-CT4, Point Squadron."

Wolf smiled slightly, and shook the outstretched hand.

"Captain Chester Wolf," he chuckled. "I'm a hunter, and not much of a commander."

"You're doing fine, sir," Arnett said with a grin.

"Do you love him?" Wolf had to ask.

Arnett nodded, not even startled by the question. "Yes, sir. I do."

The modified Runner burst through the cold polar clouds, and Beaumont Prison came into view, a massive stone castle, ringed by a thirty-foot wall of boulders, divided into four equal courtyards, each with a radius of six hundred feet. Built on top of a sheer cliffed plateau, more than nine thousand feet above sea level, the most feared prison on the planet could only be reached by air, and a special crew of demolition "polishers" routinely ensured that the cliff walls remained unscalable. In the history of Beaumont, no prisoner had even managed to climb over the stone stockade. Six thousand prisoners were held behind those walls, balancing thirty-five hours of lockdown with one hour of yard, with the exception of Bloodline prisoners, for whom yard was never an option.

"I did want the lunar," Arnett stated acceptantly. "Captain? I did. I wanted them to see my face at the end. I wanted to see their faces, see them lose."

"Did you want to see their eyes?"

"I think I did.... Yeah. I did. Am I being tested?"

Wolf nodded. "All of us are."

Wolf often felt that he had done nothing but war all his life, but his stomach was clenched as he watched the fortress growing larger. Today had been called a culmination, which in his mind was the beginning of an end. The only question was whose end it would be. People were going to die. That was just another one of those things that Wolf knew.

Twenty-six heavily armed prison guards in arctic camo formed a perimeter around the northeast courtyard landing strip. No chances were being taken.

"Beaumont Tower, this is Banishment One," Wolf intoned, as the landing geared screeched on the tarmac. "This mission is launching in exactly three minutes. Get your people moving."

"Banishment One, it will take at least ten minutes to embark the prisoners."

"Beaumont Tower, if we are being long-range stealth-tracked, we're all getting painted in about four minutes. Run. My crew is ready."

"Rear compartment, report," Arnett said into her shoulder frequency.

"Rear comp, good to go," Falcon's voice replied.

"Holding bay, report."

"All cells standing by," Corporal Ustaf said. "All mag-seal restraints read nominal."

The Runner had slowed to a full stop.

"Captain Falcon, blow the hatches, fore and aft of the prison bay," Wolf instructed. "Ladies and gentlemen, from this moment, the safety's off. Move!"

Falcon blew both hatches, simultaneously lowering the access ramps. At the same moment, the main compound door to the courtyard was flung wide, and columns of three began charging outside, two armed guards flanking each shackled and hooded Bloodline prisoner in blue coveralls, all making a beeline for the tail hatch.

"Move it, move it!" Falcon roared. "Heir and Seconds, fore cells! Heir Defenders, aft! Go!"

The first three were nearing the top of the ramp, and Falcon realized that Kressel was in the center.

"Hand off to Corporal Ustaf and Lieutenant Lewis!" Falcon instructed, grabbing The Heir's collar, and pushing him into the cargo bay, which had been converted into twenty holding cells, ten on each side of a central aisle. "Disembark via forward crew quarters hatch. In one end, out the other. No cross traffic. Go!"

He had thrown Kressel into the stern port-side cell when Wolf opened the cockpit door, stepping quickly into the crew quarters. Wolf only caught a brief glimpse of Kressel being shoved into the cell, as Falcon ripped the hood from the old soldier's head. What Wolf did see made him freeze.

The first two guards crossed into the crew quarters, but Wolf seized the first by the shoulder before he could rush down the exit ramp.

"Why are they wearing magnetic shackles?!" Wolf shouted over the still roaring engines.

"Sir?" the guard replied, puzzled.

"I wanted key locks! The doors are magnetic!"

"Orders, sir. Command wanted no chances. Highest tech locks only!"

"I told them I wanted keys!"

"Sorry, sir. You'll have to take it up with command!"

"Shit!" Wolf snarled. "Get going!"

"Sir!" the guard acknowledged, following his partner down the ramp.

"*Shit!*"

The cargo bay was flooded with jostling, shouting prisoners, all being sequentially pushed into cells, their escort guards rushing through the crew quarters as soon as the cell doors hissed shut, the magnetic locks clamping the Bloodlines inside. Wolf knew who most of the prisoners were before their hoods were even removed. Bourgeouis was second in the column, followed by Whitefeather, Curtis, and Baxter. After that came the Heir Defenders, Flaxton and Cougar at the front. Wolf could not help but feel a chill as his old friend complacently stepped into his cell, still wearing his hood. Ustaf reached inside and pulled the hood off, but Wolf's line of sight did not allow him to see Cougar's face.

Falcon was hurrying down the row, double-checking the locks of each cell. He finished just as the last of the guards charged down the exit ramp. Wolf waited for Falcon's thumbs up before sealing the hatches and closing himself back into the cockpit. From the rear compartment, Segeant-Major Cardinal locked down the prison bay, and touched his frequency.

"Captain Wolf, all hatches sealed, all cargo packaged. We're good to go."

"O Canada," Wolf replied, strapping himself into his flight chair and punching the launch activation sequence into the flight console. "Beaumont Tower, this is Banishment One. We are launching in fifteen seconds, nineteen seconds ahead of schedule."

"All personnel clear of runway, launch is a go," the tower responded. "Good luck, and Godspeed, Banishment One."

"Thank you, Beaumont Tower," Wolf said. "Start the party without us."

Banishment One blasted out of the courtyard and was soon no more than a distant speck in the blue, heading toward outer space.

Chapter Forty-One

March 1, 2191.
Prime Minister's press release,
Parliamentary Plaza,
New Shilo, Manitoba,
Canadian Exodus.

General Krunnion had never seen so many members of the press gathered in one area. Now that he thought about it, he could not remember the last time that a Canadian prime minister had made a public press statement. Even now, he wondered if Stone was being overconfident, or simply putting on a brave front for the citizens. Either way, he would have been more comfortable letting the prime minister answer the volley of shouted questions from the press studio. Indoor appearances required a lot fewer snipers.

"As I speak," Stone was saying, "the most evil enemies our country has ever faced are being taken farther and farther away, across a void they can never recross. In my heart, there is a peace I cannot remember feeling in a very long time. We have not been one nation for many years, but today that all changes. I stand here today in the open, unafraid. We still have enemies, but they will now have to learn that atrocity will not be tolerated on this planet."

Krunnion knew that RCMP units had more than fifty tactical members throughout the plaza, and fifteen snipers covering the surrounding rooftops. Even so, he was scarcely surprised when a CNE major touched his shoulder and whispered, "Sir, there's a problem."

Krunnion closed his eyes. "Where?"

"New Edmonton CNE. Um ... Edward Devane, chief maintenance supervisor on Banishment One."

"What about him?"

"His body was just found in a Chop hangar. Examiner puts TOD at two hours after Hamelin execution. No obvious cause of death."

With a heavy sigh, Krunnion touched his frequency.

"All units, this is Command Peak. Move the prime minister, now. Get her inside, take down anyone who tries to follow. Major, have a shuttle standing by. We're going to New Edmonton."

Security forces were already hustling Stone off the podium, while an aide quickly announced, "There will be no further questions. Prime Minister Stone is extremely busy today. Everyone please move out of the plaza."

"Any chance of contacting Hamelin?" Krunnion asked tiredly, fairly certain that he knew the answer already.

The major shook his head. "They passed the first sun forty minutes ago. Solar flares black them out from then on."

"Call CSIS," Krunnion instructed. "Pull everything they have on Devane, especially any habit deviations in the past two months. I want friends, associates, hang-outs, business dealings, and any private sector interactions. Find anything that stinks."

"What else, General?" the major asked nervously, following him toward the buildings.

"What do you think?" Krunnion snorted. "Until the coroner's office tells us that it was an innocent heart attack, we lock down the planet and get ready for another war. And if Banishment One comes home five minutes earlier than estimates projected, we blow her right back into space." To himself, he muttered, "Kill them, Wolf. Kill them all, *now!*"

Chapter Forty-Two

March 3, 2191.
Banishment One,
En route to The Desert.

"Captain...?"

Wolf's eyes opened, shifting his mind and body from asleep to awake in an instant. He lay still on his bunk and looked up at Lieutenant Amanda Lewis. He realized that he had not been awoken by a woman since he was a CNE corporal. The thought was depressing.

"Lieutenant," he acknowledged.

"Lieutenant Arnett said you were to be awoken when we were half an hour from destination, sir."

"Thank you," Wolf said slowly, sitting up. "Did she inform the prisoners?"

"She announced to them when we were an hour out, sir. She said 'You have sixty minutes to make your peace with God.'"

"Very well," Wolf nodded. He had slept dressed, armed, and armored, as every crew member had been ordered to.

"Sir, one of the prisoners has a request."

"I don't take a request."

"Sir, it's General Kressel. He wishes to speak to you before he's banished."

Wolf stiffened. "You spoke with him?"

"Through the cell door two-way, sir."

"What were his exact words, Lieutenant?"

Lewis replied carefully. "He said, 'Lovely young lady, before my time comes, would you be so kind as to arrange for a dialogue between myself and the wolf?'"

"The wolf?" Wolf said sharply. "He used that term?"

Lewis nodded affirmatively. Wolf stood and tightened the buckles on his forearm knife sheath. He noted that Lewis wore her chrystanium knife on her left knee boot.

"Listen carefully, Lieutenant. Are we the only ones forward, besides Lieutenant Arnett?"

"Yes, sir."

"Good. Have Hanley and Connor report here with the prisoner, and tell Captain Falcon I want him here too. Remain in the tail comp with Cardinal and Ustaf until the prisoner is returned to his cell. No exceptions, unless you hear from me."

"Sir," Lewis acknowledged, turning on her heel. She unlocked the prison bay door, then sealed it behind her. Wolf watched her cross to the rear of the shuttle on the security monitor.

The hunter splashed some cold water on his face and slowly toweled the refreshing droplets from his grey beard, then stepped into the cockpit, placing a hand on Arnett's shoulder. She looked up at him, and then they both stared through the glass canopy at the blackness

334

and stars. The Desert was clearly visible directly ahead, a golden ball of sand. At no other time of year would the planet be remotely habitable, even at the polar regions. Even now, the equatorial belt was hot enough to dehydrate and kill a human in less than ten hours.

"What do you think, Lieutenant?" Wolf murmured.

"It looks angry," she sighed. "How do you feel, sir?"

"The mission is stupid," Wolf said plainly. "And that's coming from a man who likes to take the order and shoot the gun. No one deserves what we're doing to them."

"I can't sympathize, sir," Arnett said stonily. "My uncle was at Yellowknife the day it was taken."

"I'm sorry."

"Thank you, sir."

"Kressel wants to talk. I'm bringing him to crew quarters now. Stay here."

"What does he want, Captain?"

Wolf shook his head, stepping back to the door. "Probably memorable last words."

He sealed the cockpit and sat down on his bunk, rubbing the sleep from his tired eyes.

"I can tell that you are not a talker, Captain Wolf," Kressel commented, seated on the opposite bunk.

The shackled Bloodline Heir was flanked by Private Hanley and Private Connor, while Falcon stood a wary vigil over the prison bay door. None of them had ever stood face to face with their greatest enemy before.

"Do you drink, Captain Wolf?"

Wolf shook his head, just a little, his vacant eyes never leaving those of The Heir.

"Not at all?" Kressel pressed him. "A cool, foaming lager after a hard day of killing?"

Wolf shook his head again.

"I cannot afford champagne tastes, myself," Kressel chuckled. "Keeping Yellowknife up on food stores was challenge enough, all those years. You know why your government could never infiltrate us by way of smugglers, or mercenaries? I had no use for them. I survived for so long because my trust was extremely selective. As captain of a mission as significant as this, I am sure that you can understand that."

"Very selective," Wolf said with a slow nod.

"I drink," Kressel acknowledged. "I love wine, brandy, scotch, even the odd vodk. But I've rarely been drunk, and that was more than thirty years ago. I was too busy. You were not. So, why not?"

"Because I like the taste too much," Wolf said.

Kressel smiled. "Ah, so you fear your own weakness. People underestimate the value of fear. Whether your own, or your enemy's, fear plays such a critical role in keeping us all in line. Entire countries, entire planets, can be kept in check by fear. Fear can create balance, as you well know."

"I'm not afraid of the things I love," Wolf replied. "Fear has rules I don't follow."

"But you do understand them?" Kressel asked shrewdly.

"Better than you," Falcon answered for Wolf.

"Captain Falcon, are you afraid of drinking?" Kressel asked, glancing over at the tall Cree man.

"No," Falcon said coldly. "Or smoking."

"What does scare you?"

"To you, I'll say fear itself."

Kressel nodded. "Good answer, if not very honest. These well-trained privates are afraid of me, though I doubt they'd ever admit it. They probably grew up hearing scary stories about me. Murdering, brutalizing, raping, all in a mad quest for global domination. These *half-wits* probably still believe every word of it, Hidden Hunters or not. Do you think anyone ever set out into the world with the life-goal of being scary?"

"I'm bored," Wolf said.

Kressel actually laughed. "Very good, Captain! You didn't get absorbed in my words." He had to pause a few seconds to stop chuckling, then heaved an admiring sigh. "Had I men like you, Captain Wolf ... The Mountain would have been mine. For years, Hidden Hunters were my primary vexation, faceless foes, constantly whittling away at my legion from shadows, with knives that shattered both bone and sword like icicles. I dreamed of commanding such as you, men like ghosts, slaying even those enemies surrounded by security systems and loyal bodyguards. Your abilities almost defy human boundaries, and I hated and revered you for that. Vexation, Captain, and contradiction. We needed you dead, and yet we longed to find you alive. We needed revenge and education, and we did not know how to get both.

"Then there was the day that I nearly died. A man entered my stateroom, leaving my Heir Defenders unharmed and unaware, and he pressed one of those knives to the side of my neck, as I read in my favorite chair. He told me that I had to face him. I stood, and I looked on the face of a Hunter for the first time.

"How many times have you faced death, Captain Wolf? From my understanding, you *were* death, and the dead faced you. I faced death that day, and he surrendered to my mercy, lowering his knife and offering his service. To have death surrender to you.... It is both rare and empowering.

"Do you wonder about the defection of your Vance Cougar? His offer intrigued me. Most defectors who approached me were immediately killed with my own hands. Usually, they wanted money for their services, or were too radicalized for me to even risk the association. My men are soldiers. They are savage, but that is how we must be to survive. I do not work with mercenaries or madmen. Cougar was neither. To him, life and death were simple math, and I knew that I could use a man who lived so wholly in his mind. He proved himself loyal and ruthless, and I told him that he would make the finest Hitter under my command, but he refused that. He requested Heir Defender, taking lives to preserve just one.

"It bothers you, doesn't it, Captain Wolf? One of your own, the most elite killers ever created, and one can still fall to so simple a frailty as loneliness. How can you ever trust your own again?

"You shouldn't have worked him alone. Your unit rewards killing with a life of oblivion, and tells its operatives to be satisfied with serving a greater good. You can dehumanize your enemies to help you sleep at night, but you can never truly dehumanize yourself.

Cougar tried, and you can judge his success. I thought you might want to know."

Wolf said nothing for a long moment, then stood from the bunk, watching Kressel's eyes.

"I'm sending you to the lunar module now, General Kressel," he said. "You will remain there until we reach banishment orbit."

"Coolidge never would tell me how to find you," Kressel replied, his tone bearing a challenge. "No matter how much I implored him. He did not betray your unit."

"Yes, he did." Wolf's answer was more sudden than Falcon was accustomed to hearing.

"But he did show me a picture of all of you, standing smart, and looking happy. Twelve men. I knew that I would recognize any one of you, if I ever looked on your face. That's how I knew your name. The great Captain Chester Wolf. I knew it was you as soon as my mask was taken off."

"The unit in that picture is long gone, Mr. Kressel," Wolf said.

"The planet was mine," Kressel stated, standing. "My great-grandfather's feet were in the sand before any Canadian flag was. It is mine still."

"This planet is yours, now," Wolf replied. "Don't even have to fight for it."

He and Falcon exchanged nods, and Falcon opened the prison bay hatch. The four hunters led the chained old man through the narrow prison bay, passing each windowless cell door in silence. Once in the rear compartment, Lewis and Ustaf raised the floor hatch, opening the way to the lunar compartment in the

339

shuttle's underbelly. The module itself was form-fitted to the bottom of the Runner, accessible through a small airlock, only wide enough for one person to drop into at one time. Connor and Hanley went in first, and the two captains lowered Kressel down to them. The Heir did not say another word as he was placed in the clear drop chute to await his banishment.

"Get something to eat," Wolf said, as he and Falcon climbed back into the tail comp, leaving the privates to guard the module. "We start banishing in ten minutes. The shackles never come off."

Falcon held out his hand, and Wolf shook it. They wished one another Godspeed, and Wolf stepped back into the prison bay. The moment had come.

As soon as Wolf sealed the prison bay hatch, the lights dimmed.

He froze in mid stride. There was no doubt that something was wrong. The overhead lamps were not giving off their usual gentle hum, and they were fading to darkness. In a few seconds, the entire cabin was only lit by the pale blue emergency tubing that ran along the edges of the ceiling and floors.

"Arnett, where are the lights?" Wolf said into his frequency, already feeling that knot growing in his gut. The frequency did not crackle or sputter or give a response of any sort. Wolf knew immediately that it, too, was dead.

He was running back toward the rear comp when Arnett burst in from the crew quarters, shouting the three syllables that were already running laps through Wolf's mind.

"*EMP!*"

340

Wolf shoulder-slammed the rear hatch, and it swung wide, the mag-seals useless.

"Projectiles!" he shouted, slamming the door and leaning against it. "EMP build up! Banish Kressel, *now!* Cardinal, check all shielders!"

Falcon was instantly diving for the floor hatch, yanking it open. Wolf was the only one armed with a projectile weapon. He pulled his 1911 and tossed it to Falcon, as Lewis pulled a small key from a chain on her neck, and began punching in the activation code on the cabinet of projectile weapons, which Wolf had insisted that the shuttle be supplied with.

"Chess...." Falcon said, his head the only part of him still visible as he clambered down the stairs.

"They're not winning this one," was Wolf's reply. "Banish him!"

The floor hatch dropped down, and Falcon was gone.

"Cardinal, release the lunar module moorings, except the soft-collar dock," Wolf instructed.

"Aye, sir!"

"Sir, the lock's non-responsive!" Lewis said, frustrated, tugging on the gun cabinet doors.

"What?!" Cardinal was appalled. "The lock should be released! It's supposed to be unshielded!"

"Well, it's not!" Lewis growled.

"Use your chrystanium!" Ustaf said. "We can't break the ions out from the shielders until the detonation is over."

"I'm going to secure the prison bay," Wolf said. "Use the manual charger to reseal the doors, and kill anyone. Hold this comp!"

He was already back in the prison bay, and Ustaf's shoulder was pressed against the unlocked door. He could hear shouting. It sounded like the prisoners.

* * *

"EMP!" Falcon roared, jumping down the lunar airlock, without even touching the ladder. "Fire all shielders. We're going now!"

Connor slammed the airlock, but the door would not seal.

"Sir, shielders reading on," Hanley reported, "but the soft-collar release is already gone. All other moorings released."

"Hit the manual release, as soon as we recharge the airlock," Falcon ordered. "What do we have?"

"Oxygen, heat, and gravitational generators are shielded permanently," Connor said. "But the thrust rails are dead, and so are the engines and all mag-seals. I'm charging them manually." He began spinning the brass charge wheel on the central bulkhead. "If they get loose in the cargo bay, they can drop in right on top of us!"

"Fire the emergency solar chargers!" Falcon snapped. "That'll speed things up a bit."

Falcon had the 1911 trained on the airlock, but he looked over at Kressel's clear cell, which was now unlocked, but fortunately soundproof. The Bloodline general did not know that his cell was open, but he was still smiling. His shackles fell to the floor a moment later.

342

* * *

Arnett had flipped on all emergency shielders as soon as the EMP signature had become evident, but by then the light rails, engines, lights, comm, personal ion weapons, and mag-seals were already neutralized. Banishment One was drifting through space, and Arnett was doing everything she could from the cockpit to prevent the Orbit Runner from getting ensnared by the gravity of the rapidly looming Desert.

The shielded emergency generators would take several minutes to recharge even the most essential systems, five at the very least. Until then, Banishment One was a war.

To further complicate matters, Arnett now had a clear view of the planet's northern polar region. She could see things, and they were things that were not supposed to be there.

* * *

Wolf grabbed the flexible neon light tubing, ripping it from the edge of the prison bay floor. Cutting off a three foot section with his knife, he lashed the tube through the handles of cell seven, sealing Vance Cougar inside. He did not care if he had to battle his way through all seventeen of the remaining Bloodline. Vance had to remain secured.

The door was reverberating. Cougar had managed to shake free of his weakened shackles, but was too late to stop the door from being sealed, at least for the time being.

Before Wolf could cut another section of tubing, cell six was kicked open.

"EMP!" Robert Flaxton was shouting as he lunged into the corridor, brandishing his chain shackles as a weapon. He was instantly yanking open the other doors around him, still shouting "EMP! Weapons down! Take the ship!"

Then he looked at Wolf, and there was a sadistic delight in his eyes. Knowing he would be surrounded in seconds, Wolf decided that this was one fight that would have to wait. He began to run for the crew quarters, but Flaxton's two healthy legs closed the distance between them rapidly.

* * *

"It's no use!" Lewis snapped, trying to wedge open the door with her boot knife. "Can you bar the door?"

"Nothing to bar it through!" Ustaf replied, his shoulder still acting as the only door lock, his face grimaced in anticipation of the first battering ram from the other side.

"EMP detonation complete," Cardinal said. "I'm breaking out the ions!"

When he reached for the primary weapon cache, the door swung loosely in his hand. In an instant, he knew that both the electronic and mag locks had failed. The racks of weapons inside were useless.

"*Why wasn't this sealed?!*" he screamed. "Lewis! Saw the projectile hinges! It's our only shot!"

"Soft-collar release is back online!" Ustaf reported, seeing the readout on the rebooting monitor. "But we can't release until the airlock is sealed."

"That's up to Captain Falcon," Cardinal said, spinning the manual charger. "Charging the prison bay hatches now!"

The low electric hum around the hatches grew louder at a sickeningly slow rate.

* * *

Wolf made it into the crew quarters, Flaxton a step behind him. Slamming the door hard with both hands, Wolf could see Flaxton's hand recoil involuntarily as the heavy steel hatch smashed into his forearm. With a pained cry, Flaxton's hand was withdrawn, and Wolf put his shoulder into the door. Using his teeth to very carefully unclasp his 3-6-5 Cuff, he fastened the charge through the door handles, sealing the prisoners out of the crew quarters. If they kicked in that door, it would be the last thing they ever did, EMP or no EMP. The Cuff had its own shielders, and the charge would still detonate if the band was broken.

"Arnett, what's going on?" he ordered, striding into the cockpit. "Give me an assessment!"

Arnett did not reply. Her hanging jaw would not allow words to form as she stared through the canopy.

"Arnett!"

The lieutenant could only point a finger toward The Desert. Wolf's mouth opened as he followed her gaze, but he, too, was silent.

The Desert's north pole, which should have been nothing but a single large lake of warm water, surrounded by burning sand, was capped with a brilliant green forest. Trees were growing on a lifeless planet, forming a green hedge around the lake.

"Impossible," Arnett breathed. "Nothing can live on this planet. Nothing ever lived on this planet."

Wolf could not speak at all. Eighty years earlier, The Desert had been written off as an emergency water supply. Now, a forest roughly the size of the Alberta continent had erupted from the sands around the lake.

"I've never seen a forest like that," he managed to whisper.

"Sir?"

"Look at the colour. Those trees are not Home Base transplants. They're something else."

"Captain Wolf, we're talking about alien life!"

Wolf nodded. "Yes, we are."

* * *

Robert Flaxton had now opened every single cell in the prison bay, including Vance Cougar's. The Bloodline troops rushed into the narrow passageway, shaking free of their chains.

"*Where is The Heir?!*" Flaxton was screaming. "*Find The Heir!*"

The Heir was missing.

* * *

"They're loose in the prison bay," Ustaf sighed. "They'll be in here in seconds."

"Hang on!" Lewis hissed, using the serrated edge of her knife to saw through the hinges of the projectile cabinet. Iron filings were piling on her boots, but it was still a slow process. Sweat poured from her temples, and her hands were burning and sore, but she never slowed.

"Airlocks are at fifty percent and rising," Cardinal reported, still spinning the charge wheel as fast as he could. "Comp hatches are at seventy-five. Buy me three minutes, I'll have the whole ship secured!"

"Can't you charge separately?" Lewis asked. "Prison hatches are priority."

"This isn't a Liner!" Cardinal snapped. "This isn't even supposed to be a prison transport. It's all or none. They're all on the same power grid."

"They aren't going to wait three minutes to start ramming this door!" Ustaf muttered. "How long on the projectiles?"

"Buy me one minute!" Lewis wheezed, sawing faster than ever, sparks flying from the top hinge. She was almost through.

* * *

"Where's the general?!" Flaxton kept screaming, slamming a fist into the last cell door as he opened it, releasing Major Bourgeouis. "*Coolidge!*"

Cougar pushed his way through the jostling, cheering crowd.

"Talk to me, Coolidge! How's a Prison Liner set up? Where's the general?"

"Look at the ceiling," Cougar snapped. "Demarkation line runs the length of this corridor. Those are cargo bay doors."

"Liners don't have bay doors!" Flaxton roared. "What is this?!"

"An Orbit Runner," Cougar realized. "Clever pirate decoy. But that means they have nowhere to hide. Three exits from this bay. Fore, aft, and below decks."

"The banishment module!" Bourgeouis said, panicked. "The general must be there!"

"Underbelly!" Cougar said. "I'll take Hollis."

"First tell me what we're up against!" Flaxton ordered.

"A Runner crew's no more than nine or ten, but they'll be CT4."

"I've killed CT4!" Flaxton seethed, fists clenching at his sides.

"So did a child I knew!" Cougar retorted. "They'll probably be three in each comp. Armory is aft, but the EMP must have taken out the ion cache. Otherwise, we'd be dead already. The field's level."

"Heed me, everyone!" Flaxton bellowed, cupping his hands around his mouth. "Our Mountain friends have disabled this ship with an EMP device! Weapons down, repeat, weapons down! Hollis and Camrose, below decks with Coolidge, secure the general before they can take off! Everyone else, take the aft! *Take the armory, and take the ship!"*

The Bloodline roared their consent, and fourteen troops rushed to the aft end of the bay, while Cougar's team pulled up the deck hatch.

"What about the cockpit?" Cougar demanded, as Camrose clambered down the ladder.

"Mine!" Flaxton rasped. "All mine!"

"That could be three CT4!" Cougar said disgustedly, beginning to descend the ladder, Hollis close behind him.

"Just *go!*" Flaxton barked. "The captain's an old cripple!"

"A *what?!*" Cougar blurted, but was out of sight before Flaxton could repeat himself.

The Heir Defenders Commander turned toward the crew quarter hatch, smiling with rising bloodlust.

"Hello, Captain," he mused, stepping forward. "Ready or not...."

* * *

Ustaf winced as the first wave of Bloodline hit the door he was pressed against. The door was opened an inch before he could slam it again.

"Here they come!" he yelled, pushing for all he was worth. "Lewis!"

"A few more seconds!" she screamed, sawing furiously.

The door was bashed open again. This time, an Heir Defender managed to grab the edge, momentarily preventing the door from slamming. Ustaf's knife flashed into his fist, and four of the Heir Defender's attached fingers fell to the deck an instant later, the gripping hand cut cleanly in half. Ustaf slammed the door on the anguished screams of the amputated Defender, but, two seconds later, the door was hit again.

* * *

"I've got video back online!" Arnett announced. "Coming up on security monitor."

"Prison bay," Wolf instructed. The screen lit up, showing the rather bizarre spectacle of over a dozen prisoners mobbing the aft hatch, while Robert Flaxton stood alone before the crew quarters hatch, resolutely kicking and ramming at it.

"Flaxton," Wolf muttered, shaking his head. "Arrogant bastard."

"What do we do, sir?" Arnett asked.

Wolf tightened his buckled knife sheath one more time. "He's knocking. We let him in."

"*Sir?!*"

"I will be back in thirty-five seconds," Wolf explained. "If I'm not back in forty, assume command of the mission until Falcon returns."

He left without another word, carefully closing the cockpit door behind him.

* * *

Heir Defender Mark Camrose was the first to drop into the lunar module, but he was dead before he could take a step forward. Falcon was firing the 1911, giving Camrose two .45 rounds in the sternum and one in the forehead in less than two seconds. The brain matter spattered onto Cougar's face as he dropped in behind the falling body, catching the limp form under the arms as it was knocked back against him.

"Projectiles!" Cougar shouted, but it was too late to go back up. He charged into the module, using Camrose's body as a shield. Falcon gave the dead body three more rounds before it was forcibly slammed into him, causing him to stagger against the bulkhead under the deadweight.

Connor and Hanley made a simultaneous lunge for Cougar, and he met them both halfway. Both young hunters were wielding their rifles by the barrel as clubs, but Cougar was too fast for them to hit. In an instant, he had disarmed Connor, and killed the private just as quickly with a butt-stroke to the back of the neck.

As soon as Falcon had pushed Camrose's body to the floor, Heir Defender Geoff Hollis was also in the module, seizing the gun barrel before Falcon could bring it up to fire. Doing the last thing Hollis expected, Falcon immediately released his grip on the pistol, at the same time dropping a hand to his knife hilt. Hollis had been preparing for a struggle, so the sudden release made him fall back, still clutching the gun barrel. Falcon stepped forward, smashing a palm into Hollis's nose before using a reverse-grip slash to open the Heir Defender's throat. With face contorted, Hollis toppled back in a shower of arterial spray, his carotid artery severed.

Cougar and Hanley were viciously dueling with their rifles, but Falcon's eye was caught by the green light over the airlock.

"Airlock's online!" he shouted, snatching the 1911 out of Hollis's twitching hand as he dove for the seal, driving his palm into the activation pad. With a hiss, the doors began to slide closed.

Cougar recognized the voice immediately, and his eyes locked on the face of his former teammate, realizing for the first time whom he was dealing with.

"*HUNTERS!!*" Cougar exploded, just as the airlock sealed. He could only hope that Flaxton had heard him.

Hanley had been driven back, but the flicker of distraction was all that he needed. His rifle butt smashed across Cougar's face, and the Command Second was slammed to the floor, stunned.

"Secure him!" Falcon snapped, tossing the pistol to Hanley as he dashed for the flight controls. "One up the pipe! We're leaving now!"

* * *

Flaxton had taken a run at the crew quarters hatch, but the door was pulled open from the other side before he could shoulder-slam it. An iron fist closed over his collar, yanking him inside. The door slammed, and he heard the mag-seals activate.

Flaxton only had time to see a cold pair of grey eyes before collapsing to the floor, screaming in agony. His right shoulder was dislocated, and his left ankle bone was snapped in half. He did not even know how either injury had occurred. There should not have been time.

"Be glad that I want you alive," Wolf said, handcuffing his prisoner to a bunk. "For now."

* * *

Out of the corner of his eye, Ustaf could see that the green seal light was on over the aft bay hatch, but there were too many Bloodline against the door. Hands, arms, and feet were clawing their way inside, preventing the hatch from sealing. Ustaf was being pushed back, and he was running out of strength. Cardinal abandoned the charger to help him stem the tide of Bloodline.

"*LEWIS!*" they both cried.

Lewis gave an excruciating roar as she wrenched the gun cabinet door from its sawed hinges, dropping the iron cover to the deck with a metallic clash. She had no time to be selective about her weapon. Her hand closed over the slide-action of a 10-gage shotgun.

Ustaf was thrown hard against the opposite wall as the hatch was flung wide, knocking Cardinal to the floor as well. Ustaf's head slammed into the metal bulkhead, and he slumped to the floor, dazed and exhausted.

Bloodline Captain David Whitefeather was the first to charge the rear comp, walking right into the first round of buckshot. The pellets tore into his chest and stomach, knocking him into the mob at his back. The second volley of 10-gage ripped his shoulder apart, as well as the face of Heir Defender Levitt Sterling. Both men hit the floor dead.

"Projectiles!" Lewis snarled. "Weapons hot! Return to the prison bay!"

Cardinal was instantly on one knee beside her, with a C-9 light machine gun trained on the hatch, and the Bloodline beyond.

"Projectiles!" he roared. "*Projectiles!*"

Major Powers Bourgeouis was now at the head of the column, and the old warrior knew the futility of suicide. With slowly raised hands, he stepped back into the bay, his eyes still burning with a quiet and patient fire.

"Stand down, men," he said calmly, closing the hatch in his on face. With one final magnetic click, twelve live Bloodline were resecured.

"All comps sealed!" Cardinal shouted, back at the lunar control. "Releasing soft-collar dock now. Lunar module is away!"

* * *

Falcon felt the soft-collar release the module into space. The engines were still unresponsive. He struggled to prevent the small craft from colliding with Banishment One.

"What's Connor's status?" he barked at Hanley.

"He's dead, sir!" Hanley replied, quavering with rage, the 1911 trained on Cougar's chest. The Heir Defender lay motionless, his eyes closed.

"Calm down!" Falcon ordered. "The prisoner."

"Secure, sir."

Falcon's jaw clenched, his black eyes growing even darker.

"Kill him!" he said harshly.

"Sir?"

Hanley's hesitation cost him his life. Cougar's foot came up just as Hanley's eyes flickered over to Falcon. The gun roared as it was kicked out of the private's grasp, shattering his wrist. As the bullet thudded into the ceiling, Cougar swept Hanley's legs out from under him with a kick, and both men scrambled across the floor, pursuing the skittering gun.

"Hanley!" Falcon shouted. "Kill him!"

Hanley was slowed by the flaming pain in his broken hand, and Cougar was quick to spot that weakness. Abandoning his pursuit of Wolf's pistol, he rolled hard on top of Hanley's back, pinning the hunter to the floor while placing his hands firmly on Hanley's jaw and the back of his skull.

"*Hanley!*" Falcon screamed.

Sixty pounds of torque was no exertion at all for Cougar's powerful hands.

Concern for the module was a thing of the past. Falcon was out of his flight chair and running toward Cougar, who was diving for the 1911 again. Vance rolled to one knee, bringing the gun up to Falcon's chest. Too late, he saw that the slide was locked back over an empty chamber.

Falcon's knife was in his hand as the two men collided.

* * *

"Captain, I can see the lunar module," Arnett said, pointing through the canopy. "It's still drifting."

"So are we," Wolf said. "I can't slow us down enough for an orbit. We're landing. How long on the engines?"

"About three minutes after we vaporize in a Desert crater," Arnett said frankly. "We've still only got life support and basic security."

Wolf licked his dry lips.

355

"We can't fight the gravity," he said slowly. "Maybe we can use it."

* * *

After a short grapple for the knife, Falcon and Cougar simultaneously rolled to their feet, the Cree man still holding the chrystanium blade. They circled each other warily, each one well aware of the other's abilities.

"Why do you fight, Vance?" Falcon wanted to know. "You don't believe in the Bloodline. You don't believe in causes."

With a flick of his wrist, he shot the knife toward Cougar's throat. Cougar was too fast again, isolating the blade with one hand, then driving the heel of his free palm into Falcon's sternum. Falcon chopped his forearm on top of Vance's wrist at the same moment, absorbing the force of the blow before locking his arm under Vance's bicep, tying their limbs together. Falcon head-butted his enemy before Cougar could wriggle free, stunning the Defender long enough for Falcon to wrest his knife hand loose. Cougar had to duck under the next swipe, then used his hunched-over position to charge straight into Falcon's torso, lifting him off the ground, and slamming both men to the steel floor. The impact of the landing would have blown the wind from Falcon's lungs, had it not been for the protection of his armored vest, but he lost his knife.

Cougar's arms were momentarily pinned under Falcon's body, but Falcon had no such handicap. He hammered his elbows into Cougar's shoulder blades and neck. Cougar rolled away, then slammed his right foot across Falcon's face, snapping his head to one side. Falcon could see roaming points of light as he rolled over onto his stomach and tried to rise to his hands and knees, but his head was wracked with throbbing pain, and felt as heavy as lead. He could not rise farther than his elbows, and blood dripped from his mouth.

"I fight for what I know," Cougar croaked, groggily standing, the knife in his right fist. "Ridge, you don't know anything."

"I know how to fly this module," Falcon whispered.

Cougar seized Falcon's hair and pulled him up until he was kneeling. Falcon gritted his teeth against the excruciating pain in his scalp. Cold chrystanium was pressed against his throat an instant later.

"I gave the others time to die," Cougar said gravely. "Would you rather have it fast?"

Falcon closed his eyes.

"Do you know how to fly this module, Vance?"

The knife pressed harder against his skin.

Falcon smiled. "You don't, do you? You couldn't fly this little bird healthy, let alone recovering from an EMP."

Cougar gave no reply, but the knife was unflinching.

Falcon shrugged carelessly. "We're going to be in the atmosphere in about thirty seconds, falling like a comet. Are you ready to look on the face of God, Vance? Will you ever be ready?"

* * *

"Keep angling us in," Wolf ordered. "We're going to hit the atmosphere hard and fast. Don't try to slow us down."

"Sir?" Arnett asked, while still obeying the order. "What are we doing?"

"Switch solar chargers to thermals."

"Aye, sir. How does that help us? There's no heat in space."

Wolf nodded. "But there's a lot in The Desert. We enter, light like a torch, drop like a rock, and recharge the engines off our own atmospheric friction."

Arnett swallowed the hard knot in her throat. "Aye, sir. Tell me where to go."

"We need to land in the polar lake. It's our only chance."

"Even if we can recharge the engines enough, sir, there's no way we'll have enough air time to fly to the lake. We need to angle straight to it."

Wolf nodded his consent. "Do it. Put us over the pole."

Wolf's shoulder frequency startled both of them as it began to crackle and hiss.

"Captain Wolf, this is Sergeant-Major Cardinal. Come in, please, sir."

"Status, Sergeant-Major," Wolf replied.

"We're all intact in rear comp, sir, but had some fun getting the projectiles. Two prisoners are dead, Whitefeather and Sterling, someone else lost a hand. I've got frequencies back, but main comm isn't responding. It got pretty fried. Sir, we've got eyes on The Desert. Are you seeing what we're seeing?"

"We see it," Wolf acknowledged. "We're flying straight into it. Get everyone strapped in. Can you get the lunar?"

"I can't raise them, sir. Frequencies can only recharge directly off Banishment One. The module's dark."

"I've got them on radar," Arnett noted. "They're heading for the forest. Captain Falcon must know they'll need to soft land on the water if the engines don't recharge in time."

"Keep monitoring their position," Wolf directed. "I want us to put down as close to them as possible. That's a whole lot of forest to dig through."

"Aye, sir."

"Anyone who knows how to pray, do it now," Wolf said, as Banishment One dropped into the atmosphere.

* * *

Cougar slammed Falcon roughly into the flight chair, holding the hunter's knife point against the base of his neck, like a chisel.

"Land," he whispered in Falcon's ear. "You flinch in a way I don't like, and I punch this sucker right between your first and second vertebrae. Don't think that inexplicable forest can distract me, either."

"Well, it's distracting me," Falcon growled. "I have no idea what we're dropping into."

"Just get the engines going!"

"I can't," Falcon said tersely. "We need to get over the lake, and deploy the glider. That's the only way we can get rescued. I don't know if the engines are ever going to start again, and Banishment One can't set down anywhere else."

"Can we get that far?"

"We entered shallow, so that'll give us more time, but I don't know. I just don't know."

"Try harder!"

"Engines are only at fourteen percent, Vance. Even if we were gliding already, we'd never recharge in time. It's the chute, or nothing."

"Do your job, Ridge. Do not mess with me."

"Then shut up and let me fly!" Falcon snarled. "Heading on a five degree descent. That's still too steep."

"Then level it."

"*Shut ... up!* This is not a paper airplane!"

The flames streaking over the canopy were beginning to clear, but the module was still dropping far too steeply for Falcon's liking. At their current rate of descent, he knew that they would be very fortunate to reach the lake at all. In spite of his best efforts, they were going to have to land in the forest, and that was going to be very hard to survive.

"I've got to deploy the chute now," he sighed. "You might want to belt yourself in. I can't slow us down, so this is going to be like hitting a brick wall.'

"Very well, Ridgely," Cougar shrugged, patting the hunter gently on the shoulder. "Take us down."

Falcon could not hide his shock when Cougar reached down to replace the chrystanium knife in its own sheath, and then stuck Wolf's 1911 into Falcon's belt.

"I don't really need them," Vance said dismissively, settling himself into the second flight chair beside Falcon. "Catch you on the ground. Nice knowing you, Captain Falcon."

"Godspeed, Vance," Falcon managed to reply, stunned. He took a moment to tear his eyes away from the canopy glass, and looked behind his chair at the four dead bodies on the bloodstained deck. Beyond them, he could see Kressel, still seated patiently in the drop chute, awaiting either rescue or banishment, and looking as though he did not really care which one fate decided. Falcon chose that moment to dictate fate.

Cougar was just reaching for his harness when Falcon punched the gliding chute deployment. The dual blue sails burst from the port and starboard engines, as the module still sped toward The Desert at breakneck speed. The rushing air punched into the sails with such force that the entire module was blown backward, the nose pitching dangerously upward. The strut of the port sail cracked as it deployed, and the small ship snapped sharply to the left, spiraling down around the uselessly fluttering sail.

The force of air impact launched Cougar out of the flight chair and straight into the ceiling. His flailing arms took the shock of the impact, saving him from a broken neck, but he was crashing to the floor an instant later. Falcon, secured to his seat, was driven hard into the straps, feeling each one crushing into his chest and waist, but he had no time to lose. Cougar was moaning on the floor, but already attempting to rise to his knees.

Falcon drew his knife and slashed through the belts, freeing himself. It was almost impossible to move in the tightly spinning craft, but he managed to pull himself along the wall to the drop chute. Cougar tried to crawl after him, but was pressed to the floor by the intense gravity.

"There's no landing now, Vance!" Falcon shouted over the roaring wind. "You never answered me! Will you ever be ready?"

"RIDGE!" Cougar roared.

Kressel's eyes were wide as Falcon opened the clear chute door, and then hit the auxiliary drop release, kneeling and turning his back to the Bloodline Heir. The drop chute opened under Kressel's feet. Falcon bowed his head and crossed his arms over his chest as he and Kressel were sucked from the module.

* * *

"I've got the lake," Arnett announced. "Twelve o'clock. Engines still unresponsive. We're falling at eighty-seven degrees!"

"Hold it steady," Wolf grimaced, the G-forces beginning to overwhelm the gravitational generators. "Time to impact."

"T minus twenty-eight seconds! We'll never pull up in time."

"Pleasure meeting you, Lieutenant Arnett. Fire engines on my mark."

"Aye, sir!"

"Don't call me that."

* * *

Falcon put his head down into the screaming wind as his stiff body streaked toward the forest below. Kressel's flailing form was directly beneath him. Falcon streamlined himself, closing the gap between the two plummeting men. Kressel was almost within reach.

* * *

Cougar managed to crawl back to his flight chair, but the engines were not even reading twenty-percent. The tailspinning module would crash long before the chargers could bring the power to ignition levels.

However, other systems were still coming back online in the wind-lashed cabin, and one of them was the flashing red ejection control. With only seconds before impact, Cougar lashed himself to the seat and punched the control.

* * *

Banishment One broke through the final cloud layer over the polar lake, flames still enwreathing it like a shroud of fire. Dropping as quickly and brightly as any meteor, the Runner fell toward the ocean-sized body of water.

At an altitude of five hundred meters, the light rails abruptly roared to life. The nose was pulled up sharply, preventing the ship from incinerating upon impact, but the force of the landing still lifted the ship back into the air, skipping like a flat stone across the blue surface.

Even for a pilot as skilled as Wolf, control was impossible at that point. All that he could do was try to keep the nose up and the wings level, and he kept praying.

Part Five

The Limit

April 28, 2175.
From the diary of Chester Wolf.

My Dearest Rachel,

    I look into the eyes of many of the people I kill. To be able to kill at close range in open terrain is considered a rare gift. They don't send me on capture missions. I have not brought a target in alive since Colonel Simon Cutbill at the end of the 7-3-0.

    Colonel Towers tells me that Track and Pursuit is going to drive a stake into the heart of the Bloodline, ending seventy-eight years of war. All I know is that I have been killing for five years, and there are still more of them.

    I once killed a man with a stake. Unlike the vampire fantasies, killing with a piece of wood is not simple. The heart is protected by the ribs and sternum. I drove a broken tree branch between his ribs, puncturing his left lung. That man had an ion rifle in his hands, and I tell myself that made it a clean kill, with a clean conscience. I saw his eyes. They were hazel, and they were confused. Dying is an experience that we only have once, and he did not recognize the sensation for what it was. He did not know who I was, or where I'd come from, or why he couldn't breathe. I had just thrown my knife into the throat of his fellow sentry, and the only thought going through my head was the urgency of retrieving my weapon. It was my knife, and I needed it. I left both of them dead in the woods, minus dog-tags, and I got my knife back. That gave me more comfort than the completion of the mission.

Why was that?

Your loving husband,

Lieutenant Chester Wolf.

Chapter Forty-Three

March 3, 2191.
Polar Forest,
The Desert.

Kressel had blacked out during the plummet, and it took all of Falcon's strength to hold onto the limp man, while simultaneously attempting to control the descent of his own gliding chute. Landing in a forest without the proper controls was borderline suicide, but Falcon's orders from Wolf were still being respected. Kressel was under Falcon's protection until his feet were in the soil.

He did not have a lot of time to observe the forest rushing up toward him, but what he did see was enough to ensure Falcon that the trees were like none grown on Earth or Canadian Exodus. In appearance, they were somewhat like enormous cornstalks, towering fibrous pillars, wreathed with broad, climbing leaves rather than branches.

Avoiding the trees was impossible. The glider was buffeted by the leaves, tearing the fabric. Falcon lost his grip on Kressel, and the unconscious man tumbled out of sight amongst the foliage. By then, the glider was more hindrance than help. Falcon pulled the release strap and dropped into the ocean of green, breaking his fall by driving his knife into the tree he was sliding down.

After dropping to the white loam soil, he began running. He knew that Kressel had fallen twenty degrees east of him, about one hundred meters away.

Even as he ran, Falcon was reading the hot and muggy enclosed world around him. The first thing that he read was the footprints, unlike any he had seen before. All were quadruped, some four-toed, approximately the size of large rodents. Others had only three toes, and were larger than the prints of a grizzly bear. Aside from these, there were tiny dust trails, the kind left by limbless, slithering creatures, worms or larvae. The signs of life were everywhere, and all Falcon could do was keep running. Without seeing a single creature, he had already discovered at least three different animal life forms, and he really did not want to encounter anymore than their footprints while he was only armed with a knife and an empty pistol.

From the air, he had seen two things that he deemed important. The first was the polar lake, which was nearly forty kilometers to the north. The second was the lunar module, which had crashed in a ball of fire, roughly ten to fifteen kilometers north of him. No one could have survived the impact, but if Cougar had managed to eject, that put him within twenty square kilometers, most likely between Falcon and the lake.

Falcon switched on his 3-6-5 Cuff as he ran. An unbroken signal was usually indicative of serious trouble, but he could not think of a better description for this very strange predicament.

Chapter Forty-Four

March 3, 2191.
Banishment One,
Polar Lake,
The Desert.

With just one arm handcuffed to a bunk in the crew quarters, Heir Defenders Commander Robert Flaxton had been tossed about like a rag doll as Banishment One touched down. He awoke with blood running down his forehead, having been knocked out upon impact with a bulkhead. Searing pain was shooting through his dislocated arm and broken ankle, as he gingerly tried to sit up. The deck beneath him was rocking slightly, and he realized that the ship was resting on water.

When his bleary eyes fluttered open, the first thing he saw was Chester Wolf, sitting silent and motionless on the bunk, his hands folded between his knees. Flaxton tensed, but Wolf did not even appear to notice him.

"I am going to ask you questions, Mr. Flaxton. Do not lie."

"Who are you?" Flaxton growled.

Wolf smiled, setting a nickel-plated serving tray on the bedding by Flaxton's shackled hand.

"My name is Wolf. You knew about the EMP."

Flaxton looked back desperately at the prison bay hatch, as though expecting his men to come charging through it.

"I resecured them," Wolf said. "All of them."

"Alone?" Flaxton snarled. "You're unarmed!"

"No." Wolf shook his head. "I have a knife. You knew about the EMP. Do not lie."

Before Flaxton could react, his dislocated arm was seized and yanked forward, his hand pinned flat against the tray. He bellowed with pain as Wolf's knife cut off his right thumb.

"One," Wolf said. "Who planted it?"

The knife severed Flaxton's index finger a second later.

"Two. Who planted it?"

"*Stop!*" Flaxton screamed, just before his middle finger was taken off, just below the second knuckle.

"Three. Who planted it?"

"I'll tell you! *I'll tell you!*"

Wolf continued as though he had heard nothing. Flaxton was down to one pinky on his right hand.

"Four. Who planted it?"

"Eddie Devane!"

Wolf wiped the blood from his knife onto Flaxton's sleeve.

"Interesting, Mr. Flaxton. I believe you. How did you know?"

Flaxton was biting his lip against the pain of his bleeding hand.

"He visited me in Beaumont. He said our Mountain could still be built."

That cost him his last finger, but his screams were muffled by Wolf's hand over his mouth.

"Five. Your thoughts should be firmly focused on your left hand." Wolf placed the tip of his blade lightly between the veins on the back of Flaxton's remaining hand. "Before, and after. Do not lie. I haven't even started relocating your shoulder, or setting your ankle. Round-the-clock lockdown does not have visiting hours."

"I'm telling you the truth!"

"You don't know what truth is. You've lived a lie since you were twelve years old."

"The Mountain is not a lie!"

"So, what's rape, Bobby? Truth, or a lie?"

Flaxton spat in Wolf's face, his face twisted in an evil grin. "That depends on which end you're on, Wolf."

Wolf's knife punched through Flaxton's right cheek, breaking off two molars and slicing across the top of his tongue. Flaxton could not scream through his mouthful of blood. He spewed a crimson spray across the room as the knife was withdrawn.

"Here is truth," Wolf said. "You have lost five fingers. You have five more. After that, you have ten toes, two ears, two nostrils, two eyes, two lips, two testicles, one tongue, and, because you're blonde, around one hundred thirty thousand hairs firmly rooted into your scalp. Hands at the wrists, feet at the ankles, and this knife never needs sharpening. You will bleed, and scream, and live. I fear God, Mr. Flaxton. If I slit your throat right now, I don't think He'd hold it against me.

But I haven't killed anyone in five years. Don't get me started."

Flaxton was still drooling blood, the hot red fluid making his voice slow and liquidy.

"Devane is more than he seems," he managed to slur. "Like most of us, Captain Wolf. And when we return as heroes to The Mountain, I'm going to watch your own children execute you in New Shilo Plaza."

Wolf stood, this time wiping his knife clean on Flaxton's pant legs before putting it back in its sheath on his forearm.

"Do your homework, Bobby. I don't have kids."

He stepped out of hearing range before touching his frequency.

"Arnett?"

"Sir?" the lieutenant replied from the cockpit.

"As soon as our databases are back online, run Edward Devane. D-E-V-A-N-E. I want to know any security clearances, particularly Beaumont."

"Aye, sir. Databases are way down on the automated recharge sequence, though. I'll let you know when it's back."

"Thank you, Lieutenant."

Wolf turned his attention back toward the bunk, folding his arms.

"Interrogations aren't my field, Mr. Flaxton. You'll forgive me if I'm a bit clumsy at it. Usually, I just kill people or leave them alone."

Flaxton's mouth opened to yell, but Wolf had knocked him unconscious with an elbow across the face before a word could emerge.

"But I'm learning," Wolf mused.

Ustaf was carrying a C-7 assault rifle when he entered from the resecured prison bay, a canvas duffel bag slung over his shoulder.

"We're all rearmed, sir." He flinched slightly at the sight of Flaxton. "Here's what you asked for."

"Anything from the module?" Wolf asked, taking the bag and drawing out a 10-gage shotgun.

"We picked up a 3-6-5 transmission, unbroken, thirty-eight kilometers southeast of the coastline. We're nearly at landing depth now, sir."

"Any Morse Code?"

"Just once, sir. 'Sundial.' It's Captain Falcon's retrieval code."

"That's good news, Corporal." Wolf found a Glock pistol in the duffel bag, holstered it, and then began loading his armored vest and belt with ammunition. "I want my Colt back. Browning was an artist."

"Sir, the bad news is that three prisoners are unaccounted for."

"Coolidge, Camrose, and Hollis," Wolf nodded. "That's a problem."

"And we have no locator beacon from the module itself."

"It's shielded, but more likely incinerated. But if Falcon's alive, we won't find the module intact. He'd make sure of that. Atmospherics?"

"Air's good, sir. Whatever these trees are, they aren't releasing toxins. We're in the most temperate region of the planet, but...."

"We can't hover," Wolf interrupted. "We get a lock on the 3-6-5, raft in, and go in on foot. You, me, and

Lewis. Arnett and Cardinal hold the ship until we get back."

"Then what?" Ustaf asked. "Do you really think command is going to want us to leave the Bloodline on the first known planet with extraterrestrial life forms?"

"I don't know," Wolf said plainly. "Our people in the forest are all we can think about for now."

"What about ... him?" Ustaf gestured at Flaxton's crumpled form.

Wolf shrugged. "Back in his cell."

"Should I ... treat him first?"

Wolf shook his head while opening his personal locker, removing his faded green hunt poncho and moccasins.

"I want to be on shore in twenty minutes. Let's hunt."

Chapter Forty-Five

March 3, 2191.
Polar Forest,
The Desert.

When Kressel's tired eyes opened, he was lying against the base of a tree, his body throbbing and sore. His left arm was in a wooden splint made from three sticks swathed in a bandage. When he tried to sit up, the pounding in his head nearly made him pass out. He slumped back against the tree.

"Be calm, Mr. Kressel."

Falcon did not seem bothered at all by the fact that he was in the middle of an alien forest. He was hunkered down a few feet away from The Heir, using his chrystanium to whittle a point onto a wooden staff. Three more spears, all between six and seven feet long, lay at his feet.

"We're at least thirty-five k from the coast," he continued. "You fell. The tree broke your fall, and your arm. You've been unconscious for two hours."

"What is this place?" Kressel whispered, sitting up more slowly.

"It's The Desert, Mr. Kressel," Falcon said. "At least, that's what it was eighty years ago. We just opened a whole new box. The spear I'm holding may be leaching toxins into my hands that will kill me. The air we're breathing may kill us. Or the soil, or the other smaller plants, or whatever made all of the signs that are everywhere around us. Life just got very interesting, Mr. Kressel."

"Can you tell me some good news, Captain Falcon?" Kressel croaked, and then coughed harshly, his lungs burning.

"Welcome home," Falcon smiled, tossing the spear. Kressel caught it with his good hand.

"You're giving me a weapon?"

"Chances are, we're both going to die," Falcon stated. "We have a better chance together."

"A better chance to get you home?" Kressel snarled.

"I could leave you alone, and unarmed," Falcon offered. "There's few rocks on this planet, just sand, loam, and trees. You have nothing to forge your own weapon with. Chew a spear out with your teeth? Sound fun? You need a man with a knife right now, General. I have a neutralized ion pistol, and an empty M-1911 Colt .45 with no reloads. Appreciate the primitive, Mr. Kressel. I trust it to bring me home more than any technology."

"We're walking out?"

"If Wolf made it to the lake, he'll be reading my Cuff. Assuming that everything's secure, they'll probably try to resecure the module, and rendevous with me. Did you know about the EMP?"

Kressel shook his head. "No. I guess some people still believe in me."

"Your feet are in the soil, Kressel. I am now free to kill you, and I'm choosing not to. Enough people have died. Mostly because of you, but there has to be a line. Get up. The module's about fifteen k north."

A guttural growl carried on the wind, through the lightly blown stalks of the trees. It was like no sound Falcon had ever heard from the mouth of man or beast.

"What was that?" Kressel demanded, scrambling to his feet.

"Keep your voice down," Falcon cautioned him, also standing. "Isn't it obvious? There's monsters in these woods."

Chapter Forty-Six

March 3, 2191.
Southeastern coastline, Polar Lake,
The Desert.

With Banishment One moored one hundred meters off shore, Wolf was grimly rowing the emergency raft to shore, with absolutely no idea what to expect. Lewis and Ustaf were behind him in a second raft, heavily armed, with a satchel of projectile weapons and rations for their missing comrades.

"Sir, I see smoke. About thirty k south."

Lewis was scanning deep into the forest with a pair of field binoculars. Wolf nodded.

"We just found our module," he said. "We're about to find out how flammable this forest is."

"Sir...." Ustaf's hesitant tone finished the sentence, without another word being spoken.

"Falcon came after me when he didn't have to," Wolf said, staring at the thin plume of black smoke, belching out of the distant treetops. "Once upon a time."

Ustaf blinked, and gave an acceptant nod.

"Yes, sir."

"The rules have changed," Wolf said. "We're going in knowing nothing, and believing anything. Heir Defender Command Second Vance Ryan Coolidge knows the Cuff, and he knows Falcon's retrieval code. We could be walking to him, and he could outhunt any one of us. Understood?"

"No illusion, sir," Lewis sighed.

"When we beach, flank on me, Ustaf takes the east. Hold at twenty meters, stay in visual. No frequencies, let's keep it familiar. It always complicates when we have each other's backs, but we don't have a choice. We have three rendezvouses and four targets. Seven acquisitions, and, where there's plants, there's animals. This is first contact. Safety's off, one up the pipe."

They beached the rafts on the sandy shore a minute later, pulling them close to the treeline in a sheltered gully. Wolf took one last look back at the partially submerged Banishment One, before raising his poncho hood over his head and stepping into the trees. From that point on, their march would be silent, and invisible to all but the most trained eyes.

Chapter Forty-Seven

March 3, 2191.
Banishment One,
Polar coastline,
The Desert.

Donavan Cardinal did not like things that he could not explain. The forest outside of the ship was one of those things, but the TAP Sergeant-Major realized that particular paradox was not his field of expertise. The fact that an EMP had managed to detonate without his knowledge was a field he should have been more than qualified in, and that was what really bothered him.

The gun cabinets in the tail comp were supposed to be prepared for all disaster scenarios, including EMP attack. The ion weapons were kept in a permanently shielded cabinet, while the projectiles were guarded by unshielded magnetic and key locks. The theory behind this was that any EMP device would disable all but the key locks on the projectile cache, making them readily accessible, while the ion weapons would remain sealed and operational. In practice, the exact opposite had happened. The projectile cabinet had locked down, and the entire ion cabinet had been neutralized. That kind of mistake could not have possibly happened by mistake.

"What do you have?" Arnett asked.

Cardinal sighed wearily as he crawled out from behind the projectile cabinet, holding a micro-magnetic shielder.

"It was clipped into the deadbolt ground," he said disgustedly. "It protected the locks, but left the entire keypad in the open. EMP goes off, doors lock, and we can't unlock them. Clever."

"So Flaxton was telling the truth?"

"Devane signed off on everything, including both weapon caches."

"What about the ions?"

"Shielder was rerouted right into itself. The only thing it was shielding was its own ground. Someone knew exactly what was going to happen."

"And they knew our response procedure," Arnett added. "What we'd need, and how to keep us from getting it."

"Thank goodness for chrystanium," Cardinal said sourly. "Lewis's knife just saved the entire ship. We can't contact the captain?"

Arnett shook her head. "They went in dark, just like always. No frequencies. We're waiting."

Cardinal looked at her curiously. "If I may ask, Lieutenant, exactly what directives did Captain Wolf give you?"

"He said to wait forty-eight hours," Arnett said grimly. "If they're not back by then, we launch, jettison all remaining prisoners into the atmosphere, and return home."

Cardinal snorted in disbelief. "Where did that guy come from, anyway?"

"Small town farmboy," Arnett replied, which was all she really knew. "He hunted deer as a side-job. Apparently, he was really good at it."

"Meaning?"

"According to Captain Falcon, he hunted them with a knife."

Cardinal chuckled. "And, bingo. The legend of the wolf."

"Bingo," Arnett agreed, smiling. "And it is one legend that I'm getting really, really sick of hearing."

She was still smiling as she drew her pistol and shot Cardinal in the back of the head.

Chapter Forty-Eight

March 4, 2191.
Polar Forest,
The Desert.

A full day on The Desert was only fourteen hours long. Darkness fell quickly, and began to fade just as quickly. The temperature did not seem to vary much by night or day, remaining hot and humid at all times. Falcon was grateful for the overhead tree cover, which trapped much of the moisture. Without the trees, no one could have survived more than one revolution of that burning planet. Even so, the hunter was painfully aware of how little water was left in the single-liter bottle on his vest. The fact that he and Kressel were in a perpetual state of perspiration was not helping them to stay hydrated, either.

They had been walking for five hours, most of them in darkness. Night was a phenomenon unfamiliar to both men, but they were surefooted, and most of the forest was virgin growth, with very little developed underbrush to trip them up. Falcon had long-burning phosphorous flares in his armor, but was hesitant to use them as a light source. Not only was he uncertain as to how alien forest life would react to open flame, but he also did not want to attract any undue attention from the animal life. Thus far, none had been seen, but their signs were abundant.

There was no end to Falcon's concerns and burning questions, all of which he knew were pointless to vocalize. No one had any answers on this new world.

Aside from watching his surroundings and footing, Falcon also had to constantly monitor himself and Kressel for signs of toxicity. So far, there had been none of the standard indications: increased body temperature, nausea, headaches, respiratory disorder, slurred speech, tremors, numbness. Even so, Falcon continued to be watchful. The thought of being eaten by an alien monster was bad enough. The thought of being asphyxiated by alien pollen was just embarrassing.

As the morning sun rose over the western horizon, the two weary men found themselves standing on the crusty rim of an enormous forested valley, more than ten kilometers in diameter. It took Falcon a moment to realize what he was looking at.

"I thought The Desert was supposed to be topographically level," Kressel croaked, his throat parched. "Some dunes and salt flats."

Falcon took another swig of their precious water, then passed the canteen to the Bloodline Heir.

"It is level," he said, wiping his mouth with the back of his hand. "This is a crater." He pointed to a patch of burnt trees near the center of the bowl. "And that's the module."

Although the caked soil of the crater still seemed burnt and hard, the valley was teeming with life. In addition to the trees, there was now a large amount of second growth shrubbery blanketing the forest floor, making it even harder to find decent footing as they began their descent.

"This makes sense," Falcon said, feeling his way down the slope. "I would bet you anything that we're in the planet's cradle of life. An asteroid, or even a fragment of an exploded planet, could have carried dormant seeds, frozen eggs, maybe even subterranean animals here. The impact would have cooked everything for miles around, but that could have held back the dune movement for some time. If any life survived the collision, it would have had time to start rooting in, forming soil."

"Even so," Kressel noted, "this must have grown at a vastly accelerated rate. This forest is endless, and it's not eighty years old yet. Either that, or something intelligent made it grow ... like we did."

"Anything's possible," Falcon muttered. "I'm not familiar with Home Base tropical vegetation. Who knows, maybe this planet is Brazilian Exodus."

Kressel chuckled at that, and Falcon realized that he had just joked with a man whom he had been under orders to find dead or alive for more than twenty years. People often spoke wistfully of how an alien contact would bring about world peace. Falcon did not believe that, but he could not deny that the discovery of the unexplained had made it a lot easier to call a truce. However, he was not ready to turn his back on Kressel just yet.

The slope down to the crater floor was more than three kilometers long, and every step of it revealed something new. The strangest thing Falcon noticed was that many of the treetops overhead now had huge red, gelatin-like bulbs hanging from the tips of the monstrous green leaves. He had to stop walking to stare up at them. They reminded him of bizarre Christmas trees.

"What is that?" Kressel wondered, following Falcon's gaze to the forest roof. "Some kind of fruit?"

"I don't think so," Falcon replied, looking down at the base of the trees. The fibrous roots were littered with even more bulbs, these ones dry, hollow, and a pale rose colour. He prodded the papery layers with the butt of his spear. The shell crumpled easily, almost like an oversized beehive.

"Not fruit," Falcon guessed. "I think they're cocoons. We're in a nest."

"Then let's leave the nest," Kressel decided crossly. He took a step forward, but immediately tripped over a small dugout in the dirt. Falcon caught the old man by the collar, keeping him from landing face-first in a clutch of squirming larva.

"*What...?*" Kressel gasped, staggering back, his eyes wide. The dugout was just under one meter across, packed with hundreds of thousands of writhing, yellow creatures, almost like lice, but closer to the size of a small earthworm. Falcon instinctively pulled Kressel back, but then could not help taking a step closer, hunkering down in front of the clutch.

"Alien bugs," he muttered. "Ugly." Slowing drawing his knife, he gently slid the blade into the middle of the clutch. When he withdrew it, three of the creatures were squirming on the flat of the blade. Falcon lifted the knife to eye-level to examine them more closely.

Each creature was about two centimeters long, with no eyes, ears, nose, or antennae that he could see. Their mouths were on the underside of their pointed snouts, and were constantly gaping open and then closed again, reminiscent of a goldfish. They had no arms or legs, but each had two wing-like flippers just behind the head. Their thin tails made up over half of their body mass, and ended with a slight fork.

Opening a sterile vial from his medical kit, Falcon carefully tapped one of the creatures from his knife into the clear tube, then carefully resealed it.

"What are you doing?" Kressel said, looking repulsed.

"Documenting."

"Well, let's move on," Kressel said impatiently. "These creatures are disgusting me."

"Then I would watch your step," Falcon advised, standing and carefully zipping the vial back into the med kit. "Look around."

Kressel looked out at the forest before them, and realized that the spongy floor was covered with similar clutches, hundreds of them, for as far as he could see. Most of them were less than two feet apart, making the entire ground seem to glow with pale gold.

"There are billions of them," Kressel breathed. "Why? Why are they all huddled together, not spreading out?"

"Nests," Falcon answered, pointing at the huge three-toed tracks, thickly trafficked into the narrow spaces between each clutch, while never once stepping into one. "They're waiting for Mommy to come home."

Chapter Forty-Nine

March 4, 2191.
Lunar module crash site,
Polar Forest,
The Desert.

When Wolf's team arrived at the lunar module, it was little more than a crater within a crater. The small craft was unrecognizable, a burned and crumpled compact of twisted metal, still smoldering in a smoking hole. One look told Wolf that no one inside could have possibly survived. He could only hope that his friend and crew had managed to bail.

Wolf's eyes read the forest like words on a page. The module had crashed into the dense forest at a steep angle, burning out a small clearing, which fortunately had not spread to the larger trees. Although he could not see Lewis or Ustaf, he knew exactly where they were, to the southeast and southwest of him respectively, securing the perimeter around the crash site. Wolf was very much like his namesake in that he could see things clearly without the use of his eyes. He could also see that no one had emerged from the crash site, or approached it.

"Clear," Wolf said, breaking silence for the first time since the hunt had begun. "Move in."

Lewis and Ustaf emerged like shadows from the trees, stepping closer to the wreckage.

"There's no remains to dig," Wold said. "Dust it."

Ustaf swallowed the lump in his throat, then opened his satchel of localized seismic charges, placing one of the apple-sized explosives in the center of the debris field, and setting the blast radius for fifty meters.

"Charge ready, sir," he said reluctantly. "Fully recharged."

"Set two more," Wolf instructed. "Simultaneous detonation sequence."

"Sir?" Ustaf was obviously concerned about the residual effects.

Wolf nodded. "I want powder. No stone tools."

The charges detonated without any sound or light, but sent rippling shockwaves outward for fifty meters in all directions, turning everything in their path to fine dust. Trees vanished, falling like avalanches of green powdered snow.

Standing a safe distance away, Wolf bowed his head and crossed himself as the dry cloud settled around them.

"Any lost commended to God," he muttered, eyes closed. "Bodies to corruption, souls incorruptible."

"Sir...." Ustaf's face was hard, and red.

"We're hunting," was Wolf's response.

"We have no idea which of our own we may have just dusted, sir! We owe more than that to us!"

"The job's different today," Wolf growled.

"Sir!" Ustaf took a step forward, angered.

Before he could take a second step, Lewis's shotgun was trained on his chest. He froze.

"Do not step up to the captain like that, Corporal," she said calmly.

"Amanda!" Ustaf said, appalled, holding his hands out carefully.

"Lieutenant," she corrected him. "Stand down."

Wolf took a slow sidestep, placing his own chest between Ustaf and the 10-gage. He looked at Lewis, and she immediately lowered her weapon, unable to hold Wolf's gaze. Not many could look Wolf in the eye for very long.

"We're all tired," he said. "And mad, and confused. You know your orders. You don't know mine. The country told me that under no circumstances are any of these prisoners to return. The job gets done, or we can't go home. I want to go home."

"Who doesn't?" Falcon's voice replied from behind them. Ustaf and Lewis started, pointing their weapons at the approaching forms of Falcon and Kressel, the Bloodline general in the lead with his hands raised.

"Am I interrupting something?" Falcon asked wryly.

"Thought you'd beat me here," Wolf remarked, not turning. Falcon's voice had not even made him flinch.

"Traffic was murder," Falcon said with a grin.

"Just you two?" Wolf asked, knowing who was behind him without even turning around.

"Hanley and Connor are dead," Falcon dutifully reported, his voice glum. "Cougar. I took out Camrose and Hollis, but Vance might have made it out."

"Cougar got out," Wolf assured him. "Where's my gun?"

Falcon traded the 1911 for Wolf's shotgun, Glock, and ammo belt. He could not help shaking his head as he watched Wolf reload and chamber the ancient weapon.

"A man and his antiques," he said. "You're sure that thing still shoots?"

"I keep it clean," Wolf replied. "Nice spear."

"You gave me one magazine," Falcon countered, but added, "Thanks."

"We're being hunted," Wolf said, holstering his pistol.

"I know," Falcon nodded. "We just came through a nest."

"I'm talking about Cougar," Wolf said quietly. "He can't allow himself to die of natural causes. He's getting between us and the ship."

After an uncomfortable silence, Lewis ventured, "What do we do, sir?"

Wolf took a few steps away, and stared into the trees.

"What was the wind?" he asked.

"Blowing west, fairly light," Falcon supplied. "Died soon after."

"Bail altitude?"

"No more than one thousand feet when we dropped."

"Vance?"

"On the floor. We were tailspinning."

Wolf nodded, his mind calculating and replaying an event he had not witnessed.

"He ejected at no more than five hundred feet. Light wind carried him less than two kilometers. He could see the smoke, he saw the lake, he knew where we'd beach. He knows everything."

"Let's just get back," Falcon urged. "We'll stay together."

Wolf was still staring into the trees.

"Seven times my brother has wronged me," he said to no one. "How many times shall I forgive him? Seven times?"

Ustaf and Falcon exchanged confused glances, but Lewis spoke, taking a step toward Wolf.

"Not seven," she said. "But seventy times seven."

Wolf nodded slowly, raising his hood over his head once more.

"I'll kill him," he said simply. "But he can't make me hate him."

He turned to the others, and they stared back at him in silence.

"Take an eastward sweep back to the lake," he directed calmly. "Put some trail angles between you and him. Kressel stays with you until you hear otherwise from me. If I'm not at the ship four hours after you, jettison all prisoners, and go home. Godspeed."

He stepped toward the western trees, and Falcon followed him, out of the hearing range of the others.

"Chess...." Falcon said helplessly. He was looking at the ground.

"It's okay, Ridge."

"You can't do this. He saw me. He knows it's us."

"I don't like being prey. We don't hunt him, then it's all his rules."

"There's monsters in these woods."

"People don't need monsters. We suffice."

Falcon finally looked Wolf in the eye.

"If I don't make it back, Chess ... you'll look after my little girl?"

Wolf nodded. "Don't worry. Vance wants to die. It's his only absolution."

"What if you don't make it back?" Falcon had to ask.

Wolf smiled, and it was not the half-bemused smile that Falcon was used to seeing. Chester Wolf was smiling up at the blue sky beyond the trees, and Falcon could see the deepest and truest peace in those tired grey eyes.

"'Chester Wolf,'" Wolf said, as though reading an inscription. "'December 2143 - March 2191. *He survived all but once. And that ain't bad.*' Put that on my headstone, okay?"

Seconds later, he had vanished without a trace into the trees. Falcon watched the void his friend had left, and he had to shake his head as the math caught up with him.

"Sir?" Ustaf called from behind him.

"Wolf's forty-seven?" Falcon muttered. "I could have sworn he was older than me."

Chapter Fifty

March 4, 2191.
12 km northeast of lunar crash site,
Polar Forest,
The Desert.

"We'll dig in here," Falcon said, after a couple more hours of hard marching, still having seen no other signs of life. The sun was setting again, and the short days were beginning to annoy Falcon. "Four hours. Then we push on to the coast."

"What about Captain Wolf?" Lewis asked. It was the first time that she had dared to ask. The others sank wearily to the ground, Kressel handcuffed between Falcon and Ustaf.

"All he'll ever be is a hunter," Falcon replied tiredly. "I can't stop him from hunting if he wants to hunt."

"Does he want to hunt?" Kressel asked.

"Everybody get some sleep," Falcon said irritably, rubbing the short hairs on the back of his neck. "I'm the first watch. Lewis, you'll take over in two hours. Sleep."

It was a long two hours for Falcon. The others breathed evenly as they slept, and he wished that he could lie down next to them and do the same. Instead, he not only had to stay awake, but he had to remain alert as well. He did not dare even light a cigarette. With Cougar on the prowl, he might as well have sent up a signal flare.

The sounds and smells of the forest were different from those on Canadian Exodus, even the colour of the sky as the sun sank low and disappeared. There were no birds singing, and even the grass-like blades of the trees did not rustle in the same way as leaves or coniferous needles. Nothing was familiar, and yet Falcon realized that he still felt completely at home. In a strange way, he wished that his daughter, Paisley, was at his side. No man should ever have had to be so far away from his family.

Falcon was actually startled when Lewis put her hand gently on his arm, the blackness around him masking her approach. She was as stealthy as any hunter should have been.

"I can't sleep, sir," she whispered. "Why don't you let me take over now? You're exhausted."

Falcon nodded, too weary to argue.

"I have a child," he said simply. "She lives with her mother. I barely see her."

"I'm sorry, sir."

"I have to make time for that, if we make it back," Falcon decided.

"Yes, sir."

"What is your interest in Captain Wolf, Lieutenant?"

399

Lewis knew better than to fake confusion.

"A bit star-struck, sir," she replied quietly. "He's a myth, even inside a myth. I just wonder who he is, and who really cares for him. How does he hunt so well, and kill so well, and yet remain a good man?"

"How do you know he's a good man?" Falcon asked.

Lewis shrugged. "Some things can't be taught, sir. No warrior code or ancient master can teach you how to look into someone's eyes and just know."

"I've seen the evil of hell in my own unit," Falcon sighed. "And I've seen heroism and nobility in some of the Bloodline. Without a war, it's just not simple. Black and white vanish from existence when you have to start looking for the limit of a good man. We all find our limit. Good or evil is decided by whether we decide to exceed it. Wolf told me that."

He sank to the ground, laying his shotgun beside him.

"Lieutenant?"

"Yes, sir?"

Falcon lay back in the dirt, looking up at the sky, now little more than a lighter patch of grey filtered through the black leaves.

"Wolf had a wife, when he was CNE. In the middle of a brutal war, she died in a Chop crash. Technical malfunction, nothing sinister, just a routine freight run. Wolf has had no use for the world of technology since."

"But he flies, sir," Lewis pointed out.

Falcon nodded.

"Just like she did."

His tired eyes drifted shut.

"Thank you for relieving me, Lieutenant Lewis."

Lewis shouldered her own shotgun, standing guard over the three men.

"My pleasure, sir."

The troubles and concerns wracking Falcon's mind faded into the grey mist, and he was asleep within minutes.

An hour passed, and the forest was shrouded in pitch black once more. The sounds did not stop, even as Falcon slept. His ears were still listening.

* * *

Several kilometers to the northwest, Wolf had finally found Cougar's tracks. His eyes adjusted quickly to the darkness, and he was barely slowed as he continued hunting. Cougar's trail was heading directly for the coast, and, surprisingly, was no more than two hours old. Wolf could only assume that Vance had been hindered, or possibly knocked unconscious for some time upon his ejection from the module. That made the hunt seem less impossible, but no less daunting.

Any hunter knew that the hardest part was not following the trail, but rather finding it. Knowing this, but also knowing that his time was limited, Cougar had done little to hide his tracks. His only concern was getting to the coast ahead of Falcon, and that was a concern which Wolf now shared.

* * *

"Sir, wake up."

Lewis's whisper was no more than a faint breath near Falcon's ear, but the tone of it was enough to wake him up instantly. His eyes opened to blackness, but he could feel rather than see that Lewis was standing over him.

"Lewis?" he said with an equally low voice, touching the 10-gage by his side. His eyes began to distinguish dim forms around him, including Amanda Lewis. Her shotgun was pressed to her shoulder, trained on something Falcon could not see.

"Something's here," she whispered. Falcon stiffened.

"Where?" he breathed, noiselessly lifting his shotgun into his arms and slowly depressing the safety.

"Right beside you."

The same guttural growl Falcon had heard while carving his spears with Kressel now rumbled in his ear from only inches away. Whatever the beast was, it was standing over Kressel's sleeping body, smelling him with short, whistly sniffs.

"It's confused," Falcon murmured, gingerly inching his body away from the hunched shape that was beginning to form from the shadows enveloping them all. The creature appeared to be a quadruped, and larger than a bear, but it was still too dark to make out any features. "It doesn't know what we are."

The creature gurgled once more in the blackness, this time waking Ustaf as well. Falcon heard him mutter incoherently as he floated back to consciousness.

"Ustaf, lie still," Falcon said quickly, still trying to keep his voice low. "Sidearm."

From the other side of the beast, he could hear metal sliding against leather as Ustaf's HK-USP was slowly drawn from its holster. Kressel was still breathing evenly, asleep.

"No one shoots unless I say," Falcon muttered, rising to his feet as he came beside Lewis. "The prisoner has been placed under our protection again."

The beast was moving, stepping over Kressel to begin smelling Ustaf, not in short sniffs, but with one long inhalation, sweeping its massive head over Ustaf's motionless form, head to toe. Lying on his stomach, the soldier never flinched.

"I never even heard it coming," Lewis said, awed. "It was a ghost. It's been smelling all three of you."

"Flare," Falcon quietly ordered. "We'll try to blind it."

Lewis reached slowly into her webbing, extracting a phosphorous flare from the canvas pouch.

The beast was smelling more impatiently now, alternately smelling Kressel and Ustaf, then looking back at Falcon, and drawing in more long breaths.

"Ustaf, very slowly try to move back," Falcon whispered. "Lewis, on me, light the flare. I'll get Kressel."

"I'm awake." Kressel's voice floated softly in the darkness. "What is it?"

"Mommy," Falcon replied, sighting his shotgun on the creature's massive shoulders.

The beast had turned back to Kressel as soon as he spoke. The growl that it let out was much more menacing.

"Captain...." The Heir said cautiously.

Ustaf began to slowly crawl away, and immediately the beast attacked. Giving a piercing scream, it swatted Kressel with a massive forelimb, sending him rolling toward Falcon, and then pounced on Ustaf. The soldier cried out as he tried to raise his pistol, but the beast pinned his wrist to the ground with a huge talon.

"Engage!" Falcon roared, firing his weapon. A volley of slug rounds from the two shotguns began punching holes into the creature's leathery flank. With another scream, it bounded over Ustaf and sprinted away into the trees. Ustaf rolled over onto his back and hammered three shots from his pistol into the black hole left in the charging beast's wake.

"Ceasefire!" Falcon snapped, rushing forward. "Flare!"

Lewis punched the base of the torch, sending a spray of white sparks into the air, lighting up the black woods for more than seventy meters. Already, the beast had vanished from sight. Ustaf was staggering to his feet, dazed, but Kressel lay motionless.

"Ustaf!" Falcon barked, sweeping the area with his eyes, seeking any sign of life.

"I'm good, sir," the soldier replied shakily. "He just stomped me."

"First contact is off to a great start," Lewis muttered, stooping over Kressel. The old man was moaning, bleeding from claw slashes along his ribs and skull, but otherwise seemed uninjured. Lewis quickly began preparing bandages from her kit, while helping Kressel to sit up.

"It's gone," Falcon decided, lowering his weapon. "Any guesses as to how we offended it?"

"It was hunting," Ustaf said, rubbing his wrist, still feeling the scaly talons around it.

"Hunting creatures don't waste time perusing the menu," Kressel mumbled, wincing as Lewis began wrapping his ribs with the white cloths.

"Unless it was confused," Ustaf pointed out, crouching to examine the dark droplets of blood that had been spilled by the creature. "We're aliens, remember?"

Falcon tossed him a second sterile vial from his med kit. "Get me a sample of that blood. Don't touch it. It was an animal. Animals only kill for food or territory."

"We didn't do anything threatening," Ustaf growled, scooping a small gob of the thick, purple blood into the vial. "And if it was looking for the larva you documented, it would have smelled it on Captain Falcon. It was hunting."

"Well, I hope he likes fresh meat," Kressel snapped. "Let's get moving."

"Wait a second," Lewis interjected, looking troubled. "Hunters smell blood."

"So?" Ustaf said, shouldering his assault rifle.

Lewis looked curiously at all three of them before answering.

"So that thing never looked twice at me. It should have smelled me first."

Silence fell over the clearing as they all stopped to consider that.

"So?" Lewis said, mimicking Ustaf without really meaning to. "What was it smelling for?"

Falcon looked at her, then began thumbing more slugs into his weapon.

"We're not waiting to find out."

The phosphorous flare was lighting up the woods with a brilliant white light, and none of them even saw the second creature approaching. A second later, it had bounded into the clearing, bowling Falcon over with a thick, lashing tail, his shotgun flying from his grip. Ustaf raised his rifle, but the huge reptilian creature backhanded him with a massive forearm, sending him flying against a tree.

Lewis was firing her shotgun again, dropping the flare, and the creature winced and flinched as the slugs pelted into its shoulders and neck, but it was still standing and glaring when her firing pin fell on an empty chamber. Lewis grabbed for her pistol as the beast pounced on Falcon, who was trying to rise. The crushing weight of the three-clawed foretalons slammed into his shoulders, knocking him back into the dirt. He couldn't reach his shotgun, or the Glock on his belt, but his knife was in his hand. Whipping himself onto his back, he slashed through the open jaws that were descending toward his own face. The chystanium sliced through the tongue and gums of the beast, and it jerked its head away with a deafening screech. Lewis was firing her pistol, and Falcon managed to draw his as well. The volley of .45 rounds stung the creature's shoulders, throat, and underbelly, and it leaped back, still screaming. Both pistols ran dry, yet the creature was still standing. Lewis and Falcon both made a dive, him for his shotgun, and her for Ustaf's fallen C-7 assault rifle. They both rolled to their feet simultaneously, just as Ustaf managed to raise his pistol, standing from the base of the tree he had slammed into, but none of them fired.

The reptilian lay on its side, dead. A spear was driven into its eye, the point sunk more than a foot into the beast's brain. With one arm still in a sling, Cole Dallas Kressel stood over the massive reptile, seething with a battle rage that he had not felt in many years.

"I said let's get moving!" he snapped. "There's a reason I'm a general!"

Chapter Fifty-One

March 4, 2191.
1 km south of coastline,
Polar Forest,
The Desert.

When Chester Wolf stepped into the small forest clearing after eight hours of silent hunting, Vance Cougar was sitting on a fallen tree with his head bowed, as though in prayer. He had been waiting to be found, but Wolf had not been the first to find him.

The morning sun revealed that a beast lay dead at Cougar's feet, a reptilian creature nearly the size of a rhinoceros. Its features were similar to a hyena or wild dog, but, instead of fur, its hide was coarse and scaly, a collage of dull red, silver, and black. A thick tail stretched out in the dirt behind it, and it had three fearsome claws on each of its four feet, and a long jaw full of razor teeth. But these natural weapons had been to no avail. Cougar held a chrystanium knife in his right hand, and Wolf recognized it as Hanley's. The knife had clearly been the cause of the gash in the beast's throat, which it had then bled out from. A strong smell of blood hung in the air.

Cougar did not even look up, but Wolf knew that he had been seen. He had to wonder if he had ever truly hunted Cougar, or if Vance had just grown weary of evading.

"I knew you'd be coming," Cougar said, his low voice barely carrying in the still air. "I tried to shoot Falcon with a 1911. I knew then." He nudged the creature at his feet with his dirty white prison shoe, as though ensuring that it was dead.

"I have to kill you," was Wolf's only reply. The 1911 was in his hand, but held by his side.

"Of course you do," Cougar sighed, sitting up straighter. "I've killed us seven times now. What kind of man would you be if you didn't repay death with death?"

"I'm protecting my crew."

"Are you a man of God, Chester Wolf?"

"One who's here to kill you."

"He who lives by the sword...." Cougar smiled.

"That's inevitable for me." Wolf was acceptant. "Sell your cloak and buy one."

"What can you tell me about God?" Cougar wanted to know.

"I already told you."

"Just before you shot me. You're not going to preach?"

Wolf shook his head, without blinking. "You don't need a preacher."

"Actually, no one ever preached at me much," Cougar said dismissively. "So, how did I grow up thinking that God hated me?"

"I don't hate you," Wolf said. "You don't need to worry about someone who's already died for you."

"The Bible is an impressive book, Chess. And, yes, I've read most of it. You know, there was one story that really hit me hard, because it told of a man who wielded such power to destroy, without lifting a finger in battle."

Wolf nodded. "Tell me a story, Vance."

Cougar smiled again. "An evil king sent a detachment of soldiers to seize a man named Elijah, a prophet of God, who sat alone on a mountain. The soldiers stood at the base, and their commander shouted 'Man of God! The king commands you to come down!' And this prophet, he looks down and says, 'If I am a man of God, let fire come down and consume you and your men.' Fifty men burned alive in an instant. Undeterred, the evil king sent fifty more to the mountain, and their commander yelled, 'Man of God! The king orders you to come down!' And Elijah spoke again, and fire came down on those fifty men as well. That kind of power, Chess.... Greatness that's hard to even fathom. One hundred men, soldiers, hunters, all dead from a few spoken words." Cougar had to pause, shaking his head admiringly, but giving a derisive laugh. "Elijah didn't appreciate what he had."

"You don't believe that story," Wolf said.

Cougar was still shaking his head. "Not a word of it."

Wolf had been slowly approaching, and now stood only ten feet away, the gun in his hand still unraised. He lowered himself very carefully until he was hunkered down by the gaping head of the dead beast, staring into its throat.

"Ugly, isn't it?" Cougar remarked.

"I want your knife," Wolf said. "I think it's beautiful."

"A reptilian wolf," Cougar chuckled, obligingly handing the knife, hilt first, to Wolf. "*Lupus reptilis.* Hanley fought well. You wish to honour his memory, take his knife back to a place of memorial?"

"I respected you when you were dead." Wolf repeated his words from the last time he had hunted the man.

"And yet you respect Jesus, a man who just sat back and let Himself die. He did nothing, Chess."

"We all die, Vance. He had a better reason to."

"Do you think Jesus could have killed me?" Wolf knew that no one except Cougar could have asked a question like that with a straight face.

Wolf shook his head. "No."

"Did you just limit your God?"

"No."

"Carpenters in Israel would have been stonemasons as much as woodcarvers. He would have had both strength and precision, not to mention a supposed supernatural side."

"Killing you for sport. He wouldn't do that."

"But you can," Cougar reminded him. "Or can you?"

"This isn't a game."

"What is it, Wolf? Huh?" Cougar was turning red. "What is it? The job? Revenge? Justice? Duty? *Protection?* You tell me what killing really is!"

"It's my gift," Wolf said, standing. "It's what I'm good at."

"Do you really believe that your God can use killers?" Cougar said, disgusted. "Do you really believe that? Don't ever speak to me about evil and delusion. I kept track, too. Not to the point of collecting dog tags, but I kept track. Counting seven hunters, I have killed ninety-three people. You've killed one hundred thirty-seven. Is that what a man of God is supposed to do?"

Wolf said nothing.

"Answer me!" Cougar roared, rising to his feet.

"The evil king sent fifty more men," Wolf spoke coldly. "Arriving at the mountain, their commander fell to his knees at Elijah's feet, and pleaded, 'Man of God, be merciful to me and my men.' And Elijah spared the lives of those fifty men, and came down peacefully to the evil king. It's Second Kings."

"Don't talk to me about mercy, Chess. The lack of that, and love, was what really convinced me that there is no God. If He had created them, they'd be real, and they'd be there, and we'd *know it!*"

"Careful, Vance. You sound like you want to believe in something."

"We add or subtract! We only hurt ourselves with the things we dream up!"

"Good and evil do exist, Vance. And they can't be dreamt up. Someone had to create them, and give them to us. If there is no God ... then there's no point."

"That is the point! THERE IS NO POINT!"

412

"You're dying. Accept something better than that before it happens."

"You're not going to let me know, are you? You're going to stand out of range, and kill me with a three hundred-year-old weapon."

"Suck it up, cowboy. It's just math, right?"

"So why didn't you shoot me on sight? You're that smart. Did you miss me?"

Wolf had to give a grim shrug. "Figured I'd let you see it coming."

"You ... *owed me* ... that?" Cougar almost cringed.

"Death has to be personal. It's the one thing we don't come back from. When it's real."

Cougar grinned. "Two in the chest, one in the head. You wanted to die on the 3-6-5."

"I wouldn't waste three bullets on you."

"There was no one to come back to. No Rachel, no life. The 7-3-0. Chester Wolf, the deadliest man alive. Was it worth it?"

Wolf nodded. "Every second."

"For you, or the country?"

"Me."

"It's not like you to stall, Chess. Can you shoot me, or not?"

Wolf raised the gun in both hands, leveling it between Cougar's eyes.

"Tell me about Jeffrey," he said.

Cougar's unguarded flinch was all the response Wolf needed. Cougar had to swallow hard before replying, and his voice was shaky.

"Chess ... if you know his name, you already know."

"Nine years old. Killed by the Bloodline, two months after you smuggled yourselves in from the Home Base. Random shooting, Toronto Exodus. Tell me why."

"Why I'd ever join the cause that killed the only family I had left?" Cougar ventured. "Because that was my final proof that I was right."

"Life is math," Wolf translated.

"Exactly. So kill me right now, and I'll know that I'm greater than you. Your fear proves it."

"I'm not subtracting you," Wolf said. "I'm sending you to hell. Make a choice, fast."

They faced each other in silence for a moment, and then the forest erupted with the roar of gunfire. Cougar flinched, but did not die. Wolf had not opened fire. The shooting was coming from several kilometers away.

Chapter Fifty-Two

March 4, 2191.
Polar coastline,
The Desert.

It was the first time that Ridgely Falcon had ever walked into an ambush. There were times later when he would wish that it had succeeded in killing him. That way, he never would have had to live with the memories of it.

Lewis had been pointing a finger toward the coastline as it appeared through the shallow draw before them. As she said, "There's the rafts," the forest seemed to explode with muzzle flashes and the roar of gunfire. Lewis was contorted from head to toe as bullets slammed into her from every side. Her armored vest could not stop the rounds that punched under her arm and into her thigh, or the single bullet that blew right through her neck.

"*Ambush!*" Falcon bellowed, looping an arm around Kressel's throat and using him as a shield. Stepping back, Falcon slammed himself against the partial protection of the nearest tree. Ustaf was rolling for cover behind a fallen trunk.

With a look of shock frozen on her face, and her outstretched finger still pointing toward the water, Lewis fell on her face, and did not move again.

"Lewis!" Ustaf roared, firing a burst from his C-7 rifle up the west bank. A hail of automatic fire was the only reply he received. Falcon could hear Ustaf cursing as bullets thudded into the forest from all around them.

"Stay down!" Falcon barked, firing his shotgun with his free hand, the powerful muscles in his wrist and forearm little match for the recoil of the 10-gage. He could see faces behind the muzzle flashes now, and most of them were those of Heir Defenders.

"Ustaf, two o'clock!" Falcon snapped. Ustaf popped up once more, sending another three rounds up the hill. Heir Defender John Taufield caught all three of them in the chest.

"Move in!" Bloodline Captain Garrett Baxter was screaming as he began serpentining down the bank, spraying wildly with his own C-7. Bracing against the recoil, Falcon fired again, and the slug blasted straight through Baxter's heart. He fell, but more Heir Defenders were closing in, keeping up a deadly cover fire. Falcon could count six.

Making every shot count, Ustaf flipped his rifle fire-setting to single shot, double tapping two more Defenders between the eyes in as many seconds. Another volley forced him to duck and cover.

"Getting pinned, sir!" he shouted, slapping in a fresh magazine.

Falcon turned the shotgun on Kressel, pressing the wide muzzle under The Heir's jaw, while pulling his head back by his hair. Kressel grimaced against the pain.

"Talk to them, General," Falcon rasped. "Talk to them now!"

"This is Kressel!" the Bloodline general yelled, wincing. "Hold your fire!"

"Ceasefire!" Colonel Milo Curtis barked. "Ceasefire! They have the general!"

"And I will send a 10-gage slug out the top of his skull if you don't drop your weapons!" Falcon snarled.

"Drop them now!" Ustaf shouted, still crouched behind the log.

"Send the general over to me," Curtis countered, never lowering his C-9 machine gun. "You keep your weapons, and we leave you in this nice forest. It's a fair deal."

"I'm doing the banishing here!" Falcon growled.

"Aren't you curious about the rest of your crew?" Curtis inquired innocently.

"They're dead," Falcon snapped. "Otherwise, you would be."

"I know that many consider negotiating to be a weakness," Curtis observed, "but I understand the value of bargaining chips. Your crew is alive."

"Prove it!" Falcon ordered. "I want proof of life, right now!"

"Regretfully, your man Cardinal did not survive once our mag-seals failed again," Curtis said empathetically. "But that pretty little co-pilot.... Now, that's a flower I could not bring myself to quash. *Flaxton!*"

417

Falcon could not prevent the blood from leaving his face. He felt cold and sick.

Flaxton's fingerless right hand was swathed in a bloody bandage, and his left leg was in a splint, but he could still hold a Glock pistol with his left hand. The muzzle was pressed hard into Arnett's left temple as the two of them limped over the east bank. Arnett was bound with rope, but seemed unharmed.

"Lovely," Curtis murmured, looking at Arnett admiringly. "I understand you two were quite close, Captain Falcon. Your star pupil, a pilot whose skills rivaled your own. You must have had quite a connection. Or ... was it something more?"

Falcon could not speak.

"You know what Robert Flaxton is capable of, even in the state he's in," Curtis reminded him. "You know better than most. Your sister found out. Would you like Lieutenant Arnett to find out?"

"Damn you," Falcon said, his voice barely able to rise above a whisper. Flaxton was grinning broadly, even with his grotesquely punctured cheek.

"Decide, Captain," Curtis urged him calmly. "Think of what I'm offering. Even on The Desert, a forest supplies food, shelter, clothing, and you will keep all your gear, weapons, and the lives of your friends." He shrugged. "We just want to go home. You decide."

"Don't do it, Ridge!" Arnett screamed. *"Don't let them go back!"*

"You're not dooming the country you love," Curtis said soothingly. "You know how slim our chances of survival are, with our depleted forces, and devastated strongholds. We will not last long, and your people will send a rescue mission for you very soon. You handled the 3-6-5. What's a few more months in the woods? Think of it. Your crew safe, your woman by your side. Just let us go home. We just want to go home."

Falcon swallowed hard, the sweat from his brow making him blink.

"Ustaf?"

"Sir?"

Falcon's voice was unflinching.

"Flaxton dies first, if anyone twitches. Understood?"

Ustaf nodded, smiling slightly as he lined his gunsights on Flaxton's forehead. "Aye, sir."

"Ridge," Arnett pleaded. "Don't do it!"

"They just want to go home, Jess," Falcon sighed. "Let her go."

"The general first," Curtis gently replied.

"The general gets his head blown off if she's not beside me in ten seconds!" Falcon bellowed. "Non-negotiable! Ten! Nine! Eight...!"

"Flaxton, let her go!" Curtis said sharply.

Flaxton looked disappointed, spitting blood into the dirt.

"Now!" Curtis roared, turning the C-9 toward the Heir Defenders Commander.

With a few muttered curses, Flaxton released the bonds, the ropes dropping around Arnett's ankles. Flaxton gave her a rough shove to get her moving.

Curtis now had his light machine gun trained on Arnett as she hurried forward.

"Arnett dies first," he said wryly, glancing at Falcon. "If anyone twitches. Understood?"

419

Falcon nodded slowly. "Perfectly."

Arnett was walking cautiously past the remaining rifles. Falcon could see that she was quaking, but he could not let that distract him. He had to be prepared to kill Kressel. First Kressel, then Curtis, and then whatever ammo he had left was going to make sure that Robert Flaxton was dead. Ustaf would have to handle the three remaining Defenders.

"Get behind me, Jess," Falcon said quietly. "Just keep walking to me."

"Don't try to even the odds, Captain," Curtis warned him. "Arnett doesn't touch a weapon until we're gone."

"Shut up, Curtis," Falcon shot back, as Arnett timidly passed by him. "Take your general and go." He used the shotgun barrel to nudge Kressel forward. The Heir hurried over to embrace Curtis, who warmly returned the hug.

"Welcome back, General," Curtis whispered, almost tearfully. "You swore The Mountain would not die."

"As long as there is an Heir, it never will," Kressel assured him.

"Forgive me, sir," Curtis sighed. "I had nearly lost hope."

Kressel stepped back and placed his hands on the colonel's shoulders.

"It is all right, my friend," he said kindly. "Hope is a pursuit of mist, trying to catch it in your hand. We deal with the now."

Falcon stiffened. The world around him seemed to freeze. A million puzzle pieces connected instantly in his mind.

"What ... what did you just say?"

Before Kressel could even think about replying, Falcon and Arnett were both moving. Arnett had been raising a concealed pistol behind him when Falcon spun around with the shotgun, and the two of them were suddenly staring down gun barrels at each other.

"Ustaf, cover Kressel!" Falcon roared. "Drop it, Jess!"

"Drop it yourself!" Arnett snarled.

"Arnett, what are you *doing?!*" Ustaf said, shocked.

"*Cover Kressel!*" Falcon yelled. Every Bloodline weapon was now trained on him. Ustaf quickly shifted his gunsights from Flaxton to The Heir.

Falcon had never seen such fires of hatred in Arnett's eyes.

"Drop the shotgun, Captain Falcon!" she seethed. "Do it now!"

"What's going on?!" Ustaf shouted, perplexed.

"I die, Kressel dies!" Falcon reminded the Bloodline around him. Glaring at Arnett, he said, "Curtis must be one amazing interrogator. To have the information about us that he does, without leaving a scratch on you! The mag-seals did not fail!"

Arnett actually smiled.

"I did tell you," she said sweetly. "I told you my uncle was at Yellowknife the day it was taken. I never said which side."

"The EMP wasn't on a timer, was it, Jess?" Falcon asked coldly. "You killed Cardinal!"

"Captain Falcon, drop that weapon now!" Kressel shouted.

"Don't move, Kressel!" Ustaf growled ominously.

421

"I trusted you!" Falcon snarled at Arnett, his face twisted with rage. "I loved you!"

"I still love you, Ridge!" she snapped. "So don't make me kill you!"

"I'm taking you with me," Falcon warned her.

Arnett smirked. "Sounds romantic."

"How long, Jess? How long did you have to sleep?"

She snorted at that. "How long have I been the only niece of Cole Dallas Kressel?"

"Captain Falcon, you are outnumbered, outgunned, and flanked," Curtis remarked sourly. "Commander Flaxton and Defender Peterson have you sighted in from an elevated position. Once that first shot goes off, you lose all options. Think about that!"

"Once that first shot goes off, you lose everyone who knows how to fly an Orbit Runner," Ustaf shot back. "Think about that! We all lose after that first shot. Who here wants to lose? How about you, General? You want to watch your niece die? The first shot. Someone take the first shot!"

Two of the remaining Defenders, Peterson and Francis, were exchanging nervous glances. Ustaf knew that was a good thing. It meant they were listening.

"*Someone take the first shot!*" he roared again. Even Arnett flinched.

Ustaf slowly shook his head, standing from behind the log. "That's where we are, General Kressel. We all have to die ... but no one wants to right now. You tell me where it ends, General. These men live and die for you, and I respect you for that. But you have to tell them where it ends, because they'll never learn otherwise. Tell them, General. I think they want to hear it from you."

No one could answer. No one moved.

"We live and die at the snap of a twig," Ustaf said. "Are you going to snap it, or should I?"

Falcon and Arnett were still unflinching in their burning stares at each other, but the rest of the Bloodline was clearly uncomfortable. They were losing what initiative they had left.

"I hate indecision," Ustaf said calmly. "The war is over."

His left hand opened, releasing the forestock of his rifle, as well as the single localized seismic charge he had concealed in his palm. It fell into the dirt at his feet with a dull thud. Now, even Falcon and Arnett turned to look at it.

"Ripple," Ustaf announced. "Fifty meters. Fifteen seconds."

After that, it was a race, everyone for themselves, but Ustaf had no intention of leaving Lewis behind.

Unfortunately for Robert Flaxton, he was in no shape to run. Even borne down by the weight of Lewis's body over his shoulders, Ustaf easily passed the desperate-eyed Heir Defenders Commander, as he frantically tried to limp out of range. Ustaf did not know if he could get out of range in time, but he knew with grim certainty that Robert Flaxton could not.

Flaxton's dying scream deafened Ustaf, as the ripple's shockwave bowled him head over heels, rolling him over Lewis's limp form in the dirt.

Silence followed, then a rain of dust, and then blackness.

Chapter Fifty-Three

March 4, 2191.
1 km south of polar coastline,
Polar Forest,
The Desert.

"That sounded like an ending of some sort," Cougar commented, as the distinctively hollow echo of the ripple blast faded through the trees.

Wolf stared silently to the east, seeing a world of forest between himself and the crew he had come here to save. Those three kilometers might as well have been a towering wall of concrete and razor wire. His friends lives were in God's hands now, and Wolf felt as though he had failed for the last time.

"Chess, I said that was an ending. What do you think?"

"War," Wolf replied, fully aware that his back was turned on Cougar.

"How many of you are dead already?" Cougar wondered. "You might be alone. Your ship might be destroyed, your crew dead. What do you have left? Maybe you are a lone wolf, finally. You need your own world, I think. I think you'd be happier if you were left here. Society itself bothers you."

"I shouldn't be happy here," Wolf admitted. "But it's familiar."

"Familiar?"

"Comfortable."

"I understand," Cougar nodded. "Now kill me."

"You know I don't want to," Wolf said.

Cougar laughed. "Do you know what a mistake it is to tell a target that?"

Wolf shook his head. "You're not an enemy."

"I thought it had to be personal."

"It would have been personal if you were my friend," Wolf said. "You're just flesh and blood to me."

Cougar was moving before the sentence was finished, and there was a rage in his eyes that Wolf had never seen before. Wolf could hit a moving target with ease, but he held his fire as Cougar made a lightning fast sidestep, knocking the gun aside.

A moment later, Cougar was backed against a tree, and Wolf's knife was pressed to his throat, the 1911 back in its holster.

Cougar swallowed hard, not daring to make any move larger than that. He knew it with certainty this time. He had been hunted.

Wolf's hand did not move. Wolf did not move. A silence flooded the forest, and time crept like a glacier.

"Kill me, brother," Cougar whispered the words, staring into Wolf's steel eyes. "Kill me, man of God."

For a moment, Cougar thought that he was dead. The entire world that he could see, Wolf included, seemed to have been chiseled from a block of ice.

Time was frozen, and so was everything else. However, Cougar could still blink, and a light breeze in his eyes made him want to blink. Dead men did not have such petty concerns.

Then Wolf blinked as well. That was all he did.

"What ... is this?"

Now Cougar's whisper sounded confused, but, in a strange way, delighted. Wolf still did not kill.

"Did the great Chester Wolf just hesitate?"

Wolf's hand wanted to shake. It took all of his strength to hold the knife steady and motionless.

"The deadliest man alive cannot kill me," Cougar realized, with no small amount of wonder. "Why would that be? By everything you believe, I'm more deserving of death than anyone else you know. You won't know, and I can't believe, so just end it now! My blood on your chrystanium. Blood solves everything, right? You told me that! That's what victory smells like.

"You tell me about belief, but I don't think you even know what you believe. Tell me, Chess. You came to hunt me and kill me, and you can't do it. Eternal damnation? Is that what you're afraid of? You can't justify this one. Wolf, you've lived in hell all your life. This should not scare you now. Can it be any worse than what you've always been?"

Cougar smiled. Again, Wolf only blinked.

"Speak," Cougar said.

Wolf's reply was slow and quiet.

"I am a man of God. And I was your brother. And your life ... is not worth the time it would take to clean the blood off my knife."

His knife was back in its sheath a moment later, and the pistol was in his hand, not pointed at Cougar's face or chest, but held out to him, grip first, as a gift.

Cougar was so unprepared that at first he made no move to claim the weapon.

"You don't want it?" Wolf said, raising an eyebrow. "Hmm? Neither do I."

The .45 dropped into the sand at Cougar's feet. Wolf stepped back, studying the confused eyes of a man whom he could not even look on as an enemy.

"Vance, you're probably going to hell no matter what I do, so I won't rush that. Your fate is your choice, and it's a choice you've made, whether you believe or not. I can't save you from that, but maybe you can save me from it. Man of God, or murderer. That's the only thing I need to know, and only God can tell me, because I just don't know. You know what the limit of a good man is? Mine was one hundred thirty-seven. Pick up the gun."

"What?" Cougar still could not understand.

"Pick it up," Wolf said, placing his hands on his head as he sank to his knees. "I'm done."

Cougar was beginning to turn red in the face once more.

"You'd just sit back and let me kill you? Just like that?"

"My soul's all I have left, Vance. It's more than I'm willing to risk."

"What about your friends? What if they still need you?"

Wolf just shook his head. "I don't kill people anymore."

"Wolf, stand up."

"No."

"Stand up, Chess!" Cougar stooped to snatch the fallen pistol. "Stand up, now!"

"I can't."

"Chess, stand up!"

"Jesus loves you, Vance."

"Get up!"

"I have done all the good, and all the harm, that I care to do. There's nothing left for me in this life."

"This life?" Cougar demanded. *"This life?* What if there is no other life? What then? What if this is just the end? *You ... don't ... know!"*

"Vance," Wolf sighed. "Please just accept one thing. You can't know anything if you don't believe it first. Belief and faith aren't weakness. They're step one."

"What kind of soldier are you?!" Cougar screamed, pressing the gun barrel into Wolf's left eye.

"We're hunters. I haven't been a soldier in a long time. That's not the job."

"Forgive me, Chess," Cougar muttered. "I was wrong. Your number is so far from one.... I don't know how I could have ever made a mistake like that. You are the one who is not worth killing! You're a weak child, and I execute you like the coward you have become!"

Wolf did not close his eyes as Cougar pressed the muzzle between them. There was a resounding click as the trigger was pulled, and the hammer fell on a faulty primer.

Now, Cougar was the one who could not hold himself steady any longer. His hand trembled violently as he lowered the gun. Wolf's eyes were still unblinking, and Cougar could not look into them. Cougar's mouth was dry, while sweat trickled into his eyes from his glistening brow.

"Swear to your God that you tell me the truth, Wolf," Cougar quavered.

Wolf nodded. "My yes is yes."

"In all your years of hunting with this weapon ... has it ever misfired?"

"No," Wolf said simply.

"Speak!" Cougar yelled. *"Tell me what it all means!"*

He never saw Wolf moving until an iron fist slammed into his left eye. Cougar landed hard on his back, and Wolf's moccasin was grinding into his throat before he could even catch his breath. Wolf held the pistol once more, but was putting it back in its holster. Cougar gurgled, unable to inhale.

"Speak!" he managed to wheeze, his eyes tearing. "Speak!"

Wolf dropped a knee onto Cougar's chest, seized the downed man by the collar, and immediately began raining blows with his free hand. Seven times Wolf's fist slammed into Cougar's face, smashing his nose and lips. Blood spattered onto both men until Wolf stayed his hand after the seventh strike.

Cougar weakly spat blood, coughing raggedly.

"Speak," he moaned, tears flowing from his eyes like the blood from his nostrils.

"Speak?" Wolf rasped, yanking Cougar to his feet. *"Speak?!"*

He drove his left palm across the side of Cougar's face, snapping his head to one side, and sending him crashing to the ground once more. Cougar could barely roll over to look up at Wolf. His head was swimming, and blood now flowed from his left eyebrow, blurring his vision and burning his eye.

"Speak?" Wolf mused, smiling. "There's a time for speaking. For all things, there is a season."

He lashed out with his right foot, kicking Cougar in the face as he tried to stand up. Wolf was not smiling now.

"Stand up, Vance." Wolf took a couple of steps back. "There's a time."

* * *

Ridgely Falcon could not stand, feeling the residual aftershock sensation of being too close to a ripple detonation, his extremities numb and tingling. Arnett lay eight feet away from him, moaning. He could not see anyone else, and he could not even begin to stand. He threw up when he tried to rise, nausea overwhelming him, but the only thought in his mind was that he had to kill Arnett, fast.

Arnett still held her hideout pistol, and Falcon's shotgun was in reach, but his numb hand was too weak to raise it. Gritting his teeth, he fiercely clenched and unclenched his hands, trying to renew the circulation. He still could not rise, his cheek pressed into the puddle of his own vomit.

"Don't do it, Ridge," Arnett muttered, wincing against her own nausea. Her pistol had been pointed away from Falcon, but was now sliding slowly over the sand toward him. It was an Old West shootout, a quick-draw in slow motion, and both gunslingers were barely able to move.

"It doesn't have to end here," Arnett insisted, weakly raising her head.

"Drop the gun, and I'll bring you home alive," Falcon countered wearily, still trying to move the lead weight that his shotgun had turned into.

"I still love you, Ridge," Arnett said emphatically, her pistol now pointed straight in his face. "Or you'd be dead."

Falcon sighed, releasing the weapon he could not even raise.

"What do you want, Jess?"

"What every woman wants to give the man she loves. The world. And I am one of the few who can do it in the literal sense. Just come back with me."

Falcon's eyes closed. He felt like he was being pulled into the merciful embrace of sleep, but he had to fight it.

"You're a murderer."

"Who isn't?" Arnett murmured, squinting hard, trying to keep her own bleary eyes focused. "TAP. Snipers. Covert ops. Come back with me."

Falcon shook his head. "Jess, you live your shades of grey. I have to stay in black and white."

Arnett managed to groggily rise to her knees, crawling over to pull Falcon's shotgun to her side.

"You have the option of life, Ridge. Stand up."

* * *

It is both an awing and a terrifying thing when two warriors, equal in might and skill, finally go to war with one another. Wars are terrifying for an army when it is sent into battle against an obviously larger or better army, but the truest terror, the one that is shared equally amongst both sides, is felt when the two armies are identical, and they both know it. Such was the fear and drive of Wolf and Cougar.

It is difficult to describe Wolf's final war. He was moving faster, and hitting harder, and inflicting more pain, and receiving more pain than he ever had in his life. Cougar was a mirror image, matching Wolf blow for blow, and block for block. Wolf's Colt was in the holster, his knife was on his arm, and Hanley's knife was in his belt, but neither man even considered reaching for these easily accessible weapons. They were killing each other, using only the weapons that they were.

There was no time for debate, or banter, or even goodbyes. Both men had more to say to the other, more refutes and persuasion, but both were fully aware that the time for words had passed, and it was truly a time to kill.

For the first two minutes, not a single blow landed where it was intended. The other man was always too quick for those killing or crippling strokes to meet their objectives. It was a shadowboxing match, every swing and stroke met by an opposing counterpart. Cougar's fist would be deflected by Wolf's forearm, and Wolf's upthrust palm would simultaneously be knocked aside by Cougar's blocking elbow. It was a rapid-fire war of hands, and their feet scarcely shifted weight. Anyone watching from a distance would have supposed that the two men standing in the center of the clearing were motionless, simply speaking to one another.

The balance was shattered when Wolf caught Cougar's right jab under his armpit, quickly tying Cougar's right arm with his left, and then hammering four right hooks into the side of Cougar's face, smashing the taller man's left eye socket. Blood and pained tears flooded Cougar's left eye, partially blinding him. Unable to throw a punch, he thrust his knee up, aiming for Wolf's groin, but Wolf saw it coming and twisted away, taking the brunt of the knee in his hipbone. He had to step back to keep his footing, wincing from the pain, and Cougar also stumbled back, both men trying to get a few deep breaths before the next bout.

"God doesn't hate you," Wolf had to whisper, breathlessly.

A second later, Cougar hit him with a flying tackle around the waist. Wolf threw his weight forward and lifted his feet, driving Cougar to the ground, rather than letting himself be landed on. Wolf was kneeling on Cougar's prone form, driving his fists into Vance's kidneys. Cougar screamed, but managed to plant one palm in the soil and heave his right shoulder up, toppling Wolf off him. Wolf hit the dirt rolling, and came up into a crouch, facing Cougar as the taller man lunged to his feet.

"You didn't go for the neck, Chess. It was over. Quit hesitating!"

For a man with a notable limp, Wolf had no trouble in putting his moccasin into Cougar's teeth, breaking off an upper incisor. Cougar caught the foot, a second too late to save his tooth, but not too late to drive an elbow into Wolf's previously injured left knee, snapping his leg. With a pained cry, Wolf fell to the ground. When he tried to rise, Cougar lashed out with a kick of his own. It slammed into the side of Wolf's head, and he could see nothing but points of light as he was spun around and collapsed onto his face. The dust choked him, but all he could do was lie and cough.

* * *

Robert Flaxton had been reduced to dust by the seismic charge. Everyone else had escaped the tightly-reined blast radius, but none of them had gotten far enough out of range to avoid the residual effects. All of the Bloodline men who tried to rise to their feet were shaky and lightheaded, but they managed to find their footing within a few minutes of the detonation. Arnett had a weary gun-hand pointed steadfastly at Falcon, gesturing for him to march forward. The only forms who were not moving wore CNE uniforms.

Ustaf had only managed to carry Lewis's body about ten feet outside the blast, and had received the full force of the outershock. He lay on top of Lewis in a near-convulsatory state, his head and limbs twitching uncontrollably.

"Ustaf!" Falcon yelled, running shakily to his fallen crew.

"Slow down, Ridge!" Arnett snarled. "Option of life."

Falcon knew better than to do anything rash, and Ustaf's rifle had been blown far beyond his reach, anyway. His only concern was for the young soldier's life.

"Amed," he whispered, rolling the quivering body onto his back.

Ustaf's eyes were open, but lolling back and forth, unable to focus.

"Lie still, don't fight it," Falcon ordered sharply, praying that Ustaf could understand him. "Let it pass. You'll die if you fight it. *Lie still!*"

Ustaf was trying to speak, his tongue humming and hissing against the backside of clenched teeth.

"Don't talk, either!" Falcon snapped. "That's an order! You will lie still, and you will live!"

"Sir, let me kill them," Curtis requested, trying to steady the light machine gun in his quaking hands, as he and the remaining Bloodline approached their kneeling enemy.

"No," Kressel rasped, coughing. "Hunter hostages may prove valuable."

"*Get out of here!*" Falcon roared. "You have your guns, and you have the ship. Get out of here, and take over the world! *Go!*"

"You come, or you both die!" Arnett hissed.

"I don't leave without him," Falcon shot back. "He should be stable enough to move in five or ten minutes. You can wait that long."

"No, we can't," Arnett replied. "While your heart has been diverting your senses, I have been using my ears."

"So have I," Falcon muttered. "They're getting closer. I know."

"We have two minutes, not five," Arnett pointed out crossly. "I've never liked being chewed."

"What are you talking about?" Defender Peterson demanded. *"What are you talking about?"*

"Monsters," Falcon said, putting a cushioning hand under Ustaf's twitching head. The convulsions were slower now, but still troubling. Falcon had rarely felt so useless.

"Monsters? What monsters?!" Peterson was getting panicky, and Falcon was still focused enough to note the importance of that.

"Did you really think a forest wouldn't have monsters?" Arnett snapped. "All forests have monsters!"

"Reptilian," Falcon said. "Best guess, anyway. Quadruped. One thousand to fifteen hundred pounds. Claws, fangs, attacks without provocation, soaks up slugs like birdshot. Can bound away at speeds in excess of one hundred kilometers per hour, leaves cheetahs in the dust. And I don't know why they're after us, but they're coming at us from three sides."

As if in response, a single growl rumbled through the draw. There was no more time.

"Jess, let's get him up," Falcon ordered, raising Ustaf's arm around his neck. Arnett surprised herself by obeying without pause, helping Falcon to lift the unconscious soldier.

"Fall back to the rafts!" Arnett shouted.

No one moved.

Lifting her eyes, Arnett's breath caught in her throat. The reptilis' had appeared from nowhere, without sound or even noticeable movement. More than fifty of the silent, leathery beasts stood frozen in a horseshoe pattern around the humans, less than one hundred meters away.

"General...." Curtis said shakily, raising his weapon.

"Where is Powers?" Kressel ordered sharply.

"Onboard," Curtis answered. "With the remaining Defenders."

"Where is Wolf?" Arnett growled.

"Run!" Falcon barked.

As one body, man and beast began their dash for the coastline, but it was clear which species had the advantage of velocity.

* * *

"Turn around, Wolf!"

Wolf lay motionless on his face, his poncho cloak spread over his still body, his left leg at a bizarre angle below the knee. Cougar had his hands on his knees, sucking reviving oxygen into his lungs, sweat rolling down his face.

"Chess, you look at me!" he shouted breathlessly. "You're not dead yet!"

Wolf never flinched.

Cougar drove a foot three times into Wolf's ribs, cracking two of them. Wolf still lay, as though dead.

"You're not worth my time, Wolf! You don't deserve to be killed by me!" Cougar gave the prone figure one more boot, then bent over to draw the 1911 out of its holster.

"I do this with your own weapon," he rasped, ejecting the dead bullet, and watching a fresh brass enter the chamber. "Is that how you really want it?"

Wolf still gave no response. The breeze rustled the hem of his poncho, but the man beneath it never moved.

"Wolf, you turn around *now!*"

* * *

Defender Carl Martins had been firing his C-7, attempting to cover their retreat, but he was almost instantly run down by the stampeding reptilis'. Falcon heard him give just one short cry as the beasts pounced on him.

"Don't shoot, just run!" Arnett screamed, carrying Ustaf between herself and Falcon. The stunned soldier was trying to raise his head.

"Lewis...." he moaned.

"She's dead," Falcon said grimly. "Be still."

Curtis and Kressel reached the two rafts first, the Bloodline Colonel pushing his general in ahead of himself, while Peterson sprayed his rifle into the herd. One reptilis went down in a cloud of dust, two bullets in its leathery skull.

"Come on!" Peterson shouted at Arnett and Falcon. "Move!"

Unable to be concerned with Ustaf's safety, Falcon thrust him bodily into the raft. Defender Francis caught him and pulled the body to the stern, while Arnett and Falcon bounded into the second raft, shoving off from the shore in one motion. Arnett did not even object when Falcon snatched the Glock from her belt and began firing from the bow. Another reptilis fell as Arnett and Peterson seized the oars and began furiously rowing. The rafts launched out into the lake, but not before a reptilis bounded across the expanse of water and closed its jaws over Francis' upper arm and shoulder, pulling the Heir Defender overboard. Curtis fired the machine gun into the beast, but it was too late. The bodies of the man and beast were left floating in their wake, turning the blue water to crimson.

Just before the forest draw vanished from his sight, Falcon caught one last glimpse of Lewis, as a lone reptilis took her foot in its mouth and dragged her body into the trees. With an enraged bellow, Falcon hurled the empty Glock back to the shore. It clattered harmlessly off the snout of a reptilis, which pawed angrily at the shoreline, slapping the water with its massive talons.

"Sit down, Ridge," Arnett ordered. "We're going home, babe."

Falcon still had his knife on his belt, and Arnett knew it. She also knew that, for Ustaf's sake, he would not even attempt to use it.

* * *

"Look at me!" Cougar shouted, the pistol in his hands, aimed at the back of Wolf's head. "See it coming! *Know it!*"

Giving into his frustration, he bent over and grabbed the back of Wolf's neck through the hood.

"*Please, Wolf!*" Cougar's desperation filled every word of his scream. "*YOU NEED TO SEE IT COMING!*"

He heaved on the collar of the poncho. Wolf was rolled over onto his back, and, too late, Cougar saw the rock clenched in his fist.

The stone smashed into the side of Cougar's head, fracturing his skull. Before he could even stumble back, Wolf made one final lunge to his feet, a knife in each hand. Hanley's knife struck Cougar's upper left bicep, piercing his brachial artery, while Wolf's own knife slashed through the femoral artery of Cougar's right thigh. Just as quickly, Wolf's broken left leg gave out under him, and both men fell to the forest floor. Wolf broke his fall with his palms, but Cougar landed hard against the base of a tree, half-sitting in stunned silence as he watched the blood running from his arm and thigh, and feeling it trickling down his forehead. His lips parted, but he did not speak.

Groaning from the now fiery pain in his leg, Wolf pushed himself up on his palms, drawing his good leg under himself until he could kneel on it. His eyes met Cougar's, and they looked at each other without malice, without fear.

Wolf's head was heavy, but he had to say something. When he did, he could only whisper.

"One question, Vance. That's all you've got."

Cougar blinked, and swallowed hard. There were tears in his eyes as the 1911 slipped from his quivering fingers.

"Why doesn't He just show Himself?" he whispered back. "Why?"

Wolf let out a long breath, and then shook his head.

"Because He has no use for robots," he said.

Cougar's eyes were confused for just a second, but then they slid shut, and did not open again.

"I don't know, Wolf," he quietly admitted. "I just don't know...."

His head slowly fell forward, and his chin rested on his chest.

"I do know," Wolf said. "Just this once."

Cougar made no reply. The blood had pooled all around him, and was seeping into the sandy soil.

"Vance?"

Even Cougar's chest was no longer rising and falling with life's breath. His skin was ghostly, all but drained of blood.

"Vance?" Wolf's voice was louder, and strained. He planted his hands in the earth and began tediously dragging himself to Cougar's side, wincing as the dirt was ground into the open wound on his leg, which had been ripped by the broken bone upon his fatal lunge at Cougar.

"Vance, can you hear me? He can still hear you!"

His arms buckled as he came near Cougar's body, but he mustered his strength to reach up and place a hand on the neck of the motionless hunter. The skin was cold, and no flicker of a pulse could be felt through it. Wolf's teeth gritted, his hand sliding down from the neck to the blue coverall collar. Taking a fistful of the shirt, he gave the body a single hard shake, Cougar's head bobbing involuntarily.

"Tell Him!" Wolf growled, his eyes misting. "You're not a number, Vance Cougar! Not again! Never again!"

441

Cougar's only reply was a lolling of his head to one side, as a result of the shaking.

"*VANCE!*" Wolf bellowed.

Wolf was emotional, distracted, and talking to himself. Even so, he was fully aware of his surroundings. He knew that eight of the reptilis creatures had materialized from the shadows all around him, and were forming a near-perfect circular perimeter, with him as the radial point. Undeterred, he kept talking, even as he carefully cleaned Vance's blood off the blades of both chrystanium knives with the hem of his poncho before sheathing them.

"Vance, try. Hear me."

He gently lifted the 1911 from Cougar's clammy fingers.

"Talk to Him. It's not too late. Just tell Him you're sorry. Never too late. Please. One thirty-eight is too much."

He used what strength he had left to pull Cougar into his lap, shielding the blood-soaked torso with his arms.

A single reptilis, considerably larger than the others, had broken from the ring, and was creeping toward Wolf, its movements stealthy and silent, almost as though it was floating, drawn to the injured man who faced it without fear in his grey eyes.

Wolf never broke eye contact with the beast's emerald green eyes as he gave a slight shake of his head.

"You're not touching him," he said quietly.

The gliding reptilis was very close, and its thick, scaly nostrils were quivering, sniffing the strange scents of Wolf and Cougar as it drew ever nearer. There was blood on its jowls. Somehow, Wolf knew that it was human blood. He raised the 1911, lining the sights on the flat, leathery gap between the green eyes.

That was when he heard a voice inside of himself, whether his own or someone else's he could not tell. But the voice was very, very quiet.

Let it go.

Wolf blinked, his right forefinger taking up the trigger slack. He knew that he could kill six of them with the pistol, and then use the knives on the last two. He was that good at killing, and he knew it.

Just let it go.

Wolf's hand did not shake, and he had enough strength left to fight. He did not know why he lowered the gun. The reptilis had stopped with its face less than a foot away from his own.

Just trust Me.

Wolf could feel the beast's breath whistling against his face. The breath was not foul. It cooled his hot cheeks and sweaty brow. For some reason, that cooling sensation promised him that holstering his weapon would not lead him to any harm.

He realized that the creature in front of him was no greater a threat now than his own broken body. Only then did he notice how much blood was gushing from his leg. The creature became blurry as Wolf's eyes slowly lost their will to focus.

"Thanks be to God for this beautiful day," he said tiredly, leaning back against the tree, still holding Vance Cougar in his arms.

The last thing he felt was the beast's long, thick tongue as it began to tentatively lap at the blood flowing from his leg. Wolf's eyes closed, and he slept.

Chapter Fifty-Four

March 4, 2191.
Banishment One,
Polar Lake, near coastline,
The Desert.

"Appreciate me, Ridge," Arnett ordered, shoving Falcon to the floor of the prison bay, alongside Ustaf, who was still unable to rise. "You should be dead, but you're not. That was me. It was all me."

Falcon glared. "Where's Cardinal?"

"Dead," Arnett quipped. "Why do you care?"

"Because he's us."

"A body's a shell, Ridge. Sometimes, it's better to not have a memory of it as it is, only as it was. Hollow points don't do good things for the front when they go in the back."

It took every bit of willpower in Falcon to resist the urge to touch the hilt of his knife. Arnett smiled kindly at him.

"I don't doubt you, babe. I'm out of range, holding a hot projectile, standing on guard. Your years of experience still make me wary. Kill me, if that's what you really want."

"I do," Falcon replied, eyeing her strangely. "But I don't have to, do I? All I have to do ... is wait for you. What is in your heart, Jess? You want the world. You'll need every man for that. Every last man."

Arnett laughed. "Perhaps there's just one I no longer need. Pray it isn't you."

The crew quarters hatch opened, and Kressel stepped into the bay. Bourgeouis, Curtis, and the three remaining Defenders were behind him. The Bloodline general looked at the army that remained to him, six soldiers. It was not much to take on a planet, but Kressel would never cease to quest for that which he believed was rightfully his. Everyone on board the ship knew that, and none more so than Jessica Arnett, the only child of the brother whom Kressel had spent his entire life hiding the existence of.

"I always knew," Kressel said, his smile small and sad. "I knew that the Hidden Hunters would only be taken from the inside out. Well done, niece."

Arnett's smile was wide, and without any sadness.

"Uncle," she mused. "I was just talking about you."

Kressel's eyes scarcely had time to widen before the bullets began hammering into his chest. Six rounds exploded from the Glock in under two seconds, and the general took all of them before he could even fall. An eloquent man, who had still lived his life with action before words, died without any last words at all. Only his open eyes expressed dismay as his body hit the deck, with blood pooling beneath him.

Every other face had no trouble expressing their shock and horror, especially Major Bourgeouis, who tried to catch the general as he fell, then dropped to his knees next to his fallen commander.

Arnett still held the pistol, covering everyone in the room.

"As long as there is an Heir, the Bloodline lives," she stated, standing over her uncle's body. "We need young blood for the conquest to come. I don't have time for old men who won't be able to keep up! As your new Heir, I am going to take the Bloodline to places my uncle only dreamed of. We will go global, and we will not play to the pirate's rules."

Falcon still knelt beside Ustaf, but his hand slowly closed over his knife hilt once more. He knew that, after a lifetime of flawless integration, Arnett had just made her first mistake, within minutes of her unveiling. She had already become too complacent. Arnett did not see what Falcon could see coming as she continued speaking. It was a speech which she had been writing most of her life.

"We have to do things that hurt, and I just did. That's the only way to win, in a war where we are outnumbered so vastly. Loyalty is all we have left, to our cause, and to our new Heir. This is the day when each one of us must decide what we believe."

She turned to look down at Falcon and Ustaf. Her smile was gone.

"Tell me that you love me, Ridge," she whispered.

Falcon's face wore no expression, but he shook his head.

"I did," he said quietly. "You're the job now."

Arnett blinked back one tear, but could not keep the second and third from escaping.

"Men of the Bloodline," she quavered, her voice still strong. "Maybe I don't think as conservatively as my uncle did. I do not see any value in these prisoners, except target practice. As you served my uncle, so you will serve me now. Kill these pirates. Put their bodies at my feet."

No one moved behind her. Angered by the hesitation, Arnett raised her weapon over her head and fired a deafening round into the bay doors overhead.

"Serve me!" she roared.

Major Powers Bourgeouis had disarmed her a second later, seizing her pistol and twisting it out of her hand, the trigger guard snapping off her right forefinger as it was wrenched away. Arnett cried out as she doubled over, clutching her bleeding hand.

Bourgeouis now held the pistol, plucking Arnett's bloody finger from the guard and flipping it away. His eyes were filled with flame and water as he aligned the sights on Arnett's chest.

"I served a general!" he snarled.

Never one to be trigger happy, the major only fired once.

Falcon lunged to his feet and caught Arnett as her knees buckled and she slowly fell back, toppling into his arms with a bullet in her heart.

"Jess!" he cried, settling to the floor with her body in his lap.

Her eyes had been closed, but one slowly opened, looking at the hunter she loved for the final time.

"Ridge?" she whispered.

"Be still. Lie still," Falcon soothed her. "I'm going to take care of you. *Someone get me a kit!*"

Arnett's head was getting heavier against his shoulder, but she was still trying to talk.

"I guess ... this is why we work alone. Bad things happen when we're in the same room...."

"Don't talk, Jess. Just rest. *I need that kit!*"

Bourgeouis was kneeling over Kressel again. The Bloodline men looked to him, but he only shook his head. They did not move to help Arnett.

"Paisley!" Arnett gasped, grabbing Falcon's hand. "Never would have hurt her! Never!"

"I know," Falcon said helplessly. "She loves you."

Arnett released Falcon's hand and seized his collar, trying to pull herself up. Her eyes were wide open, but Falcon knew that they could no longer see.

"Ridge," she said, speaking his name for the last time. "I want to go home."

Her body slowly went limp as she died. Falcon looked at the beautiful, bloodied woman in his arms, and he hated himself for not hating her. He kissed her still mouth, and looked into her unseeing eyes.

"It's okay, Jess," he murmured, stroking her hair with his large, rough palm. "The whole world wants to go home."

He closed his eyes, and wept. When he eventually looked up, Major Bourgeouis was approaching, still clutching the pistol. The old man's hand was shaking.

"Major Bourgeouis," Falcon said. "Where does it end?"

"It just did," Bourgeouis quietly realized. "I just ended the Bloodline. There's no one left."

"Then you can go home," Falcon said acceptantly. "You have a ship. Go to whichever world you want to go back to, and wait for someone to start another war. Wherever you go, you won't have to wait long."

"You loved her," the major stated.

Falcon nodded. "We all did."

"But you most of all?" Bourgeouis pressed him.

"I would have married her," Falcon said. "I would have married a murderer. And I would have told my daughter lies about how we met at a convention, and how we first became attracted to each other during a heated debate over a claim jurisdiction, provincial investigation versus federal. I would have worked out and coordinated ever detail of a lie so that I could have my family, and still be the job. What should I tell my daughter now, Major?"

"The truth," Bourgeouis suggested. "Or, perhaps, nothing at all. The war is over, so both options are equally valid now. Just don't hide from her."

He lowered his pistol as he spoke, stepping closer to Falcon. Ustaf's eyes were open, and he was trying to sit up, without success.

"Forgive me, Captain," Bourgeouis sighed. "You are blessed today. My men and I ... we have nothing left to go back to. Hate. Fear. I'm tired of both."

He flipped the gun unceremoniously, presenting it grip-first to Falcon.

"To have death surrender to you...." Bourgeouis smiled grimly. "It is empowering, the general would say. Please know, Captain, that I could never be at peace with what we did ... what I did at Port Yellowknife. Please, take the gun."

Uncertain of whether or not he was walking into another ambush, Falcon cautiously took the pistol. As one man, Curtis and the Defenders stooped to place their rifles on the deck.

"Thank you, Major," Falcon said, not knowing what else to say.

"I served the general with pride," Bourgeouis answered. "But not a day has gone by that I have not begged the forgiveness of God for that day. A roaming priest once told me that I only needed to repent one time, that no sin was unforgivable in God's eyes. To exclude just one crime would be to negate Christ's sacrifice. But, you see, I killed twenty-two prisoners myself that day, as they knelt before me, looking in my eyes. You see how long your conscience lets you last after saying 'Father, forgive me,' just one time. Go home, Captain. Leave us a raft."

Falcon did not know why he needed to say to the major, "Those things will slaughter you."

"These men I cannot speak for," Bourgeouis said dismissively, "but I have been ready for death a very long time. Without the module, it is impossible to carry out the equatorial requirement of your directives, but I will be banished. I will accept banishment."

Falcon stood, but did not raise the pistol in his hand.

"And what say the rest of you?" he asked.

Ten minutes later, a raft was launched from Banishment One. It carried six men, five living, and one dead, wrapped in a sheet.

From the aft hatch, Falcon watched the raft pull away, as he supported Ustaf, who was almost able to stand on his own.

"What now, sir?" Ustaf asked shakily.

Falcon nodded toward the shore.

"Now," he said, "we wait to see who brings the raft back."

* * *

From a long way off, Bourgeouis spotted two cloaked figures standing on the shore, awaiting the disembarkment of the raft, which was rowed steadfastly through the choppy water. Rain clouds were rolling in over the forest from the south, and distant thunder could be heard.

"I can only assume that is the wolf," Bourgeouis commented. "Ironic that he should be the one to bid us our final farewell. Curtis, can you see who is with him?"

The others stared hard at the shore, but is was Peterson whose breath caught in his throat, shock filling his eyes.

"That's impossible," he breathed. "I killed her myself! I saw her die!"

Chapter Fifty-Five

March 7, 2191.
Our Lady of Mercy Chapel,
Canadian Northern Eagles Garrison,
New Edmonton, Alberta,
Canadian Exodus.

"Father, forgive me," Wolf muttered, lowering his poncho hood as he quietly sat in the confessional, "for I have...."

Wolf could not go on. He did not know what to say. He did not know why he was even there.

"... sinned?" the priest's voice ventured.

"I don't know," Wolf sighed. "You tell me."

He leaned forward, resting his face in his hands. He truly felt lost, even now that he was out of the woods. A report was waiting to be filed, a general was waiting to be briefed, and a public was waiting for the story of a lifetime, but Wolf had made this chapel his first stop immediately upon landing. True, he had been forced to stick the 1911 in the face of a quarantine guard in order to do so, and was no doubt being sought by the garrison MPs, but he just did not care anymore. Nothing made sense. He was not dead, and neither was Lewis, much to the dismay of Ustaf and Falcon. They were whole, and uninjured, and that was impossible.

"Do you think you have sinned, my son?"

"I killed someone close to me," Wolf said. "I set out to kill him, and I killed him. I hunted him for hours, thinking about how I'd kill him. Then I found him, and, at first, I couldn't kill him. But then I did. I watched him bleed out, and I tried to give him the truth."

"And what is truth to you?"

Wolf leaned back into the hard pew.

"That no one's ever too lost. We screw up, figure it out, and we get ... taken care of." Wolf knew that he was not making sense, so he quit trying.

"I'm telling you a story, Father," he said. "I need you to translate it.

"A hunter woke up in the woods, when he should not have woken up at all. And a beautiful woman stood over him, who everyone else thought was dead. The hunter didn't know that. But he remembered how a beast had licked his wounds, and now those wounds were gone. Even the blood from his clothes was gone, and he wasn't where he had been before.

"When the hunter and the woman went down to the water, they met a boat filled with thieves. But the thieves meant them no harm, even offering them the boat without question. The hunter and the woman could have sailed home, but, as they rowed away, they saw that the thieves were being surrounded by beasts. These thieves, the hunter knew, were getting what they deserved, but he got out of the boat and waded back to

454

shore. The thieves were kneeling, bravely waiting to be devoured. The first beast charged at the oldest thief, and the hunter did not even have time to step between them. Instead, he stretched his hand out in front of the beast's jaws as it lunged. And the beast stopped."

He fell silent. This part of the story he still had a hard time believing.

"And what did the hunter do?" The priest's voice sounded intrigued. Wolf realized that he had never seen the man behind that darkened screen. Even church felt so threatening that he had not attended mass in years. He knew that had to change, but not here. He had to go home first.

"The hunter didn't do a thing," Wolf admitted. "But the beast stopped."

He could see it all happening. The reptilis' fangs were within centimeters of his outstretched palm, but the beast had stopped. All of the beasts had stopped, a dozen of them frozen in a circle around the kneeling Bloodline. Bourgeouis' eyes had been closed, but now were looking at Wolf.

Wolf spoke first to the beasts.

"Leave," he said. "Please."

Without hesitation, every reptilis turned and slowly disappeared into the woods. Not one looked back.

Silence. Stillness. Peace.

"You truly are the wolf," Bourgeouis said, disbelievingly. "Who are you?"

"Make your peace with God," was all Wolf said. "You may have a chance at mercy."

Then he had silently waded back out to the raft.

"And did they make peace?" the priest's filtered voice asked.

"I'll never know," Wolf answered. "Like the beasts, I never looked back. Can you translate?"

"Beasts?"

Wolf could only shake his head. "Wolves."

"I would be a fool to even try to guess the meaning of a story like that," the priest's voice confessed. "But I believe that you are blessed, maybe even in ways that you still have yet to discover. I think the beasts saw you ... well, as God sees you. You should think on that. You say you kill, and yet you showed mercy to those deserving of death. Forgiveness is not something you need for that. You were in Daniel's den of lions, and God spared you for a time yet to come."

"What do I need?" Wolf had to ask.

"Right now, I would guess a good sleep. You sound weary from time and grief. Go home."

"I have been home for five years. The weariness never goes away."

"Then maybe you don't understand what home is, what it really means. What does home mean to you?"

"To me?" Wolf said. "It means skylining."

"That is your freedom, then," the voice guessed. "We all need an oasis. To some, it is a golf course, a restaurant, an island, the arms of a loved one, or the back of a good horse. But only as a man of God can you really understand freedom, in its purest form. Do you understand freedom?"

"It is an escape," Wolf said. "Exodus from bondage. I still feel bound."

"By what?"

Wolf sighed. "By death."

"I will tell you a story, my son, and it is one you already know. A woman deserving of death was thrown in the dust at the feet of our Lord. Her accusers demanded that He make the decision, whether or not she would die for her sins. But He merely stooped down and wrote in the dust with His hand. And when they pressed Him to decide, He stood and said that only the man who had no sin should throw the first stone."

Wolf smiled slightly, and said, "Then those who heard it, being convicted by their conscience, went out one by one, beginning with the oldest even to the last."

"And what else did He say, my son?" the priest asked softly.

"Neither do I condemn you," Wolf said. "Go and sin no more."

"Feeling sorry is easy," the voice assured him. "So is apologizing, and so is truly repenting. But accepting the offered grace and forgiveness, the free gift ... that is the part which takes the most faith. Did you murder the man who was close to you?"

"I am a murderer, Father. I took money and orders from my government to commit murder."

"The great prophet Moses was a murderer, as was the apostle Paul, and King David. Did you murder that man?"

In Wolf's mind, every moment of his final hunt flashed by, every hour seen in detail in a few seconds. He could feel the knives in his hands, and see the look of horror on Cougar's face as all three of his death blows were struck, first with a stone, and then with the blades.

One last time, he could smell the blood, the smell of sorrow and victory.

"No, Father," he decided. "I just killed him."

"Tell me this, my son," the voice requested. "In your heart, how do you tell right from wrong, pure from evil? How do you know?"

Wolf smiled introspectively, placing his hands on his knees.

"I can smell it," he said quietly.

The priest continued to speak words of comfort, forgiveness, and encouragement, not realizing that Wolf had already departed in peace.

Chapter Fifty-Six

March 8, 2191.

Office of Colonel Maxmillan Towers,

Track and Pursuit Headquarters,

Somewhere in the western forests of Manitoba,

Canadian Exodus.

"Tell me it's over," Towers said, leaning back in the swivel chair behind his oak desk.

Falcon gave a slow nod, seated across the desk from the colonel.

"We traced Arnett back to a flour mill worker in Toronto Exodus. Apparently, he was Kressel's brother, died in 2180. DNA test proved the familial connection. She was the last Kressel. We believe she told Flaxton about the EMP through his cell door two-way."

"And she was right in front of us," Towers sighed. "There truly is no better place to hide. Where is Wolf?"

"In the air," Falcon said with a grim smile. "Vanished as soon as we touched down. I think he's exercising his right to terminate his commission."

"What did he say happened?"

Falcon shrugged. "He said Cougar was dead."

"And now he's gone."

"Yes, sir."

"He swore he'd never come back the first time," Towers reminded him. "We may see him again."

"No," Falcon said emphatically. "If he had sworn to never return, he never would have. I have never known Wolf to swear to anything, or take an oath. His yes is yes."

"He's a good man," Towers nodded. "That may be all he is, at the end of the day."

"Could anyone ask for anything more?" Falcon asked, raising an eyebrow.

Towers chuckled. "I suppose not. Ridge ... I am so sorry about Jessica. I know how close you two were. I hoped you would marry, someday after TAP. Evil can hide so well, even right in the open."

Falcon looked troubled. "It can, sir. It makes me start to think...."

"Think what, Captain?"

Falcon had to look at the floor as he spoke.

"It makes me think about why an Heir-in-waiting would undertake such an impossible infiltration. What would drive her to that?"

"Revenge," Towers said gravely. "We were a thorn to the Bloodline for a long time."

"We?" Falcon said cautiously. "Or ... you?"

"Meaning?" Towers asked, leaning forward slightly.

"The Bloodline does believe in vows and oaths, sir. They have a whole scale of oaths, some taken by all, some reserved for very specific times. Every soldier is required to take the Oath of Renunciation, denouncing Canadian Exodus and swearing allegiance to The Heir. They have oaths that are taken before training, before missions, leave, almost any occasion. However, there is only one that has been used just once, and it can only be taken by The Heir himself. The Oath of Blood."

Towers looked up sharply, a strange light in his eyes.

"I am aware of it," he said dryly. "It's hard to forget."

"Kressel's final televised appearance before Yellowknife was the day after you killed Frankwell Kressel, sir," Falcon said, forging ahead of his own inner warnings. "May 5, 2150. He took the Oath of Blood before the entire planet, swearing that you would be killed just as his father was. The Bloodline has never publicly targeted anyone else, sir. They wanted you. They wouldn't forget, ever."

"Say what is in your mind, Captain," Towers growled, his brow furrowing.

"I'm thinking that's what Jess was after," Falcon stated. "Initially, you."

"Initially?" Towers' cheeks were beginning to turn a slightly deeper shade of red.

"Stop lying, sir," Falcon said flatly.

"Step lightly, Captain Falcon," Towers warned him harshly.

"Lieutenant Arnett was with us for over a year!" Falcon snapped. "She had a hundred chances to take you out, and the entire job, if she had wanted to. Why would she wait? That cannot be explained innocently, sir!"

"Nothing about Jessica was innocent!" Towers shot back. "Are you trying to fathom her mind? Don't."

"I can categorize a lot under the heading of coincidence, sir," Falcon sighed. "But for her to end up as the recommended lunar pilot of Banishment One.... That's too much to believe. Too much coincidence is no coincidence at all."

"You think I put her on the ship?" Towers said it more as a statement than a question.

"Just like you put Edward Devane in charge of maintenance," Falcon replied with a statement of his own.

"Why would I do that, if I knew who she was?"

"Deal with the devil, sir," Falcon said quietly. "In exchange for your life, you offered her the Bloodline, complete with all its finest. You knew Chimney Sweep was coming, and you knew the Banishment Act was being drafted and ratified. Reinstating us into the CNE was your idea from the start, under a veil of 'only the best.' You knew that the clock was ticking on the Bloodline, so you told Jess she had a chance to turn it back. No groundwork to lay, just take over the ship and come home. The TAP infiltration alone would earn her all of the respect she would ever need to take over. It's a plan that would have worked, if you both hadn't forgotten about one major's love for his general."

Towers nodded. "Interesting theory, Captain."

"Why, sir?"

"Why what?"

"You put your life on the line, all of your life, for the country you loved. Where did that love go?"

Towers smiled sadly, folding his arms on the desk.

"Perhaps I'm evil, Captain. It can hide so well."

"No, sir." Falcon was certain. "I cannot accept that. You've done too much. Every soldier and hunter under your command loves you. You are what we all aspire to be."

"The blood on your hands," Towers pointed out sourly. "I put every drop of it there. You are not accountable for it. The blood on my hands ... I put it there all by myself. All of it."

"Sir, we all did the job!"

"That wasn't the job!" Towers snarled. "I'd still be doing the job myself if it was only the blood of the Bloodline on my hands. But our blood, Ridge. Ours. Us. The 3-6-5, Ridge! That's on me. Forty-four times, it's on me!"

"What?" Falcon was incredulous. "Sir, it was voluntary. We knew the risks."

"No!" Towers barked. "I killed us, and I was praised for it! That alone told me what I was, what I had to be! So, yes. When Jessica Arnett came to me, holding the knife I had helped her to forge, I knew what I was capable of. It was time, Ridgely. My time."

"Sir!"

"Don't call me that!" Towers shouted. "Never call me that again!"

"Sir!" Falcon seethed.

"Don't!"

"SIR!"

Towers was out of his seat, striding to his cabinet, its varnished shelves lined with awards, medals, and battlefield trophies. He stared for a long time at his reflection in the glass, his lined face mirrored over his

Purple Heart. He could also see Falcon rising from his seat.

"You sent us out to die twenty years ago," Falcon said tiredly. "We respected you for it, for what we became because of it. Then, last week, you did it again. I don't know why I still respect you, sir. I should kill you."

"On the Home Base," Towers slowly said to his reflection, "there is a small country, where honour was so deeply cherished that it was once traditional for men to end their own lives when confronted with their own shame. In this cabinet rests the very first chrystanium knife. Mine. It would work nicely. Do you support that?"

Falcon shook his head. "Connor might have, sir. And Hanley, and Cardinal. I think enough people have died because of you. Besides, your time is short. Everyone will realize what you are, and you will be forced to go away. I guess that's the core of Track and Pursuit. We just make problems go away. But don't kill yourself, or anyone else. Like you said, sir. Tell me it's over."

"I had faith in you," Towers replied firmly. "And Wolf. I was sending Arnett to her death. At least, that was my hope. That's not justification, Ridgely. That's just faith. And you won, you're here. I trained the best, so maybe my life's been worth ... well, that, anyway. It's over."

"Thank Major Powers Bourgeouis, sir. The Bloodline ended itself. We didn't do anything."

"No, Captain Falcon." Towers was adamant. "You did everything, and you did it right. I'm proud to have been with you through these years. Just like I was proud of Wolf, and Cougar. Shark. Lion. Hawk. Twelve men, half of them dead in the same year. I know you'll do great things for Canada, as you always have." He put his hand on his holster, fingers tracing the grip of his ion pistol.

Falcon shook his head, touching his own sidearm. "Don't do it."

"Be calm, Captain," Towers said soothingly. "These things happen."

"Don't," Falcon repeated. Towers simply smiled.

Both pistols were drawn, so slowly at first that neither man seemed to be moving at all. Towers' smile was almost teasing as he raised his weapon, tilting the barrel toward his own skull.

"Don't!" Barking the order at his commander was one of the hardest syllables that Falcon had ever uttered.

"There are so many things I haven't taught you yet, Captain," Towers remarked. "New ways to kill, new ways to track, hunt, survive, destroy. Twenty years isn't long enough."

The gun barrel touched the colonel's forehead for only a second. Then he opened his hand, and the weapon fell harmlessly to the floor. Falcon silently released the breath which he had not even noticed catching in his throat.

"Step back, sir," he instructed, his pistol now aimed at the center-mass of a man whom he still could not force himself to think of as a target. Towers ignored him.

"It's a marvelous art," the old soldier rambled. "Killing. Hundreds of ways to do it. Maybe thousands, millions. There is no other art form known to our species

465

that has been so exhaustively studied, and I doubt even Wolf has studied it as much as I have. There are some methods ... I couldn't even tell you."

"Step away from the gun, sir."

"But I can show you, Ridge. Just once, I can show you. One last lesson."

Falcon shook his head, his jaw tensing. "Let it be over, sir. Please."

Towers was still smiling. "Did you know, Captain Ridgely Falcon, that it is possible to stop your own heart? It is a theory which you're never supposed to ... rehearse, just because it might work."

Falcon was growing weary of repeating himself, but he had to once more, as his gun lowered involuntarily.

"Don't."

Colonel Maxmillan Towers was wavering, looking sick and off-balance as he quietly replied, "I already did."

A moment later, only one of the two men was left standing.

Chapter Fifty-Seven

March 12, 2191.
Stormy Coulee Ranch,
50 km west of White Rock, Alberta,
Canadian Exodus.

When Chester Wolf chose to go home, it was done without ceremony, tears, or goodbyes. He vanished, knowing that only Falcon knew where he was going.

There would be chaos, he knew. Everyone would want to know what had happened to The Desert, what had happened to the banishment mission, how TAP had been infiltrated by the Bloodline, how Lewis had been restored from her fatal injuries, what the reptilis really were, whether or not God was real, and, of course, where Wolf was. Investigations were beginning. Expeditionary missions were being planned. Statements were being taken and retaken. DNA was being sequenced from the larval creature Falcon had retrieved, and scientists were already in awe of its multiple pupation stages. The media was dissecting, chronicling, translating, and propagating every second of the Hamelin Mission, crying everything from heroism, to high-level corruption, to the apocalypse. The planet, and all of mankind, was on the brink of turning upside down and inside out, and Wolf could not have cared less. He had steaks to raise.

His only regret was that he had not had a chance to speak to Amanda Lewis. The two of them had been spared, while those around them had been attacked and slaughtered. Now, Wolf's leg did not have a scar. Not even knowing that he had been injured, Falcon had only briefly noted that Wolf was no longer limping. Mostly, he and Ustaf had been too preoccupied with the impossibility of Lewis being alive and well.

Even Lewis did not know that Wolf had been wounded. Sitting alone at the table in his cabin, Wolf decided that someday he would go back and tell her, but it would not be that day. It would not be that year, even. He had been given another chance at a life that was not death, and that was something to be savored first.

Wolf had been living that life for five years before, but now he felt that he might actually have a reason for living it. The beasts had never threatened him, and the one Lewis had seen had ignored her entirely. Perhaps that meant everything, or nothing. Wolf was not interested in making assumptions today. Spartan needed new shoes, and that was where Wolf's mind was when he found the letter.

He heard a very slight creaking from the raw slab deck, which made him stand up from his breakfast. He knew that creak was from a light footfall, yet he had not heard anyone approaching. That alone was enough to make him strap on his gun belt and cinch his knife onto his arm. Before he carefully opened the door to step outside, he took one last look at the mantle on which his weapons had been resting. There was a new addition to that shelf, and it was the small stone he had defeated Cougar with. On its smooth surface, he had inscribed a single word with his chrystanium knife.

ONE

He could hear the envelope fluttering in the cool breeze before he even opened the door, sweeping the area with his eyes as he eased back the latch. The letter was tacked just above the sliding deadbolt, the envelope simply marked "Wolf."

He did not touch the letter until he was certain that the barnyard was clear of intruders, and the paper was free of devices.

The letter was very short.

Captain Chester Wolf,

> *Did it ever strike you as odd that Bishop would be an exact body match to Vance Cougar? It has been a pleasure hunting you, and being hunted by you, these many years. If you are ever in need of a ranch hand, I am currently out of work. Peace is hard on our kind, isn't it?*

> > *Your friend, now known as*
> > *The Freelancer.*

The 1911 was in Wolf's hand before he even finished the last line, and he was diving for cover behind the stack of split firewood on the deck.

There was no sound but the wind, and Spartan muttering at him from the hitching rail. Wolf knew that Bishop was long gone. As in most hunts, Wolf just knew.

He stood up wearily, looking around for any tracks, misplaced items, or other signs of the hunt. There were none, and there were no gut-feelings out of the ordinary. Spartan looked up at him briefly, then returned to the patch of grass at his hooves. Wolf put the pistol back in its holster.

"Spartan," he said bemusedly. "That man can really hunt."

March 22, 2191.

From the diary of Chester Wolf.

My Dearest Rachel,

What is the limit of a good man?

The spring is warm in White Rock, and the calves will soon be born in the north pasture. I see such innocence in the big eyes of those baby cows. Unlike us, their innocence can never be corrupted.

My hunting is finished. My only duty now is to defend a herd of cattle from equally innocent predators. My enemies are banished, and the Bloodline is leaderless and fading away like the last banks of spring snow. After nearly a hundred years of conflict, Canadian Exodus is close to having peace, or at least the illusion of it.

Vance Cougar was my equal in prowess, and I do not know if his hunt ever really ended. The man was once my brother, and killing him nearly killed me. In all our years of hunting, this was the only time that we both fought on the same field of battle. Brothers one moment, enemies the next. Did either one of us survive? I do not know. Is he alive? Am I truly alive? We were both left to the mercy of wolves, and I was the one who returned, with a tale that will never be told.

Even on a new world, there will always be war, and hunters will be needed to end them. Wolves hunting wolves, something which never occurs in nature, but always in the world of men. Without the Bloodline, Track and Pursuit will outlive its usefulness, but, even after the unit is disbanded, the time will come for a new generation when the hunt will need to continue. The world needs wolves.

Your loving husband,
Chester Bradley.

Epilogue

No further Hamelin Missions were launched.

Track and Pursuit was disbanded before the end of the year. All members were redeployed to military branches of their own choosing. Ridgely Falcon chose instead to retire, citing "reasons of family."

The residential location of Chester Wolf was never disclosed to the military or government.

The true identity of Bishop was never revealed.

About the Author

A proud Canadian, Lane Bristow lives in Chetwynd, British Columbia. *The Mercy of Wolves* is his second novel, following *Slice of Heaven*, and he is currently working on several more.

Printed in the United States
116904LV00001B/13-24/A

9 781434 341877